ONE NIGHT, NEW YORK

ONE NIGHT, NEW YORK

LARA THOMPSON

PEGASUS CRIME

NEW YORK LONDON

ONE NIGHT NEW YORK

Pegasus Crime is an imprint of
Pegasus Books, Ltd.
148 West 37th Street, 13th Floor
New York, NY 10018

First Pegasus Books cloth edition December 2021

ISBN: 978-1-64313-839-8

10 9 8 7 6 5 4 3 2 1

Printed in the United States of America
Distributed by Simon & Schuster
www.pegasusbooks.com

In memory of Laurence John Thompson

Full circle then from winter's dark abyss
Towards summers of stars in golden bliss.

The tempo of the metropolis is not of eternity,
or even time, but of the vanishing instant.

Berenice Abbott

If you'll make me up, I'll make you.

Virginia Woolf to Vita Sackville-West,
23 September 1925

NEW YORK CITY

Winter solstice, 21 December 1932

16.45

Her initial shock at the height had faded, but if Frances moved close to the edge, if she tipped her head over the waist-height balustrade, the hysterical sensation returned. A few months ago she would have been terrified. Tonight she was captivated. All around, skyscrapers seemed to grow and thrust, dwarfing the cowering tenements at their feet. Fog clung to the tips of the highest towers. Snatches of street-level noise sailed up – blasting car horns, workmen shouting on their way home, swing bands tuning up in the ritzy joints on Broadway.

She could see why people jumped. The city seduced from up here, as though instead of dying on the fresh asphalt, you might leap right into the electric heart of life itself. She bent forward, vertigo swelling. It was impossible to see them from here, but she could imagine the doomed washing lines criss-crossing her crumbling street, hundreds of feet below. Soon they'd be torn down, two weeks' notice: she wondered where everyone would hang their clothes.

The wind tugged and pulled, threatening to push her off with icy hands. She stepped back and wrapped Stan's overcoat around her more tightly, glad she had brought it, comforted by the sharp sensation that her own arms were his. Leaning her head to one side, touching her chin to the rough grey wool, she imagined it was his shoulder. The smell of his Luckies was burnt into the fabric. She sucked in the fading fumes, wishing with each shaking breath that she could smell the smoke fresh from her brother's mouth again.

For the hundredth time since they'd made their promise, she wondered if she and Agnes were really going to go through with it, if she was brave and terrible enough, until a sudden gust almost stole her hat and she only just caught it, struggling with dead fingers to pull out the pins as it twisted and strained. Free at last, her hair whipped her eyes. Tears fell. She hoped she'd feel better once they'd done it, she couldn't bear the thought of this sadness sticking to her for ever. Agnes had looked at her strangely when she'd suggested they both might feel more normal afterwards. She'd gazed at the dregs of her coffee and told Frances that wasn't the point. Then she'd said she didn't know how they would feel but that either way it was the right thing to do. That was all that ever mattered to Agnes. Doing the right thing.

Frances shivered, thrust the felt deep into Stan's pocket, creases be damned, and turned, ears hollowed by the wind, breath caught, determined to take it all in. If this was the first and last time she was going to see her city from up here, if tonight was everything, then she must stain her mind with the sight of it. The dimming sky looked as though it had been stripped from the heavens and ironed flat: a thousand lit windows scattered like sequins on the dress of the night.

Agnes called to her from inside. Finally. She had said it

would only take thirty minutes. Fifteen to set up, fifteen for the exposure. She'd already been up here longer and Frances was getting all balled up. He should be here soon.

'Have you still got it?' Agnes called again.

'Yes,' Frances shouted, pushing the word away before the wind could throw it back. And yet still she didn't move. One last look.

She needed a smoke to mark the occasion. Undoing the button on Stan's other pocket, she pushed her hand in, rooting around just in case. Her fingers trembled as they brushed against damp cotton, loose matchsticks and a few mucky dimes. Finally, she caught hold of something. It wasn't a ciggy, it was the note. She pulled it out, fumbling in the cold. Whatever happened, she mustn't let it go. It was only a few lines, but they'd spent so long agonising over the words. The right tone. The most convincing lie. Without it no one would believe them. As soon as that filthy hood arrived, they'd persuade him on to the balcony. Agnes would distract him so Frances could press the note into his pocket. Then they'd both shove him over the edge with all their might.

KANSAS to NEW YORK CITY

12 September 1932

18.25

The long grass whipped and tore at her ankles. Marsh flies plumed upwards in disturbed clouds. She beat them away but didn't stop even when they stuck to her cheeks and caught in her hair. Whatever it took, however far or fast she had to go, she'd get away. The heavy bag nagged at her arm to rest. She shouldn't have crammed it so full. Perhaps she shouldn't have brought it at all – but her whole life was in there. Almost two decades of living folded up in a tattered case. More things than most people around here, thanks to Stan and his money. Nothing of her was back in the old house. Not her things, not her body, not even her mind – that had gone months ago, long before she'd run outside tonight. They could keep their memories of her, that was all. And her mother had the shoes and Frances' fading picture in that often-pawned locket wrapped around her throat. But nothing else. That was enough.

She slowed down for a second to switch arms, giving the

right one a rest until it stopped screaming. It felt strange to be running at her favourite time of day. Usually she'd have finished with her chores and pulled a chair on to the porch. She'd have taken out her sewing or her cross-stitch, or something that needed mending. She'd gotten up to 'L' in her child's alphabet. It was her favourite letter to sew. Straight down and across, a tiny curl at the top and bottom like a baby's tongue. Nothing fancy, but she'd saved her best dark red thread for it. She would have been sitting there, toes keeping the chair rocking, listening to the birds gathering, to the hooting, whistling calls of 'come home' and 'I'm here' and 'danger', looking up every now and then to brush away a fat moth, or to see if the fireflies were dancing over the scorched grass.

Never again. Now her breath caught jagged in her throat and her thin cotton dress stuck to her back. The cracked leather handle of her bag felt strangely slick in her sweating hand, so heavy there might have been a body inside, not just her clothes. Blood rushed in her ears until a shot rang out, splitting the air.

The bullet hit the old oak on the corner of the field, the one she and Stan had scratched their names into all that time ago. Rotting bark splintered. It was a warning. Father wasn't trying to hit her; he was upset, she knew that, and he was a crack shot – if he'd meant it she'd be dead by now. But it stunned her all the same. It stunned her so much she stumbled as she began to run again and fresh tears fell on to her sore cheeks, flowing down the itchy trails of all the ones that had fallen there before.

She was too far away to hear exactly what Father was shouting but she had an idea. He was probably saying she was rotten. That she was a good-for-nuthin' liar. That she could clear out. All the things he'd shouted at her a thousand times before. She knew Mother was inside trying to clean the grease off something, pretending she couldn't hear. Or perhaps she'd run out on to the porch again by now and she was clutching that dirty apron she'd worn every day of her married life and silently begging Frances to come back. Whatever, it didn't matter now. She was out and away, chasing after the sun, cresting the curve of the hill, heading down into the dust-filled ditch on the far side of the field, almost at the dirt track. Even if he was aiming, now he'd never hit her.

Her toes were dirty – not the kind of dirt that you could lick your finger and rub away, the kind that would take hours of scrubbing to shift. Blood was caked in some of the creases. Mud had wormed its way up under her nails. Worse than that, when Frances had stumbled, the strap on her left sandal had busted open and she'd had to stop outside the station and tie the two pieces of worn leather together. Heaven knows what Stan would think when he saw her. But it was no use. These were her only pair. She'd left the good church shoes for Mother. They were the same size, and Mother had let Frances wear them every Sunday for the last few years so it only seemed right to leave them behind. A final peace offering. At any rate, they were heavy. On her feet, or in her bag, they'd only have slowed her down.

The women were gossiping further down the boards. She'd seen them on the platform looking when she'd queued for her ticket. She'd even heard one whisper, 'Well, would you look at *that.*' Frances had turned away, but not before she'd seen the woman's friend roll her sly eyes heavenward. No doubt she seemed strange to them – checking and re-checking her money as she waited, covered in dust and blood and dead grass, dirty hair, mucky face. People like her didn't go on trains. Or count money. Only a handful of folks around here had enough money to travel at all. They probably thought she was some kind of thief.

They kept looking over. No doubt they'd never been gripped

by the terror of losing the only money they ever had. For them there would always be more. Stuck-up Mrs Grundys with their lightweight travelling jackets and shiny courts, yapping at each other like small, desperate dogs. The squinty one was shading her mouth with her newspaper, as though the print might soak up her spite.

Frances smoothed the side of her skirt until she felt the comforting crunch of the money beneath. The few dollars she hadn't spent felt electric in there, as though they were quivering like filaments, lighting up her ticket in the dark folds of her dress. She was too afraid to keep them in her purse in case she put it down somewhere and forgot to pick it up in a rush. Stan had sent her some extra so she could buy something to eat on the way. She wasn't sure how much shoes cost in New York City but she hoped that if she didn't eat much on the journey, she might have enough left over to buy some. He'd not asked any questions when he sent it. He didn't have to. She'd sent the telegram, and he'd sent one straight back with a one-word reply: 'Yes.' The only surprise to him was that she'd waited this long to leave.

When the package had arrived she'd snatched it out of Mother's hand and raced up the stairs to her bedroom and pushed her cane chair up against the door. Mother had hammered on it. None of them had heard from Stan for months and they were all desperate for news, or rather, for another one of his little packages to come along and save them. As far as she knew they'd never had a parcel from anyone else, so there was no hiding who it was from. She'd not seen so many dollars since that day there'd been a run on the bank. Father had yelled at Mother that they were all finished – the town, the state, the whole God-damned country. His world had fallen apart and all of theirs with it. Years ago now, and yet, like all terrible days, it seemed like yesterday.

She scuffed the earth with her toe, picked off some seeds

that were stuck to the hem of her dress and checked the station clock again. About a minute since the last time she looked up. Apart from the women there weren't many waiting to travel. It was so quiet, if she stood still she could hear the crickets in the long grass out back. Had Father realised where she was? Had he guessed what she was about to do? She checked the entrance again, flicking at a torn nail, trying to imagine what she'd do if he stepped through it with his gun cocked. Perhaps Mother had calmed him down by now. Perhaps he'd spent all his anger on her again instead. The guilt stabbed at Frances but she pushed it aside. Had Mother helped her that time Father cornered her in the barn? The old woman had seen, she was sure of it. Her shadow had paused by the window, the moonlight making a halo of her wiry hair. She'd stopped and she'd seen and she'd kept quiet. Well, now it was Frances' turn to look the other way.

She wondered what she'd have to do when the train arrived. Would there be steps up? Would someone help her on? How would she know what carriage to go in? The furthest she'd ever been until now was the Elsner farm on the back of their truck, and she'd been distracted for most of that ride by Harry's hand on her knee and his breath in her ear.

She closed her eyes and tried to remember exactly how it had felt. In a roundabout way it was Harry's fault she was here. Those first dark fumblings. The scratchy wool blanket over her lap. The hot shock of his fingers pressed on that sweet spot between her legs. She remembered saying yes and then no, and then yes again. She'd felt sick and heady, riding high on the pleasure and the wrongness of it all, bounced around by the bumps in the road, afraid they'd be caught but not wanting him to stop, not ever wanting him to stop. His hands, so rough from all the work, pressing down, his fingers pushing into her, a sharp sting and a mounting warmth, an overwhelming tide of pleasure and forgetting. Afterwards he'd casually wiped his hand on the blanket and kissed her hot cheek. He'd called her a doll, like all the men in the matinees, and promised to see her again. She remembered lying back and looking up at the gathering clouds, not caring about anything he said. It wasn't him she liked, it was what he'd done to her. She had known, even then, that she wanted to feel this every day, over and over. Yes. It was all Harry's fault.

A breeze flicked her skirt and she held off an urge to check her pocket again. Behind them the station-master had sent his boy out early to turn on the lamps. She supposed he had to do it now, in the last of the sunlight, so he could go back and set up his shoe-shine before the train came in. He dragged his ladder along, making thin tracks in the dirt, stopping beneath each globe, climbing up and flipping the metal switch, smiling each time and tapping the side of the lamp when the glow stayed put. Frances watched him until they were all lit as the minutes counted down, transfixed by the newness of that strange fizzing gleam.

A single horn blast shot a handful of collared doves skyward. Her train thundered around a bend in the track. The sight of it shocked her. She'd seen trains before, of course, whistling as they flew by out past the Pattersons' place, but never this close. It screamed as it rushed in front of her and stopped, blowing her skirt in the air, so that she had to push it down with one hand, while clutching at the money in her pocket with the other. Two guards jumped out of the doors. They wore stiff black hats like policemen, their boots shining in the mellow light. The nearest one looked her up and down, frowned slightly and beckoned her over, all the time keeping one eye on the clock.

'Where to, Miss? Got your ticket there, have you?' He looked dubious.

His face was pock-marked by some long-cured vicious disease, yet he was still handsome enough. Not much older than

her. She batted steam away from her face, distracted for a
second by a lewd fantasy of his tongue in her mouth, and smiled.
Even though the train had stopped it was still shuddering and
sighing, making her nervous, trembling on its great wheels as
though it was trying to catch its breath.

'Yes. Here it is.' Her voice didn't sound right. It was quieter,
softer than in her head.

She fumbled in her pockets, fretful that all would be lost at
the last minute. But there it was. Thin and soft, freshly printed.
The guard took it from her. She only had to worry for a second
because he nodded quickly, took hold of her case and stepped
back to give her enough room to climb up. He jumped on
behind, pulled the door closed with a bang and waved a flag at
the driver. Almost instantly, with a great creaking groan, the
train began to move again, pistons shunting, steam chuffing.
Frances clutched her throat. She hadn't had a second to think
about what she was doing, let alone change her mind. She
almost fell as the train gathered speed. The guard caught her
elbow and smiled.

'You'll be all right, Miss. Three days is plenty of time to get
the hang of it before we get to New York.'

'Thank you,' she said, righting herself, smoothing her skirt.

The guard nodded, then leant into the hall, pointing towards
the back of the train. 'Third class is that way. Keep walking
till you get to the dining car and then keep going a bit more,
right on past it. There's no reservations in third, so you can sit
anywhere there's a space.'

'Thank you,' she said again.

He tipped his hat and walked off. No doubt he'd worked
out she was some dumb Dora who'd never travelled anywhere before.

The train rocked alarmingly. Frances grabbed on to a shiny
rail by the door. For all its brass fittings, the wooden interior

was rough, with gaps in the planks and a worn carpet. The guard had left the window open to ease the heat and she was overcome with a desperate desire to stick her head out. She'd seen some boys doing that once, when a train rushed past in the distance from the back of the Pattersons' dried-up wheat field. The engine had whistled and she'd stopped kissing and seen the boys leaning out, waving their caps and laughing at each other. It had looked like fun.

She rested her palms on the wooden frame, feeling the glass vibrate, its edge worn smooth from all those other hands. Outside, the only land she'd ever known was rushing away. Tentatively she leant forward. At first the rushing gusts pushed her back, but then she felt the train slow, its strident thrusts easing into a steadier, rhythmic beat. She took a deep breath, so the smoke wouldn't choke her, and forced her head outside.

She was flying! The wind wrapped around her head, unpinned hair streaming backwards like a golden flag. She opened her eyes, squinting to ward off the sting. The sun was still there, hanging a few feet from the ground, looking like it might fall away at any minute. It coated the bare fields and shrunken corn with a deceptive sheen of hope. Liar! Frances thought. Hope had shrivelled on the vines, it had turned to dust like the soil, it had vanished from the plates on the tables and the insides of once-full pockets. It had disappeared from reflections and hand-shakes and smiles, until finally it had left her too, on that day when she'd cradled the baby – perfect, albeit for his silent heart – on the floor of the barn, and Father had found her and pulled him from her and buried him. Hope had run away from this place, like her, but now she could feel it growing. It had seeded inside and might just bloom out there along the tracks.

OUTSIDE NEW YORK CITY

15 September 1932

18.29

Frances suspected they were talking about her, so she decided to keep still and quiet with her eyes closed. Such strange voices! Their accents were queer, the words twisted and bent, sometimes stretching on for longer than they should, sometimes cut short without notice. If she hadn't been so focused on how they were speaking, she might have been more annoyed by what they were saying.

'Forcing me back here in case you miss a photo,' the woman carried on. 'Really. You could have at least let me bring my cocktail, we're almost home now.'

'I thought it might inspire you.' A man's voice now, quiet, low, slower. 'You haven't written a thing for days.' He sounded young. Mother and son, perhaps.

'Inspired by the debris in this carriage? I don't think so.' The woman's voice was getting louder. 'We need to find some characters, Dicky, some real, no-holds-barred, stop-the-press characters.

I haven't been inspired since you found that woman standing in the middle of that sorry-looking field with all those children. Now *she* was something to get worked up about.'

'You can be beastly sometimes, Jacks, absolutely beastly. I know you don't mean it, but there's no need to be rude. Inspiration's everywhere. You just have to be open enough to see it.' The woman made a scoffing noise. 'Look here,' the man continued. 'Like I said. Fine bone structure, good skin. Give her a wash and she might do.'

Frances tried not to fidget. The newspaper she'd screwed up and stuffed underneath her head to make the long hours on the train a bit more bearable no longer seemed like a good idea.

'Are you mad? She won't do at all. It's all very well for you, clicking away, with no thought to what makes a good story. I need quotes! My readers need someone they can sympathise with. I know you think otherwise, but bone structure doesn't matter a jot if they can't hear themselves when those people in your pictures finally speak.'

Frances heard the man shifting on his seat. He sighed.

'Oh, go on then.' The woman's voice was lighter now, teasing. 'Wake her up. You've convinced me. At least it'll give us something to do in the city for the winter. Go on. Poke her. See if she's alive.'

'Not yet,' he said. 'A shot first. I'll never get her to recreate this once she's awake. Look at the angle of her arm, the contrast of her cheek on the newspaper. Hold on.'

A shot? Was he going to shoot her? Frances heard a rustle and a click. Not here on the train in front of everyone? She jerked her body up. Her eyes snapped open, hands out, ready to hit, ready to run.

The man looked surprised but he smiled. No gun in his hand, just a wooden box. He had a thin, handsome face. Fine brown hair, parted on the side, not yet thinning. He was neat all over – brown travelling jacket, bow tie, waistcoat, everything tight and mannered and expensive-looking, apart from the large dark shadows under his eyes. She wondered if he'd had trouble sleeping on the train too.

'Oh look! She's smitten already, Dicky love. That's the exact reaction most women have when they see you. Terror.'

Next to the man, the woman threw her head back, blew smoke from her nostrils and laughed towards the ceiling. Frances forgot her fear and stared. The woman was like a lady from the pictures come-to-life.

Once or twice, if Frances managed to sneak away from the farm for the afternoon, she would sometimes let a boy she'd become friendly with take her to town. They'd go to the drug store and get a milkshake, and if she asked softly enough he'd agree to take her to the pictures. It was worth some fresh guy's hand on her knee if she got to sit in the dark for a while and watch the players moving around on the screen like glorious phantoms. Sometimes, if she was lucky, when a title card came up, the boy she was with would remember to whisper what it said into her ear. She liked these dates the most – the ones who managed to tear themselves away from the skin on her thigh for long enough to tell her the story. Then she could get truly lost in it. The flickering light, the beautiful faces glowing in the dark, the grand gestures and dramatic costumes, the danger and rescues and love affairs.

Somehow, this woman in front of her was all of that. She didn't just look like one of the beauties from a feature, she gave off the glamour and excitement and wonder of it all like a heady scent. Jet-black cropped hair just visible beneath a golden turban. Red lips, dark eyes, creases blooming when she smiled. Ten years older than Frances at least. Deep purple velvet jacket, the pile so thick it looked like fur, surely too hot in this heat, and yet the woman's face was powdered to perfection. Wide-legged black slacks, perched on the side of the bench, one leg up on the table between them. Frances could smell her – woody, musky, with something dirty and dangerous crouching at the back. She wanted to lean in and inhale, to close her eyes and consume her.

Now it was Dicky's turn to laugh. 'By the looks of things, I don't think it's me she likes, darling.'

Frances flushed and looked at her feet, then curled her toes beneath the bench, still sickened by the sight of them. She ought to turn her head, apologise for being rude and not replying. But she didn't. Instead, she gazed steadily out of the window.

The man cleared his throat.

Frances ignored him. Who were they to laugh at her? Let them wait. She wondered why the train had stopped. Outside, a huge factory blocked the horizon, the largest she'd ever seen, pumping purple smoke into the dimming burnt-edged sky. She wished there'd been an announcement – some warning that she should make the most of the stripped fields and rough pines before all the grey arrived. For a second she missed the farm, but the sensation only lasted a moment, because as much as it was home, it was also a kind of hell, a black place disguised by the yellow and orange land, blacker than any kind of chimney smoke, the mud as hard as brick anyway.

She let the man clear his throat a few more times, until he must have felt a little silly, and then turned to face him.

'We are terribly sorry to disturb you,' he said, 'might we discuss something while the train's stopped? Would you mind at all?' He looked around as though searching for someone. 'Is there anyone with you we might also converse with? A travelling companion perhaps? Or can we speak directly to you?'

'If, indeed, her voice works at all?' The woman held Frances' gaze and smiled with everything except her eyes.

'What's that?' Frances nodded at the box and tried to remain composed. She'd just had the sickening thought that perhaps they didn't want merely to talk. Perhaps they wanted to do her harm.

Perhaps they were planning something awful, something that Frances couldn't yet foresee.

'Just listen to that darling accent!' The woman looked like she was going to laugh again. 'Oh, go on, say something else.'

'What would you like me to say?' Frances frowned, she'd been certain to use her smartest voice.

'I don't mind, dear, anything.' The woman sucked again on her cigarette and blew smoke towards the ceiling where it clung to the polished slats.

'Please, I beg you,' the man said, 'ignore my friend. We've had a long trip and she's just itching to get off the train, and I've dragged her back here—'

'He's dragged me back here,' the woman smiled, 'because he saw how bored I was by all those Henrys in first, and he thought we might find someone interesting in third.' She leant forward. 'Are *you* interesting?'

Frances felt the woman's dark eyes roam over her. She fought off the desire to lean towards her powdered face and shout 'Yes!' Instead she kept quiet and kept on smiling until her face cooled.

'Jacks, for God's sake give the girl some space.' The man hit his hat lightly on the woman's knee, as though batting away an annoying fly. Frances wondered if they were brother and sister after all. 'She asked us a question.' He waved the box in the air. 'This is a camera. My friend Jacqueline and I are working on a little project together.'

The woman rolled her eyes at Frances as though they'd known each other for years.

'Richard Sampson, photographer, full-time resident of New York City. Charmed.' He held out his hand.

Frances tried to remember how clean her palms were, then shot out her hand all the same.

'Sorry, I haven't spoken properly to anyone for a few days,' she said. 'I'm out of practice.' As soon as the words were out, she wished she could fold them away again. Now they knew there was no travelling companion. She was alone.

'Not to worry.' He smiled at her again. He was lovely when he smiled. It broadened all his features that were otherwise a little too pointed. 'Travelling makes beasts of the best of us.'

Frances nodded. 'I'm Frances Addams. From outside Hays, Kansas. I'll be looking for a job in New York when I get there.' Whoever they were, she didn't want them to think she was lazy, just another country girl running away from another failing farm. 'My brother's meeting me at the station. I'm hoping to spot him easily – he's enormous!' If they were planning to abduct her, they might think twice if they knew about Stan. At any rate, she hadn't lied.

'Well, it certainly sounds like you've got it all planned out.' Dicky smiled at her again.

'And,' said Jacks, 'there's nothing I like more than a strapping young farm boy. Perhaps you can introduce me to this brother of yours when we get in? I'm always on the look-out for fresh meat.' She laughed.

'As I said before, while Jacks is fantastic on many counts, especially with regard to digging up a good story, it is best that you ignore most of what she says, especially once it gets along to cocktail hour. I'm not sure she can quite handle her drink like she used to.'

Jacks whacked Dicky on the arm. 'You really are a horror. I could drink you under the table any time, any place. That's why you never get jazzed. You don't want to be shown up by a woman!'

Dicky rolled his eyes and sighed, then patted Jacks' arm. 'You're right, darling, of course. Now, shall we explain to Frances why we've accosted her on the train? I'm sure she's wondering what we've got to say.'

Jacks had stopped looking at Dicky, and was instead gazing out of the window, fiddling with the end of her cigarette holder.

'I certainly hope we didn't alarm you, and I am sorry to wake you up,' Dicky said. 'Jacks and I have been out of the city for weeks. We work together, you see.'

Jacks smiled. Frances noticed a slight softening around the eyes. 'I'm Jacqueline Du Montfort, by the way. Journalist and full-time good-time girl. Pleasure to meet you.'

Frances shook her hand, aware that it was the woman, and not her, who was trembling slightly.

'Pleased to meet you,' Frances said.

'Well,' Jacks said, 'we're already off to a good start. She's polite at least, not like that last one out in Wichita or wherever it was.'

'So,' Dicky continued, ignoring Jacks, 'we've been on a little adventure, travelling around, photographing this and that, trying to get to know some of your fellow middle-Americans on their farms and in their general stores and suchlike. I take the pictures, of course' – he gestured to his camera – 'and Jacks does the words. Magazines pay us to go off and come back to the big smoke with stories from the heartland.'

'The rich never tire of hearing about those who are worse off than themselves,' Jacks said. 'And for those in New York that includes a lot of people.'

She leant towards Dicky with the holder in her mouth. Dicky drew a gold match case from his inside pocket. Frances saw that it was engraved with his initials in swirling font. If she had been the stealing kind, that's what she would have gone for. He lit the match and Jacks inhaled, the glow from the stub making her look all the more glorious. Dicky pocketed the case.

'So this time,' Dicky said, 'we boarded the train to go home and as soon as we sat down in the buffet car Jacks had an idea.'

'It wasn't as soon as we sat, I'm sure I ordered first,' Jacks said, steaming the window with her breath. 'I always order first.'

'Of course we ordered first, but really, darling, if you keep interrupting me I'll never get the words out and poor Frances will become desperately bored by the pair of us.'

He smiled again at Frances with genuine feeling. For some reason she felt she might cry; she could feel the sadness clinging to the back of her throat. Jacks drew a heart in the steam on the window and wrote J.D.M. inside.

'Her idea,' Dicky said, 'was that instead of us going to the dustbowls in the middle, or to the depths of the deep south to get our stories, we should bring the story to us.'

'It was mostly laziness on my part,' Jacks said. 'I'm just so bored of travelling, you see. And I miss New York, I miss our little house, I miss the gang. Most of all, I'm tired of standing in fields waiting around for this one to get the shot he needs. I want some home comforts for a little while.'

'And that's what this idea would allow us to do, you see?' Dicky said. 'We can continue to write and photograph middle-America while never leaving the comfort of the Village.'

Frances nodded, although she had no idea what she was agreeing with. She had a sense that she was watching a performance, as though these two strange people in front of her had said these same words in the same order a number of times before. It unnerved her.

'Can I ask how long you're planning to stay in New York?' Dicky looked truly interested.

She didn't know the answer herself. For a moment she considered lying, but then couldn't think what the use in that would be. 'I suppose for quite a long time. I'm in no rush to go home and I've missed my brother.'

'Will you be with us for the winter?'

'Yes, I should think so, definitely.'

'Fabulous.' Dicky beamed. 'In that case, I'll let you in on the plan. We want to find a bona fide farm girl like yourself.'

Frances smoothed her skirt, noticing for the first time the tiny splatters of mud on the rim of the hem. Like it or not, she was dragging the farm with her.

'Interview her, find out what makes her tick. What worries

you? What are your life plans? That sort of thing. Then, if you didn't mind, we'd make you over.'

'Make me over?' Frances didn't like the sound of that, although the idea of being asked about herself was appealing. She couldn't recall the last time anyone (apart from a boy on a date, and she wasn't stupid enough to think that was genuine) had been interested in anything she had to say.

'Yes. It's where we ...' Dicky paused, reaching for the right words.

'It's where we give you some fabulous clothes and re-style your hair, and see if you can pass as a true New York deb,' Jacks interrupted. 'We'll get you all dolled up and see if we can't get you out on the town with some dapper Dan. Dicky would take the pictures, before and after, and I'd write it up as a great little story.'

'How does that sound?' Dicky looked at Frances. 'You'd be the star in a very famous New York magazine. We went up and down this train a hundred times before we settled on you.' He moved closer until his pointed nose was a few inches from Frances' face. She smelt cologne and hair wax, the faint whiff of coffee on his breath.

The twists of suspicion in her gut started to unwind. Her, in a magazine? Make-up and clothes? Perhaps she'd get to keep them. Perhaps she'd get a job there. Perhaps this was the start of something. But as quickly as she felt the burn of excitement creep into her, she doused herself with the unlikeliness of it all, drinking down suspicion like a cool glass of water. Were they telling the truth, or had they picked her not because of how she looked, but because she seemed like the youngest, poorest, stupidest girl on the train?

'I was right, you know.' Dicky turned to Jacks. 'Astonishing bone structure.' He lifted his hand to her chin. Frances flinched. 'Sorry,' he said, not letting go. 'Would you mind if I just tilted you a little?' She relaxed slightly and allowed her head to be moved. His brown eyes were shot through with green, the edges reddened – from lack of sleep she supposed. She had felt the gaze of many men on her before, but none of them had looked at her like this, none of them had held her face so softly. 'That's it. Yes. I knew I was right. Look here, Jacks. See the way the light, even in this shoddy carriage, glances off here, and here and here. In the studio I could turn out something fine. I'm sure of it.' Jacks didn't look convinced. He smiled at Frances and patted her cheek. 'What a wonderful face you have, my dear.'

Frances grew hot and pulled away. 'I'm not sure you've explained enough for me to fully understand what you mean,' she said. Who were they to sit down and talk about her while she slept and take a picture and touch her face without being invited? Mother would have smiled nicely and agreed to anything, not because she wanted to do it, but in case she might offend. She was not her mother. 'I may well be a *farm girl*,' she continued, 'but I know about the ways of the world. I certainly don't mean to be rude, but I would very much like to see some papers that say you are who you say you are before you carry on. Things must be done properly, and in the right order. I'm not too happy about the photograph you took of me either, if that's what you did. I was asleep then. It ain't right. It's called *taking* a picture after all. You should have asked.'

Dicky stared down at his camera and smoothed his hair, then grinned at Jacks, whose eyes were drawn wide in mock astonishment. After a few seconds, in which Frances deeply regretted saying anything at all, they both started to laugh. Usually this would have angered her but there was something in the tone of the laughter that made her smile too. Jacks began laughing so hard she tried to get Dicky to hold on to her cigarette for fear she would drop it. They drew the attention of a few people sitting on the seats nearby. A young couple sitting to Frances' right looked like newly-weds, his hair plastered back with too much oil, her skirt just-sewn. Both of them were no doubt wondering why two people from first had come down to talk to someone like her. Now they were really staring, as though the laughter gave them permission to look without shame. Frances didn't care. She was grinning too, all suspicious thoughts pushed aside, thrilled that she had pleased these two astounding new acquaintances.

As the laughter died, Dicky said, 'Why Jacks, I think we've found her.'

Jacks was dabbing at the corners of her eyes with the edge of her velvet jacket. 'I think you're right, dear. I didn't believe we'd find someone, not this fast, but thanks to those eagle eyes of yours I think we've done it. I thought she'd be a real flat-tyre, but it turns out she's a bona fide flapper.' She turned to Frances. 'You should get angry more often. I've never seen someone come alive so fast. Church mouse to snarling hell-cat in a second. If you keep that attitude up, my readers will love you. They really will. There's nothing a New York woman likes more than hearing about a Midwest girl with gumption. Anything that terrifies the men, delights the women, that's the way it works. You'll give them something to chew on over breakfast, no doubt about it. Quite right you should ask us who we are. Who the hell are we? Dicky dear? Can you remember?'

Dicky was patting himself down. He drew a small card from his breast pocket and handed it across.

'I must apologise again. I'm not sure what came over me. Perhaps it was the long journey. Perhaps it was because I've been stuck with this one' – he nodded at Jacks – 'for the past few weeks. The first thing I should have done was give you this.'

Frances looked at the small rectangular card. It felt soft and freshly printed, like her ticket to board the train, except the writing wasn't simple. It was small and slightly curved, the ends of each golden letter curling like twitching cats' tails. She could make out the R at the front of the first word and the S at the start of the second, so that must be his name. The word underneath began with a P and was fairly long, but she had no idea what it said.

Where was the 'F' for photographer? The address at the bottom was a mystery of curving lines and numbers. Strips of molten ink ran around the edge, straight and neat, just like the card's owner.

'Now, take that and keep it safe,' he said. 'The address of my studio is on the bottom. To prove to you that we mean you no harm I'm not going to ask where you'll be staying. Once we get into Penn I want you to wave goodbye to us, go on your merry way with that brutish brother of yours, and not look back. Get settled in the city, have a few steak dinners, see the sights, think over what we've said. Then, a few days from now – I hope no longer than that – drop by the studio and let me know what you think. You can have a look at your photograph. If you don't like it I'll burn it there and then, the negative too. There's no rush.'

Frances nodded. It didn't matter that she couldn't read the address. She'd work it out.

'Like hell there's no rush!' Jacks was gazing at her intently. 'There you go again, Dicky, being selfish. You might only need five minutes to get this girl in the right positions, but I need to know her. If I don't like her, neither will my readers, and to see inside someone, to really understand who they are, you have to spend time with them. I'm not just going to be able to knock up this story at the last minute. Now, Frances – that's your name?' She turned it round in her mouth as though working out if it was good enough to swallow. 'Fran-ces. Not too bad, I suppose. It certainly makes you sound older than you are, which is never a bad idea. The main thing I need you to do is not to change yourself at all, not until we see you again. No hair cutting. No make-up testing in department stores. No buying new clothes. When we see you, I want you to look exactly the same as now, preferably in the same dress. Can you do that for me?'

Frances wondered at the way two people like them could so wrongly assume she had enough money for those sorts of things. Steak dinners and make-up in department stores? But there was nothing to be won by letting on, so she nodded. 'I think so, yes, although I was going to buy some new shoes when I got the chance.'

They looked at her feet. She blushed.

'Ahh yes,' said Dicky, 'I see what you mean. Well, I suppose you can sort yourself out with something appropriate for the city, can't she, Jacks? We don't want you burning yourself on the fresh asphalt.'

Jacks nodded, assessing Frances like a bug behind glass. 'All right, but make sure you bring those sandals with you when you come to the studio. Don't throw them away. Nothing says Midwest to New Yorkers more than a broken shoe and a dirty foot.'

Dicky looked over Frances' shoulder. 'Ahh, here he is.' The conductor was winding his way down the carriage at speed. 'My good man, could you tell us what the hold-up is? My friend here's desperate to get in.'

'Mr Sampson, my apologies.' He was a little out of breath. 'I didn't recognise you there. And Miss Du Montfort. Hello again.' He tipped his hat in Jacks' direction.

'Rogers, isn't it?' Dicky said. The man was looking about, edging himself towards the back of the carriage. 'I was hoping you'd be able to tell us what's going on. Surely we're not still being held at a red signal? We're usually home and pouring a second bourbon by now.'

'Yes, sir. Sorry, sir. Bit of trouble on the line.' The conductor pursed his lips. He looked like he didn't want to keep on talking.

'Mind me asking what sort of trouble? Or at least how long it might be until we're on the move again?'

If Frances had asked, no one would have told her anything. She thought of Stan waiting on the platform for her and wondered if late trains got announced. Would he know where she was? What if she couldn't find him when they got there? What if he thought she'd changed her mind at the last minute?

'Well, sir, it's a bit difficult, I'm afraid.'

'Okay, Rogers, now we're all interested. You'll have to tell us, I'm afraid.'

'Very sensitive, sir. We don't want to alarm the other passengers.' He leant closer and lowered his voice. Frances smelt coal dust and heat. 'Death on the line, I'm afraid. A young girl, the driver says.'

'Oh dear, how terrible.' Dicky looked distraught. 'Jacks, did you hear that? A young girl. Accident, was it?'

'Not sure at this stage, sir. Nothing the driver could do. She just stepped on to the line. Looks like she'd been waiting for the train. Driver said she wasn't running, and no one came after her.'

Frances looked out of the window. A girl. Dead. On the front of her train. The conversation continued around her. Jacks and Dicky with their sadness and surprise, the conductor desperate to get away, tired of their questions about how long it would take to get in and how far they were from the station. Rogers rushed off and they kept on complaining that they would be late, that they'd miss dinner, going on and on about the inconvenience of it all, the damned bad luck that it had happened on the front of their train.

Outside, Frances could no longer see the stacks and the smoke. She imagined the girl, half an hour before, standing there, for some reason in a white nightshirt, her long hair drifting round her waist. Then the whistle of the train on a bend, the smell of the coal, the gravel beneath her feet, the straggling grass drifting against her bare legs, the compression of air on her thin body as the rails shook, the deep breath, the step forward, the twist and crack and rip of bone and flesh. The noise and the silence, then the girl's face, still lovely at the end of it all, her body torn beneath the wheels. Frances might have done the same thing if Stan hadn't saved her. She wondered if they'd have to clean the train before they took the girl away, if any of her blood was still stuck to the wheels, if some part of her would be dragged back to the city she'd been desperate to escape. The same city Frances had risked everything to see.

PENN STATION to
THE LOWER EAST SIDE

15 September 1932

19.03

Church was small and plain compared to this. Golden light poured in through sky-high windows, shafting on to marble floor tiles in angular patterns. Frances had never seen the sun do that. The sun she knew stripped and bleached and withered. She had never been in a place where the ceiling swelled in deep shadowed arches hundreds of feet above her head, where the pigeon calls from the eaves could barely be heard, where people were dwarfed by the buildings they had constructed.

She stood still with her back against a cool pillar and allowed the bodies to move around her. Stan had said he'd meet her off the train. He'd promised. Panic fluttered in her chest. She brushed it away and stood on tiptoes, scanning the crowd. Was that him over there? Strong arms, bag aloft, head turned away. No. Stan wouldn't tip his hat like that.

She searched the throng for the right shoes, the right shade of leather, the perfect shine. Stan was tall but the rest of him was forgettable. He had one of those regular faces people tended to confuse with others. Thick-set jaw, ruddy skin, sun-bleached hair, but his shoes stood out. On the farm, where everything was fraying and needed fixing, every Sunday he would spend hours shining his only good pair – they'd look fine even here.

Sunset made magic of it all. Three young girls chattering side by side on a stone bench beside a ticket office, their heads locked in friendship, became a trio of angels, the yellowed light dappling honey on their cheeks. A giant stone bird on a plinth looked so real it might take flight. A man nearby brushed her shoulder and stepped away at speed, his hat tipped low, a murky river smell eddying in his wake – a sailor, perhaps, a stowaway, a thief.

Stan must be here somewhere. Perhaps he'd gone to a café and lost track of time. He was probably eating a nice plum pie somewhere. She wondered what had held him up, how far from here he lived, how much of the city she'd be able to see before it got too dark. She thrust her hand into her pocket and pulled out Dicky's card. The light caught on the golden lines. What would Stan say? Perhaps it was best to keep quiet when there was a chance he'd forbid her from going. But without Stan's help, how would she ever find her way? She pushed it back into the folds of her skirt as deep as it would go and jumped a few times to see over the crowd, then screamed without meaning to. There he was.

'Stan, Stan!' she called out, although it was useless at this distance. She could see him about fifty feet away, the russet shine on his shoes gleaming against the milky tread of the stone staircase. He turned, although he couldn't have heard her – the rush of people and announcements and chatter in the station was almost deafening – and for a terrifying moment Frances feared it wasn't him. Pale not ruddy, the hair beneath his hat dirty blond, almost brown, not yellow. He looked confused; then he saw her arm in the air and transformed. His eyes softened, his cheeks warmed, he waved.

Frances waited for the relief she'd expected but it didn't come. It was Stan, but it wasn't. She struggled to remember how long it was since she'd seen him. One year? A year and a half? Maybe two? And yet, so much of him had changed it might have been ten. His walk was the same, and his smile, and his eyes, his height, his shoes. But that was all. Everything else was different. His cheeks looked hollowed out, as though they'd been pressed with the back of a cold spoon. He was still bigger than most of the other men in the station, but his suit hung from him, his body reduced in size, like a scarecrow with the stuffing pecked out. He probably hadn't been eating enough. He'd probably been working so hard he kept forgetting to have a proper meal.

As he moved closer, dodging past baby carriages and fast-walking men with newspapers tucked beneath their arms and girls in twos and threes, linked at the elbows, gossiping, Frances realised that the most striking change was his skin. It looked sallow, even in this heavenly light. Drained of colour like a much older man.

He carried on smiling at her until he got close, then he frowned. At what she wasn't sure. He'd never been good at hiding his feelings, at least that hadn't changed. She looked down at her dress, wishing she'd had a clean one to change into, then rubbed her hands on her hips trying to get rid of the worry. Would he hold her? He'd only done that once before, on the day she almost drowned in the lake. She remembered how warm he had felt. How her clothes had been wet through, her eyes icing over in the cold, frost spidering. He'd held her while she'd gasped at the sharp air cutting the back of her throat, every breath an agony. The snow had felt soft beneath her – she must have been so frozen not to feel its cold. Her fear had drained away, as though Stan was melting it.

Now here he was, almost beside her, and there was no more distance between them, no track left to travel, no more remembering. She craned her neck all the way back.

'You made it,' he said. 'Sorry I'm late.'

'I managed,' she said. 'Did you think I'd chicken out?'

'No, but I thought Father might find out and stop you coming.'

'I'm sneaky. And fast.'

He laughed, and it was only then that she realised how much she'd missed the sound.

'I know that. I've not been gone so long I've forgotten how much trouble you are.'

Moments passed and they didn't speak. He smiled down at her and looked around for the exit. She shifted on her feet.

'This way,' he said, finally filling the silence, picking up her case, a beam of fading light forcing half his face to shadow.

The noise and the smell. The motion. Nothing could have prepared her.

The widest street she'd ever seen, at least four lanes across, thundered with packed trams, gleaming flat-top motorcars and closed-back trucks. At first everything seemed to shine, but then she noticed the tar on the wheels, the chipped paint, the peeling lettering.

She tried to steady herself, leaning into Stan, breathing deeply, then coughed on the thick air. She could smell newspaper from the stall beside her, its shelves stacked high with freshly inked words she couldn't read; doughnuts from another stall, sweet and sticky, pooling saliva in her mouth, and tomatoes from the grocer opposite, mostly red and ripe, but some going over, the rot just there at the back of her throat; and dust – an earthy smell but more like rubber; and somewhere, beneath it all, the tangy taste of metal, as though she'd caught her cheek with her teeth and drawn blood. She closed her eyes, but Stan was moving now, his hand on her shoulder, urging her forward into the chaos.

'Are you hungry?' he shouted. 'If you are we can get supper on the way. Or did you eat on the train?'

She nodded. 'Hungry.'

'Don't worry,' he said, sensing her shock, 'it's not always this loud. Once we get off Eighth it all calms down.'

They moved away from the station, weaving between the crowds. Frances kept misjudging the distance between herself and others. Bags crashed, elbows jolted, heels tripped. Naturally, she apologised, but no one ever said sorry back. Even when it wasn't her fault and she managed to stop gazing up at the blocks of dark blue sky between the buildings for a minute, or ceased wondering at all the things one could buy in all the shop windows – the meat on hooks, the jackets on dummies, the books on shelves – even when she concentrated they still pushed impassively past, and not one person turned and smiled or rolled their eyes or murmured sorry under their breath.

It sure did make her mad. No matter how long she lived here, if it was her fault, she was bound to apologise, and so their journey towards Stan's apartment was accompanied by a steady stream of regret, a rhythmic 'so-rry, so-rry, so-rry' that began to merge with the blasts and yells and spinning wheels, until through voice alone, Frances felt herself beginning to keep time with the tempo of the city.

For the most part Stan was silent, and she worried she'd made the wrong decision, that he hadn't really wanted her to come. Then every so often he'd stop and point out a landmark, and relief would course through her like a swift river. On the right, a vast department store, with a name she forgot as soon as he told her, but which sold things she'd always remember: fresh lobsters shipped in from Canada, Dutch cheese as large and round as tractor wheels, diamond rings that cost a thousand dollars. They didn't go inside, but she could imagine it – cool and quiet, dim electric lights casting a sheen of beauty over the flesh and fabric and stones, men and women like Jacks and Dicky wandering around, discarding silk scarves, selecting dark wool jackets, requesting delivery.

Stan walked fast like he did at home, but here he kept his hat tipped, his eyes locked on his feet. She wondered if he was ashamed of her, if he was worried someone would recognise him and he'd have to introduce his farm-girl sister. Down another side-street, he pointed out the angular vaults of the El Train, straddling the street like some giant iron beetle, the windows on either side blackened with smoke, the sun wedged between its feet, turning steel into gold.

They passed church after church, squashed between the homes and offices of those who ignored them until Sunday, the shifts in faith marking their journey, cathedral to chapel to synagogue, Stan said; pointed slate spires to glittering golden domes. All those Gods, Frances thought, all that praying. And all the while, as they walked, she could smell the dirty heat lifting off the sidewalk.

They turned from West 31st on to Broadway and Stan grasped her shoulder, pivoting her body. 'Look up,' he said. Between the streets, above the cotton dresses and felt hats, past the shining hoods of silver Greyhound buses, higher than the freshly chiselled statues and growling gargoyles, a skyscraper, the tallest she'd ever seen, the tallest anyone had ever seen, rose up and needled the darkening sky.

'Empire State. A hundred storeys. Forty million bucks to

build.' Stan marvelled at it beside her.

Next to them, two women, both with curved horn-rimmed glasses, stopped to look too.

'Well, Marjorie,' one of them said, 'I told you it was big.'

They walked on. The light softened and waned. Crowds scattered. One by one the streetlights crackled on around them. To Frances it felt a little like magic, as though each time they passed beneath a lantern, it sensed they were there and flicked on.

'Are they all electric?' she asked, nodding upwards.

'Of course,' Stan replied. 'Have been for ages. Imagine how long it would take someone to light all of these.'

Inside the restaurants they passed, waiters lit candles on the tables, and flipped switches by their awnings, dousing the sidewalks in more light.

'Can we go in here?' Frances asked outside a particularly appealing café, the diners burnished by lanterns, the waiters passing each linen-covered table with pristine cloths thrown over their forearms.

'You crazy? To eat in there, even if we shared a dish, some bread and cheese, a coffee, it'd cost ten times as much as back home at Joe's place. Probably cost me a month's salary.'

'Oh,' Frances said, embarrassed.

'We're still in a rich area, you know. If you hang on a minute, we'll get downtown and there'll be somewhere good. Somewhere that'll make your eyes pop. Lafayette and Third, I think. Not far now.'

They walked past a small hidden park that Stan said was locked, the sparse trees a shock after all the concrete. A single starling chattered on a twisted branch, sounding lost.

A man squeezed between them, his nose so crooked Frances wondered how it was still attached. Two young women, around Frances' age, nudged her shoulder, elbows twined, hair pinned, lipstick on, heading uptown. They giggled when Stan flipped his hat, and stared at Frances. What an awful drudge she must look. She wondered how far Stan's place was, whether it was too late to ask him if they could pick up something to eat and take it there instead of dining out. But just as she began putting together the right words, Stan stopped.

'Here we are,' he said. 'What do you think of that?'

A few steps ahead a store front was glowing, casting a pool of burnt light across the sidewalk outside.

'It's an automat,' Stan said. 'One of the best eateries around. Horn and Hardart.'

Frances stared at the giant sign above the shop front.

'Neon,' Stan said. 'Not sure how it works, but it sure does light up a lot of the city these days.'

There were a few tables down the centre of the room and lots of people: old and young, some in fancy frocks, lots with scuffed shoes. A small boy by the door, his pants torn, drank soup from a bowl as if it was his last meal on earth. Some people were eating standing up next to tables too high to sit around. Strangest of all were the little cupboards around the walls where folks gathered. She watched one fat man put his hat on a small shelf in front of him, his hair thinning, his moustache small and oily. He reached up, pushed a few coins into a slot, opened a little cupboard and took out a piece of pie.

They went in. It smelt of stew and coffee, of cigarettes and baked apple.

'So,' Stan said, 'it's a pretty simple idea. You work out what you want from the signs, put your money in the slot and unlock your food from behind the door. No need for a cashier, no need for a waitress. If you ain't got the right change you go over to the nickel thrower.' He nodded towards the corner of the room where a young woman, around twenty, sat behind a large till. A group of people were lined up in front of her. 'You give her a dollar and she breaks it down for you, then you feed in the right amount.' He reached into his pocket and gave Frances a handful of coins. She smiled, teasing him. He shrugged. 'I don't like to queue, so I save 'em up in case I'm passing. Knock yourself out, see what you feel like. There's enough there for a few plates. I'll get us some coffee.'

He walked towards a row of five or six fancy silver taps sticking out of the wall with a sign above each one. Frances guessed they said things like 'Coffee', 'Milk' and 'Hot Water' but she couldn't be sure.

She peered into the tiny glass doors. It was easy enough to see the lines of cupboards were divided into cakes, pies, sandwiches and soups. The hard part was working out what the flavours were. The cabinets were awful shiny, the glass and chrome and tiles so polished she could see her reflection. Not like the farm. The minute you cleaned anything there, the dust always drifted back.

She could see people outside on the street, reflected in the glass, speeding past, and she could see her own face, twisted by the curve in the metal. She ran a hand through her hair, her fingers snagging on the knots. It wasn't like home. No one was going to see her and talk behind her back. No one was going to bump into Mother after church and say they'd seen her looking like she'd been pulled through a hedge backwards. She didn't need to hide away at Stan's, eating supper in the dark, fixing her clothes and hair. In the city she was a shadow. A nobody.

A hand on her shoulder. Stan beside her with two cups of steaming coffee, apologising.

'Sorry, I forgot,' he said. 'I'll help. What are you smiling at?'

'Nothing. Glad to have made it is all. And I don't need your help. I'm working it out.'

'I know, but . . . ' He paused, and she knew he was trying to find the right words to sound kind. 'Did you have any more lessons before you left?' he asked.

'No, but maybe there'll be someone in the city who can help.' She didn't want to tell him Mother had started using the money he'd sent for reading and writing lessons to buy food. She didn't want him to know how bad things had got.

'I'm sure there will be.' He smiled. 'It's a question of how many bucks it'll cost. I could teach you.'

She laughed. 'You can barely read more than me.'

'Don't be like that,' he said. 'A lot's changed since you saw me last.'

'I don't mean anything by it, I'm just saying there's no point in the blind leading the blind. Better for me to get a job and get someone to help in the evenings. I know the basics, the shape of the letters, some of the sounds. It wouldn't take that long.'

Stan looked dubious. 'All right, I'll ask around. Maybe one of the Jewish families can help – I keep hearing them trying to teach the kids out on the stoop. Or Ben, I know he used to teach the boys at the club, or Mrs Bianchi might know someone.'

Frances nodded. She wondered who these people were but was too tired and hungry to ask and Stan didn't offer to explain.

'So,' Stan said, 'what do you feel like? Chicken soup? Vegetable? A beef sandwich? A piece of pie?' Frances nodded, distracted. He laughed. 'What? All of them?'

She thought for a moment, watching their fellow diners. 'Chicken soup, I think. And pie. Definitely pie. I don't mind what filling.'

Stan found them a seat and she watched as he raced around the room with a tray, feeding in coins, opening cabinets, collecting food. He came back looking proud, as though he'd cooked it all himself. The coffee was hot and strong but watery. The soup was good. Not like Mother's, but salty at least, with chunks of real chicken. While they ate, Stan asked her about her journey, how she'd gotten away, what Father had done. He didn't need to ask about Mother. They both knew she was probably still crying herself to sleep at night. Frances hoped that a small part of her might be glad her daughter had escaped.

'Once I'm settled I'll send a telegram,' she said, wondering why he hadn't taken his hat off.

'Good idea.' Stan nodded, pushing wedges of sandwich into his mouth. 'I don't want them thinking I talked you into it. Or worse, Father thinking Mother was in on it too. He'd make her life even more of a misery than it already is. Were they as bad as ever when you left?'

She paused, the truth sticking to the roof of her mouth.

'Surely not worse?' he asked.

She shook her head. Not quite a lie.

'Well, that's something I suppose. Although, I don't know what's happened to you since I've been gone. You were never this quiet before.'

'I'm tired is all.'

Pieces of chicken drifted to the top of her soup while she stirred. When she looked up he was staring at her in a queer way again and she knew he was building up to saying something.

'At any rate, you're quiet too,' she said.

He looked away and sipped his coffee. 'I'm tired, like you. Work's busy.'

He leant back on his chair and went to link his hands behind his head, almost knocking over a woman carrying a tray of food behind him.

'Oh, my!' the woman said.

Stan jumped up and began apologising. 'I sure am sorry. I didn't intend to startle you. You haven't spilt anything, have you? I'd be glad to replace anything if you have.'

The woman, who was a little older than Frances with rusty just-curled hair peeking out around the sides of a bottle-green hat, looked all the way up at Stan and smiled with her lids lowered. 'Oh no,' she said, 'it was my fault. I was in such a rush to sit down and eat with my friend over there, I didn't really look where I was going.'

This was the Stan Frances knew. A wink and a smile and they melted. Stan watched the woman walk back to her smirking friend on the other side of the room, then folded himself into his chair.

'I don't know how you do it,' Frances said.

'Do what?' He was acting innocent but she could tell from the merry look in his eye he knew what she meant.

'You know. All the . . .' She mimed Stan's shocked face and the woman's bashful eyes.

Stan laughed and shook his head at her. 'Like I said, I've missed having you around to keep me in line.' He reached across the table and tapped the top of her hand. He didn't usually do that. He must have sensed her shock because he only touched her for a second then went back to his food.

Frances gulped her coffee so fast it scalded her throat. She coughed, and Stan clapped her on the back.

'You might as well tell me, then,' he said when she'd finished choking.

'Tell you what?' She was dabbing at the corners of her mouth with a paper napkin, worrying about a splash of coffee on her already dirty skirt.

'Whatever it is that's bugging you,' he said, eyebrows raised.

'Nothing.' Frances laughed. Not now, she thought. Not now. She didn't have the energy for his judgement, couldn't bear the possibility that he might ruin the fantasy and forbid her to see Jacks and Dicky.

'Well?' he said.

But then, maybe if he looked different in the city, he'd think differently too. And if she wanted to see them, she'd need his help. So she told him what had happened on the train, the truth for the most part, although nothing of how she had felt, of how if she closed her eyes she could still see the shine on Jacks' lipstick, the darts of green in Dicky's eyes. The more she spoke, the more it sounded, even to her, as though she'd made up the whole thing.

'So this Joe Brooks, this fella, this Dicky, wants you to go down to his studio so he can take pictures of you for some paper?' Stan raised his eyebrows.

'Yes, sort of,' Frances said. 'But I think Jacks would be there the whole time. They always work together.' Frances had no idea if this was true but it seemed right to make sure he knew she'd never be alone with Dicky.

'And how much did they say you'd be getting paid for this inconvenience?'

'They didn't.' Frances felt herself grow hot. Stan shook his head and began mopping up his soup with a piece of bread. 'I think that'll get sorted out later.' Her voice was quiet.

'I can't believe,' he said, still chewing, 'you've been here barely five minutes and you've already been duped.'

'That's what I thought first of all. But honestly, Stan, I was ever so careful. I asked them for evidence that they were who they said they were. Look.' She fussed in her pockets and brought out Dicky's card. She smoothed it for a second then passed it across, not wanting to let it go.

'Hmmm. Let's see. Richard Sampson, photographer. Very fancy.' He turned it over, then held it up to the light and sniffed at it.

'There's no need to be such a tease!' Frances hated him then. For a brief second she wanted to hurt him, like she'd done every time he mocked her as a child. She held out her hand. He made as if to pass it back, then whipped it away just as her fingers touched the edge and held it up too high for her to reach.

As he craned his neck, Frances noticed a tiny scar underneath his chin that she'd not seen before. It was so small no one else would have spotted it. Fresh and pink, about half an inch across. Perhaps he'd done it shaving? But he never cut himself – he was always precise about that, even when he was fifteen.

'What's that?' She shot out her hand and pointed.

'What?' he asked, his fingers flying up to the blemish.

'That, there, on your neck.'

'Cut myself.'

'I can see that, but how?'

'Oh, I don't know. Shaving probably.'

'Hmm.'

'What's all this? You turned detective? It's nothing.'

'If you say so.'

'I do.'

She sipped her coffee. It was obvious from the flush in his cheeks, the way he couldn't look at her now, that something was up, but she knew better than to push him about it. This was information that would need to be teased out – like pulling a long trail of thread through tight cotton. She would wait for the right moment and tug carefully until the truth came free.

She pointed at Dicky's card. 'You're just jealous that the second I arrive something exciting happens and you've been here for months drudging along in the same job, doing God knows what with not even a hint of drama.' She paused, waiting for the row to ignite as it always had, for Stan to shout and her to cry and them to make up and walk through the dark streets together. But he slid the card across the Formica towards her, then looked down at his plate and carried on chewing in silence.

She spooned the last of her soup into her mouth and started on her cherry pie, wondering what was the matter. It was too sweet, but not bad, the cherries halved, the jam congealed.

'Pretty good pie,' she said. He ignored her. 'Come on.' She tugged on the edge of his sleeve. 'I didn't mean anything. There's no need to give me the silent treatment.'

After a long pause he sighed and said, 'I think you need to be careful is all. There's things that happen in this city, things a girl like you can fall into without knowing it. Terrible things, some of them.'

'So you won't let me go?' She clenched her fist beneath the table. If Stan banned her, she'd go anyway, she'd figure it out, but she'd also have to lie to him, she'd have to sneak around like back home, and she didn't want to do that.

He peeled the lid off his pie and shovelled the contents into his mouth, as he'd always done. 'I'm not saying that,' he said. 'I'm saying that we've gotta do this right. I don't know, maybe there is money in it, maybe these folks are the bee's knees. Then again, maybe they're not. Either way, I'm coming with you.'

Frances took a deep breath. 'But what about work?'

'Don't worry about that, it's mostly evenings these days anyway.'

'You still haven't told me what you've been—'

A commotion behind Frances stilled her words. The door crashed open as though someone had pushed it too hard and now a woman was shouting. Stan looked past the side of Frances' head, frowning, his spoon hanging in the space between his mouth and the plate.

'You're good for nothing! I told you outside. I'm hungry. I'm coming in to eat by myself. If you touch me one more God-damned time, I swear you'll regret it. I swear to God himself I've had enough of this!'

Frances twisted on her seat and stared. By the door a woman with a fur coat slung over her shoulders and bare legs was trying to stop a man from coming into the automat. Her arms were holding him by the shoulders, pushing with all her might. Long pearl necklaces and jade beads dangled from her neck. Her hair was bright blonde, her reddened eyes ringed with kohl.

'I mean it, Joseph, I mean it this time,' the woman said. 'No more, I said, no more! You can't keep doing this!'

Some diners watched silently, others were pretending not to notice, as though they were still occupied by their food. A few of them inched towards the edges of the room.

The man, who was now halfway inside the diner, still hadn't said anything. His hat had tipped at a precarious angle. One more shove, Frances thought, and it would be on the floor. He was thin, much smaller than the woman, his hair dark and slick, a smear of a moustache. He was breathing deeply, his cheeks flushed. Then he seemed to rise up and gather his strength and he pushed the woman so hard her feet lifted off the floor and she crashed into a table on the other side, knocking the contents flying. The people sitting nearby jumped back, then grabbed their coats and hats as fast as they could. On the floor, the woman began to moan.

'You've done it now, Joseph,' she said between sobs. 'That's it, now you've done it. Wait till I tell him. Wait till I tell him what you've done.'

Frances waited for Stan to stand up, but he didn't move. He had tipped his hat even further down his face and was staring at his plate.

The man strode across the room to where the woman was lying. He looked taller now, his fists clenching as he moved. He didn't look around. When he got to the woman he bent down, grabbed the lapels of her coat and dragged her up. One shoe fell off. Her stockinged toe scraped the floor.

'Say sorry, Joseph, say sorry, that's all you have to do,' the woman said. 'You gotta apologise to all these people at least. Look what you done to their food. Never mind me, look what you done.' She was pleading now, shrinking away from him, her voice quieter, and she seemed much younger than Frances had first thought, maybe even younger than her. Her make-up was smeared across her face, her eyes wet and wide.

'What's wrong with you?' Frances hissed at Stan. Back home he would have been across the room by now, giving that man a piece of his mind.

'Nothing, leave it. It's not our business.'

Frances scowled at him. 'That never stopped you before.'

She stood quickly, then, brushing Stan away when he tried to hold her arm, and walked to the couple without thinking.

The man slapped the woman hard across the face. Frances stopped and raised her hand to her cheek as though she was the one who'd been hit. She knew that sting. She knew how the welt would rise up and the skin would swell. She knew how sore it would be for days after, how the eye might bloom in rainbow hues for weeks. How everyone would stare.

She was next to them now. 'Let her go,' she said.

The man didn't seem to hear, he didn't look at her. Instead he shook the woman, then hit her twice more, harder each time, the cracks echoing around the tiled room. The woman fell silently to the floor, her legs collapsing beneath her like a marionette.

'Enough!' Frances said.

She stepped between the two of them. Some of the other diners were breathing loudly, shrinking behind their cups. Somewhere someone cleared their throat but no one said anything. Up close she could see a thin film of sweat between the man's feeble moustache and the top of his lip. He grinned at her. Until then she'd not been afraid, but the way the smile cracked his face in half sent her shivering. He pulled his lips all the way back like a child, but his eyes stayed cold – black and white, no colour. Some of his teeth were missing. He grabbed her arm. She waited for Stan. He'd be behind her by now. She wondered why she couldn't hear his footsteps. The man pressed his nails into the soft part of her wrist. She tried to twist away, to see where Stan was.

'I think your girlfriend wants you, Stanley.' The man's voice scraped at the back of his throat as though, like her, it was desperate to escape.

For a moment the sound of it distracted Frances from what he had said. *Stanley.* She tried to pull away. Her brother still hadn't looked up.

'I said,' the man went on, 'I think she wants your help.'

'Leave it, Joseph.'

There he was. So they knew each other.

The man grabbed her close and she could smell his sour breath, the rot in his gums. There was a wild stillness about him, his black eyes flicking over her, his body barely moving.

She scowled at him. 'Let go.'

He laughed. 'You sure know how to pick 'em, Stan.'

'Leave her be, Joe.' Stan again. 'Boss'll hear about it otherwise.'

'I ain't afraid of him or you.'

'I know that, but you want to get paid, don't you?'

The man paused.

'I suppose I do.'

'Well that's that, then,' Stan said.

Frances twisted her head as far as her neck would allow. Stan still had his hat tipped, but she could see his hands, splayed upwards on the table; he was shrugging at the guy, as though he was making peace.

The man let her go. She made out like she was walking away, then spun and spat as hard as she could in the direction of his face, like Stan had taught her. Strings of it, tinged pink from her pie, clung to his tiny moustache. He wiped it off with the back of his hand and laughed again.

'Classy. Real classy.'

'Off you go, Joe,' Stan said.

'It's all right, I'm going. I'll see you at the club some time.'

The door banged the wall as he left and the diners started talking right away, their chairs grinding on the tiles, people running over and helping the woman on the floor, all of them staring at Frances but not one of them coming close.

Frances walked back to Stan, frowning at him, rubbing her wrist where the man's nails had caught.

'Sorry,' he said. His jaw was pulled tight at the edges.

She tried to catch his eye but he didn't look up from his dirty plate. 'I should think so. Some welcome that was.'

'You should have left it.'

'You shouldn't have. How'd you know him?'

'Work.'

'Must be some fine place. I can't wait to see it.'

He started gathering their things. 'You've got to calm down.'

'Strikes me you're being too calm. Sitting still while a woman gets hit, while I get hurt.'

He wouldn't look at her. 'Things are different here.'

'From what I've seen, not that much.'

'Trust me, Frances. You can't act here the way you did on the farm.'

'I'll act any way I God-damn choose.' She was livid now, the anger rising up and flushing her cheeks till they burnt.

'We'll see,' he said.

NEW YORK CITY

Winter solstice, 21 December 1932

16.49

Frances turned away from the city and climbed back inside. Her temples ached. From the cold, she supposed. It was barely any warmer inside than out. She blew on her hands and watched her friend work. Agnes was still setting up her camera. In the dim light from the paraffin lamp, her fingers were bleached, as though death had come early to strip away the flesh and now there was nothing left but bone. She crawled over the camera, twisting metal screws, polishing glass, releasing the bellows from their nest; checking height and angle and distance.

Frances wanted to smooth her friend's cheek, to wrap her arms around her. She wanted to go back and see her again for the first time at the door in the square, to sit side by side in the picture house, to get lost in the city, to smell the darkroom. She walked over and stilled Agnes' hands, rubbing her frozen fingers between her own chilled palms, pressing them back to life. Agnes looked up, exasperated that she'd had to stop, then softened when she saw the way Frances was searching her face.

'It'll be all right, you know,' Agnes whispered. 'We're doing the right thing.'

'Then why do I feel so awful?'

'You'd be mad if you didn't.'

'We could stop now, there's still time,' Frances said. 'We could take a photo, of the city, of us, of anything, and go back to the Village and think of another way.'

Agnes pulled her hands away and walked around the camera, checking for faults.

'There is no other way,' she said. 'We've been over it and over it. I've been round my own head with it a thousand times. You might be able to go on living with him in the world, but I can't. And if we're going to do it, this is the best way.'

Frances closed her eyes for a second, hoping that she wouldn't see his body, but as the light vanished, there he was. It was the reason she couldn't sleep, the reason for the headaches, the reason she drank and drank before bed until she blacked out. That image of him on the ground burnt behind her lids, as though the popping flashbulb had scorched it there, and no matter how much she tried she couldn't rub it away. A sliver of hope. If this man goes, if he disappears, maybe the picture in her head would too, maybe some of the pain.

She opened her eyes, relieved by the glowing light.

'You're right,' she said, 'I couldn't keep living either.'

'If there was another way, any way at all . . .' Agnes said. 'If telling the police would get him punished, if getting him locked up would work, we'd do it. Obviously we would. But we both know that would never happen now. *We'd* be accused of something instead. He'd find a way to get off the hook and he'd find a way to destroy us. No. I've never been more certain of anything in my life. I've never thought about anything so much. We've got no choice.'

Seventy-two floors below, a siren wailed, making the two women jump. Frances giggled, and put her hand to her mouth, the same hysterical sensation rising in her stomach. Agnes rolled her eyes and held her finger to her lips. They listened intently, looking at the window, holding their bodies as still as possible until the sound faded to a distant sigh.

Frances wondered what it might feel like to run across the room and jump. First there'd be wind. Then air. Her innards would lurch, the windows and buildings would rush past. Would she feel weightless? Like that time beneath the ice when she feared she'd never see the surface. Would she black out? Or would her eyes stay open all the way down so she might take in the lights of the city one last time? From this height she was certain you wouldn't feel much when you hit the sidewalk. Even if you did it'd be over in a second. Perhaps she'd land on top of some ritzy car and her hair would pillow against the twisted metal and her stockinged feet would pitch at strange angles and her pearls would stick to her neck. Perhaps they'd put her picture in the paper. Another glamorous dead girl for them all to gawk at.

Behind them, the door creaked. The air shifted, light flickered. A shadow cut across the room. In the doorway a man stepped towards them and stretched out his hand.

LOWER EAST SIDE

28 September 1932

19.50

The cotton drifted in the breeze from the window. Frances' fingers slid on the needle again. She cursed the unusual heat, put down her sewing, wiped the sweat from the back of her neck with her handkerchief and walked to the window, then tugged at the rotting sash until it slid up another inch or two.

A group of children were playing on the street beneath the washing lines, using the light from the windows to see what they were doing. In this heat none of the women wanted them inside. Mrs Bianchi's eldest grandson Marco was there, ordering the rest of them around. And the Tonioni twins from Apartment 4. The older kids were playing some kind of baseball game without the diamond or the stumps. They ran and screamed and pushed each other over, their shirts too small, the knees of their pants ripped, torn laces trailing in the dirt. There was even a baby in a large perambulator, sitting upright with a dirty cotton bonnet and a stern look on its face. She wondered whose it was, watching its fat fingers fiddling with something, imagining holding them, kissing them; then whipped her thoughts away when they drifted back to the farm, to the tiny mound she'd had to walk past every time she went to fetch up water. She closed her eyes for a second, folding at the edges of the memory until it was small and hidden and she could look out again without crying.

She leant towards the gap and sucked in the almost-fresh air, enjoying the way it caught on the damp patches beneath her arms, then returned to her chair and bent close to the fabric, checking over her work. It was only the second day she'd managed to keep going since lunch without having to plunge her hand into iced water. When Mrs Bianchi had told her she'd get used to the pain she hadn't believed her, and yet here she was, at nearly eight, taking some pleasure in it still. Stan had fixed up the job for her a few days after she arrived. Mrs Bianchi needed someone who could sew fast and neat, but who could also make up some of the designs herself. Someone who didn't fuss too much, who didn't ask too many questions. That had suited Frances just fine.

She turned the wooden frame over and tightened the metal screw a little to stop the fabric sagging. Nearly finished. She hoped the old woman would like her design this time. The last one hadn't gone down too well – too fussy, too fancy, she'd used too much thread – but whoever it was for must have liked it because a few days after she'd been told off, Mrs Bianchi had come knocking and asked for two more pillowcases and a 'Home Sweet Home' in the same design.

She pushed the needle back and forth, going over the pencil lines she'd sketched out earlier, enjoying the tug and strain of the thread against cotton, the pressure and resistance, the way the dark green gathered and built and spread, until it unfurled across the edge of the fabric. A Garden of Eden – as close as she'd ever get to reaching out and running her hand through fresh leaves, to hearing them rustle.

Stan called from the other room. She slid the needle into the cotton, tucked her hair behind her ears and walked through. He was lying on the daybed with two old cushions propped behind his head and a book in his hand. Their chess game was still on the table. He kept trying to teach her, but she was no good.

'Yes?' she asked, fighting to keep the annoyance from her voice. A fortnight of living together and she was already tired of being at his beck and call. 'Are you hungry?'

'No,' he replied, not looking up. 'I mean yes.'

He glanced at her but didn't carry on so she filled the kettle from the faucet in the corner of the room, then set it on the stove and checked to see if there was paper and kindling. There was. She set a match to it, and rinsed out a chipped bowl while she waited for him to speak and for the kettle to boil. At this time of year she was thankful that the stove didn't throw out much heat, but she worried what it would be like in the dead of winter.

She washed the bowl for longer than it needed, then turned to talk to him but he'd gone back to his book, so she started peeling potatoes instead, stripping the old skin away, revealing the clean flesh beneath, the motion almost as soothing as sewing. She dropped the peelings into a pail at her feet, and swivelled to wash what was left. Part of her enjoyed the tiny kitchen now, the way she could reach everything she needed without moving, but another part still hated how small it was, how dreary the wallpaper looked, how the peeling flock seemed to soak up the light.

At first she'd been so overwhelmed by the sound and feel of the city around her, by the engines and shouts, the patter of unknown feet on creaking stairs, the noise stretching the space between the walls, she'd not noticed how their two tiny rooms – front parlour and back bedroom – made the farmhouse seem like a palace. But with each day Stan asked her not to go outside, she longed for dead fields and empty skies a little more and struggled with his closeness, with the smell of him and the strange hours he kept, with his half-formed thoughts and strung-out silences.

When dinner was ready she dragged over the little side table. They ate bending forward like when they were children. Stan held his plate underneath his chin and chewed in silence until a shout from down the hall cocked their heads. The Tonionis arguing again. She giggled, and Stan mustered a half smile. The best she'd seen in a week.

The walls were whisper thin. It was impossible to escape from the crying babies and incessant muttering, from the deep-throated anger in foreign tongues and the high-pitched sighs. Frances had learnt the rhythm of the tenement without ever going into the passage. She knew the makeshift school had ended when the twins clattered in and called for food. She knew Mr Tonioni was back from hawking metal when his door banged and his wife shouted at him, and that it was time to sleep when Mrs Tonioni eventually relented and let him use her body to relieve the stresses of the day. The creaking bed, the wail of relief, the thickness of a snore in the dark.

'It's good,' Stan said, shovelling great mouthfuls of cold meat and potato salad into his mouth. 'Not as good as Mother's, but not bad. I'll make a great cook out of you at this rate. Some guy'll be thanking me one day.'

Frances rolled her eyes. 'Read me something, would you?' she asked. This, at least, remained unchanged. This, they still shared. He could be the patient teacher and she his devoted student. What must it be like to be able to cast swift eyes over the letters, to trace a finger beneath swirling black lines and know what they said?

'Can't, I'm afraid,' he said. 'This one's far too hot for a little thing like you. It'd burn your ears off, some of it.'

'Like what?'

He flicked back a few pages, frowning. 'Like, "Was she jealous?"' he read. '"She was . . . and domineering, and spoiled, and

suspicious, and greedy, and mean, and unscrupulous, and deceitful, and selfish, and damned bad – altogether damned bad!"'

Frances laughed. 'It doesn't sound too awful to me.'

'Too rough for you,' he muttered, already distracted, staring
at the lace on the window. He folded his corner over and put the
book down.

'It's hot,' she said.

'Sometimes is this time of year.'

'I didn't think I'd miss the farm but in this heat I do. I'd give
anything to go down to the lake, although it didn't have much
water in it when I left.'

Stan smiled at her. 'More like a puddle.'

'Yeah. More like a puddle of piss.'

His laughter warmed her like hot coffee – strong and thick and
stuck to her insides.

'But you still miss it?' He raised his eyebrows, almost frowning.

'Well, perhaps not the lake, so much as the sky.'

He nodded, and looked back at his plate, building up a
mound of food in the centre with his fork. 'Now that, I can
understand. I longed for the sky at first. Twilight ones especially. Remember those great dull rainbows that stretched away
from the farm so far you felt like there was nothing else out
there, nothing else you needed? All those colours. Now it's just
brown and grey. Here and there a sliver of blue. Sun? Forget it.
Damned buildings everywhere. Too many folks going about all
over the place. Funny though. I can cope in the day, it's mostly
night-time I get stifled. I hate it when I can't see the stars.'

She nodded and crushed a warm potato between her teeth. He
was right. About the sky and her food. It was overcooked. Like
chewing flour if you didn't eat it with a lump of ham. Nothing
like Mother's.

'You finished?' He was looking out of the window again.

'Almost.'

'Hurry up, I wanna show you something.'

He got up and threw his plate in the sink without scraping. It riled her when he did that. She cleaned hers and sloughed some water on the china then followed him to the window.

'You wanna see something great? Something you'd never see if you were still sloping about on the farm annoying Mother?'

'Sure.'

She hoped he wasn't going to point out the tenements across the street. They were all she'd stared at for days.

He slid the window up as far as it would go, then stuck his leg out into the sky.

'Stan!' What was he doing?

'Calm down. Look.'

He stepped all the way out, wincing when some part of him hurt. She ducked her head beside him and looked down. How had she not noticed before? There was a cage running all the way under the window. She'd seen the metal from inside but hadn't realised it was a platform. Stan pointed over his head. Ladders criss-crossed all the way up. Right to the top of the building.

'Fire escape. Wanna see?' He held out his hand.

She took it and stepped out. The metal creaked. She didn't call out but he laughed at her fearful expression.

'Why didn't you show me this before?'

He shrugged. 'I dunno. Didn't think of it. Come on.'

He let go of her hand and started going up, slowly at first, wary of another jolt of pain, she guessed, then faster, his slacks flapping, thinning arms still so strong he barely had to pull on them. Slowly, carefully, she put her hand on a bar. The shock of the hot metal on her palm made her call out.

'Ow!'

'Move fast and it won't hurt so much.'

'You could have warned me.'

She watched his tan heels all the way up, the leather so worn and cared for it looked like it had turned back into living skin, pursing her mouth at the pain in her hands, too fearful to look down.

At the top she caught her breath, brushed off her skirts and turned to see what all the fuss was about.

For a while she didn't speak. She stood and stared and rubbed at the pain in her palms. Then she looked across at Stan's beaming face.

'So this is where the sky went,' she said.

He nodded and grinned even wider. 'Take it all in. I'll be here, beside these giant Garcia Grandes, having a smoke.'

He stepped back a few paces, lit a cigarette and leant against a huge advertisement, the cigar on the sign bigger than he was.

Frances nodded and kept staring. She could still see the other tenements, but they were beneath her now, almost cheerful-looking, with all the strings of washing flapping in the soft wind like carnival flags. Beyond that were more buildings, mostly the same size and shape, but jagged on their flat tops, covered in signage and water towers and chimney stacks. Then further still, past them, she could see the city proper, the buildings so much taller there, all of them straining heavenwards, and one, taller than all the rest, thrusting straight up, as though it was pointing at the sky she had so longed to see.

She stretched her head a little more towards it all, drinking in the chaos, the air a little cooler up here, watching the buildings blacken as the light failed. Somehow, like a snuffed candle, the sky kept glowing. The streets were still noisy but everything was muffled, as though not a damn thing beneath their feet mattered.

'It's something, isn't it?' Stan was sitting with his back against the water tower now, his feet crossed at the ankles, catching the drips from one of its curved wooden slats in his palm, sipping at what he held.

'It is.'

'Worth the trip?'

'Almost.'

'What more do you want, woman?'

'To be in it.'

Perhaps now, when he was fed and smiling. Perhaps now was a good time to ask again.

'About Dicky,' she began.

'No.'

'Can you at least tell me what part of the city he lives in? We could get a map. I don't need to go, I'd just like to see where it is.'

'No.'

'Why?'

'Like I said yesterday, and the day before. I don't want you going around with people like that.'

'But you didn't say that before and you don't know what he's like.'

'I know enough and I've been thinking about it. Any man that approaches a girl on her own on a train and fills her head with nonsense isn't the kind of man I want you seeing.'

They looked out in silence for a long time, the sight of it all stopping her from yelling. Then Stan stubbed out his cigarette and they climbed back down. He held the lace aside for her. She refused to look at him.

Frances cleared the rest of the food away, gripping the edges of the plates, clattering them in the sink.

'What was the point in saying I could come if all I'm allowed to do is stay indoors?' She spoke with her back to him. If she saw his face she'd scream.

'You can go out. You can go shopping with Mrs Bianchi, or one of the Annas. You can go for a walk with them.'

'But not on my own?'

'No.'

She started scrubbing the dishes, using her nails to get rid of the grease, grinding them against the china until they started to split.

'Why?'

'I've told you. The city's a dangerous place. Until I've got time to show you properly, you'll have to make do with the Bianchis.'

'Fine.' She dropped the plates on to the drainer and marched into the bedroom. She tried to slam the door, but it was too light to make much of a sound.

The edge of the sewing she'd finished last night lifted in the gust from the door. She wrapped the fabric in brown paper, but didn't tie it – there was no point when Mrs Bianchi was going to check over her work in front of her the minute she got there – and went over to her dresser. The few possessions she'd brought from the farm were scattered on the top. She'd tried to arrange them in a pleasing pattern, but there was only so much you could do with scruffy things. Her brush was good enough, but some of the enamel on the back had flaked off. She picked it up and ran it through her hair, the bristles scratching at her scalp, staring into the small water-damaged mirror while she yanked the knots. Next to her brush were her best gloves – cream with pearl buttons. A sweet-sixteen gift from Mother and Father before all the trouble began. She'd told Mother she'd lost them so they wouldn't be sold, then hidden them under her mattress.

Beside them was a photograph of her and Stan as kids, taken by a passing photographer in the back yard with the old tin bath hung up behind them, and next to that was Dicky's card, propped up against an almost-empty bottle of Mouson Lavender that a friend had given her years ago. She snatched up the card and pushed it into her pocket. If Stan wouldn't help her, perhaps someone else would.

Frances waited. Two small bright canaries, one green, one yellow, swung in individual cages from the ceiling, chirruping at each other through the bars like talkative prisoners in adjacent cells. In a third, a large grey parrot eyed her and cleaned itself. As it nipped and pulled, feathers drifted down and littered the floor of its cage. One of them fell through the bars, as though the bird had passed her a gift, and she quickly grabbed it before anyone noticed, smoothing the soft plume between thumb and forefinger.

Two of Mrs Bianchi's three sons were sitting at the table by the open window, muttering in their own language, playing cards. They'd eaten her with their eyes when she first arrived, then gone back to their game without a greeting. They both had long, tan, thick fingers, their knuckles so dry they looked like they were dusted in icing. Frances pushed down an urge to rush across the room and lick them – to suck at their fingers like fat sugared lollies.

The tops of the morning glories rippled on the sill, yellowed lace ebbing. She dabbed at the back of her neck, listening to the two brothers' wives outside on the fire escape, settling their children down for another hot night.

The weather didn't bother her as much as it did most people. She was used to it, after all, used to waiting for it to rain, to giving up praying when it never did. At least the storms couldn't get her here. The silent ones had been the worst. Black blizzards. No warning except a slight shift in the thickness of the air. Noon sunlight mottling to muddy twilight. And then before you knew it they were upon you, thousands of feet high, sweeping across the broken plains.

She remembered crouching indoors beneath her thin cover, knees to chest, the house shaking all around, tiles flying from the roof, the darkness as thick as a velvet blindfold. And then afterwards, the tiny particles swirling in the new light, the dust seeping through panelled walls, the cupboards and closets coated in the stuff, faces as black as if they'd been pressed into soil, hair as grey and stiff as a dying man's. Dirt grinding between your teeth when you called out for help.

She dabbed at her top lip and pushed the memories away. She hated the way sweat collected there. It made her look common. Like the man in the automat. This was not the new start she wanted.

Mrs Bianchi returned. The old Italian woman was as fat as an overfed cow and almost as bad-tempered, but she could be warm and she always smelt of flour and aniseed, and not much ruffled her.

'Now, I've given you a little more than last time,' she said.

Frances brightened.

'Not much more, mind you. Don't get silly about it. I still can't agree about all that extra thread, but you can sew. There's no doubt about that. And you're convenient for me. It's not often someone with your skills moves next door.' She handed over a small envelope.

Frances itched to look inside but was too proud to do it with the old woman watching. 'Thank you.'

Mrs Bianchi bustled past her and busied herself at the sink.

'Not known heat like it since home, have we, boys?' One of her sons grunted but didn't turn. 'Good for business though. Sheets get used and used in this weather. All that tossing and turning wears everything out. Better than in the winter, that's for sure.'

Frances took a deep breath. 'Mrs Bianchi?'

'Yes?'

'Can I ask you something? A favour?'

'Not if it involves more effort or more money.'

'It doesn't.'

'Well, go on then, girl.'

'I want to visit a family friend while I'm in the city, but Stan's too busy with work to take me. Do you know this address?'

Frances' fingers shook against the card as she held it out.

Mrs Bianchi wiped her hands on her apron and took it from her. She squinted down at it, then walked to a rough wooden dresser in the corner of the room and took out some spectacles.

'A family friend, you say?'

'Yes.'

'Must be someone well-to-do.'

Mrs Bianchi eyed her. Frances tried not to squirm.

'Yes, an old friend of my father's.'

'Hmm.'

The old woman fingered the edge of the card and turned it over.

'And your brother's too busy to take you, is he?'

'Yes, that's right.'

She handed the card back to Frances and walked through to the other room without speaking. Frances wished she'd not mentioned it and looked up at the birds, wondering whether the woman would tell Stan, trying to decide how angry he'd be.

The old woman returned with a small parcel in her hand.

'I can do you a deal,' she said.

'What sort of deal?' Frances was immediately suspicious. Mrs Bianchi might be as fat as a cow but Frances suspected she was not as stupid.

'The kind where I help you and you help me. This parcel needs to go to the other side of the square from that friend of your father's. I'll tell you where the address on your card is if you deliver it for me free of charge.'

Frances exhaled. 'Yes, I could do that.'

Mrs Bianchi leant close and tapped her nose. 'And we can keep this between you and me. No need to bother your brother with the details, no need to—'

Someone knocked at the door.

'Thank you,' Frances said, taking the parcel and smiling at Mrs Bianchi's ample behind as she pushed past her, trying to keep a hold of the hot excitement in her chest.

'Well, who can that be?' Mrs Bianchi said. 'Are you expecting anyone?'

'No, Ma.' Both men called over from the table without looking up.

Mrs Bianchi opened the door and gasped. On the other side a Negro was smiling at her. He was short and stocky, like Mrs Bianchi's sons, his white shirt rolled up to the elbows revealing muscular arms. He wore a black tie and black slacks. At his feet, two large cases blocked any means of escape. Frances moved backwards until the curve of her back touched the dresser.

Mrs Bianchi threw her arms in the air and Frances thought she was going to scream, but the sound that left her mouth was more like a wail of pleasure.

'Ben! Is it really you?' the old woman said. 'You're back! How long it's been! Boys, boys – look who it is!'

At the door, the man bowed and held Mrs Bianchi's outstretched hand between his. Their skin was almost the same colour.

'Mrs Bianchi. How wonderful it is to see you looking so well.' When he spoke, his words rounded in a Midwest way that made Frances think of home. 'I'm sure you haven't aged a day since I've been gone. In fact I'd say you were looking even younger.'

Mrs Bianchi scoffed and ushered him into the room. Frances saw her face had flushed. The man walked in, bringing his two cases with him.

'Are you just back, then?' Mrs Bianchi asked, busying herself putting the kettle on. She seemed to have forgotten Frances was still there. Her sons had stopped their game and were scowling and whispering at each other, occasionally glancing in Ben's direction. 'Have you been all over this time?'

'Yes, I'm afraid so,' Ben said. 'Six states.'

'Six! You must be exhausted.'

'I am, but it was worth it. We got to play in some great places. Folks in the big cities seem to appreciate what we do almost as much as the boys back in Harlem.'

He glanced across at Frances and smiled. She tried to smile back, but was distracted by the way he held her eye. Not like the Negroes back home. The ones she'd seen walked with their heads down and their hands behind their backs. She remembered Father chasing a young boy off their farm once. He'd gone after him with the shears through the parched grass until the child fell, and she'd been afraid Father would run him through. He hadn't though. She'd heard Father shout and the little boy's cries, but she'd carried on with her chores and there'd been no sign of the boy since. She wondered what had become of him, whether he'd convinced any of their neighbours to let him rest a while in their barn, whether anyone had given him the food he'd looked so desperately in need of.

Ben turned back to Mrs Bianchi. 'I sure am glad to be home though. I'm looking forward to my own bed tonight. Wanted to check in on you first and see how things have been.'

'Oh, you know.' Mrs Bianchi poured out two cups of coffee. Frances had never known Mrs Bianchi not to offer her a drink. 'Nothing changes here.'

Frances watched Ben closely. His neck looked tense, veins ticked across the taut skin.

'Glad to look after the place for you,' Mrs Bianchi carried on. 'I've been in now and then to water your boxes.' She passed him the coffee and saw Frances. 'Oh, sorry, dear,' she said, without much feeling. 'This is Ben, he lives across the way. Ben, this is Frances. Stanley's sister. She's fast becoming my best seamstress.'

Frances tried to smile again. Ben moved towards her, holding out his hand, and she fought off the urge to run away.

'Pleasure to meet you at last. Stan's told me all about you.'

Her reply was a whisper. 'About me? Stan?'

'Sure has. He wasn't sure when you'd be coming last time we spoke, but he guessed it'd be soon. How's the city treating you so far? Has he been showing you the sights?'

She stuttered. Mrs Bianchi saved her.

'We've not seen much of him. You know how he is – work, work, work. But this one's been doing a fine job of looking after him.'

Ben looked concerned again, then he smiled. 'I'm sure she has. Is he in tonight, are you able to receive visitors?'

'Well, I guess so,' Frances said. 'I mean, when do you think you'd come to call?'

'Later? I'll go home and clean myself up. Then if my bed doesn't steal me, I'll be over to see him for a game of cards, chess maybe. Will you tell him? If it's no trouble?'

'No, no trouble at all.' Frances hoped she'd kept the shock from her voice. 'I'm sure he'll be pleased to see an old friend. To have some male company.'

'No doubt,' Ben said. 'Has no one else been to call? No other friends?'

'No,' Frances said, 'no one.'

Ben nodded. He reached into his back pocket and pulled out an envelope. 'I can't tell you how much I appreciate what you've done for me,' he said, handing it to Mrs Bianchi.

The old woman tucked the envelope into the folds of her skirt and smiled. 'Nonsense. After what you and Stanley did for my Vito, helping us up and down the stairs in his chair every day before we lost him, looking in on your place is nothing.' She nodded at her sons, who had resumed their game, then raised her voice. 'The things you did for him that his own sons wouldn't do.'

'I should get back,' Frances said.

'Yes, dear, off you go.' By the door, Mrs Bianchi held Frances' elbow and murmured in her ear. 'Come by tomorrow and I'll point you in the right direction.'

When Frances walked back into the parlour, they still had their arms wrapped around each other. She thought to leave, but figured she'd make too much noise. They parted but kept their heads close, whispering at each other like lovers. She coughed and walked across the room to make coffee.

'None for us,' Stan said. 'I think we'll have those last few beers.'

He was smiling, his energy renewed, bouncing around like a puppy. Frances pulled out the bottles then cleared and wiped the table by the window.

'For God's sake stop fussing,' Stan winced. 'No need to tidy up for this one. He was in the war, went all the way to Europe. He's lived in far worse. The 369th, wasn't it, Ben? The Harlem Hellfighters. There ain't a vet I've spoken to who doesn't remember what they did.'

'Yes, that's right,' Ben said, frowning, his eyes shifting away from them both. Frances wondered what he was remembering.

'Those Frenchies loved you, didn't they?' Stan said. 'Great brutes, running around France, killing Germans for them. He's got medals and everything. What was it they called you over there? Men of Gold?'

'Men of Bronze,' Ben muttered.

'Yes, that was it,' Stan said. 'Men of Bronze. Think of that, Frances. Doubt they'd let them go now, but back then ... Well, everything changes in wartime. What medal was it?'

'The Croix de Guerre.'

'That's the one. You'll have to show it to Frances some time.'

Ben nodded, but he'd turned his face away so Frances couldn't tell if he wanted to or not. Stan settled in a small chair on one side of the table at the window. He motioned for Ben to sit opposite him.

'I thought you were a musician,' Frances said.

'He is,' Stan answered for him. 'Greatest sax player I ever heard.'

Ben grinned, his thoughts back in the room. 'I played in the Infantry band. A small group of us still tour. That's where I've been these past few months.' He glanced at Frances.

She opened the beers for them and washed her hands at the sink. They were waiting for her to leave.

'I'll be in my room if you need anything. Mrs Bianchi's set me a few more pillowcases.'

Both men nodded at her. She walked through to the bedroom and pulled the door closed.

The two men started up discussing things as soon as she was gone. The sound was more muffled than she'd expected, considering how thin the walls were, and she couldn't make out anything they were saying, even with her ear up against the wall. They must have been watching the volume of their voices so she wouldn't hear.

How did they know each other? Ben lived next door, but that didn't explain the closeness, the whispers, the shared glances. Surely even in New York it was strange to get along this well with one of them. And there weren't any others living in the block that she'd seen. They usually kept to their own over in Harlem, wherever that was, or so she'd heard Mrs Tonioni saying.

She ran her hands over the crochet coverlet on her bed, sticking her fingers into the larger holes and twisting until the tips started to purple and swell. She didn't know why she laid it out every day only to kick it off in the heat each night. She wished she'd remembered to make coffee to distract her from all the sewing – for once it seemed like a chore to be avoided. This wasn't how New York was supposed to be. She'd felt more trapped since she got here than she ever had back home. That first evening was the only one that felt the way she'd imagined New York would – Jacks and Dicky disappearing into shadows at the end of the carriage, the roads and the people and the horns, the automat and the screaming woman and the man's pitching eyes.

She heard Stan laugh. A proper chuckle. The kind he used to do all the time. She lay down on the bed, curled her throbbing fingers around Dicky's card and closed her eyes.

One more night, then she'd break free.

GREENWICH VILLAGE

Frances turned out of the end of their alley and on to the main thoroughfare. At night the street was more raucous than ever, the sky a darker shade of indigo but the sidewalk brighter, multi-coloured from all the electric light. She pulled her cotton bag in front of her and checked Mrs Bianchi's parcel was safe then repeated the directions in her head and waited to cross the road. She'd left half an hour after Stan had gone to work so it was unlikely he'd followed her, but she couldn't be sure. The speed and number of vehicles set her heart hammering. A young man next to her skipped across as soon as a gap widened and she raced after him, only just managing to set her sandalled toe on the kerb before a bread truck almost clipped her heel. She hoped the strap wouldn't break again before she got there.

As she walked she tried to keep distracted, quelling her rising panic in front of windows that sold curious things – a pet shop with a miniature wind-up monkey in the window that

chattered as it swung from a rainbow-coloured parrot's cage;
another full of giant bottles, some almost as tall as she was; a
third packed with every kind of knife, the blades curved or
toothed or straight, some as short as a little finger, others as
long as a forearm.

A few times she paused at crossroads, going over Mrs
Bianchi's instructions, counting off the roads on her fingers,
worried she might falter, but she didn't. Her memory never
failed – it couldn't when signs and notices were nothing more
than vicious squiggles etched with doubt.

A left, then a right, into a small, dingy street, a single lantern
lighting her way through the piles of rubbish. The alley thinned,
as Mrs Bianchi said it would, then connected to another. A few
more steps and she was in a small tree-lined square. It was cob-
bled all the way around. A few electric lights in old lanterns lit
up a group of gnarled trees, skulking in the centre like a bunch
of bored old men. Six trees, exactly as the old woman had said.
The buildings were as high as her tenement, two or three storeys, but everything looked neater. No peeling paint, no drunks
on the kerb, no forgotten washing trailing on the lines.

It was darker here than the rest of the city. She walked slowly
around the square, looking for a yellow door. The colour of
primroses, Mrs Bianchi had said, but it was hard to tell the
shade in the dark. She had to walk up to each house to be sure.
What a heel she must look, traipsing up and down people's paths
but never knocking, like a frightened Bible salesman, doubting
his own faith.

Finally, down the fourth path, she found it. Primrose door.
She paused and looked at Dicky's card again. It was starting
to look grubby. His place didn't have a number either. At least,
there wasn't a number on the card. Mrs Bianchi had said to ask
Jacob, the man she was delivering the package to. She said he'd
probably know where it was. The door knocker was shaped like

a large hand holding a ball. It was stuck, so Frances used her knuckles, wondering what Jacob would look like. No answer. A single light behind the arched glass above the door, another in the basement. She knocked again and leant forward, listening. Nothing. She rapped a third time, as loudly as she dared, so hard she winced in pain and rubbed her fingers.

Inside someone yelled. It was more like a groan. Frances stepped back, nerves jangling.

'Arghhhhh!' Another shout. A man's exasperated voice, muffled on the other side. 'What? What? Why must I be constantly interrupted?'

Still the door didn't open.

'Sorry, sir, sorry, won't be a minute. Stay still, whatever you do don't move. I'm at a pivotal point.' Footsteps coming closer. 'I've got to answer this. It might be Anthony. He's bringing our supper. Probably forgot his key.'

Frances made up her mind to leave the package on the step, but before she could do so and run away, the door swung open.

'Yes? What do you want?'

The man peering at her wore a long white smock like a priest or a sick person. It was splattered with grey smears, as though it had been dragged through chalked earth.

'Sorry to bother you,' she stammered, hating her voice again – too God-damn soft! 'I've brought this from Mrs Bianchi. It's for Jacob.'

'I'm Jacob. Bianchi, you say?'

He took the package from her, frowning, turning it over in his hands. He wore large yellow glasses. His brown hair stuck up all over his head like a raccoon's. As he stepped to the side, Frances caught a glimpse of the room behind. It wasn't a hallway as she'd thought, but a large space with dirty wooden floors and a great big block of some sort of mud at its centre. Next to the mud was a chair with a stained dust-sheet over it, tools scattered all around, and over to one side was a man sitting with his back to the door.

After a moment, Jacob shook the package in her face and pointed at her, grinning, the anger gone as swiftly as it had arrived. 'Bianchi! Of course! My eiderdown!' He leant towards her and tapped the side of his nose. 'We've all been waiting for this.'

'Oh good, I'm sure you'll like it,' Frances said, mustering a smile, glancing over his shoulder. When she thought about it, that lump of clay looked a lot like a man's head, only ten times the size. The guy in the chair fidgeted but didn't turn. He had blond hair, as yellow as Stan's used to be, a thick neck on top of straight shoulders. Navy blue suit, rich-looking thread.

'Oh, I'm sure we will,' Jacob said, winking at her. 'Wait here, one second. How much is it again?'

Frances had been dreading this moment. She'd asked Mrs Bianchi over and over if she was sure it was that much. At these prices the old woman should have been paying Frances twice as much for her sewing.

'She said twenty-five.' Frances' voice was almost a whisper.

'Twenty-five!'

Here it came, this was what she'd been worried about. No one right in the head would pay that for an eiderdown, however warm it kept you.

'One moment.' He fished around in his robe, counted out some notes, then peered into the drawer of a table near the door and pulled out a few more. 'That should do it. Thank you very much.'

He started closing the door.

'One more thing,' Frances said, shoving the money into her bag, her voice mustering strength now that he'd given it to her.

'Yes?'

'Do you know where Richard Sampson lives? Where his studio might be?'

'Dicky? Of course! Got an order in with Bianchi too, has he? No doubt he has. Look down there in the corner. Dark green door. Black paint on the window frames – very de rigueur, very modern.'

Over in the far corner of the square an old townhouse was all lit up.

'Yes, I see it, thank you.'

'You're welcome – and thanks to Mrs Bi—'

'Can we get on?' The man in the chair had turned slightly, revealing a blunt profile, his exasperated voice booming around the room.

Jacob swept his hand over his hair, neatening nothing, looking worried. 'Sorry, sir, of course, coming now and we can get back to it.' He was already closing the door. 'Thank you, young lady, many thanks, many thanks.' It shut in Frances' face and she was alone again.

She frowned at the closed door and began walking towards the house he'd pointed to. There was lavender all the way down the path. She ran her free hand through it and lifted her fingers to her nose, spreading the scent into the warm air. Music thudded softly through its open windows.

She stopped outside, her hand hovered. The music was louder now, but soothing. Voices rumbled. A woman laughed. Next to the door, a small, neat bronze sign was nailed to the wall. She peered at the letters. An 'R' on the first word, an 'S' on the second, a 'P' on the third. It matched Dicky's card exactly.

The wind crept up from the trees in the centre of the square and blew against the sweat on the back of her neck. Her hand wavered above the brass knocker, this time in the shape of a delicate woman's hand, palm-side up. Layers of sound, the city still so very awake, even at this hour. Voices murmuring inside and out, a car honking a few blocks away, the soft pat of her light soles on the cobbles as she shifted from side to side.

All she had to do was knock. She willed her hand to do it, to lift and hold and hit, but the sound of it still shocked her – too loud in this hallowed square, this place that might save her.

'Get the door, darling, would you?' A voice shouting from inside. A voice she knew, a voice that somehow she had missed. 'I know I'm closer but my make-up will spoil if I stop mid-way. It always does.'

Jacks.

Relief flooded Frances, setting her hands shaking again. It *was* their place.

Bolts slid on the other side of the door. She stepped back, preparing herself for Dicky's thin face, his neatness, his heavy-lidded stare. She wondered how surprised they'd be, if they'd be pleased, if they'd even remember her.

The door opened.

It wasn't Dicky. It wasn't Dicky at all.

A slight dark-haired woman stared across the threshold.

'Yes?' she said, eyeing Frances. 'If you're here for the party, you're early. If you're serving, you're late.'

The woman was a little older than Frances. She looked annoyed, as though she'd been interrupted in the middle of something very important. A strange smell wound its way out of the door from her. Not unpleasant, but not wonderful either. It reminded Frances of Mr Jameson's chemist shop back home, all those glass bottles filled with different-coloured liquids. The two-cent soaps piled high on the counter. The strange little pots of pills that promised so much but fixed so little.

'Sorry,' Frances said, 'I'm not here for neither. I'm here for Dicky.'

The woman frowned.

'Not *for* him,' Frances blustered, 'I mean to see him. He's expecting me. At least he was expecting me a time ago.' She worried her hand through her hair. She sounded like a fool.

What an awful state she must look. This was a terrible idea. She shouldn't have come.

'Who is it?' Jacks called from inside. 'If it's August here early again, tell him to clear out until a reasonable hour. We haven't uncorked anything yet, let alone laid out the food.'

'I don't know who it is,' the woman called over her shoulder. 'Who are you?' she asked, looking Frances straight in the eye.

Frances paused. She felt like the woman was asking for more than just her name. Her hair was cropped short and straight and came to a point in the middle of her forehead. Her eyes and eyelids were dark. Red lipstick, slightly smudged. Wide hips in wide cream slacks, a black shirt tucked in, sleeves rolled up, a colourful scarf tied like a man's. As creased and strange as Dicky was neat and rich.

'I'm Frances, Frances from Kansas. I met Dicky and Jacks on the train to New York a couple of weeks back.'

The woman nodded and shouted over her shoulder again. 'It's Frances from Kansas. She met you on a train.'

'Kansas?' Jacks shouted back. 'I don't know anyone from Kansas. God-forsaken place.' She paused. 'Don't tell me it's one of Dicky's projects. One of those poor folk he forced me to shake hands with in that field?'

Frances felt her cheeks heat.

'She doesn't look like she came from a field,' the woman called back. 'Although, her shoes do.'

'What's that?' Jacks called. 'Shoes? Frances? ... Golly! I'm coming! Agnes, don't let her run away. Dicky will kill you.'

The woman's eyes widened. She leant forward and whispered, 'Sounds like you're in high demand.' From the look on her face, Frances wasn't convinced she was happy for her.

'Darling!'

Jacks' turbaned head appeared around the side of the door. It was black satin this time. She was wearing a billowing red velvet dress. It swamped her yet somehow managed to look revealing.

'It really is you!' she said, eyeing Frances up and down, just as the woman had. 'I didn't think those shoes could look much worse, but you've managed it.'

'Hello again,' Frances said, flushing. 'I'm sorry, I meant to come sooner.'

'Oh, don't worry, darling, you're here now, that's the main thing. Dicky will be glad you've still got those awful things on. He loves metaphors, you see. Although I must say, you've caught us on a rather bad evening. We're about to have a party! It's my birthday, you see.'

'Oh,' Frances said. 'Happy birthday.'

'It's not her birthday,' the other woman said, still leaning on the doorway.

'Don't be beastly, Agnes,' Jacks said. 'It was only a few weeks ago. We were away. Didn't have a chance to celebrate. What a sour puss you are.'

The woman, Agnes, raised an eyebrow at Frances.

'I can come back,' Frances said, fiddling with the hem of her dress, 'I don't want to bother you. I was passing and saw this was the address on Dicky's card.'

There was no point begging, in explaining anything, in asking for help. She wanted to crawl in and curl up on their carpet, safe and coddled like a spoilt house cat.

She looked up and found Jacks smiling. Out of pity or warmth she couldn't be sure. Jacks threw her arm over Agnes' shoulder and kissed her cheek. Agnes made a noise as though she was going to be sick. 'Oh, don't complain so,' Jacks said. 'You love me. Everyone does. Come in, Frances, we can't have you out here loitering on the doorstep when the guests arrive, no matter how delightful you look in the moonlight. Dicky *will* be pleased.'

Jacks led them into the hall. 'The house runs over four floors.' She pointed to a frayed runner. 'Down there is the basement – Dicky's darkroom – although it smells worse than any basement

I've ever been in. All those God-awful chemicals. It can't be good for you.' Jacks leant across and pinched Agnes' cheek. 'No wonder this one always looks so pasty,' she said. 'All that time spent in the dark with no fresh air.'

Frances suspected from the look on Agnes' face that it wouldn't take much for her to knock Jacks' hand away.

Once Jacks had released her, Agnes offered her hand to Frances. She shook it. Her palm was small and warm, but her fingers were rough like a field-worker's and she held on with a firm grip.

'I'm Agnes by the way.'

'Oh yes, sorry, darling,' Jacks said. 'How rude of me.'

Agnes shrugged. 'I'm used to it.'

'Oh goodness me. Don't be like that.' Jacks turned to Frances. 'She's jealous of all the time I get to spend touring around with Dicky. Aren't you, darling? If you weren't like you are and he wasn't like he is, you'd be set up in a nice little marriage by now. As it is, you've got to make do with helping him out.'

'I'm his assistant,' Agnes said. 'It's a bit more difficult and important than simply helping him out.'

'Yes, yes,' Jacks said, 'and one day you'll be as good a photographer as he is. I've heard it all, darling.' She looked at Frances. 'This floor is where we live. One floor up is bedrooms. Right at the top is Agnes' room and where Dicky takes photographs. You'll see it later. That's where the best light is. In the daytime, of course.'

Jacks started moving down the hall. Once she was out of earshot, Agnes leant towards Frances and whispered, 'I won't be *as* good as him – I'll be better.'

Frances smiled politely, and turned to the pictures that lined the hallway. Some were landscapes: prairie fields stretching into the distance; thick woods split apart by twisting paths; glassy lakes reflecting sharp snow-capped mountains. In between these were shots of New York: kids playing on stoops; barbers sweeping hair on to the street; old men pushing carts laden with scrap. To Frances it looked like Dicky had mixed up her old life with her new one – her past rubbing shoulders with her present like two strangers on a packed train. There, the open stillness, the dust, beauty and boredom of before; here, the suffocating closeness, the people, the rush and danger of the present. The contrast shocked her – the distance between her two lives at once huge and impossibly close. She felt giddy.

'Oh God, Agnes, it's the ones in the parlour you ought to show Frances, Dicky's ones, not yours, although she might not be quite ready for them yet. Why don't we get a drink first and I'll go and gather him from wherever he's collapsed upstairs. Make me a large cocktail, would you? We've still got an hour or more before everyone arrives. If I can rouse him there'll be plenty of time to take a few test shots while I ask Frances some questions.'

'Fine,' Agnes sighed.

Frances was awed. 'You took those?' she whispered.

Agnes nodded her head, the first flicker of a smile brightening her melancholy face as she led Frances to the parlour.

'What would you like to drink?' Agnes asked.

Frances' reply stuck in her throat. The room they had entered was large and cluttered, stretching from one end of the building to the other, as though at some point all the inner walls had been knocked down. There were paintings everywhere – covering cracks, stacked next to piles of books, lining the backs of shelves – but these weren't of old men or animals like the ones Frances had seen in the foyer of the picture house back home. These were of shapes and patterns and colours, crazy angles and black splodges, thick paint flowing in drips to the edges, as though it might still be wet. In a corner a woman's throaty voice sang a jazz ballad from a large brass gramophone that bloomed obscenely against peeling wallpaper. The room looked rich and poor at the same time, adored and ruined like a wedding dress trailed in the dirt.

In between the paintings were photographs of people, some dressed in fine outfits and wide-brimmed hats, the men in Oxfords, the women in pearls. In others (and Frances guessed these were the ones Jacks thought she might not yet be ready for) the people clearly had no clothes on. They were posed at jaunty angles, the women's loose hair saving their modesty, the men grinning at the camera, their broad chests as square and exposed as their teeth. She wondered if they'd try to make her do that, if all the niceness was actually a trick, if Stan had been right all along.

Frances frowned, and began planning how she might get out of it without making a scene, but almost as quickly her outrage softened. It was no surprise that the men in the pictures looked like they were having fun. It was the women who made her stop. All of them were staring directly out of the picture, at Frances, at the world. They didn't look ashamed. They looked proud. Like they wanted to be seen. Frances stared back. She realised part of her was jealous of them, of their refusal to do what was proper. In truth, a small part of her might like to pull her own dress over her head as Dicky and Jacks and Agnes watched. Somewhere inside she wanted to stand motionless while the camera shutter clicked, to come back into this room one day and see her own flesh, her own face, staring resolutely out from one of these frames.

'I suppose Dicky's private prints are a little shocking, even for the Village,' Agnes said. 'Not quite my taste.'

'The Village?'

'Yes, the Village. Greenwich Village.' Agnes spoke slowly again. 'That's where we are, you silly thing.'

Frances bristled. 'I don't know much about the city. I've not been here long.'

'I can see that,' Agnes said. 'Don't worry, Jacks and Dicky will have you feeling like a native in no time.'

Agnes walked to a small polished wooden cupboard and opened the top. Inside it was all mirrors and satin, like a jewellery box. The lamplight caught on cut-glass flutes and delicate triangular glasses that looked a sip away from cracking. There was so much liquor it was a wonder the cabinet didn't collapse. Frances watched her pouring different liquids into a silver tumbler.

'I'll make you the house special,' she said. 'That'll take the edge off. It's like a Singapore Sling with an extra kick.'

'I'm afraid I don't know what that is,' Frances said. She didn't want to seem stupid, but she was too tired to care what this woman thought of her.

'It's Jacks' favourite cocktail. A few of these each evening keep her happy. And if Jacks is in a good mood, we all are.' There was something in Agnes' tone that made Frances doubt that was true.

'Frances! You found us. How wonderful.'

Dicky was in the doorway. He looked much like he had on the train, except he was wearing a strange dressing gown with a swirling green pattern over the top of his shirt. Frances walked towards him and shook his hand. His eyes were as darkly rimmed as before but this time they were blood-shot too.

'Terribly sorry I wasn't up when you got here. I was going through some prints and then thought it wise to have a little lie-down before our guests arrive. I always think it's a good idea to be properly rested ahead of a big party – one never knows how long it might go on for.'

'That's okay,' Frances said. 'You weren't to know I was coming.'

'No, indeed,' Dicky said. 'In fact I'm afraid to say Jacks and I had somewhat written you off as another lost soul, another stranger passing in the night. It was a romantic thought, but I much prefer being wrong. And here you are in the same shoes.

How wonderful. I suppose neither this one nor Jacqueline has thought to ask you how you are?'

'Quite the opposite.' Agnes turned swiftly from where she was making drinks. 'I was giving Frances some space. She's just arrived in this mad house and already you and Jacks are like the Spanish Inquisition.'

Frances twisted her hair around one side of her neck. 'I've been fine. Busy.'

Agnes handed a glass to Frances with a wink. 'This will help,' she said, 'whatever you've been through.'

'To Frances, for finding us,' Dicky said, clinking his glass, 'and to a long and happy working relationship.' He took a large gulp and sighed.

Frances took a small sip. It was strong and sweet but not as overwhelming as the bootleg stuff she'd had before. She managed not to splutter.

'So,' Dicky said, 'do you think you have enough energy for me to take a few shots now? You look so authentic at the moment, we could get some great first pictures. Do you remember what we talked about on the train?'

'Yes, I think so,' Frances said, squeezing her glass until she felt her fingertips numb. 'About the photographs of me looking like I was from the country and the ones of me looking like I belong here?'

'Exactly,' Dicky said. 'First we'll shoot you as you are, then we'll doll you up. Go up to Agnes' room and she'll help you pick some things. Between her and Jacks we'll find something that works.'

They were in the eaves, as high up the house as it was possible to get. Frances sat on the edge of the bed wishing she could disappear, watching Agnes pile clothes around her.

'Not that, that won't suit you. Your hips are thin, that won't work. This would have been good but your skin's too tan, it'll make you look yellow – not that that'll matter for the pictures. They'll be black and white, but if I bring it up Dicky will only throw it out. He hates his eye to be distracted if a colour's off. No point wasting time.'

The higher the piles got the angrier Agnes seemed to become. Apparently, nothing about the way Frances looked was right. Perhaps if she asked something Agnes might soften a little. She cast her eye around the little attic room. Clothes littered the floor. Half-dead plants lined the dusty window sill. Dirty cups and plates were piled on the nightstand. Ashtrays overflowed, teetering atop stacks of books, their spines splayed, pages threatening escape. Photographs of broad-leaved trees and deserts and camels and queer buildings and foreign-looking people in strange clothes were pinned without frames in the gaps between the wooden roof struts.

'Did you take all these?'

Agnes looked up from the shiny black dress she was holding up for size.

'I wish. They're all Burton Holmes. I'm guessing you don't know about him.'

'No.' Frances wished she hadn't asked. Whatever she said, this girl, this woman, made her feel stupid.

'He's an explorer, of a sort. Goes around the world taking pictures. I went to his lecture series a few years ago at Carnegie Hall. Changed my life. Before that I was aiming to be Dicky. Now I've set my sights a little higher.'

Frances marvelled at her tone. No woman she knew spoke like this. Not about herself.

'What do you mean, higher?'

Agnes threw the dress on the pile. 'That might work.' She sighed. 'I mean, if I'm going to spend all this time learning the craft, I might as well put it to good use. There's enough people photographing this city and all the people in it. I've been doing it too, apprenticing with Dicky, helping out around here, but now I've nearly finished taking shots of all the new buildings going up, what's keeping me? How many photographers do you know who are out there?' She pointed at the window. 'How many are on trains and boats, how many are trekking over deserts, dancing in Paris, freezing their behinds off in the Arctic, risking their lives in wars to show people what's really going on? Not enough. Certainly not many women, that's for sure. Holmes is one of the few who've gone out and come back. If he can do it, I figured I could too.'

'Won't that cost a lot of money?' Frances thought of all those dollars Stan had sent her to ride a single train to New York.

Agnes' eyes widened, anger brimming at their edges. 'It will. And what of it? I'm worth it. I've done my time with these two, mixing cocktails and making prints of all those skinny rich girls so older, fatter, richer women will go gaga over them in magazines and waste money on clothes they don't need that won't fit them.'

She looked away, and Frances sensed a shift in her. A shiver rippled her body, then she gathered the clothes, her fairy face barely visible over the top.

'This will do,' Agnes said. 'Jacks'll bring some of hers. Off we go.'

'That's it,' Dicky said, his head beneath a black cloth, half his body hidden by a large wooden box, 'left, left, left, and hold, hold, hold.' He squeezed something attached to the box with a wire. Like a hose, Frances thought. A hose or a snake or a rope.

Her neck ached. She daren't ask what time it was in case they thought she was bored but she must have been standing on the wooden crate for at least an hour. She'd have to go soon. She couldn't risk Stan coming back from work and her not being there.

Once she'd got over her initial fear, once her body had stopped feeling so tight, it had been fun. She'd enjoyed them all tending to her – Dicky shouting instructions, Agnes helping her change behind a lacquered screen of black and gold and pink, blossom shedding across it like snow, Jacks running in with armfuls of clothes – damask, tulle, velvet – the rich fabrics so strange, silks skimming over her skin like river water, nets scratching, all three of them watching so intently she wondered if they could see the hairs rising on her arms.

First, Dicky had asked her to pose in the clothes she'd turned up in – a cream smock that had once been white and her old leather sandals that Stan had fixed for her. Dicky made her sit down on the edge of the box and think about something sad. He said to pick the first thing that entered her head, but that had been the baby, and she didn't want to think about all that right now, so she'd thought about the time Father shot Yeller instead.

She'd been five then and Stan ten, but she could still feel the way the gunshot had ripped her from a dream, how she had instantly known what Father had done, how Mother must have tricked her into sleep so he could go out and do what he had to do without her making a scene. She could remember the rage rising in her chest as she'd run down the stairs, could feel her mother's coarse hand on her wrist and the way she had to twist to get away. When she got outside, Father had made no effort to stop her coming close. She'd sunk into the dirt and pressed her face to the old dog's neck and Stan had come out a while later and patted her on the shoulder. That night was the first time he'd come into her room and told her a story. Perhaps he'd heard her crying. All she could remember now was the bed creaking beside her as he sat on it, the sound of his voice soothing her back to sleep.

Dicky must have been pleased with what she looked like because while she was thinking all this, he kept saying 'Wonderful, that's it, just like that, one more time. Now, look away from the camera and think about it again. Did you ever see such a face, Jacks? That'll have your readers weeping into their teacups . . . '

After that they started dressing her up. Behind the screen with Agnes and Jacks she'd stripped down to her underclothes and tried to hold her nerve. They were women after all. She'd done fine until Jacks had wedged her holder in the corner of her mouth and pushed at her breasts. 'We need to hoist these, eh Aggie? You might as well not be wearing this, darling, it's doing nothing for you.' Frances had jumped away. Jacks had laughed. Agnes had scowled at the floor. After that she'd kept one eye on them both, holding her body tight in case it was touched again.

They put her in a green dress of such thick satin she'd started to sweat. She wished she could have washed before they began, but as soon as the dress was over her head and hitting the floor, she forgot her embarrassment. She felt taller, more important somehow. It spilt down her body and stuck to her skin. She could tell from their faces how good it looked. She'd held her breath while Jacks bent close, adding flicks of kohl to her eyes, smudging rouge on her lips and cheeks. When she emerged from the screen Dicky had whistled, not like the boys back home on their stoops, but like a man standing on a hill looking out over fresh pastures.

'Isn't she something?' Jacks had said, and they both nodded.

Agnes had silently held her hand as she climbed up on to the box. Dicky fiddled with his camera and turned on some lights. He'd warned her about the flash before the first one, but it had still shocked her, the pop blinding her for a second, and she'd worried her eyes would be closed in all the pictures and they'd be ruined.

With each outfit they did the same thing. Up on the box, look this way, that way, stick out your foot. Click, click, click with the camera, pop, pop, pop with the lamp. Even though there was no mirror in the stuffy attic room, she could tell how well the dresses suited her from the looks on their faces, could sense how much she had managed to transform into the vision Dicky desired. His smile made her proud.

But now? Now she wished she could get down. Now she didn't want them to look at her any more. The expensive clothes were piled in the corner like rubbish and Jacks was sitting on them smoking, looking out of the window, waiting for party guests to arrive.

'I can't believe no one's come yet. I thought August would be here. Or Jane, she's always desperate to get going.'

'You said that already,' Dicky murmured. His voice had taken on a solemn tone and he'd stopped standing on his tiptoes and clapping when Frances moved the way he wanted.

'What about these?' Agnes poked her head out from behind the screen. She wasn't holding a dress, she was waving something that looked like a pair of men's denim overalls.

Dicky raised an eyebrow and twisted something on the side of the box. 'Why would I possibly shoot her in those?'

Jacks left her perch and went to Agnes, her hand outstretched. 'Wait a minute, don't be so hasty.' She flicked out the denim slacks so they unfurled in front of her. 'Agnes might be on to something, you know. I've seen women wearing these down south, but I've never seen them in a magazine. It might be just the thing to catch someone's eye. You're always telling me to bring you something different. Well, this is new. Especially if we match them with one of my silk shirts. Even if Claude won't take it, one of the girls at *Vogue* will and that'll double our revenue. They're always desperate for something no one else has. You'd think they were positively starving.'

Dicky tilted his head to the side and smoothed his hair. 'All right, darling, if you say so.' His eyes looked emptied out. His thumb tapped a nervous rhythm on the camera.

Frances glanced at Agnes. She was standing with her hand on her hip looking triumphant, as though this was the one outfit she'd wanted to see Frances in all evening.

Jacks waved the overalls at Frances. 'Here you go, then, get them on.'

She stepped gingerly off the box and took the stiff pants behind the screen, then lifted the dress over her head and laid it carefully on a crate. It was the first time she'd ever worn pants. She was surprised how difficult they were to get on. Men always looked so free strolling around the farm in them. She pulled the starched fabric up over her thighs, wiggling this way and that. Thank goodness Agnes had wider hips than her otherwise she'd never have gotten them on. The zip and button were impossible – her fingers got sore from pulling.

Agnes poked her head round. 'Need a hand?'

'Thanks.'

Agnes came close and twisted the waistband. 'Breathe in a bit. You're tiny compared to me. This should be easy.'

Frances could smell her again. A little bit orange blossom, a little bit acid. Right on her hairline she had a small off-white birthmark Frances hadn't noticed before. It looked like a drop of milk.

'There you go. Jacks wants this on top.' Agnes slid a creamy silk button-down over her head.

The contrast between the two fabrics on her skin was shocking. Her bottom half felt caged in, while her arms and chest felt like they were swimming in custard. She'd not realised clothes could make you feel like this, that they could change the way you stood and walked and felt.

When she came out, moving stiffly, feeling strange and on display, but also protected somehow, as though, for once, her body was safe, Jacks didn't say anything. She just smiled and nodded and smoked and helped her up on to the box, then went back to her window seat again.

Dicky ducked his head beneath the black cloth. 'Right as usual, my dear. Now, hand on hip, Frances, pretend you're Agnes. Imagine you're walking down Fifth Avenue as though you own it.'

Jacks said, 'Hang on, here's Jude. We'll have to stop now.' She walked quickly across the room and held Frances' hand. 'You were wonderful, dear, magnificent. I don't doubt the photos will be divine. Now, if you'll excuse us, I've got a party to host. We'll save all my questions for next time.'

'You can't just kick her out,' Agnes said, frowning.

Frances fidgeted on her box, picking at a thread on the denim that wasn't there.

'Absolutely right,' Dicky said. 'Frances, you must stay for the party.'

Frances glanced at Jacks who made no effort to hide her horror.

'Oh no,' Frances said, 'I couldn't. I must get back to my brother.'

'Of course she must,' Jacks said. 'You see, Dicky, not every-one's holding out for an invite. It'll probably be terribly boring for you, darling, a bunch of law men and a couple of artists, nothing special.'

Frances heard Agnes muffle a laugh.

'You will come to the next one, though, won't you?' Dicky asked, packing his camera away. 'It's the least we could do. Tell that brother of yours ahead of time then he won't worry. It's my birthday next. A few weeks' time. Jacks is planning a big one.'

'I'll try to come,' Frances said, not looking at Jacks for fear of her expression. Agnes came to help her off the box and she waddled behind the screen.

'How did you find it, dear?' Jacks asked from behind the screen. 'Was it as fabulous as you thought it would be?'

'Yes,' Frances said, the lie stinging her tongue, her fingers frantically tugging at the stiff button at her waist. 'Thank you so much. It was more wonderful than I could have imagined.'

LOWER EAST SIDE

11 October 1932

21.17

'I won't do it.'

'You will because I've asked you to, and this is my place you're staying in.'

'You sound like Father.'

Stan sighed and looked away from her, trying not to rise to the bait, then walked to the daybed and shrugged a jacket over his shirt. There'd be a chill in the air by the time he got back from the club.

'I thought you wanted to learn.'

'I do, only not with him.'

'What's wrong with Ben? You barely know him.'

'Exactly.'

'He's one of the good guys, Frances, can't you take my word for it? I know it's strange seeing me friendly with one of them, but it's different in the city. We're not on the farm now. I was terrified the first time I walked into the club. So many of 'em all over the place, dancin' and singin' and playin' – nothing like the land boys back home.'

She folded her arms and stood between him and the sink. He pushed her aside. Not in a mean way, but hard enough so he could reach his beer on the drainer.

She tapped her foot. 'How did you two get so friendly anyhow?'

'He plays at the club, I told you. He's helped me out a few times is all.'

'And you helped him get his place here? That's what Mrs Bianchi said. She said no one wanted him to come and you talked them all into it.'

'Maybe I did. So what of it?'

'So it's strange is all. I ain't never seen you talking to one of them back home.'

'Well, Ben ain't them.'

He drained his beer and handed the empty bottle to her. She considered throwing it into the sink, but if it broke she'd be the one who had to clean up the glass. It wasn't worth the trouble.

'How often would I have to go?'

'Once or twice a week.'

'And how do you know he's on the level? How do you know he won't make some pass at me while I'm concentrating on my A, B, Cs? How do you know he knows how to teach anyone anything?'

'Because I seen him teaching some of the young ones in the club. He brings in books, kids' ones some of them, ones a schoolteacher might use. Then he tells Willie he's taking the boys outside to clean their instruments and while he's round the back he goes through some words with them, that's how. As to whether he'll make a pass at you, I'm certain he won't do that.'

'Oh yeah?' She sensed the joke before it came.

'Ain't no man in their right mind gonna make a pass at you.'

She hit him on the arm and finished off the washing while he paced around the room gathering the things he needed.

She watched him put his hat on. 'Can't I come with you?'

'No.' He was fiddling with something in his jacket pocket and he didn't look at her. Even his fingers seemed thinner. She wondered if he'd still be able to shift the giant bales. Some of the girls in town used to come up when it was harvest time just to watch. They'd sit on the gate and swing their legs and chew long strands of grass and cheer when he managed to drag the last one into place. She doubted he'd manage it now.

'Why not?'

'Because the club ain't no place for a girl like you.'

'And what sort of a girl is that?'

'The sort that manages to find trouble where there isn't any and make trouble worse when there is. The sort that should stay home and learn to read.'

'I'd be real quiet, you wouldn't even notice I was there.'

'You wouldn't be and I would. I don't need you acting the way you do around Bianchi's boys with any of our regulars. They'd see your slow looks and that cherry mouth and think you knew more about the world than you do.'

He walked across the room and pecked her on the cheek. She wiped his kiss away with the back of her hand.

'But I'm bored.'

'I thought Mrs Bianchi gave you more sewing?' He was opening the door now, not really listening, his mind already halfway across town.

'She did, but—'

'Well then, do that.' He raised his hand and closed the door, shutting her words away.

A corner of one of the maps lifted as Frances brushed past. She reached up and pressed it back down, annoyed by the shake in her hand. It wouldn't stick. The glue must have failed in last month's heat. On this side of Ben's parlour the wall was covered in a large map of New York. At least that's what he said it was. It looked more like a living thing to her: roads in a deep, furious red; subway lines in vein blue, pumping, she imagined, beneath the skin of the city; housing blocks in a quiet shade of stony grey; green patches suggesting grass and clear skies and fresh air, the city hemmed in by rivers that strangled while teasing escape. When she really thought about it, Manhattan looked like a ballet dancer's foot tipped high on its toe – precarious and delicate, but stricken with pain, bleeding into Long Island and New Jersey and Brooklyn along those straight bridges.

Ben walked into the room and she pulled her hand away. Another white shirt. Brown slacks. Almost the same as before, like a uniform. She tried not to step back from him, but could feel her body inching away of its own accord.

'The whole world's up there, you know.' He pointed across the room at another map, twice the size of the first. 'Seven continents, God knows how many countries, and I've only been to two of them.'

She nodded, but wasn't convinced. Surely the world was bigger. And it must be more beautiful than these blotches of mucky colour. The countries or contents, or whatever he'd called them, looked like stains. Like a collection of accidents from a luncheon gone wrong. Beer and gravy and cherry juice spilt all over.

He busied himself at the table. She stepped across his thinning rug so she could trace her finger over a fading patch of burnt-coloured land. The word in the centre began with an 'S' but perhaps that wasn't a country at all. Without names to recognise the places, she felt lost. The letters and shapes blurred until the whole world swam.

'Soviet Union,' Ben said, looking up. 'That's one place I'm not sure I want to go.' He leant across and tapped the map. His dark forearm strained at the rolled cuffs on his sleeves.

She held her breath, then forced herself to speak. 'Why not?'

'Not the kind of folks I'd like to meet. And look how far north it is. I think it's cold most of the time. I hate the cold.'

She nodded. That was one thing they could agree on. The dust storms back on the farm had been bad, but summer was nothing compared to winter. In winter the wind tore the breath from your throat. Frost stole fingers, toes too, if you weren't careful. Snow could trap you in your home for weeks, and that home would fast become a tomb if you ran out of firewood or tins of food, or if the pipes froze up. Waking up in winter was a curse because you had to endure another day, but it was also a relief because it meant you'd lived through another night.

'Would you like a drink before we get started?'

'Just a water, please.'

He filled a tumbler from the faucet and passed it to her. His hand shook. Perhaps he was nervous too.

'Thanks.'

He motioned her back to the table by the window. Vines and creepers lined the sill. Not flowers like at Mrs Bianchi's, or dead sticks like on theirs, but lush plants that looked like they didn't belong in a city. More like the ones at Jacks and Dicky's place. She still hadn't asked Stan about the party. There wasn't much point. Better to sneak out again, only this time she'd need a better dress. She was desperate to show them, especially Agnes, that she could look just as fine without their help.

Ben offered her a chair opposite and she sat down feeling uneasy, looking at the top of his strange head. Stan had waved his hand at her when she'd brought up the rumours. The whispers slipped from lips. Hints of violence. Even Ben's biggest fan, Mrs Bianchi, had stopped Frances in the hall one day last week when she heard he was going to help with Frances' reading and told her to be careful. She'd said he was a fine man, but that there were things he'd seen in the war and things that had happened in the city that had harmed him. She said he was unpredictable. Trustworthy, yes, but sometimes that wasn't enough. Sometimes even people with good hearts did bad things.

'Let's get started.'

He checked his watch and picked up one of the small books from the table. Two children and a dog on the front. It looked like a collie. She thought of Yeller again.

'How much time do we have?' she asked.

'About half an hour until I've got to leave for the club. I'm playing the late shift tonight. Midnight to daybreak. Hopefully next time we'll have longer.'

He opened the book and the lesson began. 'I'm going to run my finger beneath some words and say them aloud, then I want you to do the same.' He slowly traced his finger under a few words and said, 'This. Is. Jane.'

Frances copied and repeated. After that he went through the book and asked her to point out any time she saw one of the same words. If she did she had to say it and pass her finger underneath again, then he'd pick a new sentence and do the same thing all over. It wasn't like what she thought. There were no alphabets and there wasn't any writing. He said that would come later. She didn't get bored or feel awkward like she thought she might. He was patient like Stan said and, although she should have been embarrassed learning from him, she wasn't.

After a time he asked if he could sit beside her because it would be easier for him to hold the book. She nodded, but made sure their legs didn't touch under the table. She didn't care what Stan thought, but there was nothing to be won by Ben getting the wrong idea. She needed to keep things nice between them, but not too nice. That way she'd get the information she wanted.

He picked up another book.

'Is it far to the club?'

She glanced at him as she spoke. He was searching for the next sentence to teach, his brow a furrow of concentration. What had those eyes seen? What pain had those hands given and received? Until now the war had seemed far away to Frances. She'd had no idea men like Ben had been made to go and fight. Only a few soldiers from her town had gone and come back. She'd been a child and life since had been so hard, no one ever really talked about it, except in hushed whispers. Once, when she was small but old enough to listen, Frances had been shopping with her mother and they'd passed a cripple begging in the road. Mother had stopped and handed him a few coins. She usually never did that. Most of the time she ushered Frances past the down-and-outs, afraid they'd be there themselves before long, but this time she had made an exception. She said he was war-wounded, that someone ought to be looking after him but everyone had their own trials to bear. Frances remembered almost tripping as she skipped on because she kept turning round to stare. There was nothing left of him below the waist. He'd smiled and waved at her, but she ran away without looking back. When Mother caught her, she'd boxed her ears.

'Quite far, yes. Uptown, across the park.'

'How long does it take you to get there?'

'About forty minutes if I walk fast enough.'

'Have you worked there long?'

'Longer than your brother. Willie, the owner, went out of his way to employ ex-servicemen like me when everyone else refused. He served as a gunner in the 350th – the Buffalo Soldiers. They say he used to roar when he fired his weapon. That's why they call him "The Lion". Finest pianist you're likely to come across. Hired a fair few from my regiment to play. Hates it when we all go off on tour at the same time though.'

She nodded, smiled, tried to read a few more sentences.

'So, you got my brother a job?'

'I did.'

'How did you meet him?'

'Didn't he tell you?'

She shrugged, trying to decide if a 'no' would mean he'd stop talking or if a 'yes' was a lie she was ready to tell. The lamp on the table spluttered. Ben got up, went to the drawer by the sink and brought out some oil to refill it. His face burnished as he lifted the glass. So much of the city was electrified, and yet, down here in the tenements, they were all still groping around in the dark. The flame picked out his features – thick nose, plump cheeks, a surprising flush of freckles on his temples, black hair coiled as tight and soft as a lamb's. He smiled at her. His teeth were the opposite of that guy in the diner. So white. She wondered how he kept them so fine when everyone else's were crumbling.

He tilted his head at her. 'He didn't tell you, did he?'

'No.'

'Well, I'm not sure I should. It's not my place to explain another man's business.' He looked at his watch. 'And I've got to end the lesson there, or I'll be late and all those good people who've come to see us play will be disappointed, not to mention the hiding I'll get from Willie.'

'Thank you.'

She had to figure out a way to make him talk. If she could learn about Stan's work, she was sure she'd find out why he was acting so strangely, why he was so thin and distracted and bleary-eyed all the time. It couldn't just be the late nights.

'I've got to get going. There's a walk ahead of me, although at least it'll be a pleasure going through the park. My soul's crying out for trees. You did well today. So we'll meet once more this week? Thursday sound good?'

She smiled, less wary of him now, an idea pushing up from somewhere inside, as rampant and unwieldy as the vines at his window. 'That sounds swell,' she said. 'I didn't think I'd enjoy myself, but I did. Thanks for taking the time.'

He moved towards her and held out his hand. She was surprised to see the pinkness of his palm, as though top and bottom were split in two. It was a strange thing for a man to offer his hand like that to a girl her age, and she tried not to wait too long before looking him straight in the eye and grasping it in what she hoped was a firm grip. She'd feel bad following him, but what choice did she have?

The park was a shock. So many shades of green. The gloom suffocating, the air thick and saturated with scent – pine and damp moss and leaves on the turn. On either side trees and bushes crowded in. Where lamps had been lit, heavy boughs blocked most of the light. The winding path curved away into the distance.

Frances stepped resolutely on, her nerves locked in the rigid muscles of her hips and thighs, feeling the dust compress beneath the thin soles of her fixed sandals, fallen leaves crackling under her heels, and some distance ahead the same crunch repeated by Ben's feet – the only comforting sound.

She was terrified he would turn and see her but he hadn't looked back once. In fact, he was walking faster than she'd expected, striding over crossings, switching his saxophone case between his hands. Perhaps he was late after all. Approaching a clearing he sped up again and Frances found herself almost running to keep him in sight. If she lost him, she might never find her way out.

Past a group of trees on the left a huge space yawned at her, a kind of desert amid all the dying greenery. In the sparse light she could make out the roofs and walls of a small group of makeshift buildings nestled in the curve of a giant dustbowl. After all the leaves, and before that all the buildings, the openness was shocking, the size of ten ball-parks, the emptiness more frightening than the whispering trees. The small buildings scattered across it were made out of all kinds of material – wood, glass, old bottles, giant oil cans, anything the homeless could lay their hands on, she supposed. Beyond the buildings, the dust expanded, empty and barren and just like home, familiar, until the dry edges touched the grand trees, until those trees touched the great stone skyline.

In the tallest towers a few lights were still on, so high up they looked like stars. Inside was someone rich, no doubt. Someone like Jacks and Dicky. In New York, height meant money. A good view from a window cost more than the land it looked at. Stan said the only space left on an island like this was above their heads. It was the opposite of home, the opposite of the ramshackle village in front of her, the opposite of everything she'd known before. With each step she moved closer to those buildings, closer to the money, closer to the sky.

She watched Ben's back, his confident gait, the air of calm. She couldn't imagine him hurting anyone. Not like Mrs Bianchi had suggested. Not even in a war. She wondered what he had done to cause folks to talk like that, what had happened to make him and Stan so close.

Around another bend Ben paused and looked back. She jumped behind a bush, scratching her calf on piercing thorns, cursing under her breath. He said something but she couldn't make out who he was talking to. She waited a moment, then peeped out. He'd gone. Another beat, then she stepped on as quickly and silently as she could, looking all around, her fear of being abandoned in the park at night far greater than being found out.

A man stepped close in front of her. 'Late to be out for a stroll,' he said.

Frances could see the dirt on his face, the mess of his teeth. She smelt his rag-a-muffin stink – clothes encrusted with sweat, the stench of bootleg hooch spilling from wet lips, a hint of something worse, of something soiled.

'Very late. I don't suppose you've got a donation to help rebuild our homes?'

So there was to be no messing, Frances thought. No introductions, no lies. There was a strange kind of honesty in that. She glanced towards Ben, this time begging him to turn around and see her. He kept walking, moving out of earshot.

'Not tonight,' she replied. She felt her hands shake. 'Perhaps another time?'

'Ain't no time like the present,' the guy said, holding out his hand. 'A small donation to Hooverville over there and you can get on your way.'

But then, out of nowhere, she was angry. Angry like the time she'd found Yeller. Angry the way she'd been every day at home living with Father, watching him do up his boots or stoop to light a cigarette, eyes narrowed at the vanishing daylight, his brow as furrowed as the earth he looked out on. Waiting for a harsh word or a thick ear, or worse. How dare this tramp make her afraid.

'I'll be on my way *now*, thank you,' she said, the force in her voice surprising her, not a hint of hesitation.

The guy laughed. 'Well, you're as feisty as you are pretty. Lucky man, your beau, whoever he is. What a lady. In a dress like that, you must be on your way to work. Perhaps I can be your first job?'

'I won't be giving you anything,' Frances said, her voice firmer than she'd heard it in months. 'Now move out of my way, or I'll start screaming, and my friend over there will come back and start hitting.'

She felt the power of what she had said rise up. After all, what could this man do to her that Father hadn't already done? What could he take that hadn't already been taken?

The man shifted his feet and glanced across to where Ben was almost through the gates, judging the distance between him and them.

'Your friend, is he? Why's he not walking with you? Ashamed? You courtin' and don't want Papa to find out you're dating a Negro?'

She'd not waste her breath on him. She pushed past and started to run. He stepped backwards, tripped and fell in the dirt.

'All you women are the same,' he called after her, his voice getting fainter as she approached the park gates, her breath pumping from her, heart in her temples now, eyes scanning left and right, until she caught sight of the top of Ben's head disappearing down a side-street. 'Never think it'll happen to you, do ya?' he carried on, but she didn't turn. 'Those above always gotta spit on the ones below. Always thinkin' the worst. Heads in the sand. Go on, then! Keep running. We'll be seeing you down here in the dirt soon enough.'

Back into the heaving city. She raced across crowded streets, struggling to keep Ben in her sights.

Only once did he almost see her. An old woman stumbled on one of the strange steam grates and he rushed forward to help. The elderly lady gasped and raised her hand to her mouth, as shocked at his hand on her elbow as at the fall itself. In that instant Ben turned his head towards Frances and she ducked into an alley. His face had pushed through the steam and he'd looked kind. Kind and open and almost beautiful with the white cloud of hot air blooming around his dark head, as though Frances was seeing his features in relief for the first time, as though until now the light hadn't done him justice. The woman had changed in that moment too. She'd thanked Ben and smiled, he'd nodded and walked on. It was small things, Frances thought, tiny kindnesses, not grand gestures, that changed the way one person saw another.

The further they went, the more the people on the street changed too. Italians and Jews on her own block to dark-skinned Spaniards and Negroes as they approached Harlem. Slowly, she began to realise that the roads of Manhattan didn't just divide buildings and districts and wealth, they also marked out divisions in origin and skin. Unwritten rules. She felt invisible one minute and exposed the next. It was a curious sensation, as though she was shedding clothes as she walked, until she turned into 133rd naked and conspicuous. She wondered if Ben felt the opposite, if the whole time he was in the tenement he felt on show and now, among his people, he felt safe, invisible. She wasn't sure she could live as he did, always on display.

The final street was wide and dusty – far broader than theirs, but just as busy, with couples walking arm in arm up and down the sidewalk and children playing way past their bedtime, sucking on oranges as big as their heads.

Between Lenox and 7th it got crowded, people's clothes got fancier and the music got louder. Newly washed cars lined both sides, as ready for the night as their owners, the fenders and bonnets so shiny it might have just rained. Groups of old men and women sat on stoops and passed the time of day, gossiping. Now and then Frances caught snatched phrases – 'You'd do well to ignore him – kick him out!' 'Not that lame Joe – God save us. If he opens that place the street'll be finished.'

Ben waved at people and stopped a couple of times to talk. Frances stayed as far back as she dared. It was only due to this distance that she noticed a few people whispering behind their hands as Ben passed. She even overheard one woman say to another, 'The gall of the man. Honestly, Bettie, can you believe he still comes down here? I heard Willie say he woulda got rid of him before now if he didn't play so darn good.' Frances wished she could have asked what they meant.

She moved on, passing a row of brownstone bar fronts, awnings stretching on to the sidewalk. Men stood underneath shouting out their crazy names, touting for business: 'Edith's Clam House', 'Tillie's', 'Basement Brownie's', 'Mexico', and on the opposite side, 'The Nest'. Near each bar groups of much younger men and women gathered, smoking and laughing. She'd never seen such a sight. All these black folk in one place. All of them happy, joking, enjoying the promise of the night. The smell coming off the place was heady – perfume and smoke and liquor and sweat. Steam from the vents. Dust from the sidewalk.

Finally, Ben stopped up ahead, shook hands with a fat doorman and ran up some steps. The bar had a strange wooden entrance like a log cabin. The name above it began with a C, but that was all Frances could make out. She clutched her purse to her chest and looked around, on guard in case Stan was nearby. Most of the men queueing wore hats, but those that didn't had slicked their tight curls into side-partings as shiny as those of the Italians who roamed her own street. The women were a sight. Lots wore cloches but some had left their hair free – flowers and ribbons of different colours adorned their heads like exotic crowns.

Frances waited over to one side of the steps, shivering, although she wasn't cold. When the door opened, the scent of sawdust and hog maw and sweet liquor flooded the street. Her stomach rumbled. She waited for Ben to go inside, then joined the line, relieved to see not just black faces but whites in the crowd too, everyone mixing, elbows rubbing, hands clapping, sending their excitement up and away and into the black sky.

The doorman winked at her as she went past, her heart hammering, in case, for some unknown reason, he wouldn't let her in. On the other side of the wide front door a girl greeted people and took their hats and coats. She had tan skin the colour of tenement bricks and curious half-frizzy hair tucked beneath a cap. Frances waited for the group ahead of her to go past a thick velvet curtain, wondering what to do now she had gotten this far. The girl checked the last coat, handed over a ticket and disappeared from view behind a wooden counter. Frances smoothed her skirt and inched her purse back on to her shoulder. If she went in now she might bump right into Ben or Stan. She needed a vantage point, somewhere she could . . .

'You gonna stand there all night fidgeting, or you goin' inside?' It was the girl behind the desk, although Frances couldn't see her.

'I'm waiting for someone.'

'Oh yeah? Who?'

'My brother. I'm meeting him here.'

'Huh. Is that so?'

The girl popped her head up. Frances thought from her tone she might have been frowning, but she wasn't, she was grinning a smile so broad, Frances couldn't help smiling back in spite of her nerves.

'And who might your brother be?'

'Why should I tell you?'

'Oh, no need, no need at all, only I might let you come back here and sit on one of my stools while you wait if you talk to me and put a stopper in my boredom for my trouble.'

Frances felt the weight of the walk in her aching feet and realised there was nothing she'd like more than to sit and rest a while, to work out what to do.

'All right, thanks.'

The girl lifted up part of her counter so Frances could duck behind, then lowered it again and kicked out a stool. It was almost as close to the floor as a child's and meant, Frances supposed, that the girl could rest without anyone being able to see her.

'I don't let just anybody back here, you know. I liked the look of you is all. And my sister's got a purse like yours, so I thought you'd be a good bet. Especially considering how shifty you were looking.'

'Thanks, I think.' Frances lowered herself and sighed, the pain in her feet ebbing as soon as the weight was off them.

The girl giggled. 'I don't mean nothing by it, you don't have to look so worried, I just thought you seemed like the right sort to keep a girl company. So, who you waiting for? Your brother you say?'

'Yes, my brother.'

'And your brother's name is?'

'I'd rather not say.'

'Ooh, a mystery. I knew you were the right one to pick. Where you from?'

'Kansas.'

'Oh my, you're a country gal, are you?'

'Yes, I guess so, although I've been in the city a while now.'

The girl nodded, as though she understood everything, as though there was nothing Frances might say that would ruffle her.

'Have you worked here long?'

'At the Catagonia? For ever. Least that's how it feels. And before that I was workin' tables at the Nest. I been all over this street.'

A man came in. Older than Frances, older than Stan even. Giving off a confident air, although something about him put her on her guard.

'Missy, you back here?'

The girl jumped up. 'I'm here, Walt, how you been?'

'I been good. You wanna take a drive?'

'I'm workin', you know that. Remember what Willie said last time?'

'Don't worry about Willie. I helped him out last week. He owes me. Come on, I've got the car outside. Can't leave it too long, the natives'll put their paws all over it.'

The girl looked down at Frances, then back up at the man, trying to decide what to do. After a beat she reached over Frances and grabbed her jacket.

'I'll come, but I wanna take a walk first, all right? I need some air.'

The man shrugged, but looked annoyed. 'If you have to.'

'Will you watch the coats for a while?' the girl whispered.

Frances felt stunned. She couldn't watch the coats. Was she crazy? But the girl was looking at her in such a sweet way, her eyes wide, excited to get away. So Frances nodded, even though she had no idea what to do.

'You're a doll. I'll be right back.'

Frances nodded again and shifted awkwardly on her stool, scraping patterns in the sticky floor with her sandals, watching the girl pulling her cap off and smoothing her hair, seeing the way she craned her neck so the man could kiss her cheek. Before she left she leant back over the desk and winked at Frances.

'I'll be fifteen, maybe twenty, tops. There's nothing to it. Take the coats, hang 'em up, give them a ticket. Easy. If Willie comes out tell him I stepped out for some air. And put this on.'

The girl tossed her cap at Frances.

'I knew you were on the level the second I saw you.'

She turned and walked out, arm in arm with her beau, leaving Frances poking at her cap.

The coat-check was inside the front door, in between two sets of moth-eaten red velvet drapes. Frances had eavesdropped on the doorman. He told some delivery boy that the first curtain was there to keep the cold out in winter and to give them a few extra seconds in case they got raided, although so far they never had. The second was there to keep the music and lewd language in, to block the whooping and hollering from the street. Part of Frances thought that was a shame. Surely the sound of the place was what made people want to go in.

The girl, Missy, had said twenty minutes, but it had already been a lot longer than that. At least there'd been no sign of Ben, or worse, Stan. She wondered where he was. Why had she agreed to do this? She stretched out her legs and tried to breathe slowly. It was almost impossible to stop her heart racing in a dress this small. She longed to unbutton it, but daren't in case she couldn't do it back up fast enough. Mrs Bianchi's daughter-in-law Anna had lent it to her. It was too tight in some places and too loose in others, flattening her breasts and billowing around her waist, but the pattern was handsome enough – light blue forget-me-nots – and the fabric was in far better condition than anything she owned.

She reached behind her head and ran her hands over the coats on the rail. Not many. A light tan men's overcoat with stains on the cuffs. An expensive-looking fur. A black satin jacket, worn at the elbows. Must be someone's favourite. She picked up the pelt and brushed the sleeve across her cheek, then leant back and rested her head on it. Soft and grey, like a wolf's belly. As she moved her head from side to side smoke and perfume added to the club smell of onions and whiskey.

'Excuse me down there.' It was a man's voice. 'Are you going to take our coats or should we hang them up ourselves?' The sound of women giggling.

Frances jumped up. Behind her the fur swung on the rail and slid to the floor. On the other side of the counter a lovely-looking man smiled. He was surrounded by five girls. He wore a light grey suit with the finest pressed shirt and striped tie Frances had ever seen. He was leaning on the counter and holding his hat in his hand, occasionally spinning it. The action reminded her of Dicky. A crisp cotton handkerchief peeked out of his top pocket. His hair was freshly cut and slicked back to one side. She could smell the pomade, his just-washed freshness. The girls all had short dark bobs, no hats. They were covered in lace and long pearls. Most had alabaster skin, unmarked like they'd just been born, but one, who was draped over him like a fine mink coat, had freckles all over her arms that bloomed in beautiful hand-drawn patterns. Frances held back the urge to lean over and stroke her.

'I said, would you be a good girl and do your job and take our coats for us? Myself and the girls are dying to get inside and sit down. Willie will be starting soon. And Benny's in tonight, isn't he? Wouldn't want to miss it if they all get up and play together like last time.'

'Perhaps she's a mute?' the freckled girl whispered. The others laughed.

'I don't care if she is,' the man replied, 'as long as she takes our coats.'

Finally Frances found her voice and reached across the counter. 'Yes, sir,' she said. 'Sorry, sir. I'm new.'

'I can see that,' he said. 'So new they've not even given you a proper uniform yet. Not to worry. You'll soon get the hang of it. Bright little thing like you. Not much to learn. Now, the way it works is people come in through these curtains looking for a good time.' He pointed towards the door. He'd begun speaking slowly as though he was worried she still might not understand. The girls kept giggling. 'We, the patrons, arrive and pass you our coats like this.' He gave her a fine lightweight overcoat and a pile of flimsy velvet, satin and embroidered jackets. 'Then you turn around. That's right. Just like that. You place our coats on the rail, nice and tidy – there you go.'

Frances picked up the fur then hung the coats. Her cheeks were burning.

'Good job!' The man leant over and patted her on the top of her head. Two of the girls fell about laughing. 'You see, girls, encouragement, that's all some of you need. A kind word and a soft touch.' He ran his palm up the girl's freckles. She was the only one who hadn't laughed. She rolled her eyes and winked at Frances.

Frances felt her blush burn brighter. She stood, as though frozen, while the little gang pushed their way through the second curtain and entered the club. As they disappeared she heard the man greet someone.

'Well if it ain't old Benji! Sure have missed you these past few months.'

Frances heard someone click their fingers, a few more muttered words, and footsteps behind the curtain. Seconds later Ben pushed his way through the velvet. She ducked down low behind the counter just in time. A band started up behind him. The music was loud, upbeat and brassy. It was nothing like the music Father listened to back home. No banjo, no fiddle. This was a piano, a horn and a set of drums that sounded like they were being thumped so hard the skin might tear. The sound pushed up and through her body, reminding her of the feel of the subway trains beneath the city.

'Missy?' Ben called.

Frances held her breath, squeezing herself further under the counter, softly reaching for a jacket to throw over the tips of her toes.

Heavy footsteps on the other side of the velvet. A man's voice, real loud. Someone different.

'Okay fellas, cool it. Take ten. No point in wearing ourselves out early. Sounds good.'

Frances swivelled her head a little and found a crack in the wood she could see through. An older man came through the curtain and grabbed Ben's shoulder. His skin was lighter than Ben's, but still dark. His brown suit was creased, white shirt a little stained, tie twisted. A fat cigar puffed from his wide smile. His eyes darted all over, as though the beat was playing them.

'My man!' He squeezed Ben's shoulder more tightly and shook him a little. Frances could tell it annoyed Ben. 'The Mayor's just told me how sad he is you're not on tonight. Sure I can't persuade you?'

Frances sank down a little lower. She felt hot. So that guy, the one with all the girls, had been the Mayor? She'd just spoken to the Mayor of New York? Of the whole city? Folks like that should go around with a sign on their necks. It didn't seem fair.

She would have put on a better voice if she'd known. She was still stung by the way he'd spoken to her – as if she was a fool, as if she was too stupid to know what to do.

Ben sighed. 'All right, one set, but then I gotta go help Stan.'

'Oh yeah, that was tonight? Now, like I was sayin', ain't no point you going inside too. Go with him, fine, but stay back. If they see you, it won't make no sense to them. All they want is the bag. Stan can slip in and out quiet as can be. And when you see him, tell him to stop defending girls he doesn't know, it ain't good for business. His honour'll get him in real trouble one day. Got two minutes before you play? Mo thinks something's stuck inside his horn. Says you're the only one knows how to fix it.'

'Sure, why not,' Ben said. 'That kid – I've been telling him for months to take it in for a service. Thinks it'll fix itself. Five minutes, all right?'

'All right. Where's Missy?'

'No idea, I was lookin' for her too.'

'That girl! If she wasn't my sister's niece, and the guys didn't like her so much, I'd kick her out.'

'I'll send another out before I go.'

'Thanks, make sure it's a pretty one. The Mayor's here already, but we got some big hitters in tonight. I heard Mae's coming. Maybe even the commissioner.'

They carried on talking and disappeared behind the curtain again.

Frances picked herself off the floor and sat back on the stool. What were they up to? Where was Stan going? It sounded like he wasn't working at the club at all.

'What you got in there? You waitin' for eggs to hatch or sumthin'?'

She looked down and realised she was squeezing her purse tight to her chest. She dropped it and stood up. If only the curtain was a door she'd have heard the next man come in.

'Oh no, sorry, sir.'

He was large. Not fat but broad. Like Stan used to be. When he moved his head to the side to see if the two men behind him had appreciated his joke, his neck barely swivelled. He looked familiar but she couldn't place him. Another expensive suit, this time bright blue. The two guys behind him sniggered as they pulled off their jackets and helped him out of his. The large man leant over, real close, and clutched her shoulder so she couldn't move.

'I'm feelin' lonely tonight,' he whispered. Hot brandy-breath in her ear. Just-shaved skin on her cheek. His cologne was so strong she felt faint, flooded with the smell of money and good times and danger. He was drenched in it. Tufts of his yellow hair brushed her forehead. 'You think there's some other dame can watch the coats? I like your dress. Those flowers make me think of my ma. And I only got good things to say about her.' His blue eyes seemed electric in the dim light. Like neon. Older than Stan but not as old as her father. 'What do you say? Don't mind about old Willie if that's your worry. Me an' him got an agreement. We share. Hell, he'd be pleased I was showin' one of his girls a good time.' The two men behind him laughed.

'I'm sorry, sir, I'm waiting for someone,' Frances said.

'I thought you were workin'.'

'I am, I mean, I am until they come back.'

'Well, where's this person gone to?'

'She's stepped out.'

'Well then, in that case, it all works out fine.' He leant back and pulled up the counter so she could duck under. 'We can go in and find Willie, get him to send another girl. He won't mind, I'm sure.'

Frances didn't know what to do. The man assumed she would go. Another couple walked in. Young this time. The man tipped his hat when he saw the older men by the counter and slid past, holding his girl's hand tight, as though he was worried she might stay behind if he let go. He threw their coats on the counter but didn't stop for a ticket.

As the couple went through the second curtain, Frances caught a glimpse inside. All the tables were draped in red and white checkerboard cloths. On the small stage a band was tuning up. Tiny lights glowed behind dark red shades, rouging the light. Girls in short skirts and small caps snaked between the tables.

What would one drink hurt? If she didn't go with him, she might never get inside. Stan practically owed it to her, making her stay home all this time. She said she'd watch the coats for that girl, but she didn't know her. Twenty minutes, she said she'd be. It wasn't Frances' job. And this guy. There was something about him. He reminded her of Mrs Bianchi's sons, or some tough guy from the pictures, or one of the characters from Stan's books. But then again, going in meant she might run into Ben, and he'd tell Stan and then she'd be in all sorts of trouble.

A girl walked through the curtain. Cherub face, tight blonde curls haloing her head. She looked at Frances, confused.

'Ben sent me,' she said, 'said Missy had gone again. Who are you?'

'I was just . . .' Frances stuttered.

'Here's someone come to save us.' The guy's hand was already on Frances' shoulder, leading her away from the coat-check.

The girl shrugged. 'I needed a break from the noise.'

Frances put the cap on the counter and let herself be taken. Behind her, the man's body pressed against her back.

That beat. The thump, thump, thump jerking the ice in her glass, flicking the check cloth against her bare knee beneath the table. Boards creaking from the weight of all the kids dancing. Black and white and every shade between, arms knotted. The clarinet winding around her as sweet and hot as the liquor in her belly. The guy had his arm on her but he hadn't gotten too friendly yet.

When he lifted his palm away from her shoulder she felt the air cool on the sweat he left behind.

He was leaning forward again, shouting a conversation she couldn't hear towards his two friends on the opposite side of the table. Ignoring her. She didn't care. She only liked him when he looked at her with those electric eyes. From this angle he was just another thick-set man. Another average Joe.

The dim lights held her eye like fogged stars. Music and talk; slapped thighs and chairs pushed back. Layers of sound. Smoke swirled, so thick she was convinced if she held her hand above her head it would disappear. One of the man's friends had offered her a drag on a cigarette when she sat down. She'd waved him away, not wanting to put her lips where his had been. Since then he'd kept blowing smoke in her direction. It smelt strange, sweeter than normal and thicker somehow, and if she took a breath at the wrong moment her chest filled with it until her head swam and she coughed and all the men laughed.

Still no sign of Stan. Ben was in the shadows by the stage, fiddling with his horn. Everyone was right. He did play well, so well she'd barely been able to take her eyes off him, stunned at the sound he'd forced from a twisted lump of brass. He'd still not seen her though. Lucky the guy she was with liked to sit at the back in the dark.

One of his men said something to him. He threw his yellow head back and slapped the table. He had this way of laughing where he kept his eyes on his friends the whole time, like he was checking to make sure they thought it was funny too. Like he'd be mad if they didn't.

'I wouldn't worry about that. We've got our best man on it.'

'He ain't what he used to be.' The guy with the cigarette snorted and flicked ash at his feet.

'I've still got faith in him. You should too.' It sounded more like a threat than a piece of advice.

Frances pretended to push her hair from her eyes and looked at him between her fingers. His mouth was firm and pinched on the glass when he sipped his drink. He put it back on the table a little harder than he needed to.

'I've vouched for him before and I'll do it again.'

'I don't trust him.' The cigarette guy again.

'What you got against him? Jealous of his luck with the ladies?'

'He ain't had much luck lately.'

They all laughed except her guy. The mirth didn't last long.

Her guy turned his cigarette pack over and over on the table. His voice slowed down and he stared at the man smoking. 'Like I said, earlier, let's see how he gets on tonight. Then you can cast judgement on our friend Stanley.' He leant towards her. 'I'll be back.' His breath was hot and salty in her ear. 'Hurry up and finish your drink so I can buy you another.'

Did he mean her Stan? She wanted to grab hold of his lapels and ask but she didn't. Of course she didn't. Too many drinks to count. Hours passing by in a rush of liquor and heat. She had no notion what time it was. It had probably gotten so late it was early again. His blue eyes flashed at her, leaving a bright trail in the air as he moved away. The smoke shifted as the three men left the table and she began to cool. She watched as they wove between the tables towards a packed booth at the back of the room. Someone stood up to shake her guy's hand. It looked like the Mayor. He moved out from behind the bodies of what seemed like a hundred girls, stark limbs in piles, and the two men embraced. He must have meant someone else. There were probably thousands of Stanleys in this city. At any rate, if he did know Stan he liked him. She was worrying over nothing.

A song started up that moved her. She banged her hand on the table to the beat, softly at first then harder as the mood took her, nodding her head, rocking the fringe on the table lamp, not caring who saw. A girl twisted past, done up like a cigarette seller in a movie theatre, and offered her a drink. She waved her on. There was no money in her purse, and at any rate, if she had any more to drink she'd not be able to stand let alone dance.

She checked her guy was still busy and squeezed her way to the edge of the dance floor. What looked like hundreds of people (but were probably more like fifty) were crammed into a small space in front of the band, all of them moving and twisting and jumping up and down. The men's ties swung from side to side as they grabbed at the girls they liked and flung them into the crowd. The girls wore flat shoes with laces and wide skirts that let them lift their knees up. They always landed on their feet.

Before she knew it a tall Negro with a line down his head (that gave the look of a parting in his hair) wearing a pin-stripe suit crumpled from all the dancing offered her his hand. It was too loud to speak so he bowed at her and smiled instead. She glanced round. Her guy was still busy. Ben had disappeared. She nodded at the man and grabbed hold of his soft, hot fingers.

Her feet lifted off the floor. She was swung and jerked until her head grew dizzy and her palms burnt from the effort of holding on to him. He was a fine dancer and she could see from the way his friends winked and clapped when they passed by that he was proud she'd agreed to partner him. He jumped and twirled, as light on his feet as a tap dancer. The more they danced, the more she felt their differences fall away. The band took up a heady rhythm and he spun her so fast she lost her footing and fell. This was why all the girls wore flats. Before she had a chance to get up, someone grabbed her arm. Not her dance partner – Ben. She was too lit to be shocked.

'What are you doing?' he said.

'What?' she shouted back. She wondered how angry he was: she didn't know him well enough to tell.

'Get up.'

He pulled her until she was on her feet and her head hit the smoke. She was standing. A miracle – her buttocks had felt welded to the floor, as though the liquor she'd drunk was made of lead.

'Move fast before he sees us. Go.' Ben held her hand tight and dragged her past the tables.

'I want to stay,' Frances said. 'It's early. Please?' Her voice sounded as though it had split from her throat, like she'd changed into one of those dummies at the fair.

Either Ben didn't hear, or he was ignoring her, because he kept walking and pulling her, looking over his shoulder at the guy who'd bought her all the drinks, until the velvet curtain brushed up the hairs on her arm and they were on the other side standing next to the coat-check. She felt sick. The lights were too bright. She lay her head on the counter. No sign of Missy or the girl with yellow curls.

'What the hell are you doing?' So he was angry.

'Having a drink and a dance, that's all.'

'How did you get here?' He paused, the truth of it dawning. 'Did you follow me? No doubt Stan knows nothing.'

'No. He's not my keeper, and neither are you. You've no right to grab me.'

'You have no idea.'

'About what?' Her voice was muffled. The cool counter comforted her hot head. The darkness soothed.

'It doesn't matter. Let's go. I'm already late and now I've got to get you home as well.'

'I want to stay,' Frances said. 'My guy was going to buy me another drink.'

'You don't need any more drinks from Kane. Now pick up your purse and let's go. The air will do you good.'

As soon as her feet hit the sidewalk, she leant over and lost her stomach in the gutter. A sliver of shame sliced through the fog inside her head. Ben laid his hand on her back.

'Too much?' he asked.

'Of what?'

'Of everything.' Not so angry now, she thought. His voice sounded softer. 'We'll sit here a moment and then we'll have to get on, okay? Stan'll kill me if I'm any later. Although he'll probably kill me anyway when he finds out about you.'

Frances nodded and sat on the stoop, clutching her knees. It was totally dark now, hardly any streetlights left. She was glad the real night had come to hide her.

'Do you have to tell him I was here?'

Ben didn't answer. He lit a cigarette and stared out, not looking at her. Guys and girls were milling around, some of them still lining up to get into the club. No one seemed to care she'd made a fool of herself. He passed over her purse.

'Will you?'

She didn't want to beg. She felt stupid. And what had she found out? Almost nothing. All she knew was that Stan wasn't here. All she'd done was drink and flirt. She held her head and cursed herself.

'I don't know. Can you walk?'

'I think so.'

'All right, then, I'll put you in a cab.'

'Where is Stan, anyway?'

A girl screamed.

Missy, the coat-check girl, was standing at the top of the steps beneath the awning. The man she had left with earlier was holding her by the wrist. Even in the darkness, Frances could see her fingers changing colour as he squeezed.

'Make a fool out of me, will ya?' the man yelled.

Missy's lip was cut. Blood dripped down her chin and splattered the porch. She was crying. The man pulled her down the steps past Frances and Ben, giving no care to everyone's stares.

'If you keep making a scene,' he said, 'I'll take you out back and give you a proper hiding. Now shut your mouth and get in the car.' He opened the door of a shiny flat-top parked in front of the club and tried to push her inside.

'Hold on,' Ben said, standing up. 'You can see she doesn't want to go.'

'Keep out of this. You don't know nothin' about it. Why don't you get back inside and play your sax some more.'

The guy was talking tough, but Frances could tell from the look on his face he was more frightened of Ben than he cared to admit.

'She's supposed to be working. Willie won't be pleased if you take her off someplace.' Ben leant on the car. Frances could see his fists flexing inside his trouser pockets.

'I don't give a damn what Willie wants. We made a date and that's that.' He pushed Missy again. 'I said, get in the damn car. Don't think you can go all doe-eyed on me now. Bearcat one minute, dud the next.'

'That's enough, Walt.' Ben's friend hopped down the steps beside Frances, moving with the bouncy strides of a much younger man. He was still chewing on his fat cigar. 'Like Ben said, Missy's working, and I sure would appreciate it if you'd let her get back to it. I don't pay my girls to leave before the evening's barely begun.'

A small crowd had gathered around the car.

'I told Ben, and I'm telling you, Willie,' Walt said, 'me and her made a deal. It ain't like she's one of your best girls, is it? Dirty half breed. Neither one thing nor the other. If she weren't usually so obliging, I wouldn't be interested. Next time I'll take myself someplace there's not so much mixing going on.'

Frances felt a rush of air beside her as Willie jumped forward and grabbed the man's lapels, forcing him over the bonnet of the car. He raised his fist over his head, anger dissolving his age. Walt shrank back. The crowd jostled, trying to get a better view. She glanced at Ben. He was swaying a little, as though trying to pull free of an invisible rope. His body teetered but his feet didn't shift.

'All right, Willie, old friend, all right,' Walt whined, 'no reason to get hot. No reason to turn on your pal.' He was holding his hands up.

'Now, Walt, like Ben and I were sayin', leave her alone and get in your car. Time to go home and sleep it off. No need for all this. If you've got a problem with the kind of girls I employ or the type of folks that come into my place I suggest you get your bigoted ass down to the Cotton Club with the rest of those phoneys. The likes of us ain't got no time for you.'

Willie released his hold and Walt shrank away. Willie helped Missy out and shoved Walt into the driver's seat. The door slammed. Walt wiped his brow, checked his wide-eyed reflection in the mirror and accelerated away. Frances had never seen someone look so relieved, like he'd outrun a dust storm. But it was strange. All the while Willie had been holding him, he'd been staring at Ben, as though it was him he was worried about. But Ben hadn't moved.

The crowd began to drift away. Willie walked Missy back up the steps. The girl was sobbing into his shoulder, pressing his crumpled handkerchief to her mouth. The blood stains looked like lipstick.

Ben sat back down beside Frances. He bent over and worried at his hands.

'You didn't help,' she said, unable to keep the scorn from her voice.

'No.'

'Why not?'

'Fightin' don't solve most things.'

'You sound like Stan. At least, Stan how he is now, not how he was. I guess fighting doesn't solve everything but it helps enough. Did you see how fast that piker moved once your boss went for him? Most men like that are weak. They like beatin' on girls but they can't take a beatin' themselves. Didn't take much to make him run.'

Ben shrugged. He wouldn't look at her. What was it about this city that turned good men into cowards? How long would he wait to tell Stan what she had done? She smoothed her dress over her knees and ground her heels on the grime between the steps, clenching her jaw, trying hard not to be sick again, watching the couples walk to and fro, letting the soft beat of the city settle into the silence between them.

*

Frances asked the taxi man to let her out on the main street. It wouldn't do for her to be seen by someone from the tenement. Not at this hour. Ben had put her in and waved her off. He'd looked melancholy. She wasn't sure why. She could barely see where she was walking – no streetlights past a certain time over here. At least, for once, if she looked up high enough she could make out a few stars. Finally she was feeling a little less woozy.

She turned the corner on to their block, dodging past the upturned barrows waiting for morning goods, keeping her fingers crossed that none of the dirt would ruin Anna's dress. As she passed she heard whispering from underneath one of them. Street urchins, she guessed. Young ones without a mother or a home. They were all over the tenements like stray cats, too poor even to get inside, as dirty and sorry-looking as the barrows they slept under. She'd seen some of the older men kick at them as they walked past. Mrs Bianchi handed out scraps but she kept it quiet so her friends in the tenement wouldn't get annoyed.

She felt strangely calm. The liquor was still pulsing softly inside her, taming the panic. She had her story straight, and after all, Stan wasn't Father. Even if he was home, it was unlikely he'd hit her. And it sounded from what she'd overheard Willie saying to Ben that Stan was out anyway, doing some kind of job elsewhere. Either way, if she was truthful to herself, however exciting the night had been, the thought of giving Stan cause to worry, of adding to his problems, whatever they were, made her stomach clench more than the thought of his anger.

At the foot of their building she took out the large iron front-door key and quietly twisted it in the lock, all the while looking around and listening hard. Once inside it was quiet enough to hear the mice scuttling in the walls, the ones that made Mrs Bianchi so crazy she'd put a trap in every cupboard.

Best to pull off her sandals. She carried them in the crook of her arm, padding lightly up the worn stairs. Once she got to their floor, she paused at each door, listening. There was Mr Tonioni snoring, the giggle of one of Mrs Bianchi's grandchildren tussling to sleep beside their siblings. Behind Ben's door it was so quiet all she could hear was her own breath. Finally she stopped outside their apartment. She couldn't hear anything. No pacing footsteps, no worried sighs. She found the key and turned until it caught.

Now she could see into the parlour. Her throat tightened. Stan wasn't out. He was crouching on the floor with his back to her. It was such a strange position to find him in she almost laughed. He was concentrating on something and didn't turn. She pushed the door a little more and stepped inside. She could see half of him now, his body pivoting in swift repetitive movements. In the floor a small board was missing. Next to him, on the other side, she saw an open package. Another step and she'd be able to see what he was doing.

Voices behind her in the hall. Stan paused mid-swing. Frances pulled herself backwards and tugged at the door, flattening her body on to the wall outside, trying to stifle her startled breaths. She didn't think he'd heard her but she'd seen what he was hiding. Money. Hundreds and hundreds of dollars. Sheaves of it slipping beneath the boards.

NEW YORK CITY

Winter solstice, 21 December 1932

16.51

'You're not ready?' Ben said, a wave of frustration passing over his face like a scudding cloud.

'Almost,' Agnes replied, exhaling loudly, her relief warming Frances' cheek. 'We'd probably be moving a lot faster if you hadn't terrified us. Why are you here? Why didn't you call out?'

'I know. Sorry. I was worried in case he'd already arrived. I didn't want to ruin it.'

'He's got a point,' Frances said. 'We didn't think of that.'

Agnes shrugged. 'We can't think of everything. No harm done, although if my nerves get any more wrung out I won't be able to operate this thing, let alone do what we're here for.'

Frances watched the rise and fall of Ben's chest, his deep breaths clearly visible beneath a thick woollen coat. If she hadn't known better she might have thought he'd run up the stairs, but Ben never ran. The relaxed motion of his limbs remained even in a situation like this. No need to hurry. Only his breathing gave his fear away. Not like Stan.

Her mind reached for him. His hands curling round a mug of coffee. The tap of his foot in time to the wireless while he read the paper at the window in the morning, the light turning his blond hair into a halo. His great big body spread out on the daybed, feet crossed at the ankles, smiling at her, asking for another beer, another plate of ham and eggs, another story from home. She clenched her fist around the cotton handkerchief in his pocket. The suicide note crackled against her knuckles. She would not cry again.

'What happened?' Agnes asked.

'I had to give them more money,' Ben said.

'Them?' Agnes looked startled.

'His buddy came to change shifts. He tried to ask for more, but I said I didn't have it. Luckily, he believed me. They're in the diner across the street. I thought I'd better come up and let you know. They said they'd get some early dinner and be back around six. We'll have to be gone by then and we'll have to hope they're both so worried about keeping their jobs they'll stay quiet. It might work as long as none of us ever run into them.'

'Not much chance of that where we're going,' Agnes said.

Ben nodded and pulled his collar up against the violent gusts shuddering the glass.

'What are you going to do?' Frances asked. She didn't think his plan for after was as good as it could be. Perhaps he'd changed his mind.

'I told you. I'm going on tour. Be gone for a few months. By then it will all have blown over. It'll be out of the papers.'

'If we do it right, it might never be in them,' Agnes said, fiddling with a screw on one side of the bellows.

'Maybe. But folks'll wanna read about a man like him, dead or alive. And if I had to stay for some reason, even if I saw one of the guards on the street, to most white folks, one black man looks the same as any other. They wouldn't be able to pick me out of a line-up if they tried. As it was, one could barely stand to look at me. And all the other one was thinking about was how much pie he was going to buy with those fresh dollars in his pocket. I'll be fine. It's you two I'm worried about.'

He said two, but Frances knew from the look on his face he was only thinking about her.

'What time is it?' Frances asked.

Agnes glanced outside. 'Almost five. I can tell by the colour of the sky.'

'Where is he?' Frances wondered out loud. 'Perhaps he's not coming.'

'He'll come,' Ben said, walking back through the door. 'You don't need to worry about that. I'll keep watch. He won't be able to resist.'

GREENWICH VILLAGE

20 October 1932

21.36

Frances gripped the sides of the crate she was sitting on and tried not to fidget. The more they talked the more nervous she felt. The longer they sat here, the closer they got to Dicky coming up to do photographs and the nearer they were to going down to the party. She'd never been so desperate to get somewhere, yet so scared of what she might find, of how she should act, of who to be.

'I'm confused,' Jacks said. 'So are you sad to leave the Midwest or relieved?'

Frances frowned. She'd already answered three questions like this, and before that a hundred others. Surely Jacks had all she needed now.

'Both, I guess. I'm happy to be in New York, but I'm a small part sorry to leave home too.'

Jacks scribbled in her notebook. Every time she did it, Frances flinched and regretted saying something.

'Why? What's back there in all that dust for you? Hell, what's there for anybody? As I remember it, most girls like you who could escape already had and the ones left behind were so hungry and depressed and desperate, they'd have sold their children and strangled their husbands and dragged themselves all the way to New York on the back of my kimono if they could.'

Frances uncrossed her legs. She stared past Jacks' sculpted face and looked up at the tiny window behind her head, wishing that the view beyond held something other than darkness. Dicky's studio at the top of the house felt more like a cave than an attic. The large statue in the corner of the room seemed to shift in the dusty light. Every now and then the stone woman seemed to move, as though she was edging closer and trying to listen.

It had taken a lot for Frances to sneak out on Stan again, not knowing if they'd really meant for her to come along to Dicky's party at all. She'd tried to ask his permission to come earlier but that had been a mistake. She'd seen flashes of the old Stan all day. He'd even sent her down to buy cinnamon buns for them both when the seller had called out. Frances had run down and run back and they'd gone out on the fire escape and stuffed thick wedges of warm dough into their mouths. He'd even made her laugh. Then she had asked about the party and he'd gotten mad and she'd promised not to go, then snuck out anyway when he went to work. It was agony being inside the apartment when he wasn't in it – all that money sitting beneath the boards, calling out to her, but she was too frightened to look, too scared she'd disturb something and send him over the edge. She'd waited for him to go then taken her time to get ready, washing her hair in the parlour, running across the way and borrowing a dress from Anna again, swearing her to secrecy, then making her way across town, wondering all the while if she dared to rap Dicky's brass knocker again. She'd paced up and down his path, trying to decide what to do, imagining what kinds of people might be inside, what photographs Dicky might ask to take, then before she'd had a chance to run away, Jacks had opened the door, looking flushed and wild. She'd asked Frances into the hall then called to Agnes and told her to take Frances up to the studio at once, that she wanted to ask all her questions before Dicky took his shots. Jacks had barely smiled at Frances the whole time she was shouting orders at the caterers. Agnes had led her straight upstairs then disappeared to get ready.

'Maybe I'm not explaining it right.'

'You think?' Jacks raised an eyebrow. 'Take a deep breath and give it a try.'

'I guess,' Frances sighed, 'I miss the way things used to be, not the way they were when I left.'

'Go on.'

'I miss being a child.'

'Yes. What was that like?'

'It was safe.'

'Really?'

'Well, not all the time, but mostly. And the things that scared me, or worried me, I could see them coming, I could be ready.'

'Like what?'

Jacks scratched on her pad again. Frances squeezed the crate so hard she felt a splinter press into her thumb. She didn't let go.

'Like fresh guys and nasty girls and chores I didn't want to do and Mother worrying at me, and Father's bad moods. And most of all the work. The cleaning and scrubbing. Helping out on the farm. The welts on my hands, the tiredness dragging at me until I felt like no amount of sleep would ever fix it.'

'Good.' Jacks paused and wrote something down. 'Sorry, not good; I mean, I see. And then your brother left and everything changed?'

'It changed before that.'

'When?'

'When the bank lost all our money. When the crops dried up. When Mother started crying over where she'd get supper. Stan leaving was the end of all that, not the start.'

'But things got worse after he left.'

'Of course.'

'You missed him.'

Frances didn't answer. She couldn't. The truth was, she still missed him, even though he was sleeping next door to her every night. She missed him reading to her and laughing at her. She missed his anger when she snuck into his room and upended things; she missed the sunshine that followed when he forgave her. She had hoped it would all go back to how it had been once she got to the city, but everything seemed worse. He was further away than ever. And all her sneaking around with Jacks and Dicky and Agnes was only making it harder. Every night the guilt piled on to her, but the next day her stifling life in the tenement made her want to run away all over again. And now he was hiding money from her too.

'Yes, I missed him.'

'And finally, what do you think about our crazy city so far? What do you hope to do while you're here? What are your dreams and desires for the future?'

'That's a lot to think on.'

Jacks clipped her pen on to her notebook and cocked her head. 'It is, but it's important for my readers to see the future through your eyes. They need to know that whatever they're dreaming of, you're dreaming it too. That whether they were born in a mansion uptown, or picked up their skirts and ran all the way to the city from the deep south, they're just like you. They need to hear an echo of their own voice in your words.'

'Should I make something up?'

'God, no, dear. Just tell the truth.' She paused. 'But make

it spicy.'

'Spicy?'

Jacks sighed. 'Just tell me where you want to end up, what you want to see, who you want to be.'

Frances looked from the night in the window, to the statue, to Jacks' black eyes. She squeezed the splinter deeper into her thumb and took a deep breath. 'I want to go everywhere, see everything, be everyone. I want to dance. I want to live in the pictures. I want to stretch my hands out and not touch the walls of my room. I want to fly.' She looked Jacks straight in the eye. 'I want to be you.'

Everywhere strange men and women huddled, talking, laughing, smoking, drinking. Some wore fine clothes, the kind Frances imagined came from the stores on 5th Avenue, the kind that glittered and slid. Others looked less fancy – creased jackets, badly sewn skirts, monocles. One man even had an eye patch. These were the artists Jacks had mentioned, she supposed, the writers and poets and painters who covered the walls and filled the shelves. Poor in funds, Jacks had said, but rich in spirit. The ones, Agnes had whispered to her, that Dicky funded with his family's money.

Lots of them talked to Frances. Some of them complimented her dress (navy silk, hesitantly borrowed from Jacks after Dicky's shoot because they'd all told her Anna's wasn't quite right), then asked her to dance. She had decided to say yes to anyone under forty. If they looked older, she smiled and asked them to get her a drink, then she made sure to disappear into the crowd before they came back.

A few of them asked her to pose for them. One old man with a lazy eye and salmon-pink slacks said he was painting something and she had just the kind of look he was searching for. She said she might be able to help, but that he'd have to speak to Dicky. Another started reciting poetry. She'd never heard it spoken so seriously. To her, a rhyme was something to laugh at – to scrawl on a wall or finger in the dust. Here it was murmured. Here a rhyme could trick you into bed, or describe a sunset as though you'd never seen one. It could make trees greener or the sudden twilight sky last for ever. So far she'd liked the poet the best, but in the end he'd seemed too melancholy to kiss.

The man beside her said something. He had a stumpy nose and fine brown eyes, the sort of eyes she might once have got lost in. He said he wrote copy, whatever that was, for Jacks' magazine. They were squashed together, sitting on the back of a sofa, their feet on the seat cushions, next to a couple who were kissing. Frances nodded in reply, although she wasn't sure what she'd agreed to and didn't really care. Somewhere in the throng a group of musicians were playing a frantic jazz tune but it was so busy she couldn't see the piano.

She gazed at the photographs of nude women on the wall and felt a flare of annoyance that Dicky hadn't taken a photo of her like that. She wondered what this said about who she was becoming. Here she was in the middle of a real New York party, the sort of party she'd never have believed until she was in it, and all she was really thinking about, apart from Stan and the money, was why, when she posed for more pictures, Dicky hadn't asked her to strip.

She tilted her head back and drank the rest of her drink in a single burning gulp. When she opened her eyes, Jacob, Dicky's crazy neighbour, walked past and nodded at her. He was swaying all over the place, knocking into people and spilling their liquor. He had the same yellow glasses on and the same stuck-up hair.

'Got any more deliveries for me?' he asked, tapping his nose at her, shouting over the hubbub.

'Not today.' She smiled at him and held out her hands to show there was nothing in them.

'Fair enough. It's probably for the best.'

Frances nodded as though she understood, her eyes drawn back to the dance floor. A handsome woman with dark skin wearing a tight, one-shouldered white gown was spinning and twirling and clapping her hands to the music. She kept laughing and waving at a stern-looking Negro in a tweed suit with perfectly circular glasses. Jacob followed her gaze.

'That's Alta Sawyer Douglas and her husband Aaron. He's one of the finest painters to come out of Harlem. They've been in Europe. Came back at the end of the summer. She really is something, isn't she? Quite a handful for Aaron, but you can see why he married her. Stops life getting too serious.'

Jacks danced by, blocking Frances' view of the twirling woman, her velvet dress bunching, arms thrown around the shoulders of two young men who were taking it in turns to steal her cigarette holder and suck on it. She winked at Frances but clearly wasn't going to stop, until Jacob caught hold of Jacks' hand and said, 'Your friend is on his way over. He's getting cleaned up.'

'You've finally finished your ode to that monstrosity, have you?' Jacks eyed Jacob with one eyebrow raised then pushed the young men off her. 'Go and get yourselves some candy from the kitchen. Mummy needs to talk.' The men sloped off looking forlorn. One of them turned and winked at Frances. A flicker of a frown crossed Jacks' fine brow, then her face smoothed again.

'I thought you'd want to know he was on his way,' Jacob said.

'Why would I care about that?'

'Dicky said—'

'Oh, Dicky said, did he? Well if Dicky said I'd mind then I'm sure I must do. He is my keeper, after all. I'm just his lowly female sidekick, not a single thought in my pretty little head.'

'That's not what I meant.' Jacob looked affronted. 'I wouldn't have agreed to make the thing in the first place if you and Dicky hadn't—'

'Oh Jacob, I really don't care. Stop being so sensitive. Have a drink. Have something stronger. Either way, please stop whining at me, you're ruining the mood.' Jacks' tone was light but Frances could see her edges flickering – anger and something else, something she'd not sensed around Jacks before. Sadness, perhaps? Panic, even?

'I didn't mean to cause any trouble,' Jacob said. 'It was such a big commission, I couldn't very well say no. Not if I want to make it through another winter.'

'I know, Jacob. I said I don't care. Now run along.'

Jacob sighed, shrugged his shoulders and removed his glasses. He cleaned them with the edge of his sleeve, then put them back on and wobbled slowly towards the bar in the corner of the room. Jacks twisted her chin towards Frances, her lips as dark and shiny as ripe cherries, and Frances felt, not for the first time, the full force of her gaze. It was a blaze of attention, as though the sun had changed course and now it was burning Frances' face.

'How's your night been? You've set the party alight in that dress. I can't tell you how many people have come up and asked after you. I hope you're enjoying all these lingering glances.' The compliment was lined with spite – as rough and loving as a cat's tongue.

Frances let Jacks' words sting for a moment. Her body hummed from the drink.

'It's all thanks to you and Dicky. You have such fine dresses. Although, I can see you prefer things that are a little looser now. I suppose we all have to change our style as we age.'

As soon as the words were out, Frances regretted them. This woman was helping her. For a second their eyes locked. Jacks' nose crinkled as though she was smelling something sour and Frances feared she might shout, but then she threw back her glossy head and laughed.

'My word,' Jacks said, 'you really do tread a fine line between bravery and insanity, don't you. I'll take the first half of that as a compliment and forget the rest, I think.'

Frances wanted her drink. 'Sorry,' she said, 'I didn't mean—'

'We both know exactly what you meant.'

'I'm having a really good time.' Frances paused. Why did she always find the word so hard to say? 'Thanks.'

'Only good? Well, we'll have to do better than that next time, won't we?' Jacks started to walk off, then twisted round and tapped the side of her glass. 'The cure's in there. They'll all tell you it's not, but it always is.'

Frances watched her sashay away then leant over the guy next to her and reached for a half-full bottle. She drank, almost retched, then drank again.

Against the opposite wall she could see Agnes talking to a group of people. Two were women in long, loose dresses in peacock colours. The third was wearing a suit. From the back, the person's wide shape made them look like a giant penguin. Every now and then Agnes looked bored, downcast even. Frances watched her look away from her friends and stare into the crowd. She caught Frances' eye, smiled and waved her over. Frances stumbled from her seat, her feet more unsteady than they'd been when she sat down, and moved through the crowd towards her.

As Frances approached, Agnes pointed to the women in dresses who turned out to be identical twins.

'Frances, this is Angel and Adeline. They live on the other side of the square. More artists.'

Frances shook their thin hands in turn. The women nodded at her and smiled, but didn't speak. Their eyes looked far away and they were both swaying out of time to the music, as though they were listening to something only they could hear.

At first, even up close, Frances couldn't tell if the third person, the penguin, was a man or a woman, if they were young or old. They had a large patchwork quilt around their shoulders from which their chubby head was poking. After a second Frances saw the swell of a large bosom beneath a partially hidden three-piece suit. The woman's hair was cropped short, much shorter than Agnes' and greying on the temples. A homemade cigarette was stuck in the corner of her mouth. She blinked, her small eyes still bright somehow behind large black-rimmed glasses.

'And this is Sue. Meet Frances, she's Dicky's newest.'

Frances held out her hand. The woman ignored it and, bending forward so her quilt wouldn't fall, pulled Frances into a tight embrace. She smelt of cigarettes and musty straw. For a second the scent reminded Frances of home. The woman pulled away and held her at arm's length.

'Pleasure. Dicky said a new girl was coming to pose, but he didn't mention it was someone with a face like yours, so this is a nice surprise.' Sue sneezed, pulled a ragged-looking hanky from her pocket and blew her nose. 'Sorry, I'm in recovery. I gave blood again at the start of the week and I'm still feeling terribly weak. I'm sure they took more than two pints.'

'You're not on that scam again?' Agnes scoffed.

'I have to. No one comes into the shop any more. What choice do I have?'

'No one came in before.'

'Yes they did. Don't listen to her, Frances. I was doing a roaring trade this time last year.'

'Sue runs an antique shop,' Agnes explained. 'But she ought to give it up and carry on with her painting instead.'

'I've got some of the finest antiques in the city between my walls. I told you last time, Ag. It's all the fault of that damned subway. If a new one hadn't opened up a block away, everyone would still be trooping past my place on their way home from work. Funny sort of progress, putting honest people out of business. I'd go and give blood every week if it was allowed. I don't know why more people don't do it. You should go. Five bucks a pint isn't to be sniffed at. And you're helping those in need at the same time.'

'I'm not a fan of needles.' Agnes feigned a shudder. 'I'll be suffering from something awful soon enough, no doubt, so I'd rather not go into hospital before I have to.'

Sue eyed Frances. 'How about you?'

'I can see the sense in it,' Frances said. 'A little pain to help someone else and your own pocket sounds like a fine idea.'

'Well,' Sue smiled, 'if you stick around I'll take you. We can hold hands.'

Frances glanced at Agnes, but she wasn't listening, she was staring over Frances' shoulder. 'Watch out.' Frances went to turn her head but Agnes held her arm. 'Don't look.' She bent close to Frances' ear. 'And don't trust him.'

'So, how are you finding it?'

The man had sidled close. With a shock, Frances realised it was the Mayor. He looked more casual than before, but his slacks and shirt were just as crisp. The beautiful girl with the freckles was still on his arm. Apart from a flush at her neck like a lace collar, most of the spots were hidden by the long sleeves of her black beaded dress.

'Oh fine,' Frances said, 'just fine.' She tried to sound breezy, but the truth was he made her more nervous than anyone else here. She was barely used to talking to folk like Jacks and Dicky, let alone a man of his standing. She was surprised to see some of the same people here as at the Catagonia.

He smiled at her. He didn't seem to recognise her from the

club, though. That was a relief. She supposed he was dripping in girls, that in this dress she looked the same as any other. At least now she was free to make herself up however she pleased. Now she could be the person she wanted, instead of who she was.

Agnes wasn't looking at her any more. The three women had twisted their bodies away from the Mayor as he approached and now they edged a little further away.

'Dicky's been telling me all about you. He took the time to show us some of his photographs of you in the darkroom. Fine dresses suit you.'

'Thanks.' For some reason this annoyed her. 'That's nice of you to say, but in my book, the person in the photographs should be the first one to see them. Surely a picture belongs to whoever's in it and that means they should look before anyone else.' What was she doing? The damn drink was loosening her tongue. 'I don't mean to be rude.'

'Not at all. I understand what you mean, I think.'

Frances could see he wasn't listening to her. His eyes slid around her dress, as though they were slipping on its inky oil slick. She wondered why Dicky had shown him the photographs. Now the Mayor and this girl, and God knows who else, had a notion of her she didn't have herself.

The girl was leaning away from him, talking to someone else, her long fingers lingering at the man's shoulder. They both seemed to know everyone. The girl laughed, then shouted at the man she was talking to.

'Vous êtes écœurant!'

The Mayor leant closer to Frances, his scent so sharp she thought of Mother taking out her woes on the front step with a scrubbing brush. 'Colette's French.' So the girl, Colette, was foreign. This explained most of how she stood, her long nails, the golden pins she wore in her hair.

For a moment Frances wished Mother could see her now, in

the midst of all this. She would have dropped dead at the door had she looked in. Frances had a sudden urge to send a telegram, to ask Dicky to take a photograph and mail it. Things had been so bad before she left she knew she had almost forgotten the good times – those rare moments when they had sat together sewing on the porch, not talking, just listening to the wind beat branches on the roof. Or when she'd been small and Mother had confided in her, whispering worries as though Frances was her best friend. Or the time she'd found Mother weeping at the bottom of the coal box and she'd helped her out and cooked for her and Mother had eaten the eggs she made and cried and folded Frances into her arms like when she was a baby.

'And New York? What do you think of our city, young lady? Standing up to scrutiny, is it?' The Mayor was half smiling at her. Some would find him hard to resist. He was much younger up close.

'Oh yes,' Frances said.

She struggled to think of something clever to say. She must try and be polite. But why? Everyone who knew her was far away. She could do what she wanted here, say what she liked. Beneath the title and the fancy suit, he was just a man, after all. And though he was talking to her, he still wasn't listening. He didn't really care what she said, so she might as well tell the truth.

'I mean, I like some of it.'

'Like what?' He had one eye on her and one on Colette.

She thought for a moment. 'Like the way the sun falls through the high buildings on to the sidewalk. The smell of all the fruit stalls. I've never seen so many tomatoes in one place. I like the rush and all the people, and I went to an automat with my brother. I like those.'

'How sweet,' the Mayor said.

Frances frowned. 'And then there's all the things I don't

like too.'

'I don't believe it. This fine city? The greatest on earth. At least I'm working to make it that way. What can you possibly not like about it?'

'Chéri, why are you interrogating this girl?' Colette had finished her conversation and leant her head on the Mayor's shoulder. She smiled at Frances.

'I'm not sure,' Frances said. 'Sometimes people act in ways I don't like.'

'Come now, I need more detail than that. I'm the Mayor, you know, I can take criticism as much as compliments. It's my job to make things better around here. I'm asking everyone, but the opinions I care for the most are those of beautiful women.'

Frances looked quickly away when she saw how he was looking at her. She felt like his gaze might sear off her dress. She wondered if Colette enjoyed or endured his wandering eye.

'She's right,' Colette said. 'People here are not like in Paris. In Paris, if they don't like you they tell you so to your face. They cross the road to avoid you. Here, someone who hates you would run towards you with open arms.'

'That's just it,' Frances said, liking this foreign girl. 'You never know if what someone is saying is what they really think. It's not like at home.'

'And where is home?' Colette asked, absentmindedly running one of her sharp nails along the edge of the Mayor's jaw.

'Hays, Kansas.'

'A farm girl,' the Mayor said. 'Yes, I remember now, that's what Dicky said.'

Frances narrowed her eyes at him and wished for another drink.

'Well,' Colette said, 'this Kansas, wherever it is, sounds a lot like Paris.'

Frances laughed then. 'I'm sure it's nothing like Paris, but thanks all the same.'

Colette smiled even wider at her. 'When you laugh you remind me of my sister. I love it. It sounds high and clear and true. Like you don't care who's listening, like you don't mind how your face screws up when you do it.'

Frances felt herself blush. She eyed the Mayor. He'd lost interest and was waving at someone over her shoulder.

Colette seemed to sense the shift. She stopped smiling, leant close to the Mayor's cheek and said, 'Let's dance.' Her dark brown eyes found Frances'. 'It was lovely to meet you.' The Mayor grinned, patted Frances on the head as if she was a child, which made her want to slap him, and allowed himself to be dragged into the middle of the party.

Frances watched them dance for a while, Colette shaking and shuddering and swinging her hips, the Mayor trying to mirror her flowing movements but only managing to look awkward and out of place, until Dicky raised a hand at her from across the room. He was perched on an open window sill, legs crossed at the knees, locked in deep conversation with a lovely-looking wide-eyed dark-skinned young man who was wearing a strange smock with embroidery on the front. Dicky mouthed something at her but she couldn't make it out, then he stood and swayed so that the man caught his arm. For a moment Frances feared they would embrace, but then Dicky moved away and began to wind through the dancers towards her.

'You look like you could do with some fresh air.' He seemed weary, heavy-lidded.

'Yes, all right.' She was angry at him for showing the Mayor her pictures but she didn't let it show.

He nodded at her, then took her hand and walked her through the dancers and into the hall. She thought they were headed outside, but then he started walking upstairs. At the top he opened a little cupboard in the wall, took out two glasses, then clinked some ice into them. He reached inside the little cubby-hole and lifted out a large bottle.

'Lemonade,' he said, 'my own private stash. If I left it down-stairs those hooligans would mix it with some God-awful bootleg rum and ruin it. Same with the ice box. Drink up, then we'll run back down and no one will be any the wiser.'

Frances did as she was told. The thought of the tart liquid brought water to her mouth before she'd even tasted it. She sipped the cool freshness, then gulped it with Dicky's encouragement.

'Are you enjoying the party?' he asked.

She nodded. 'You sure do have some interesting friends.'

'Most of them belong to Jacks.'

'Don't you like them?'

Dicky sat heavily on the top step and sighed. 'I don't know. I do and I don't. One party drifts into all the others these days. If you spend enough time with the same people, one friend starts to speak and think like the next.'

'But this one's for you. All these people putting on their fancy clothes, making all this effort. That must make it special. I'd chop my own arm off to have someone organise a party like this for me.'

'God, Frances. Apologies. Ignore me. It's probably my age. What an ungrateful lout I must sound. Birthdays are terrible, aren't they? One looks forward to seeing all one's friends, to being the centre of attention, to feeling, for once, perhaps, that one is loved. And then one spends the whole night stricken with anxiety, with the fear that everyone is judging you and having a terrible time, but also with the sensation that no one is really here for you at all, that every gift, every kind word, every slap on the back is not for your benefit but for theirs.'

'Why would they do that?' He looked so sad, she almost touched his shoulder.

'Because it makes them feel generous. And generosity, regardless of what most would have you believe, is one of the most selfish inclinations going. Around here, one does not give to receive, but to give and give again, for with each gift the giver feels righteous, superior, Godlike, even, if only for a moment. They have done something for which you should be grateful. You are in their debt. And so, any sense of one enjoying one's birthday, of relaxing, of feeling loved, is lost.'

Frances sipped the lemonade. If she'd not drunk so much she would have stayed quiet. 'I've never felt like that, at least not at home, not with the people I truly called friends,' she said. 'Where I come from folks have to work so hard to give a gift of any kind, you're grateful for anything.' She saw his forehead crease, then he smiled at her, and the warmth of it was more of a comfort than a soft blanket or a stiff drink. She didn't want him to feel too bad, so then she lied and said, 'Of course, I've never given it much thought, not really.'

'You're right, of course. What a tonic you are, Frances. I don't know if you realise it or not but you speak like someone beyond your years. For some reason I feel like you'd always tell me the truth. I'd like us to be friends. What do you think?' He drained his glass without waiting for an answer. 'I don't know what came over me. I knew you'd be the one to set me straight. Good. Yes. Socks up. Back to the fray. Be grateful. Come on, don't take too long. They'll send out a search party for me.' He stood up and held out his hand for her glass.

She drank it down and passed it to him. 'Thanks, so good. I could drink ten.'

Dicky laughed. 'Glad to be of service. I knew you'd appreciate it. Everyone else turns their noses up at soda at a party. All they want is to get plastered on car oil and pass out. This is the stuff that'll keep you dancing until dawn.' He shut everything away in the cupboard again and they walked back down the stairs.

When they got to the landing they heard shouting outside. Frances craned her head towards the open sash, the arched halo of stained glass glowing in the lamplight from outside. Dicky paused beside her.

'You're not welcome!' Jacks was shouting, leaning on the front gate, her body half collapsed over the top of it.

Frances stepped closer to the window. At the end of the garden path she could make out the outline of a large man retreating into the darkness. Thick-set, smart suit, neck as thick as a boxer's thigh.

'Go!' Jacks screamed, sobbing now, the shock of seeing her like this catching at the back of Frances' throat.

The man seemed to change his mind and began walking back towards the house. The light from the lamp overhead caught on his eyes and Frances knew it was Kane. The guy who'd bought her all those drinks at Stan's club.

'They've had a falling out.' Dicky was sitting on the landing step looking at her.

'Oh yes.' Frances felt her face heat, embarrassed she'd been caught staring.

'Used to date, ended badly, you know how it is.'

'Yes,' Frances said, 'of course.'

'Let's keep moving, give them some privacy.'

Frances nodded at him, feeling queer, unsure what to say. Kane must be one of those men, she thought, the kind that could send even a woman like Jacks crazy.

They walked back into the party. Dicky disappeared and Frances danced with a few people, the music calling at her to move, the feel of the dress shifting against her skin so strange and exciting, her eyes closed, hair shaking across her shoulders. A song she didn't like as much started up and she went to get another drink. Before she got far, a commotion by the door stopped her.

A tall man walked in, the light glinting off the top of his fair hair. Frances felt her throat constrict. Was it Stan? Surely not. Or Kane? She couldn't tell. The light was too dim and the music too loud. The drink swirled in her head – billowing, brightly coloured clouds blurring her vision.

The guy's head disappeared then popped up again. No, it was someone who looked just like them. His hair a warm shade of russet, not blond. From inside the crowd, Jacks screamed.

'Frank! It's you!'

Frances felt the music lull. People before her parted, as though a gust of wind had split a field of corn. Jacks ran down the gap and jumped into the man's arms.

'You came!' she shouted. 'You came – I knew you would!'

Another beat and the music was loud again, almost too loud to bear. Frances watched as the couple embraced. The room moved back together like a sewn seam, until Frances suspected she was the only one still watching them kiss.

'He's a judge, you know,' Jacks said.

'He can't be a judge,' Agnes reasoned, 'he's too young.'

'Not if you come from the kind of family he's from,' Dicky said.

'Okay,' Jacks said, 'maybe he's not a judge, but he definitely works for one. At the very least he's an attorney.'

Frances chewed on a salty piece of ham. The four of them were standing in the kitchen. Next door in the parlour a few people were still swaying to soft music, stopping each other from falling over with cocked elbows and sweaty palms. Everyone else had gone home. Through a gap in the door, Frances could see poor Frank, the guy in question, sitting in a cane armchair, awkwardly sipping a drink. He looked stiff, as though he didn't trust the chair enough to support the whole weight of his hefty body. She wondered if he could hear their loud whispers.

'Why do you want to go around with a lawyer?' Dicky asked. 'Aren't they awfully boring?'

'Not in the slightest,' Jacks said. 'You think too little of me. I like my brain to be expanded from time to time. I'm not just clothes and gossip and headlines.'

'Don't be ridiculous,' Dicky said. 'Those are the cornerstones of your existence.'

'Those are the things I choose to regale you with. They are not the entirety of my being.'

'Perhaps not your entirety,' Agnes said, 'but gossip is pretty fundamental.'

'Oh, you can shut up,' Jacks said. 'I saw you talking to Helena.'

'I was being polite,' Agnes said. 'If I hadn't gone over and said hello she might have made a scene again.'

Jacks rolled her eyes and billowed smoke towards the single bulb hanging above their heads. Frances watched, mesmerised, as the cloud drifted up from her smudged lips and kissed the glass. She reached for another piece of ham. The scraps were always the best part, but the smear of cold grease on the china beneath almost turned her stomach. What time was it? Not that it mattered. All she knew for sure was that whenever she got home Stan would be mad at her.

'Where did you meet this wonderful man anyway?' Dicky asked, refilling his glass.

'Oh, I can't remember – I've seen him around for aeons. He's been all over town. You'd have recognised him instantly if you looked up from Carlos's doughy eyes now and then.'

Dicky flushed. Frances felt herself redden too. She wondered if she'd got it right. Perhaps Carlos was the young guy she'd seen Dicky talking to earlier. She'd heard about those kinds of men, but not thought she'd ever meet one. She eyed Dicky over the rim of her glass. There *was* something different about him. A lightness, a sense that he was genuinely listening when she spoke, a feeling of safety when he touched her, a lack of lust when he paid her attention. He only seemed to want what his camera could take.

'We're not talking about me,' Dicky said, 'we're talking about you.'

Jacks stubbed out her cigarette on a dirty plate and lit another one. 'I suppose I only *really* met him last week. He's been terribly busy working on some case for Seabury.'

'*The* Seabury?' Dicky said.

'One and the same,' Jacks said, smiling. 'That's why I thought he was a judge. Whatever he does it's terribly important. Apparently they're about to blow open a corruption case. It'll even affect the Mayor.'

At the mention of the Mayor, Frances tensed. The sharpness of his suit, the weave of multi-coloured limbs on the dance floor at Stan's club, the freckles scattered across Colette's skin like spilt peppercorns.

'The Mayor who was here tonight?' she asked.

'There's only one Mayor of New York, darling,' Jacks said. 'Frank said something about our friend the Mayor being in a spot of trouble.'

'Do you know him well?' Frances asked.

'Everyone knows the Mayor,' Jacks said. 'Frankly, I'm surprised he hasn't gotten hot and heavy with you yet. He doesn't discriminate by class, dear. He's all over town, too. Always got the next hot young thing on his arm. Rumour has it he's started dating some Ziegfeld girl.'

'Colette?' Frances asked.

'Not Colette, darling. Colette's his trusty steed, his Jeanne d'Arc. This Ziegfeld girl's new, not here tonight. It's all right, Frances, don't look so perturbed, it's hard enough for me to keep up, you've only just arrived.'

'I've met him before,' Frances said. She had begun to hate it when Jacks talked to her as though she was a little girl, as though she knew nothing.

'What?' Agnes looked at Frances, surprised. At the mention of the Mayor she'd grown sullen and started cleaning plates, ignoring them all, but now she was lively again. 'When? She's got one up on you, Jacks.'

'Not in the slightest,' Jacks said. 'He's been here dozens of times – long before you were around, my dear, and long before he ran for office.'

'I was in a club in Harlem,' Frances said, conscious that Agnes was studying her, warmed by her attention. 'He came in with Colette and a group of girls.'

'Harlem, eh?' Jacks said. 'My my, you do get around, Frances. Here I was thinking we were the only ones showing you a good time.' She paused and filled her cheeks with smoke. 'He is fun, but he's also got his fingers in an awful lot of pies. Nasty pies, some say. Pies the likes of us wouldn't want to taste.'

'Oh,' Frances said, her stomach tightening. She tried to catch Agnes' eye again, but she was studying her drink. 'I didn't see anything like that. He was having a good time. I thought it strange he was there.'

'Without men like him slumming it in Harlem, clubs like that wouldn't exist,' Dicky said.

'And he says that from the point of view of a photographer *and* an avid newspaper reader,' Jacks said. 'The Mayor's antics distract our minds as much as sell our souls. Why, his social calendar alone has helped my magazine sell a mountain of copies.'

'Which brings us right back to your new beau,' Agnes said, coming out of her trance.

'I don't know what you're implying.' Jacks looked offended.

'I'm implying,' Agnes said, 'that the only reason you're with our lawyer friend Frank in there is because he might be at the centre of a story about the Mayor and you want to be the first one to sell it.'

'Ha!' Dicky said. 'Bravo, Agnes! Touché!'

'Who, me?' Jacks said, placing her hand over her heart. 'Well, I've never been so offended.' She winked at Frances. 'I suppose it doesn't hurt that Frank's damn good-looking into the bargain.'

'What do you think, Frances?' Dicky looked at her, his usual languid stare so piercing she felt skewered.

'About what?' she mumbled, trying to rid the ham from her mouth.

'About Jacks' new man.'

She felt them all watching, waiting for her reply to reveal something. Her jaw ached from chewing and talking. Exhaustion dragged at her, an all-consuming tiredness brought on as much by being constantly observed as by the shock of the night. She wanted to go home and sit in her dark room alone, to lie back on the little bed and pull the crochet throw over her head – even if it meant facing Stan.

'It's hard for me to say,' she said. 'You mean, do I think he's handsome?'

'Yes,' Dicky said. 'And the rest. Should Jacks here be dating someone solely for the potential of a good story? I mean, is it morally right?'

'I think,' she said, 'that Jacks should do exactly as she chooses. Most men can look after themselves – and isn't he getting something too? As long as whatever she writes doesn't lie or invent or tell something the wrong way round, I see no harm in trying to find things out. I'm sure he wouldn't tell her anything he wouldn't want the world to know. Most people, especially men, keep their worst secrets so close it would take more than a fine-looking woman to draw them out. At any rate, I doubt that a man would take too long thinking on such things. They'd just do it.'

A strange kind of silence filled the kitchen. Jacks looked at her with a cocked head and a raised eyebrow, as though Frances was a crow who'd just learnt to talk. Agnes was staring at her too, but Frances found it impossible to judge what she was thinking. Dicky must have seen the look, though, because then he said, 'Well, I am glad I asked. You've cleared it all up for us again, Frances. There you go, Jacks, no need to feel guilty at all – permission to snoop duly granted. Agnes, I've just had an idea. If Frances here agrees, I thought it might be nice for her to accompany you on one of your photographic trips. It might help her get better acquainted with this fine city of ours. I'm sure she wouldn't mind helping carry some of your equipment.'

Agnes nodded. She was sitting up on the counter looking down at her feet. 'Do you think that might be something you'd like to do?' she asked, her eyes not leaving the floor.

'Yes,' Frances said. There was no point pretending to consider.

'Right,' Dicky said, 'now that's settled let's work out how to get you home, Frances. You look ready to drop.'

It was almost pitch in the hall. Odd strips of light slithered from beneath a few of the doors. For once Frances couldn't hear the Tonioni twins. Perhaps they'd been bribed into sleep. She wondered what the promised reward had been – sherbet from the cart out front on Saturday, perhaps, or two shiny nickels for a trip to the pictures. She stepped lightly along the passage, not wanting to disrupt the quiet with a sound of her own. Jacks' dress shifted silently up and down as she walked, licking at the back of her calves. Ten more steps. She'd only lived here a matter of weeks but already felt as though she'd snuck along this walkway as frequently as she'd run between the farmhouse and the old oak at the bottom of their field back home. She knew the dent in the wall the size of a fist about halfway along. She knew the place on the floor just before their door where a tile looked like it had cracked in the summer heat. She knew the weight of their small iron knocker in her palm.

Quietly she unlocked their door and stepped inside. No one ran towards her shouting. No one huffed from the daybed. Stan was out again. His shoes were gone from the little upturned wooden box by the door. Where was he? At the club, or somewhere else doing something he shouldn't? At least now there'd be no hollering. She waited for relief, but none came.

She went through to the bedroom and slipped off the dress, taking care to hang it right, delicately tugging at the edges. The pulls in the thread weren't as bad as she'd feared. Jacks probably wouldn't notice anyway. It smelt less of orchids now, and more of nothing – of herself, she supposed, whatever that was like – so she took it over to the window and hooked it over the rail to air. She put on her nightdress and sat down on the edge of the bed and brushed her hair, thinking over the party and the Mayor and Agnes, lodging the feel of it all so she'd never forget, watching the dress billow and twist in the soft breeze, as though her body was still dancing inside.

She had wanted to avoid a row. She had wanted the quiet. But now she had those things she didn't want them at all. She brushed until her lap was covered in fair strands, until her arm ached, until she felt she'd go mad from wondering where Stan was. Outside, a sliver of moon inched over the tenement roof. Perhaps she should check on the money. Perhaps she should slip a little into the back of a drawer. Perhaps she should make sure she'd not imagined it all. She stood up.

Yelling behind the front door. She rushed across the room and hid in the tiny hall, her heart beating hard enough to quiver the cotton on her chest.

'You're in a mess.' Ben's voice, firm and low. 'Get inside. You need fixing up. We can figure out what to do tomorrow.'

'You don't understand.' Stan's voice now, almost shouting. 'You've got no clue what's going on. You're no use to me.'

'No use, huh?' Ben said. 'I'm of no use. Well, in that case I'll see you in and be on my way. You can bleed out all by yourself. I'd leave you too, if it wasn't for your sister. She doesn't deserve to deal with you like this alone.'

'I know your game!' Stan said. He was slurring; she hated it when he got this lit. He sounded like Father again. 'You're after her. I know it. I won't agree to it. Keep away from her, you—'

'Let's get inside before you say something I don't want to hear,' Ben said.

A key in the lock. What had Ben meant? Frances jumped back. What blood? She slipped across to the bed and messed up the eiderdown, making sure to throw the crochet blanket on to the floor. As they barged in she slid beneath the sheet and pretended to stir.

'Frances!' Stan shouted. 'Frances! You here?'

She got out of bed and slapped her cheeks a few times so they'd look slept on.

'I'm here, where've you been?' she said, stepping through the doorway. 'I fell asleep waiting. I was worr—'

The rest of the word hung in the air like an axe.

Stan's arm was cocked over Ben's shoulder. Without support she could see he would fall. His face was purple down one side. Purple and swollen and covered in mud. His eye oozed. She watched as the blood, bright even in the lamplight, dripped from his face and spotted the rug. There was something wrong with his arm, but she couldn't tell what. It hung at an odd angle and he winced and clutched at it as Ben dragged him across to the daybed.

'What happened?' she asked.

'A brawl,' Stan muttered. 'Nothing to worry about. Fetch a

bowl.' He wouldn't look at her.

She filled a dish at the basin and ran to get a washcloth from her room. As she passed her old mirror, she caught herself in the glass and wished she hadn't.

'Here,' she said, tilting his blanched face and dabbing at the place on his cheek where she thought the wound might be. It was hard to tell under all the filth.

Ben still hadn't said anything. He was pacing up and down, making tracks in the rug.

'I'm glad to find you here,' Ben said, watching her, 'but that's not the worst of it.'

Ben's face looked almost as bad as Stan's, except all the hurt was inside, in the way he was looking at her. He walked over and lifted up Stan's shirt. Underneath was a makeshift bandage. He started unwrapping. Stan cried out.

'Here,' Frances said, her hands shaking, 'I'll do it.'

'My fault,' Stan said, closing his eyes, 'it's all my fault.'

The dressing was damp to the touch. From his sweat, she hoped. Frances had seen enough injured animals on the farm to know that if anything got infected, he wouldn't last. She peeled away the layers of torn cotton – an old shirt, she guessed, crisp with blood – tensed against what she might find.

Underneath was a thin red slit about an inch across that gaped a little when she touched the sides. The skin around it had begun to mottle to a greenish-yellow – bruising blooming already. The knife wound – she was sure that was what it was – had almost stopped bleeding, thank God. She dabbed at it, ignoring Stan's cries, feeling strangely calm and outside herself. From certain angles, in the dim light, the wound looked like it had always been there. It already had the appearance of a permanent feature – of a pursed mouth, or a sly eye, or a half-listening ear. Part of Frances was repulsed, but part of her wanted to stick her finger inside, to whisper into it, to lean her head close and listen, as though she might learn more truth from the wound than from Stan himself.

She looked at Ben. 'Go and get Mrs Bianchi.'

'No,' Stan moaned. 'Not her business.'

'I don't care if it's her business or not,' Frances said, 'she'll know what to do.' The old woman had three sons and eight grandchildren, six of them boys. A neighbour with a knife wound wouldn't worry her. Frances could already imagine her brown hands, as large and coarse as ears of corn, moving over Stan's pallid skin, the wound healing as if by magic.

Stan moaned and twisted. The slit opened, blood escaping again, dark and fast, staining the cotton bedspread.

'Go and get her,' Frances said to Ben. Why hadn't he moved?

'I know what to do,' Ben said.

'He does,' Stan muttered, looking weaker by the second. 'The war.'

'I thought you knew how to make these, not heal them,' Frances spat.

'We need a needle and thread,' Ben said. 'Alcohol for the pain if you've got nothing else.'

Frances looked at him, horrified. 'I can't sew him up like a torn jacket.'

'You've got to. If you don't he'll keep bleeding.'

Frances stared at Ben, wishing what he'd said wasn't true, knowing in her heart it was. She got up, ran to the bedroom and pulled out her box from beneath the bed. A needle. What sort of needle did she need to sew skin? The thought almost made her retch. Her hands shook. She fought to open the old tin box where she kept her sharps. Inside, a hundred pins and a dozen needles, all different sizes, stuck in an old scrap of cotton. She'd need something fine of course, long too. Something she could grip.

'Frances,' Ben shouted. 'Hurry.'

She didn't reply.

All the needles were straight except the leather one she hardly ever used. It was the strongest needle she owned, as curved and sure as a sickle. She pulled it free and grabbed a roll of fine white cotton, then ran back through to the other room. Ben was sitting next to Stan. He'd put a cold towel on his forehead and was bent close to his ear, whispering. Frances held on to her rage. More secrets.

'I've got it.'

'Good,' Ben said, moving aside. 'I've given him some whiskey, poured some on the wound as well. It was the strongest thing I could find.'

Stan growled some kind of thanks and opened one eye. Frances could see he was trying to muster a smile but it looked more like a grimace. He held her hand. 'What would I do without you?'

She leant over and uncovered the wound again. The fresh dressing was already red and sodden. She'd have to work fast. Should she pin it first? Bile pooled in her mouth. The thought almost made her laugh. Course not. She wished Ben wasn't watching.

'Can you step back?' she asked. 'He needs room to breathe and I need space to work. You're blocking the light.'

Ben's feet didn't shift. He pulled a rusty brass lighter from his pocket. 'Take this,' he said. 'Heat the needle with it.'

It was heavy in her hand. A strange shape for a lighter. More like a bullet.

'It's a trench lighter. A friend made it for me the day before he got shot. Never fails to light.'

She tried to click it but it wouldn't work.

'Here,' he said, taking it from her, 'like this.'

She couldn't see what he did, but suddenly a flame lit up his hand. He passed it to her and she made the needle hot with it and gave it back.

He walked to the other side of the room but didn't sit down. Once he turned his back she took a deep breath and pressed the wound together like two pieces of fabric. Blood smeared on to her fingers. Stan cried out again.

'I'm sorry,' Frances said, 'I'm sorry. I'm so sorry.' She held the tears and panic at the back of her throat, choking herself.

'Here,' Ben said, coming close again, 'bite down on this.' He pushed a wooden spoon between Stan's teeth.

Frances studied her brother's face, unsure if she should keep going.

He took the spoon out, breathing heavily, his deep voice little more than a whisper. 'It's all right,' he said, grasping her shoulder, 'it's all right. You can do it. I trust you. Wouldn't let anyone else touch me.' Then he leant back, put the spoon in his mouth, closed his eyes and nodded at her to begin.

Ben stepped away and she pinched the flesh again, bracing herself this time in case Stan yelled, but he didn't. She could tell he was straining every part of his body, could see well enough he was bound up with fear and pain. She wished she didn't have to be the one to give him more of it.

She made a knot in the cotton, then squeezed the skin hard and began to sew without pausing, her fingers shaking, the skin joining more easily than she thought, softer than she'd imagined, slimy and hard to hold, pretending as she went, as Stan twisted in agony and the blood ran down her wrist, that it wasn't his body she was sewing but a purse or a chair or a saddle, a soft old saddle just like the one they'd owned on the farm.

It only took a few minutes, but by the time she tied the last knot she was sweating.

'I'm done,' she said.

Stan opened his eyes, beads peppering his own colourless brow. Ben walked over and took the spoon from his mouth. Stan wiped his lips with the back of a shaking hand.

'I knew you could do it,' he said, gulping cold coffee from a leftover cup on the side.

'You should have some water.' Frances tried to stand up, but the room swayed and she sat back down.

Ben came to her side. 'I'll get it.' He picked up the bowl and the dressing and the needle and took them over to the sink.

Frances sat with her head in her hands, forcing herself to breathe. 'Who did you fight with?' She hoped the drink and pain might loosen Stan's tongue.

'Men,' he muttered. 'Takes more than one to make such a mess of me.'

Ben came back with the water and passed it across. Stan took it with a shaking hand, gulped and handed it to Frances. She sipped slowly until she felt a little better, then redressed Stan's wound and propped him up on some cushions.

'I should go,' Ben said. He leant down and shook Stan's hand with both of his. 'You were right, she did a good job. You'll be back on your feet in no time.'

'Sorry,' Stan said, 'not your fault, or your fight. I'm too fast with my mouth sometimes.'

'Shame you're not as fast with your fists,' Ben said.

'Watch it,' Stan muttered, his voice falling away, his body slumping until all he could muster was a weak salute.

'I'll walk you out,' Frances said.

'What happened?' she muttered, once she was sure Stan wouldn't hear.

Ben leant on the door frame. He looked ready to drop. When his eyes met hers before he spoke, she knew he wouldn't say much.

'I'm sorry,' he said slowly. 'It's not my business.'

'Not your business?' she hissed, anger replacing the worry. 'If it's not your business I don't know what is. You sneak around at all hours with my brother, you plot and plan and scheme with him, whispering all the time, and now you say it's not your business?'

'I'm sorry,' he said again.

'Is that all you can say? Sorry? Sorry? How would you feel if it was your brother? If it was someone you loved in there bleeding all over the eiderdown and I knew what happened? Would you let me stay silent? Or would you force out the truth somehow? Would you stop asking?'

He wiped his cheek with the back of his hand and stared at her. 'No, I wouldn't.' He paused. 'I wouldn't stop asking until I found out. But I'm the wrong person to ask and you ain't asking the right questions. You did a good job tonight.' He patted her lightly on the shoulder. 'Most women would've flinched. They wouldn't have been able to go through with it. I'm not surprised Stan loves you like he does.'

She wished he'd put his hand on her again so she could knock it away.

'Fine,' she spat, 'leave.'

He stepped out and closed the door, the sadness behind his eyes softening the edges of her rage. Once he'd gone, she walked back to the parlour, expecting with every step to find Stan passed out, but when she got there he was crying. The sight was so strange, so unexpected, so impossible, at first she wasn't sure what to do. He was curled up with his head between his knees and his nose dripping, a vision more shocking than all the blood. She knelt beside him and cradled his head.

'Won't you tell me?' she said softly, as though she was speaking to a child. 'Won't you tell me what's wrong? What happened?'

'Can't,' he barked. 'I can't, and don't ask. Don't say anything.'

'About what?'

'About any of it – the money, the fight, me here now.' He raised his head. 'I know you know about it. I've seen the way you step across the parlour, as though you're worried it might reach up and grab your ankle. Nothing to no one, all right? Forget it all. I shouldn't have let you come. You shouldn't be here. Should have stayed safe at the farm.'

'Safe at the farm?' She almost laughed. 'I was only safe there when you were around.'

'Well, I'm the last person you're safe around now.' He dragged his good hand across his face. 'Pass me the water and get to bed. It's late even for the devil to be up, let alone you.'

She watched as he kicked off his pants. The veins on his thighs stood out like the wide blue rivers on Ben's maps, splaying and spidering all the way to his flaking knees. He was even thinner than before, the muscles wasted, his skin covered in large red welts as though he'd been beaten with a buckle. She bent down, picked up the pants and tried not to stare, hiding the shake in her hand with the folds of fabric. He closed his eyes and leant back.

'Water, Frances, please. More water, then get to bed.'

She got him the water then walked through to the bedroom with the pants all screwed up and went to toss them into the washing sack. They were heavier than usual. Something large in the pocket. She reached inside. A flick knife. Blood all over the handle. She nearly dropped it. More blood on her hands now. And something else, something at the bottom, deep down in the dark. She pulled it out. A knot of rope. Hair entwined. Long, red, curly hair. So long it must have been dragged out from the root.

MIDTOWN and the LOWER EAST SIDE

4 November 1932

22.13

The movie was almost over. Frances could tell from the way the music was swelling, the way the woman's movements were getting more and more frantic. Soon there would be a surprise or a release, a thoughtful moment, a reckoning perhaps. Then he would embrace her and they'd die together in a hail of bullets and that would be that.

Her legs twitched. She could feel the itch in them, the urge to run. She wanted to get up and race down the dark aisle and break into the little room at the back and strangle the man making the projector work until he agreed to start the whole thing over.

She'd have done the same thing with the day if she could – re-lived it somehow – from sewing in her room that morning, to where she was now, distracted, sitting in the rough velvet seat, flicking her eyes from the woman's wide-eyed face on the screen to the one glowing gloriously beside her. Perhaps, if she went over it enough, she could fix the day and revisit it whenever she chose, not in fits and starts, but exactly as it had occurred, leaving nothing out; no glance, no footstep, no cast of light, just everything as it had been, whenever she wanted – her own private picture show from now until she died. All she needed was this day, over and over. For ever. She watched the screen, but her eyes didn't see it.

Frances held the cloth lightly in her hands and looked over both sides. How could she only be up to P? She'd neglected her alphabet. She knelt on the floor by the bed, looking for her sewing box, twisting and pulling at her thin skirt as it wrapped around her thighs.

For two weeks there'd been no air. However slowly she moved, however much she sat and rested, she felt like she was struggling for breath, like her limbs were caught on the floor. Outside, the cold sky hung lower than usual, a leaden blanket threatening to smother the city.

She found her sewing box and laid out all the thread on the bed. What colour was P? She closed her eyes, trying to see it. P made her think of Dicky's business card, of the townhouse, of him. And Dicky was definitely a vivid shade of green – the colour of fresh grass – a shade from her childhood, from a time when water fed crops and quenched thirst. She hovered her hand over the tight spools, selected the closest match and sat down on the crochet to stitch. In, out, over and back. In, out, over and back. The prick of the needle in her finger instantly soothing. Slowly the letter took shape. Her fingers moved where she commanded. It pleased her to make something from nothing, to build and mould and fashion.

She worked for a few minutes, turning the frame back and forth, checking as she went, humming, trying to push her thoughts away. Stan was snoring next door. She'd already done his breakfast and he'd gone back to rest. She knew what the day would hold once he woke. She'd spend her time caring and listening and nudging and teasing and hunting for clues, walking back and forth over the creaking floorboard where the money was hidden, unable to look. He'd be more silent than ever. A fat lot of good all the asking had done. She'd learnt almost nothing except that the night he'd been stabbed, Stan had driven Ben somewhere in a car that belonged to a rich man, and she'd only gathered that from a conversation she shouldn't have heard.

On the other side of the room the washing sack bulged offensively, taunting her while she worked. She wanted to move it, to hide it or keep it safe, to get rid of it somehow, to throw it out of the window. Each night she'd allow herself a peek at the contents, but still, she could barely resist the urge to rush across the room and empty the contents on the floor, to check that what she'd seen was still there. At some point she was going to have to touch those things again. The thought of it turned her stomach. That night she'd put Stan's clothes in the bag and washed her hands and tried to forget. She'd said nothing to Stan. She knew it was pointless. He'd pulled himself in like a tight stitch, as though when she'd sewn up his belly she'd also sewn up his mouth. She'd kept the washing bag where she could keep an eye on it, like a large insect she was too afraid to rescue or destroy.

These past few days, when she drew close to Stan she could feel the pressure in the way he moved and the looks he gave, as though his whole body was being slowly, silently squeezed. She closed her eyes and saw the blood from the knife on her hands splattering the porcelain, darkening the stained cracks in the old sink. She forced the thought away and tried to concentrate on today's clean fingers, on the neat white crescents of her nails, on the swelling green thread. In, out, over and back. In, out, over and back.

A knock at the door.

She waited. Perhaps they'd go away.

They knocked again. If she didn't answer they'd wake Stan.

She set down her sewing and stepped lightly to the front door, making sure he was still sleeping as she passed. He was flat on his back on the daybed with his arms across his chest as though he'd hugged himself to sleep. She put her ear to the door and listened.

Soft breathing on the other side.

A pause. Another knock, louder than before. Feet shuffling.

Frances gathered herself and opened it.

It was Agnes. She was almost smiling, tucking her hair behind her ears. Somehow the short strands looked even blacker than before. She had on a blouse, the same scarf as before, loose slacks and neat brogues – a man's shoes, really, Frances thought, but they somehow looked girlish on her. She was clearly nervous, and this was more surprising than anything else.

'Hello.' Frances tried not to sound surprised.

'Hello,' Agnes said.

'You found me.'

'I did. It took some doing, but I managed it.'

'Did Dicky send you?'

'Yes and no. When you didn't come back he suggested it might be a good idea to see if you got home okay. I'd been having visions of you sleeping in some dingy alley, so I came. You were tricky to find. I visited almost every tenement on the street before someone recognised your name.'

'Oh,' Frances said, glancing behind her, pulling the door a little tighter. 'Sorry.'

'You don't have to be sorry.' Agnes shuffled from side to side. 'I'm not a great detective to be honest.' She paused and looked at her shoes. 'I stand out a bit too much.' She clicked her heels as though standing to attention.

They smiled at each other.

'You don't mind being found, do you?' Agnes asked.

'No, I'm sorry I didn't come back.'

'It's all right. I was a bit worried we'd scared you off. It was a crazy party even by Jacks and Dicky's standards.'

'I really enjoyed it,' Frances said. 'I would have come when I said, but my brother's not been well.' She glanced behind her again, her eyes scanning the room from Stan to the loose floorboard, then turned back and saw Agnes watching her. 'Can we talk in the hall? I don't want to wake him.'

'Sure,' Agnes said, a look of concern sweeping away her smile. 'Not too ill, is he?'

'Oh no, he'll be all right in a few days, I just don't want to disturb him.'

'Frances! Who is it?' Stan yelled.

Her heart sank. She tried to smile at Agnes who mouthed 'sorry' at her and looked away.

'A friend,' Frances called over her shoulder.

'You haven't got any friends. Who are you talking to?'

Agnes raised an eyebrow.

'Agnes.'

'Agnes who?'

'Never you mind.'

'I do mind!' He was teasing her now, Agnes knew it too – Frances could see it in the soft smirk on her lips. 'Bring her in, I'm bored. I don't want you to have friends I don't know about.'

She looked at Agnes. 'I'm sorry,' she whispered. 'Do you mind coming in for a time? He'll only go on if you don't.'

'It's fine.' Agnes shrugged and smiled a little wider. 'I've come this far . . . ' She bent down, and Frances saw that she had brought a large canvas bag and a big brown box, the same kind as Dicky had on the train.

They walked in. Stan was easing himself up on to some cushions. Frances cast her eye around the room, relieved she'd neatened it earlier, pleased to see he was yet to make another mess. Agnes didn't look like she was disgusted by the place. She kept smiling slightly, her eyes flicking from this to that and back to Stan again. As usual, there was little hope of knowing what was really going on inside her.

'So this is Agnes, pleased to meet you. I'd get up and shake your hand, but as you can see, I'm ... ' Stan held up his arm and showed her the sling.

'Oh, that's all right. It's great to meet you. How did you hurt yourself?'

Frances wasn't surprised at Agnes' directness, at her disregard for what was proper, but she could see Stan was, and a part of her enjoyed watching him try to come up with a lie.

'This? Oh, a little accident at the club where I work, nothing to worry about, at least not when you've got a sister like mine to look after you. How do you know each other?'

Now it was Frances' turn to squirm. Before she could open her mouth, Agnes said, 'We met at the market. Frances asked for directions and I helped her. I had my camera with me and she asked if I'd bring it along and show her some time. I was free today so I thought I'd come and find her. I know she's not been in the city long.'

The lie flowed so smoothly from Agnes' lips, by the time she stopped speaking, Frances had started to believe it herself. She glanced at Stan. He was rubbing at his stomach. Probably trying to scratch the wound as it healed, too busy thinking up his next lie to think someone else might be deceiving too.

'A camera, you say?'

'Yes, medium format. I've got to go and take some photographs for my employer. I wondered if Frances might like to come along and lend a hand.' She raised her eyebrows at Frances.

'Oh, I couldn't,' Frances said without a beat. 'I can't possibly leave Stan today.'

Agnes shrugged. Frances could tell she was trying to stop her shoulders from sinking.

'Ah well,' Agnes said, 'not to worry. I know where you are now. Maybe next time I'm going out I'll drop by again.'

'Fine,' Stan said, 'nice of you to come by. It's good to hear Frances is making some friends.'

Agnes nodded and stepped back towards the door. 'Good to meet you too. I hope you get better soon.'

Frances showed Agnes into the hall and closed the door behind them. She felt awkward now she'd said she couldn't go.

'So,' Agnes said. 'Apart from your brother, how've you been?'

'Not too bad. Thanks for bringing your camera.' She wanted to say she felt desperate. She wanted to say she'd thought about Agnes and Jacks and Dicky every day since the party. She wanted to say each night she lay in bed and worried over Stan, before drifting off thinking of the townhouse and the artists and the liquor in her belly and the way everyone looked at each other. But she didn't.

'No problem.' Agnes looked down at it. 'It's one of Dicky's old ones. To be honest, I was going out shooting before I thought to come and see you. I've still got a fair bit I want to capture before I give up on the place. The light's nice and flat today. I should be able to get some clear shots of a few buildings going up.' She paused and looked Frances in the eye. 'I'm sorry you can't come, but I can see you're all right now, not languishing in despair somewhere awful. And I know where you live. I'll report back. Dicky will be relieved. Jacks too, although she wouldn't admit it.'

Frances nodded. Agnes shouldered her bag and picked up the box.

'That looks real heavy,' Frances said.

'It is, but I'm strong as an ox.' Agnes held up her thin arm like a boxer showing his muscles.

Frances laughed. 'Thanks for coming,' she said. 'Any other time I'd have been glad to go along.'

'Not to worry,' Agnes said, walking down the hall, 'there's nothing so important as looking after family.'

'Say hello to Jacks and Dicky for me, won't you?' Frances said. 'And thank them again. They've been awful kind and I had such a fine time.'

'Will do,' Agnes called back as she rounded the corner. 'Stay safe.'

'I won't,' Frances yelled, one hand on the door frame, trying to think of something thrilling to say, craning her body into the hall, watching Agnes until she disappeared.

She must have yelled a little too loudly, because Mrs Tonioni came out to see what the commotion was. She was worrying at a stained dishcloth in her hands. Frances couldn't remember ever seeing her without it.

'Sorry,' Frances said, 'I was saying goodbye to a friend.'

'That's all right,' Mrs Tonioni said, 'it's fine to have friends, but try not to shout – these walls are thin as old lips.'

'Yes, sorry,' Frances said again, although she wanted to roll her eyes and remind Mrs Tonioni that it was actually her and her husband who kept everyone awake at night.

Frances walked slowly back inside, trying to guess where Agnes was going to take pictures.

'You want to go, don't you?' Stan eyed her as he repositioned his pillow, getting ready to go back to sleep.

'No.'

'I'm fine here, you can go if you want.'

'I told you, I don't want to. I don't know her very well anyway.'

'Get to know her.'

This wasn't like Stan. All these weeks of trying to keep her in, of saying she couldn't go anywhere. She narrowed her eyes at him. 'Why are you so keen to get rid of me?' Perhaps he wanted her gone so he could do something with the money. Or the sack.

'I'm not. I thought it would be good for you to get out.'

'Since when?'

'Since I realised I rely on you too much.' For once he wasn't looking at her with mirth in his eyes. 'Since I decided I don't want you fading away in here with me like some cut flower in a vase with no water. Go out and have fun with your friend, even if she does look strange. Men's shoes? I ain't never seen such a thing.'

'Oh go back to sleep, you fool.' She walked over to him and pulled the blanket up around his chest. If only he'd be this honest with her about everything else, if only he'd tell her what had happened. 'But just so you know, you're not the boss of me. I'd go if I wanted.'

'Just so *you* know, yes I am.'

She squeezed her fingers against her palm. It was a small action, barely a clenched fist. She frowned. 'Why do you have to do that?'

'What?' He looked genuinely puzzled.

'Talk like that to me?'

'Like what?'

'Like Father.'

She turned and went to the sink, wishing there was something there that needed washing. She folded a damp cloth instead, taking her time, letting what she'd said settle between them both.

When he finally spoke, it didn't sound like him. His words twisted as though he was wringing them out. 'I ain't nothing like him.'

She whipped her head round, squeezing the cloth. 'You think you ain't, but you are. All your secrets.'

His eyes widened but he didn't speak. He rolled over and pulled the blanket up.

'Is that all you've got? Ignoring me? I care for you night and day and you can't even bring yourself to talk. I suppose you're saving up all that money under the boards for a new pair of shoes. You don't want to share it? Is that it? Well, don't trouble yourself. I can make my own money.' She watched his shoulders tense but he stayed silent. 'All right. You can cook your own lunch. Dinner too.'

She threw the cloth into the sink, stomped into the bedroom and grabbed her purse. If he didn't need her, if he didn't trust her, she might as well go. But she couldn't leave him, not in this state, could she? He'd had his breakfast, though. She could ask Mrs Bianchi to look in, but not tell him that. She felt the closeness of the walls, the thickness in the air. She'd suffocate if she didn't get out, she was certain of it. Suffocate, or faint, or go mad from it all – the loose floorboard, the pants screwed up in the sack, the lies, the worry. Him. All of it.

She stepped to the window and looked out on to the front sidewalk. Agnes must be walking slowly with all the equipment. She stuck her head out. Some pedlars had set up their carts on the street below, selling kitchen things – old coffee pots, buckled metal whisks, saucepans that had seen better days.

No sign of Agnes. She craned her neck further.

There she was! Almost right under the window, a little over to the left. She was leaning against the wall having a smoke, the bag and box at her feet. 'Agnes!' Frances called. 'Agnes!' She didn't care if she upset Mrs Tonioni. She didn't even care if Stan told her not to. She had to get her attention before she lost her nerve.

Finally, Agnes looked up, shielding her eyes, trying to work out who had called. Frances waved frantically, almost falling out.

'Hello!' Agnes called back, seeing her waving, smiling.

'I'm coming!' Frances shouted. 'Don't go!'

The box was so heavy it reminded Frances of her suitcase. However she tried to carry it, either by the stiff handle or out front with both arms, some part of her body soon began to complain. She didn't care, though. Agnes saw pictures everywhere and it took her a long time to set up, so Frances had plenty of opportunity to rest in a patch of shade on a clean-enough square of sidewalk and watch her work.

Each time they stopped, Agnes would point to a place and Frances would ease the case on to the sidewalk, rubbing whatever part of her hurt the most as she straightened up. Then Agnes would pull out the wooden legs of the tripod and set its little brass feet on the ground. If they were somewhere busy – an intersection perhaps, or behind the barrier of a construction site for another skyscraper – other people might stop and stare, murmuring to each other, asking Frances what was going on. Agnes would ignore them as she walked around checking the light, then she'd hoist the box on top of the tripod and start to pull and twist, flicking catches and popping out hidden compartments, the concentration adding lines to her smooth face. Once or twice Frances was certain she saw Agnes whisper to the camera, as though encouraging it to do a good job. If a little crowd gathered they'd ooh and ahh like an audience in front of a show, except they never really got to see the part when the curtain went up. That would come later, Agnes said, down in Dicky's darkroom, where she promised Frances could watch as she conjured the pictures from nothing.

Frances already felt like she'd seen half the city being built. Agnes had taken pictures of the new Rockefeller Center going up, of its vast balustrades and huge iron girders, of ton upon ton of concrete poured into wire frames that looked like giant chicken coops. She'd pulled Frances underneath the metal legs of the El Train, hunting for the right pattern of shadows, shouting when cars refused to slow enough for her to freeze them in time. She'd shot old men in rags pulling carts of scrap and young women in fine clothes jumping on to the backs of buses, their skirts hitched up so they wouldn't catch on the wheels.

Set up on a corner by a church, Agnes had laughed so loud she scared a few pigeons into the air, and she'd beckoned Frances over and let her dip her head beneath the black cloth. Only then had Frances understood the magic of it all. She hadn't felt the wonder until she'd seen the world turned for herself, as though the sidewalk was crushing the buildings, as though they were crushing the sky. She'd not realised the power of that little wooden box until she too laughed out loud when a man walked past, striding along, hanging from the asphalt like a bat side-stepping across a branch.

Early on Agnes had explained that it was contrast that mattered. If a photograph was going to make the cut, if it was good enough to print, it had to have something of the old and the new in it, of the past and the present in the same frame. Agnes was desperate to capture old New York before it shifted into something else; or rather, she wanted to see if she could keep hold of the change itself, that precious moment when a shop or building or person would show up the city for what it was – a place of ceaseless motion, of crumbling bricks and worm-eaten wood, of stinking asphalt and walls of glass. If the photographs worked out, Frances didn't doubt they'd be as fine as Agnes hoped.

Now, though, they were opposite a regular-looking barber's. Frances still wasn't exactly sure why they had stopped. Agnes said she was taken with the stripes on the thing turning by the door – the thing that meant you could tell it was a barber's from all the way down the street. It looked normal to Frances, boring even, like the ones in Kansas, but Agnes had lit up when she saw it.

A young lad was leaning on a metal box by the door of the barber's, trying to ignore them. Behind him a red and white sign advertised the prices. Ten cents for a shave and hot towel, thirty for a 'ladies hairbob'. A lot more expensive than Kansas, but then, Frances thought, they were in New York after all. An electric massage, whatever that was, was twenty cents. It sounded painful. Next door was Blossom restaurant. Ham and eggs was eighteen. Agnes said she had enough to share a plate for lunch.

'Almost ready,' Agnes called, her back to Frances, her head beneath a cloth behind the camera.

'Don't worry,' Frances said, 'I'm in no hurry. Take your time.'

'Well, I'm hungry,' Agnes said, twisting something, her head still hidden. 'The smell of those ham and eggs is driving me crazy. Okay, here we go.'

As Agnes closed the shutter, a man walked up the barber's steps and looked at them. The owner, Frances thought. Perhaps he was going to tell them to go, perhaps he didn't want his shop in a photograph. She waited for him to say something, to shout, to wave them away, but he didn't move or speak; instead he stood perfectly still with his hands in his pockets and his white coat tucked around his back and one foot on the step above, staring right at the camera, as though simply by looking put out he might scare them enough to stop.

Agnes started counting down. She'd taken to doing this earlier in the day, when Frances had asked how long each photograph took to make. It gave the whole process a note of excitement.

'Ten, nine, eight, seven, six ... ' Agnes began. Still the man didn't move. The lad buried his head in his hands. 'Five, four, three, two, one.'

And it was done. Agnes pulled her head out and grinned back at Frances. 'That'll be a good one, if I've got the exposure right.' She didn't seem to notice the man's hard stare.

Frances walked over. 'Do you think we should say sorry?' she said. Something in her gut tightened at the thought of anyone taking her photograph without permission, as though they'd steal something. She thought back to Dicky on the train, to the Mayor seeing her picture before she had.

'Who to?' Agnes asked. She was already taking down the tripod.

'To him,' Frances said.

Agnes looked over. 'Him? He should be thanking us. You still don't understand, do you? I'm immortalising him. He thinks this is an inconvenience, that I'm doing some kind of scam, that I'm conning him somehow, that I'll make money from him, when in fact, years from now, when we're all long dead, someone will be looking at his ugly mug on a wall or in a book, just because I thought the way he was standing with that sour look on his face worked for my shot. I could have waited, I could have asked him to move. I thought about it. I didn't know he'd stand there. But there was something nice about his height next to the window. It balanced the frame, made it more pleasing to the eye. A happy accident. Serendipity. He helped me. He doesn't know it, but he did, and now I'm helping him. He'll live for ever, or at least for as long as this negative and the prints I make from it last.'

Agnes grew when she got excited. Her eyes widened, and when she stood her body seemed to get taller, stretching upwards as she spoke, like the newborn buildings she loved to photograph. Frances couldn't look away – if she did she might miss some part of the transformation.

'You're looking at me funny,' Agnes said. 'You think I'm crazy.'

'Sorry.' Frances looked at the ground. 'It's not that.'

'Arrogant then. Arrogant like some fresh guy who's too big for his boots.'

'No, not at all.'

'Well, I'm not sorry,' Agnes said, collapsing the camera back into its box like a magician at the end of a trick, 'even if you do think that.'

'I don't, honestly,' Frances said, surprised at how quick Agnes was to anger, watching the stern man cuff the boy by the door round his ear and march him back inside the barber's. 'You're surprising, that's all.'

'Well, coming from someone as curious as you, I'll take that as a compliment,' Agnes said. 'I'd rather die than be normal. Typical, average, usual – that's not for me. Unexpected is a good thing.'

'Yes,' Frances said, smiling. This was the first time she'd ever heard another woman explain exactly how she felt, without a shred of shame. 'I suppose it is.'

'Now,' Agnes said, shouldering her bag, 'stop staring at me and be a good girl and grab that tripod. Let's get some of those ham and eggs before they run out.'

Frances got up from the buttoned leather chaise and walked closer to the painting. The backs of her thighs made an embarrassing sound as she stood, but she didn't notice, and if she had, she wouldn't have cared. The room was almost empty now. Only herself, Agnes and an old attendant remained. Her legs were sore from all the sitting. She rubbed them absentmindedly as she gazed, edging closer until her nose almost touched the paint. How had this man, this Bonnard, done it? She checked the plate on the wall pretending to read, as though that might reveal his secret. She didn't need to understand what it said. She'd already memorised what Agnes had told her – his age and where he lived and what the painting was called – but none of that revealed anything important. It didn't tell her *how*. It didn't explain the feeling.

From far away on the chaise, the delicate multi-coloured dashes merged, mottling the woman's naked flesh into a sea of almost-believable colour. Up close, the paint swirled. Her body seemed to shake. She was all the shades of a field of wheat. Sunflower yellow, cornflower blue. She was every shift of dusk from sharp orange to deep blue-grey. It looked like she was putting some kind of ointment on her skin, standing next to a bath, in a pink-tiled room, concentrating on an almost scandalous part of herself without a care, as though the painter had happened upon her, and instead of being startled or embarrassed the woman had simply carried on, distracted by her own flesh.

Until this room, this painting, Frances had thought the gallery was nice enough. Agnes had stopped outside the building to take an image of a man on a stoop talking to his friend. At first when she yelled Frances had thought something was wrong and she'd rushed across the road from where she was leaning beneath the awning of a cake shop, narrowly avoiding a speeding car. Agnes was waving her arms around on the other side of the road, pointing to the large building behind her.

'It's the last few days of the exhibition,' she said, 'I almost forgot it was on. I try and go every year.'

'Exhibition of what?' Frances had asked.

'Of painting, silly. Well, painting and sculpture, and all the up-to-date art from all over the world. It's the Museum of Modern Art. Do you want to see?'

Frances hadn't been that interested in going inside. She was so taken with watching Agnes work, she'd have much rather carried on doing that, but Agnes' face had lit up. She'd gotten that exciting air about her again, like when she was about to take a picture. It was impossible to say no.

Agnes had paid for her – a present for helping out, she said – and they'd started wandering through the high white rooms. At first all Frances had really enjoyed was the relief from the cold. The paintings and objects had been interesting but not striking. There was a strange one of a woman with sky blue eyes and no pupils Frances had been struck by – a Modigliani, Agnes said, a wonderful painter, very famous – but it didn't fill Frances with joy, it made her feel anxious and afraid. The woman's face was manly and long. She looked stern, like an old school mistress, like an uptight Mrs Grundy casting judgement. It drew Frances in, but it didn't hold her, it pushed her away.

Then there was a large sculpture of a woman's body she liked, made in bronze, Agnes said, the dizzying cost making Frances draw back, as though she might damage it and be held accountable just by looking. That people spent this much time and money on something made only to be looked at shocked her. It was fine, beautiful even, the skin hammered flat, the curved stomach crying out to be cupped, but it was headless, and Frances realised it was hard to feel anything for a body without a face. There was something wrong with the way the artist had sliced it clean off – or, according to Agnes, not bothered to make it in the first place, as though that part of the woman didn't matter.

Nothing had really taken her until they'd walked into this final room. Frances had spotted the painting from outside. Everything else seemed to be pointing towards it. Agnes had nodded and smiled. They'd walked closer.

'It's my favourite too,' Agnes said after a while. 'Bonnard really understands the way women feel, the way they look, the way they want to be looked at. Let's sit and take it in for a while.'

'Are we allowed?' Frances said, eyeing the attendant by the door.

'Of course we're allowed, that's what I've paid for,' Agnes said. 'The guards are here to protect the paintings from hands, not eyes.'

So they'd walked over to the leather chaise and sat down; and now Frances knew they'd been in the room for ages, that Agnes was probably bored, desperate to leave and take more photographs or go and get some dinner, and she cared about that, she didn't want to upset her or seem ungrateful, but still she couldn't bring herself to move. Once they stepped out she might never see this painting again.

It made her feel as though the woman's insides, her thoughts and emotions, were on the outside, as though her body wasn't only a body but a map of who she was, a puzzle to be unravelled simply by looking. It felt like when she got lost in her sewing, when she wove and stitched and built and made something from nothing, but she couldn't work out how it did this when she hadn't been the one who painted it. Most of all, it made her feel free and it made her forget. For the first time since she came to the city, since all the trouble with Stan, in front of this painting she could breathe again, she could think, she could be herself. With her nose so close she could smell the paint, Frances finally knew why all this art cost so much, why people cared, and she also knew that once she left, all those feelings would disappear. With every step she took away from it, the painting would lose its hold on her, and in turn, she'd lose herself again.

'You've never liked anything this much before, have you?' Agnes whispered, standing by her shoulder.

'No,' Frances said, 'but I've not seen much. Only the paintings at Dicky's place, and they all seemed to be of shapes, not people.'

'They make Dicky feel the way you do now, though,' Agnes said. 'He says they sing to him. That's the thing about art. There's something for everyone, it's just most people don't know that. Most people are afraid. They think you have to be able to explain it, to know the names of the painters, to recite the kinds of paint they use, but none of that matters. All that matters is how it makes you feel.'

Frances nodded, her eyes drawn back to the swirling colours, to the fields and skies and rivers that made up the woman's body.

From where Frances perched on the edge of the window sill next to the one Agnes was shooting from, she could see almost all of Herald Square beneath them. Rich women wearing bright hats milled in and out of Saks at 34th Street. On the opposite side crowds pushed down into the subway on their way home after a busy day at work, shuffling past giant advertisements encouraging them to spend their hard-earned dollars on nuts and stockings and bank loans, on ten-cent shaves and trips to the seafront, wherever that was. Of course, Frances could only guess they were selling these things from the pictures. They might, she thought, have actually been selling nut crackers and shoes and ledgers, beard wax and bathing suits. When you couldn't read it was impossible to be sure.

Down on the street, shiny cars hurtled along beside yellow-bellied taxis. Packed trams shuttled up and down, their drivers leaning out now and then to shout at the rushing businessmen who were too important, too stupid or too hungry perhaps to get off the rails when the clanging bell rang out. Further up, against the horizon, giant metal signage boards – for Coca-Cola, a new movie and a grand hotel, Agnes said. It was this that she was photographing now, leaning so far out of the window with her large camera it made Frances fearful.

Agnes had seen all this from down on the street. The last photograph. The whole evening, dusk seemed to have fallen faster over the city than usual, the speed of the failing light colluding in the sense that their time together was ebbing away. Agnes had grabbed Frances by the sleeve, looked up at the apartments above the street and said, 'I have to shoot from there before the light goes. Can you see the way the sun's sitting between those

two buildings? The way the shadows have lengthened? Can you
see the sign, the criss-cross of the metal? I need to get up there.'

Frances had noticed the shadows but not much else. A dark
mood had settled over her as she walked further away from the
gallery, a nagging guilt over how Stan was, over what he might
say when she got home – a dull fear that however wonderful
this day with Agnes had been, it wouldn't be worth what was
waiting for her.

Agnes didn't notice the shift in Frances' feelings, or if she had,
she didn't say anything. When she suggested stopping, Frances
nodded, eager to take advantage of the chance to stay out for
as long as possible. Agnes had raced away to ask a shop owner
who lived in the apartment. He pointed to an old woman sitting
outside a café next door who looked like she was talking to her
tiny dog. Agnes made a beeline for her, leaving Frances standing
on the sidewalk with the equipment. She couldn't imagine how
Agnes was explaining it, how she might ask if she could take a
photograph from inside someone's home. It was daring, risky,
manly even. If Frances had been the woman, she would have
thought Agnes was mad, or at the very least trying to steal from
her. As it turned out, it was the woman who was crazy.

Frances sneezed. Agnes muttered her blessings from behind
the camera. Frances wished she could work out what was
making her nose itch. The room was crammed so full of animals
and junk it could be anything. A fat Siamese cat purred behind
her at the base of the window, one of five she'd avoided touching
so far. Frances didn't like petting cats the way other people did.
Not because she didn't like them, but because she suspected
they were cleverer than everyone thought. The idea of stroking
something so fancy and mysterious seemed absurd. Dogs, on
the other hand, Frances loved. Dogs were simple things. Dogs
were hungry or thirsty or tired. They were angry or afraid or
content. They had basic needs, obvious desires. Before all this

business with Ben and Stan, before she met Dicky and Jacks and Agnes, Frances had liked to imagine all dogs were men and all cats were women. Now she wasn't so sure.

The old woman wandered back into the room with a tray and made a noise Frances decided meant 'help yourself'. She set it down on a rare patch of empty table. At first the woman had milled around muttering at them, moving vases and old boxes and ashtrays from one teetering pile to another while Agnes set up, trying to tidy but only making more mess. Frances had felt like they were taking advantage of her. She was obviously simple, her mind addled from age or liquor, struggling to recover from some long-past horror. A lost love in the war, perhaps.

But Agnes shared none of Frances' concerns. All she could see was the photograph. From her point of view they weren't hurting anyone – like she said before, they were doing the woman a service: without Agnes and her camera, no one would ever remember the view from her window.

For Frances, it didn't feel so simple. It was why she preferred it when the photographs they took involved things, not people, when she and Agnes didn't have to deal with anyone but each other. The worst thing was that somehow the old woman reminded Frances of her mother. She could see her in the curl of the woman's lip and the shuffle of her feet, in her wide-eyed stare and the way she gripped Frances' elbow, offering dry crackers and past-its-best milk without a word. The similarity taunted her. The guilt of running away, of leaving Mother alone, darkened her mood further. She stared out at the dusk, unmoved by the rushing beauty of it all. She shouldn't be here looking out at New York with Agnes, she should be home in the dirt protecting Mother, or back in the tenement seeing to Stan. She hugged her knees and watched the city smoulder.

'Almost got it,' Agnes called over her shoulder. 'Then we'll go eat.'

Frances nodded needlessly. Agnes wasn't looking at her.

On the edge of Frances' vision next to the looping Coca-Cola sign, a giant globe lit up. She'd never seen anything like it. It turned slowly, illuminating the sky, reminding her of Ben's map. Beneath it four words flicked on one at a time.

'Can you see what that sign underneath the world says from where you are?' Frances asked.

'Yes,' Agnes replied. 'Can't you?'

'The angle's not great from here,' Frances lied.

'It's an advert for a new film. *Scarface*, I think.'

'It doesn't look like an advert.' Frances couldn't see any words beginning with S.

'No,' Agnes said, fiddling with the camera, not really paying attention, 'Jacks was telling me about it. They've done this new thing where they've taken a moment from the movie and used that instead of a photograph.'

'What do you mean?'

'I think the world is important to the storyline. The writing underneath means something in the picture.' Agnes looked up and read aloud: '"The world is yours . . ." It makes people ask questions, encourages them to go and see it. I thought it was a clever idea.'

'How are people supposed to know it's got anything to do with that movie, though?'

'Word of mouth, I guess,' Agnes said, 'people like you asking people like me. People like me asking Jacks, and so on.'

'What is *Scarface*?' Frances asked, watching the world turning brightly against the gloom, stretching her legs over the sill and dangling them cautiously into the air.

'It's another gangster flick, I think.'

Frances heard Agnes stop what she was doing. Her pause stretched between them.

'Would you like to see it?' Agnes asked, finally. 'We could go now if you like.'

*

The picture ended.

Frances was still dizzy from the movie, her head full of the sound of gunshots, of Cesca's dark lips, of the frenzied, bloody ending, of the shiver along her back when Agnes brushed her hand as they got up to leave. For all that she wanted to stay, she also wanted to go out into the world again, to see if she still felt this good outside on the brightly lit street, hoping she could re-live the day over and over. She wondered whether Agnes would walk her home, and it was this wondering that meant she didn't see the woman fall.

They walked into the middle of a fight.

A man was yelling. Sometimes, Frances thought, it seemed like they never stopped.

'Get up, bitch. Get up! Play-acting again, are you? Entertaining the crowds?'

On the ground in front of them, directly outside the entrance to the theatre, a woman was sobbing, her skirt hitched up, the contents of her purse strewn across the sidewalk. Frances ran forward and stood between the couple, her mind emptying so swiftly she might have tipped her head to the side and poured out the thoughts.

'Who the hell are you?' the man snarled.

'No one,' Frances said.

'Get out of my way.'

'No.'

The man paced back and forth, jerking his arms as though he was trying to shake the clench from his fists. Frances could see the rage behind his eyes. Still she didn't move. Agnes was at her elbow.

'Back off,' Agnes said to him, her voice low and firm and fearless.

A little crowd began to gather, hemming them in. No one

stepped in to help. The man kept pacing. Frances eyed him, watching his body, tensed in case he ran at her.

'She's nothing, you know,' he said, 'not worth bothering with.' He spat on the ground in front of them and wiped his lips with the back of his sleeve.

Behind them the woman sobbed louder.

From somewhere in the crowd, someone shouted, 'That's enough, buddy.' It started a cascade of calls, a hail of 'stop's and 'time to go's and 'leave her alone's. The man seemed to cool a little. His shoulders slumped. He took his hat off and wiped his brow, then swayed to the edge of the sidewalk and tried to hail a cab. Frances didn't take her eyes off him. She felt hollowed out, as though she was floating, almost invincible, like when she got lit. A taxi arrived and the man stepped inside. As it pulled away he wound down the window.

'You bitches are all the same,' he spat. 'God-damn hookers, the lot of you. Burn in hell.'

And he was gone.

On the sidewalk, the woman was sliding around, trying to collect her scattered belongings. Frances knelt to help, struggling to gather up the lipstick and coins and handkerchiefs. She turned to smile her relief at Agnes, but she couldn't see her. She stood on tiptoes and twisted towards the crowd in front of the theatre, searching for her dark head, then stepped up and down the street, walking backwards and forwards, wringing her hands. Where had Agnes gone? The canvas bag was still there on the sidewalk next to the camera and tripod. Where was she?

For the next few minutes, Frances distracted herself putting the woman in a cab. The crowd left quickly and she was soon alone on the sidewalk, standing beside Agnes' equipment, wondering what to do. It was late now. Folks hurried past in blurred bursts – quickened feet speeding towards home. Eventually, for a brief moment, the sidewalk seemed to still and the traffic lulled.

In this rare instant of quiet, Frances heard crying from the alley next to the theatre. She shouldered the bag and the box and went to look, dragging the tripod behind her.

Agnes was leaning against the wall in the dark. As Frances approached she lifted her head. Her face was streaked black from wet liner.

'Whatever's the matter?' Frances asked.

Agnes shook her head and hid in her hands. Frances put down the bag, box and tripod and put her arms around her.

'It was a shock, I know,' Frances said. 'I never get used to men like that, and I've met enough of them.'

'It's not that,' Agnes muttered from Frances' shoulder.

'What is it, then?' Frances said, afraid. 'Are you hurt?'

'No.'

'Well, what then? You can tell me.'

'I can't tell anyone.' Agnes pulled away and fished in her trouser pocket for a creased handkerchief to blow her nose.

'Well, that's silly. Whatever it is, you can tell me. I won't gossip. Who would I tell? I don't know anyone, least of all anyone who'd be interested.'

'It's not that,' Agnes said. 'I trust you, I do, but I can't risk it.' She scrubbed at her eyes, trying to wipe the smears away.

Frances stilled her friend's hand and cupped her face, then touched the hanky to her tongue and delicately dabbed at the smudges on her cheeks. They stared at each other, until the rise and fall of their chests fell in time. After a moment, Agnes gathered herself and stepped back.

'I can't tell you,' Agnes said, 'but I could show you. Can I see you again later this week? Can I come and collect you?'

'Yes, all right,' Frances said, balling the cotton tightly in her fist. 'Will we be taking more photographs?'

'No,' Agnes said. 'We'll be looking at some.'

UPPER EAST SIDE

7 November 1932

22.21

They watched the nurse tend to Agnes' mother through a crack in the doorway.

'How long has she been like this?' Frances whispered.

'Not long,' Agnes said. 'A few months, although she's always been a nervous wreck.'

The nurse, a middle-aged woman, her dark arms so plump Frances imagined they might pop if pricked, dipped the flannel in warm water, squeezed off the excess, and smoothed it across the woman's forehead. She didn't move. Her wrinkled face stared forward with unseeing eyes, her head and body motionless except for thin lips that were silently muttering.

'I'm sorry,' Frances said, mesmerised by the air of emptiness.

'It's all right,' Agnes said, 'not your fault.' She took down two tumblers and filled them with fresh ginger ale from a wide refrigerator in the kitchen. Frances gaped at the size of it but didn't say anything. It was the largest one she'd ever seen. Agnes handed her a glass. 'She gets night-sweats so Esther brings her in here to cool her down then takes her back to bed again.'

'What does the doctor say?' Frances asked, sipping slowly, enjoying the fizz on her tongue.

'Not much. It could have been a mild heart attack or a stroke, some other mental problem maybe. He said a big shock can do that to a person. All I know is she's not my mother any more and none of the drugs they've tried has made a damn bit of difference.'

The nurse was lifting Agnes' mother now, her body so frail, she might have been cradling a small child. Her arms and legs were skin and bone, her high-necked lavender nightie clinging crudely to buttocks that were barely there. The nurse carried her through a wallpapered door beside a grand stone fireplace. The birds and trees and tall grasses on the dark green paper split apart and came together again as the door closed softly behind them. Like something from a fairytale, Frances thought, as though instead of walking into another room, the two women had disappeared into an enchanted forest.

'I don't know what I would have done without Esther,' Agnes said. 'She's here night and day, caring for her as though she were her own mother. She was in hospital at first but it was awful. Neither of us could bear it there. All the noise of other people's pain. So I brought her home. I tried for two days, thought we could manage on our own. I didn't want anyone else in the house. I knew Mother would hate it – not that she's noticed.'

'How did it happen?'

'Follow me,' Agnes said, 'that's what I want to show you.'

They put their glasses on the marble and left the kitchen, passing through the living room with its giant grandfather clock, the heavy tick following them down a dark hallway. Along the walls were photographs of Agnes and people Frances assumed were her family. Uncles and cousins and parents, sitting stiffly in high-backed chairs, running on beaches, climbing mountains. Here and there she recognised Agnes' mother, although in the pictures she was a different woman entirely – a smiling, laughing, beautiful woman with neat hair and fancy clothes who bore only a mild resemblance to the shell of a thing Frances had just seen.

In one photograph Agnes posed alone as a child with a fishing net at the seaside. In another she was opening a present at Christmas, a huge twinkling tree setting her face a-glow. In all the others, next to her in every picture, was a blonde girl, the exact opposite of Agnes in every way – as tall as Agnes was short, as fair as Agnes was dark, as joyful as Agnes was serious. Before Frances had a chance to ask who she was, Agnes stopped and opened a door.

Soft streetlight filtered into the room beyond through gauzy curtains. A faint rush of sound drifted through the closed window. They stepped inside and Agnes switched on a lamp. It was a young woman's bedroom – Frances could tell from the hint of patchouli clinging to the air, from the soft pink of the satin bedspread, from the cuffs of lace and damask and velvet eddying from the half-open wardrobe. Two single beds on either side of the room. On a dressing table beneath the window a scrolled mirror reflected their serious faces along with glass bottles, fine brushes and sparkling jewellery. In the middle was another photograph in a silver frame. Agnes walked across the room, picked it up and sat on the bed. She motioned for Frances to join her.

The picture was of the girl and Agnes as young women. Agnes looked stiff in it, her body tight and rigid in her mannish clothes, but the girl looked carefree. She was wearing a long dress and had her arms wrapped tightly around Agnes' waist, grinning at the camera. Agnes smoothed the edge of the frame.

'My little sister,' she said, tears welling. 'This was our room before I moved out.'

Frances was afraid to ask, suspecting the answer already, but she had to. The question burnt inside.

'Where is she?' she murmured.

'Dead,' Agnes said, the tears falling now, patterning her slacks with tiny black spots.

'How?' Frances asked.

'Murdered.'

Frances gasped and put her hand to her mouth.

'Well, not exactly murdered,' Agnes said, 'but as good as.'

'What do you mean?'

'Stella wanted to be an actress. She would have made a great one. Mother always said she was a little ball of energy, that if we ever had a power cut we could hook Stella up and the lights would come back on.'

'She looks lovely,' Frances said.

'She was,' Agnes said, sighing, 'that was part of the problem. Everyone loved her. I tried not to. It wasn't easy having a younger sister who looked like that, but even I couldn't help falling for her no matter how much we used to fight. It was always me who started the rows and Stella who finished them. She used to make me these tiny "I'm sorry" cards with flowers round the edge. I've kept some – I'll show you later if you like.'

Frances nodded, holding her breath.

'Like I said, everyone loved her, but Stella knew it. She could be bossy and arrogant. Stubborn too. When she was fifteen, around when this picture was taken, she started courting. Young men would come and call. Sometimes Mother was annoyed, but mostly she was flattered, especially if the men were charming or rich. I think she liked it. She always saw herself in Stella, you see. I was too much like Father. Sometimes I'd catch her looking at me sideways and I'd know she was thinking about him. He ran off with one of Mother's friends. A painter. They went to Mexico, and two weeks later he crashed a car up in the mountains somewhere and that was that. Dead and gone, and Mother never said his name again.'

'I'm sorry,' Frances said.

'It's all right,' Agnes said, 'I hardly saw him when he was here. Always in his office or at the bank, out for drinks with friends. Not much time for noisy children. More of a passing acquaintance than a father. I never really mourned him. All the tears I cried when he died were for show. With Stella it's different. I feel like I'll never be myself again, like I can't cry enough. Taking pictures and hanging around with Jacks and Dicky and all those guys in the Village is all I can do to distract myself. Whenever I'm alone the sadness swallows me up.'

Frances held Agnes' arm while she cried, then leant across to a side table and pulled a tissue from a china holder.

'Thanks,' Agnes said. 'I knew I'd cry if I told you, but not this much, and I haven't even got to the worst part yet.' She took a deep breath. 'Like I said, Stella started going out and she never stopped. Parties, dinners, dancing, a different man wherever she went. I was jealous of her – jealous and proud. But at home she was wonderful. One day about a year ago she came into the room and said some guy had promised her a part in a picture. I can see her standing there now, so excited she couldn't keep still. I said I was worried she'd ruin my rug if she didn't stop moving. She said not to tell Mother, that she wanted it to be a surprise, that nothing was guaranteed. From that day on everything changed. She started losing weight. She looked gaunt and sour. Her skin turned grey and her hair thinned. I kept asking and asking what was wrong but she wouldn't tell me. Then one day I came back from the studio and she was in here crying. She'd laid out all her jewellery on the bed and was stuffing it into a bag.'

'What for?' Frances asked, thinking of Stan.

'To pay off these guys who were blackmailing her. It was a

scam, you see. It took a while, but she finally told me. Some policemen were after her and she didn't know what to do. They'd threatened her. Said that if she didn't pay what they asked, they'd arrest her and tell everyone she was a whore. She wasn't, of course, but that wouldn't matter – once the lie was out no one would have any time for the truth. Years ago she'd had some fairly racy photographs taken to help her career, and they had them. They were nothing, really, at least not compared to the sort of stuff on Dicky's walls. All she was guilty of was being a beautiful rich girl with everything to lose.'

'Policemen?' Frances asked, trying to hide her shock.

'That's why I got mad outside the theatre the other night,' Agnes carried on. 'Whenever a man talks like that about a girl I can't cope. Hookers, whores, prostitutes. I don't feel so bad when women go on about it, but men ... They're always shouting it at us, right? As if selling sex is the worst thing someone could do. As if they're not the ones buying. It didn't matter that Stella never took a dime for a kiss in her life. As far as I know she was still waiting for a prince to sweep her off her feet. Old-fashioned. All the flirt, all the promise, none of the action. Anyway, Stella was frantic. She made me swear not to tell Mother. She was worried the shock would kill her – and she was probably right. So I kept quiet, and for a while things seemed okay. She put a bit of weight back on, did some acting lessons, but every now and then I'd notice something was missing – a gold candlestick one minute, Father's old pocket-watch the next. And Mother had started to notice too. She even blamed me for taking a pair of her earrings.'

Agnes paused.

'And then what?'

'And then I went to meet Stella in a diner for lunch one day and she didn't turn up. I looked all over, even went to the Mayor's office and asked after her because someone told me – Jacks, I think – that she'd been stepping out with him. I couldn't get to speak to him, of course. No one had seen her. Two days later they told us. She'd been hit by a train outside Penn Station. Walked right on to the tracks, so a witness said. There was nothing the driver could do.'

Frances stared down at the photo. She couldn't speak. The girl on the train line – the one she'd imagined dressed in a nightie, long hair drifting across the tracks. Had it been Agnes' sister's blood on the wheels? Or another desperate girl? Her thoughts began to congeal, any words of comfort sticking at the back of her throat. Lost in her own grief, Agnes didn't notice.

'When did she die?'

'February. The sixteenth.'

Frances sighed, relieved. The coincidence would have been almost too much to bear. But then she felt even sadder. That meant more dead girls. More blood on the tracks.

'The thing is,' Agnes said, 'now they're after me.'

'What?' Frances said, tearing her eyes away from the photograph.

'The policemen. At least I think it's them. I got a letter last week. Anonymous, threatening.'

'Can I see it?' Frances asked.

Agnes nodded. She left the room for a moment and came back with a creamy envelope. The writing on the front was small and neat, but some of the letters slanted, as though written in a rush. Inside, the letter was short and to the point. Agnes read it aloud, the paper shaking in her hand.

'Your sister may be gone, but we know the money is not. If you don't give us what we are owed we will ruin her even in death. You must deliver one thousand dollars to us. If you don't we will hand your sister's name to the papers. She will be disgraced and so will your family. We are watching.'

As she finished reading, Agnes screwed up the paper in her

hand. She brushed the tears from her face.

'I'm sorry,' she said. 'I had to tell someone, it was eating me up.'

Frances put her hand over Agnes', stopping her from ruining the letter. 'That's all right,' she said. 'No one knows me here, and even if they did, I've got nothing to give them, no family to upset.'

Agnes smiled thinly. 'I know, but still . . . '

'What are you going to do?' Frances asked.

'I don't know,' Agnes replied. 'Find the money I guess. Mother's so ill now, I don't think she'd notice a few more pieces of jewellery going missing, although we've not got anything here worth that much. I even asked an old friend of Father's to value a few things. Lots of what I thought was worth something is costume jewellery. Looks like Stella sold all the good stuff already. So now I'm in a fix. I've already borrowed loads from Dicky. Where am I going to get more?'

Frances stood up and started pacing the room.

'You're sure there's nothing here worth that much?'

'I'm sure,' Agnes said. 'And anyway, I don't want to pay them. Why should I?' She strode to the window. Frances could see her shoulders tightening. 'Why should I give them anything when they've taken everything from me? Stella gone, for what? God knows how many other families they're doing this to all over the city, how many more innocent girls are lying in their beds waiting for a lie to ruin their lives, wondering if death might be better than shame. I wish I could teach the men doing this a lesson. If Mother and Stella hadn't cared so much about keeping up appearances they wouldn't have had any power over them. Mother would be herself, Stella would be alive. Whoever's done this, whoever sent the message as good as killed them both. I'd give anything to get hold of them, to catch them so they can't hurt anyone else, to make them understand what they've done.'

Frances nodded. She was treading up and down, her old

shoes making patterns in the thick pile, lost in her own thoughts.

Then the two women stood in silence for a moment in the dimly lit room. The grandfather clock in the living room down the hall kept ticking. After a time, Frances said, 'If you're to find them, you need to trick them.'

'What do you mean?' Agnes asked.

'I mean, you'd have to tell them you had the money, then wait until they came to collect it and catch them out.'

'But that's the problem,' Agnes said. 'I don't know where to get the money from.'

LOWER EAST SIDE

'Where've. You. Been?' Stan paused between each of the words, hitting his hand on the back of the chair. Bang. Bang. Bang. Frances could see the anger flickering in his neck. In fact, she thought, now he'd lost so much weight, his whole body looked like it was pulsing, as though there was a wild animal clawing at his insides, eating him from within. Thanks to the neatness of her sewing, the wounds on his skin had healed to a murky russet, but he was more broken than ever.

'I told you,' Frances said, 'out with a friend.'

'That girl again? The one who looks like a man?'

'I don't think she looks like a man.'

'She does. She's strange. I don't like her.'

'You don't have to like her; she's my friend, not yours.'

'I can see that,' Stan said, his eyes narrowing.

They were standing in the kitchen. A single bulb illuminated the little table beside the window. There were papers all over it. Stan had tried to stuff some of them into his pockets as she walked in. It was a funny thing to do when he knew she couldn't read them.

She could smell the ends of his dinner. Something fried, something oily. The pans were piled in the sink ready for her to wash. Empty bottles clinked beneath the chair as he swayed. She wondered what he'd done with what was in the washing sack, if it was burnt or buried. Either way it was empty now.

'I don't want you to see her again,' he said.

'That's not for you to decide.'

Frances could feel her anger rising. They were teetering on the edge of a full-blown fight, had been dancing around it for days, and now she had no idea how to hold back. Part of her was desperate to scream at him, to rip at his body and release whatever was poisoning his insides. Perhaps then he'd tell her what was going on. Perhaps the truth would leap from him and lodge its fangs in her throat.

'It is while you're living here with me,' he said. 'You're under my watch.'

'Well, you've not been watching me very closely, have you,' she said. 'You've barely paid me any attention since I got here, except for when you want me to cook your dinner or stitch you up.'

'I had to ask you to do it,' he said, 'there was no other way.'

'And I did it gladly, but now you're going again and God knows how many holes I'll have to fix when you come back this time.'

'That's enough,' he said, gripping the back of the chair.

'Perhaps I should follow you. Perhaps I should come along for myself and see what it is you're doing when you say you're at work.'

'I said, that's *enough.*' His knuckles blanched against the wood, the veins in the back of his hands bulging, the tips of his fingers turning a bluish shade of purple.

'I might end up like you did, stabbed and bleeding, and you'd have to fix me and watch me ebb away to nothing, till I'm skin and bone, and I wouldn't tell you what was happening. Then you'd know how it feels. Then you'd know what it's like to watch someone you love turn to dust before your eyes—'

'Shut your mouth!' Stan picked up the chair and hurled it across the room. It smashed into the wall, shattering two of the chipped cups that hung on hooks beneath the shelf, and clattering the salt pot to the floor, its contents spilling across the wood like fine white sand.

Someone hammered at the door.

Frances wondered who they'd woken up. Stan slumped at the table, his head in his hands. She fixed her face into an apologetic smile and opened the door.

It was Ben, his forehead creased with concern.

'All okay?'

He tried to peer around her. She could hear Stan at the table gathering his papers, forcing them into an envelope. Before she had time to say anything, he was beside her, pulling on his shoes.

'Nothing to worry about,' Stan said, wrenching up his shirt sleeves. 'I pushed over the chair in a rush to leave.'

'Where are you going?' Frances asked. She could tell from the look on Ben's face, from the way he glanced at the salt and shards of china, he knew what was going on.

'I forgot I've gotta go meet someone.' Stan shouldered his way past her into the gloomy hall.

'I could come?' Ben offered, looking from Stan to Frances and back again. 'I've been cooped up all day. I could do with some air.'

Stan paused for a moment, still fiddling with his sleeves and checking his pockets, folding the envelope and shoving it into the back of his waistband. He looked up at Ben, a flicker of relief crossing his face, reminding Frances of the old Stan, the one that was warm and grateful.

'All right,' he said, 'come.'

Ben nodded, and smiled at Frances. She imagined he thought it comforting.

Stan took two steps then turned. He met Frances' eyes as he walked towards her and for a moment she saw the anger slip away. Ignoring Ben, he smoothed his hand over her hair. Then, taking her by surprise, he pulled her close, hugging her to him so forcefully she couldn't catch her breath. She sighed against him, his shirt pressing against her face, his smell – Luckies, sweat and polish – filling her up before he let go and stomped away.

'What about your coat?' she called after him, but he didn't look back.

'Don't be too hard on him,' Ben said, 'he's not himself.'

'I can see that,' Frances said. 'He's my brother, you know. I can tell when he's unwell. I can see what's going on.'

'Can you?' Ben asked. 'Can you really? I hope not.'

'What do you mean?' Frances asked, fear rising in her belly, threatening to stifle the anger. 'If you tell me what's happening I might be able to help. At the very least I might understand.'

Ben raised his eyes to her, a look of defeat on his face, a weariness weighed down with sorrow. 'I can't,' he said. 'Telling would put you in danger. There's nothing to be done. I'll follow him, it's all I can do.'

She nodded, and watched him walk away until he merged with the darkness at the other end of the hall, wishing as she closed the door and slid to the floor that she had the strength to run after them, to scream in their faces, to make them talk. Her heart forced a vicious throb to her temples. Blood rushed through her arms and into her hands, pushing against her fingertips as though it was trying to escape.

She flexed them, trying to hold on to the anger. If she lost it, she wouldn't be able to do what she had promised herself. How dare Stan speak to her like that? Who was he to tell her what to do and who to see? Who was he to keep all this from her? She was glad she had shouted at him, glad she had pushed him into throwing the chair.

She raked her nails through the salt on the floor, licking it from her fingers, making patterns with it, pushing it into little mounds. So much was lost between the cracks. If Stan didn't trust her enough to tell her what was going on, why should she put her faith in him?

She had to do it now, quickly, before she cooled, with the ash of the anger smoking inside her. If Ben was right, if Stan was too far gone, lost from her already, if he refused to let her in, at least she could help Agnes.

She picked up her purse and walked over to the middle of the room then lifted the threadbare rug. One of the boards beneath had a larger groove around it than the others. When she bent down she could see little dents against the edge. She slotted her fingers between them and pulled. It came up almost instantly, tipping her on to her heels. She rocked there for a moment then thrust her hand into the gap. Cobwebs clung to her fingers, sticking dust and crumbs to their wet tips, the smell of softening wood, of the past, of death, rising up.

Empty.

Deeper perhaps? She peered in and held her breath, panic rising. Slowly her eyes adjusted to the gloom. Weak strips of light slanted through the boards. There it was. Right at the back. She stretched her arm in and grabbed the money, fisting it into her purse before she lost her nerve, scrabbling at the stray notes that fluttered around her knees, making sure she got every last dollar.

NEW YORK CITY

Winter solstice, 21 December 1932

17.04

Heavy feet pounded up the last few steps. Ben ran into the room. Frances was so shocked by his speed she backed into Agnes and almost knocked over the camera. His usually calm eyes stretched with panic. A blast of wind sailed through the open door.

'I was right, he's here,' he said. 'On his way up. Ninth floor and rising. He lied though, broke his promise to Dicky: he's not alone, there's one guy with him. I couldn't tell who. Two minutes.' His words pumped out in stuttered bursts.

Agnes exhaled. 'All right,' she said, 'it's time. Everyone calm down. What do we do?' She squeezed Frances' shoulder, as much for her own benefit as Frances'.

For a few panicked seconds the three of them stared at each other.

'I'll take his goon back down with me, distract him with a smoke,' Ben said. His voice sounded firm, but his eyes betrayed him.

'You think that'll work?' Frances asked.

'It'll have to,' Agnes said.

'And what about after? What'll we do with him?' Frances said.

'I'll sort it out,' Ben said. He cocked his head and nodded at her. Something about the way he did it made her scared.

'All right,' Agnes said, 'that's agreed. Now, we don't have long. I want to ask both of you, one last time, before he gets here, if you're sure you want to go through with it. No hard feelings if you back out now. I can do it all on my own if I have to.'

Frances wheeled round. 'You don't think I've come this far to stop now? This was my idea more than yours. I'm doing it.'

Agnes nodded at her, then leant over and softly ran her thumb along Frances' cheek. They both looked at Ben. He'd already hidden himself in the shadows between two rolls of carpet, his body primed, like a runner before the gun.

'I'm not moving,' he said. 'I want to see this through as much as you.'

Frances rubbed the tops of her arms again, trying to squeeze some warmth into them. She pictured the man's face – his deceitful, cheating, murdering smile. His lies echoed around her head. She wished she could throw her doubt off the edge of the building, that it would thunder to the ground along with his body. The joyful splatter of both would be a tonic for her troubles.

'Help me move the camera, would you?' Agnes said. 'Once it's out there I won't be able to come back in. The wind's so fierce if I don't hold the box steady it'll get ripped off the ledge.'

Frances nodded. They bent down and lifted the tripod together, struggling to the window. Agnes stepped out first. Frances watched her face as they fumbled. Brutal gusts tore at her. She frowned, casting dark shadows over her eyes. Her skin was almost see-through. Veins crawled across her temples, and yet, still she was so beautiful. Frances willed Agnes to look up so they could smile at each other one last time before he arrived, but she didn't. Her face was a distracted mask; pale and doll-like, perfect and terrifying.

Murmuring on the stairs, steps behind the door. A deep laugh, echoing against the concrete.

He stepped inside. 'Well, well, well.' He was out of breath.

Frances cocked her leg back over the sill and managed to walk towards him. She smiled hello but didn't speak, willing him to suffocate right there in front of her so they wouldn't have to do anything.

'Sure is a long way up,' he said.

How she hated him. She'd not prepared herself for the force of the feeling. She wanted to run at him and claw his face, smother him with Stan's coat, drown him with her tears.

Ben stepped out. Frances could see he had also cast a mask for himself – a solid surface as petrified as the bronze in the gallery. He walked towards the man's friend.

'Good to see you again,' Ben said.

The goon swivelled. Frances recognised him straight away. Relief washed over her. She'd not mind whatever Ben did to him. The worse the better.

'Benny-boy!' the man said. 'What are you doing here? Good to run into you again. I've not seen you since Stanley.'

She wanted to rip her brother's name from his lips.

Ben looked at the floor. Frances glanced at the window but could only see the back of Agnes' head.

'Wanna walk back down for a smoke while they take the picture?' Ben said. 'It's freezing up here. They won't take long.'

The guy shrugged. 'I guess I could take a walk.'

The man they'd come to kill inclined his head. 'Fine by me,' he said. 'I'm sure the girls will take good care of me.'

Frances forced her mouth to smile again.

Ben left with the stooge trailing behind. Frances wondered how many Luckies they'd smoke before the body landed on the sidewalk in front of them.

She held up her arm and gestured to the window. When she spoke, the steadiness of her voice surprised her: 'Agnes is waiting outside. She's got everything ready.'

GREENWICH VILLAGE

11 November 1932

23.06

'Drink up, darling. Whatever it is, it can't be that bad.'

Jacks circled behind Frances' chair again, trying to top up her glass. Frances held her hand over the rim, denying her access for a second, then gave in. It was making her feel better, after all. If only there could be a moment for her and Agnes to be alone so she could tell her about the money. Every time they'd looked at each other since Frances arrived at Dicky's place she'd seen the hope in Agnes' face, the way her eyes searched Frances', hunting for a sign that she had come to save her. The sooner she could tell her, the better.

Except, if Frances was honest with herself, they'd already been alone. When Frances arrived, Agnes had answered the door. When Frances had spilt wine on her skirt, Agnes had helped her sponge it out by the sink. When Dicky got up from the table to make a call before Jacks came down from upstairs, they'd sipped quietly together for at least five minutes. But on none of these occasions had Frances said anything about the money. She couldn't bear to. She knew that once she did she wouldn't be able to take it back. So instead she drank and held the purse tight between her knees and watched and listened to them all talk, pretending to herself that she was waiting for the right moment when in fact she hoped that moment would never come.

'She won't tell me, Dicky, love. I've tried and tried.' Jacks called through to where Dicky was mixing more drinks in the kitchen. She'd been drunk when Frances arrived; now she was swaying, her words beginning to slur.

'Leave her alone,' Dicky called back. 'We're not all like you, desperate to reveal everything at the drop of a hat. Ignore her, Frances. What she means to say is, we're here when you need us, if you want to confide.'

'Like I said,' Frances replied, 'nothing's wrong. I just remembered a little later than expected that Agnes had invited me for drinks with you, that's all.'

'I see,' Dicky said, walking back into the room with a tray full of clinking glasses. He didn't look convinced. It was he who looked sad, Frances thought. He'd given off an air of melancholy since she arrived, nodding at the conversation but not listening. On more than one occasion she'd caught him staring into the distance, frowning at one of their exuberant plants, paying more attention to the splay of veins on the back of a leaf than to what Jacks was talking about.

'Whatever happens, he's going to have to resign,' Jacks said when they were all sitting down again.

'Who?' Agnes asked.

'Have none of you been listening to me?' Jacks sank her drink and banged the glass on the table, her black lacquer holder sticking out from the corner of her mouth. 'The Mayor, everyone's sweetheart. He's in it up to his neck.'

Frances saw Agnes' eyes flash.

'What's he done?' Agnes asked, staring at her drink.

'Maybe nothing, maybe something,' Jacks said. 'Frank's convinced it's the latter, that he's got something to do with the Gordon case.'

'I thought they already found those guys,' Agnes said, 'and they got off.'

'Exactly,' Jacks said. 'Greenhauer and Stein both had alibis, but Frank said that doesn't matter now, that it's less about who did it and more about who ordered them to do it.'

'Surely the Mayor didn't kill the woman?' Dicky said. 'And I can't believe he'd have the time to ask anyone to do it either, what with the number of nights he spends blotto down in Harlem with all those chorus girls.'

'Frank isn't sure how involved he is in everything yet, although he said it might help once the police release the name of the woman killed in the same park the other night. Anyhow, even if he's not directly involved, it's on his watch, isn't it? And Frank thinks the corruption goes all the way to the top.'

'Another woman was killed?' Frances asked.

'The night of our party, darling. Didn't you read about it? There we were dancing, while some poor woman's life was ending at the hands of God knows who. Heads will roll, Frank said.' She pointed her holder at Dicky. 'If you had any sense about you at the moment, you'd be out there with me getting interviews with all of them – the hoods, the molls, the lawyers. Soon everyone will be jumping on the case. With Frank's contacts I could get us another scoop.'

Dicky rubbed his eyes and slowly sipped his drink. 'I don't feel like working now.'

Jacks turned to Agnes. 'Can't you do anything with him?'

Agnes shrugged, her eyes flicking to Dicky, but she didn't speak.

Frances' mind whirled. She stared at the lamplight glittering the liquid in her glass.

'Goodness me, what a bunch of sad-sacks you lot are tonight,' Jacks said. 'I've half a mind to go out and see if I can round up some new friends to drink with. I know what's wrong with him.' She pointed at Dicky, spilling some ash on the moth-eaten silk kimono they were using as a tablecloth, smouldering another hole in the fabric. 'Carlos has gone back to Brazil and he's all alone again. But I didn't expect you two to turn up looking like this.'

'Shut up, Jacks.' Dicky sounded weary.

'Did you say the woman was murdered on the night of the party?' Frances asked.

'Oh, look, she lives!' Jacks said. 'Yes, the night I introduced you all to Frank. Another redhead apparently. No witnesses as usual, jet beads strewn all over the grass. Frank said it was awful, that it turned his stomach to hear what they'd done to her. Apparently she'd been dragged behind a car by her neck, same as poor old Vivian Gordon. Although they haven't found the car or the rope yet. He thinks it must be the same gang's work, that she knew something about the Mayor and the whole prostitution scandal, that they might have been worried she'd testify. Anyway, he wouldn't tell me her name, but that'll come out soon enough. I'm thinking of doing a piece on gangsters' molls for the magazine. You know the kind of thing, glamorous, young, scandalised, half of them dead before they're twenty-five. My readers will adore it.'

Frances glanced across the table at Agnes, barely hearing what Jacks was saying. Their eyes met. Her friend looked like her body was bound up so tight she might suffocate.

The night of the party. Frances felt the gin begin to curdle inside her.

Dicky faked a yawn. 'Well, I'm beat,' he said.

'Don't lie,' Jacks said. 'You had a nap this afternoon, you can't be that tired.'

'I'm tired of you, darling,' he said, raising an eyebrow. 'As unlikely as I know that sounds, I really am. I'm going upstairs to read.' He got up and began walking towards the door.

Jacks flew past him like a dervish and stood in his way. 'You're disgusting when you speak to me like that, you know. If anyone needs to go to bed early it's me.' She pushed past him and raised her hand to the room without turning round. 'Night, you two, I wish I could say it's been fabulous.' She disappeared, and Frances heard her stomping up the stairs, water running, cupboards banging, then the twang of springs as she presumably threw herself on her bed.

Dicky rolled his eyes at them from the doorway. Frances thought he was going to make some comment about Jacks but he didn't. Instead he said, 'Agnes, why don't you take Frances down to the darkroom and show her some of the prints from your jaunt around the city before she goes home. They really are rather good.' Then he smiled and softly closed the door.

Agnes rolled back the balding rug in the hallway. Beneath it, a large trap door with a rusting iron ring was squared into the floor. She pulled at it, heaving the wood on its hinges, pushing it back against the wall. A chemical smell tainted the air, the same, but stronger, as the way Agnes had smelt the first time Frances met her. The tangy stench rasped at the back of Frances' throat – vinegar and rusting iron and latrines. Medicinal, but the kind of medicine that makes you feel worse before it makes you better. She was glad of it. The burning air almost distracted her from thinking about Stan. She shook the thought away. Not Stan. He wouldn't hurt a woman.

'It's awful, isn't it?' Agnes said, mistakenly thinking the wretched look on Frances' face was caused by the smell.

'It's not too bad,' Frances lied.

'It is. I don't think I'll ever get used to it, but it's worth enduring it when you see what the chemicals do to light-sensitive paper. It's the only true magic that exists, the only way to see a miracle unfold before your eyes in real life.' Frances wasn't convinced. Her doubt must have shown because Agnes said, 'Come on. Not afraid of the dark as well, are you?'

'No,' Frances said, peering into the depths.

'Down we go, then,' Agnes said.

They'd not spoken about anything yet – not about Agnes' sister, or what Jacks had said about the Mayor, or about the money. Agnes was quiet, so Frances was too. At any rate, she didn't know what to say. The shame of taking Stan's money licked at her insides like a lit match.

She followed Agnes down the creaking stairs into the darkness, holding her purse tight against her chest. About halfway in, Agnes reached up and flipped a large metal switch. A dim bulb spluttered into life. The basement was smaller than Frances had imagined. It ran the full length of the house, but since the building was fairly thin it wasn't as big as the cellars back home. In Kansas in the winter some people kept cows beneath their floors. Here there was barely room for chickens. There were none of the usual things people stored in basements, either. No buckets of coal, no tools, no cans of paint. Instead, large wooden tables ran around three sides of the room at waist height. Trays of liquid, cameras lined up in order of size, piles of dark waxy envelopes and a few large mysterious machines were stacked on them. To Frances it looked more like a laboratory than a cellar, like a room in a picture she'd once seen about automatons and scientists and experiments and electricity.

Above their heads, strings hung from the ceiling covered with photographs. Frances walked around staring up at the strange washing lines. Each row held photographs of a similar type. On one, Frances could see images from a party – Dicky and Jacks and all their friends, sprawling and smoking and dancing and clutching at each other. Some of the people looked familiar, but no Agnes. Perhaps she had taken them.

On another were some high society shots. Women in fancy frocks and pearls. Long gloves, lit cigarettes, billowing smoke. Gardens and flowers and tea parties. Tight dresses. Jaunty angles. The good life. These must be Dicky's, the ones he sold to magazines, the ones that kept everyone in clover. Frances still found it hard to believe it was possible to make a living from this; from simply looking and waiting and pressing. It seemed the exact opposite of work.

Agnes beckoned her to a string along the back wall. Kansas. She knew it from the first picture. The particular curve in the trunk of one of the trees, the way the bark peeled, the bright slant of sunlight, the pattern on the woman's cotton dress, the way the crying child clutched at her mother's knee, the hunger chiselled into their muddy cheekbones. Home.

'I think Dicky took these before he met you,' Agnes said. 'He and Jacks toured around the dustbowl looking for poor people to make the rich feel guilty. Dicky hopes a few will send cash, help somehow. Jacks is less bothered about that and more concerned with how famous it might make them. The story isn't out yet, I don't think Jacks has even written it, but the magazine has already paid up on the strength of the negatives alone. The money will keep them both in cigarettes and booze until Christmas.'

Frances nodded but didn't speak. She focused on each image in turn, staring at the farmsteads and upended cooking pots, at the aprons and shoeless feet, at the hollow eyes and wailing mouths. She gazed at what she had escaped, trying to feel something other than empty.

'Sorry,' Agnes said, 'I didn't mean to make you feel homesick.'

'It's not that,' Frances said, 'it's more that I don't know this place any more. I didn't realise that if I left it would leave me too. I thought I could come here and stay with Stan, be in the city, get away from Kansas but still go back some day. I thought where you were born would always be home. I've only been here two months and it already feels like some place I don't remember truly being in the first place. Like a dream. A nightmare. I don't ever want to go back.'

Frances could feel Agnes staring at her as she spoke, the heat of her gaze burning her cheek, but she didn't turn. She was aware of a tightness in her chest, as though her insides were bound with a rope of silk and every time Agnes looked at her she tugged on the ends.

Agnes moved away to the other side of the room.

'How about these, then?'

Frances followed her and gasped, her hand at her mouth. It was her. There she was in her old smock looking like a lost child. There she was in all Jacks and Agnes' dresses, the colours turned black by the print, fat white pearls wrapped around her throat.

'None of them look like me.' She pointed to the one of her sitting on the floor in her ruined sandals. 'Not even that one.'

'I think they do. It's just that Dicky's caught a version of yourself you've not seen before.' Agnes pointed to one of Frances staring right at the camera, her chin up, the dress cut low, her collarbone jutting out, hands on her hips. 'I love this one. I'm going to ask Dicky for a copy. You look like someone from the pictures.'

Frances stared at herself. 'I got it,' she said, her face still hot from what Agnes had said, the words bubbling up, unbidden, whispered but somehow loud in the small space.

'What?' Agnes said, concentrating on the photograph of Frances in front of her. Frances was relieved she didn't turn.

'The money.'

'What?' Agnes said, facing her. 'How? Where from?'

'Don't worry about that. I'm not certain, but I think it'll be enough. Here.' She shoved her purse at her, relieved she wouldn't have the weight and the worry of holding on to all those dollars any more.

Agnes looked inside. 'I can't believe it, Frances. There's probably enough in here to pay twice what they're demanding.' She tried to hand it back but Frances shrugged her arm away. 'I can't take it,' Agnes went on. 'You hardly know me. It's too much. Where did you get it?'

'I can't say.'

'Did you steal it?'

'No. Sort of.'

'Well I definitely don't want it then. I've got enough problems. Thanks, but no thanks.' Agnes put the bag on the bench and started fiddling with something, twisting the mechanism on a machine in front of her.

'Don't be like that.' Frances felt her throat tighten. This was not how she'd imagined Agnes would react. She was supposed to thank her. She wasn't supposed to look away. 'Can I explain?' She wished there was something for her to do while she talked, some sewing, a cigarette, something to busy her hand.

'No need,' Agnes said.

Frances took a deep breath. 'I want to tell you about Stan, about my brother.'

'Okay.'

'He's connected to the money, you see.'

'Right,' Agnes said.

'I saw him take it.'

'Take what?'

'The money.'

Agnes looked up, her thick brows furrowed. 'From where?'

'He works at a club but I don't think that's the only place he's been working. I saw him taking money from a parcel and hiding it underneath the floorboards.' The words tumbled out of her as though they were rolling down a hill. 'I can't work out what's going on, what he's up to. And he's been getting thinner, and he's angry all the time. He looks ill. He's not himself. I've been

so worried. And then the other day when you told me about
your sister, I started thinking that it sounded so similar, the way
she changed, the way she started stealing. And then Jacks said
all that about the girl getting killed in the park the same night
Stan got hurt and now I'm worried, I'm worried ... that ...
that ... ' Frances started to cry then, the tears coming so swiftly
they took her by surprise and she couldn't hold them back.

Agnes held her. 'It's all right.'

'It's not,' Frances mumbled, her voice stifled by the pressure
of her nose on Agnes' shoulder. Every time she tried to take a
breath, Agnes' shirt stuck to her face. For a moment she dreamt
of suffocation, of dying right there in the strange basement, her
nose full of Agnes. 'I don't know what to do.'

'Neither do I,' Agnes replied. 'Did you hear what Jacks said
about the Mayor being involved somehow? Sounds like we're
both in a fix.'

She drew Frances from her, holding her at arm's length. They
stared at each other for a second, then Frances turned away,
afraid of what might happen if she kept on looking.

'One thing I do know is I can't take this money from you.
You'll have to take it home and put it back. All right?'

'Are you sure? But what will you do?'

'I'll think of something. I always have done.'

'But what if they come after you? I'd never forgive myself if
something happened and I could have helped.'

'We can't take this money, Frances. It wouldn't be right. God
knows what kind of trouble you'd get into. We've no idea what
your brother needs it for, where it came from, who's involved.'

Frances sighed. Agnes was right, she knew she was. 'All right.'
She wiped her nose, relieved she wouldn't have to betray Stan
after all.

'Enough of this.' Agnes smiled, but Frances could see the
effort. 'Let's take our minds off everything for a while. I've been

hiding down here since Stella died. Not sure what I would have done without it. Come and watch this. I've got to put the red light on before we start. Try not to be alarmed, okay? I don't want you getting all jumpy and knocking over one of Dicky's ritzy cameras by accident. He'd kill me.'

Frances followed her to the bench. Agnes was holding a large rectangle of see-through film in her hand. She held it up so Frances could see it more clearly. The image looked strange. At first Frances couldn't tell why, then she realised everything that should be black was white, and everything white was black. The world reversed. Agnes fanned out a pile of them. In one, the iron and rubble of the Rockefeller Center emerged from the ground like some man-made mountain. In another, the barber was on his step, hands in pockets, frowning. In a third, the giant Coca-Cola sign curved above the skyscrapers, the curl of the letters making it seem to flutter like a celebratory flag. It was their perfect day.

'Negatives,' Agnes said. 'Now watch.'

She walked back to the light switch and for a moment they were plunged into darkness until a deep red glow lit up the room. It reminded Frances of the club in Harlem, of the frantic jazz beats and languid interlocking arms, of the way the liquor had swirled inside her. Agnes looked strange as she walked back across the room. Frances couldn't see her eyes properly. Her clothes were stripped of colour; fabric, hair and skin trans-formed, everything a trembling, murky shade of red.

Agnes curled her finger, encouraging Frances to follow. They walked over to one of the machines. Frances watched her take out a thick piece of paper from one of the dark envelopes and put it under the machine. She slotted the negative into a little shelf above, twisted a few dials at the side, adjusted the position of the paper and pressed a button. For a few seconds an image of the photograph appeared on the paper, a building, a window, a person perhaps, then it disappeared again.

'Did something go wrong?' Frances asked.

'No,' Agnes said, picking up the paper and walking over to one of the trays, 'keep watching.'

Agnes submerged the sheet in the liquid and started lifting the tray up and down, making sure that the paper was getting wet. Frances stared at the sheet, made pink by the light. The liquid slid all over, washing over the surface and skidding back again, the way she imagined the sea might spread over her feet then race away.

'Keep watching – whatever you do, don't look away,' Agnes said, a note of excitement lifting her voice. 'I've wanted to show you this since the day you came to the door. I knew you'd think it was special.'

Slowly, Frances thought she could see something changing on the surface of the paper. Another few seconds went by and she was sure of it. A dark shape emerged. First a building, then a window, finally someone's legs hanging over the edge of a sill.

She sucked at her breath in shock, sensing Agnes looking at her again, shivering when she felt her friend's hand on her arm.

Frances looked back at the paper and now she could see the photograph clearly: the dark lines of the bricks, the flaking paint on the white window sill, and there in the centre of it all her own body, legs hanging over the drop, serious face staring forward, hair streaming down one shoulder.

'When did you take it?' Frances whispered.

'When we went up to that crazy old woman's house at the end of the day. I was setting up for the shot of the sign and I saw you there, staring out, and I knew I had to get the picture.'

'Why?' Frances asked.

'Because I'd never seen someone look so much like themselves. You were serious and thoughtful and still, so very still. Nothing was hidden, you were just looking out and wondering at it all. It was the opposite of those monstrous women Dicky has to shoot, slinking around town with their tight shoes and fixed grins.'

Frances smiled. She looked down and watched as the image grew darker. For the first time she saw herself as Agnes must see her – young and stubborn, staring at the world as though it was ready for the taking, as though she was the one who might take it. Agnes' eyes were on her again.

'Oh no!' Agnes cursed.

She fished the paper out and pushed it into another tray of liquid. As the water eddied over it a different, stronger smell overwhelmed them. Frances coughed.

'What is it?' she spluttered.

'I almost left it in too long. If you'd distracted me any more, it would have got darker and darker in the developer until you couldn't see anything. I'd have destroyed you.'

Agnes paused for a moment, swirling the paper, then pulled it out and pinned it over their heads. Frances could see why she had taken it. It wasn't only the look on her face, but the angle of her body, the way her legs hung against the line of bricks. Her chin thrust forward into the sky, the sunset hitting the dark window behind, haloing her head.

'You're beautiful,' Agnes said, her breath a whisper on Frances' cheek, raising the hairs on her arms.

Frances turned, no longer afraid. For a few seconds they stared at each other, then Agnes cupped Frances' chin with both her hands and kissed her.

Afterwards, as she walked up the basement steps, leaving Agnes to tidy up, Frances could only remember what had happened in bright pockets of sensation: the rustle of her skirt as Agnes lifted it; the shock of the cold table against her buttocks; the pressure of Agnes' lips on hers, their strange softness.

She touched her mouth now, as she stepped quickly up the creaking boards. Surely it looked different? The heat must have left some mark? As she moved she felt the wetness on the tops of her thighs, her cotton knickers saturated with her own desire, the sliding texture at once heady and shameful. She flushed, although no one was looking, and opened the front door, praying she wouldn't bump into Jacks or Dicky on her way out.

Somewhere above her head she heard a glass shatter, a howl of pain. Man or woman she couldn't tell. She put a foot on to the top step. If she went now no one would know how late she had stayed. No one would suspect anything.

'What is it?' Agnes called. She was still packing things away.

'Nothing.' For some reason Frances didn't want to see her face in the light. It might break the spell.

Footsteps creaking overhead, another shout. But what if someone was in trouble? What if Jacks or Dicky needed her? What if some guy had broken in while she and Agnes were distracted?

The shock of what they had done forced blood back to her face. She wondered if she'd ever be able to face Agnes again, but still, part of her wanted to rush back down the basement steps.

'Bye,' she called down.

'Bye, then,' Agnes yelled back. Perhaps she didn't want to look at Frances either.

Softly Frances closed the door and, taking care to place her feet only in the centre of the stairs where the carpet was, she padded up towards the commotion.

At the top she stopped to listen. Beside her a black lacquer door was slightly ajar. She crept closer and put her eye to the tiny gap. The room beyond was neat and glorious. A few beautiful clothes were slung over a peach-coloured chair; a large dresser covered in bottles and watches and brushes in front of a scrolled mirror. Everything shone in the lamplight. Dicky's room, she guessed. He was sitting on the bed with his head in his hands. Jacks was standing in front of him holding what looked to Frances like a pillowcase. On the floor at their feet, a broken glass, the shards pricked by the light.

'I told you, that was enough. You promised. You'll ruin everything.' Her voice was bitter, unforgiving. Frances felt shocked by the force of it, hurt even though she wasn't the one being spoken to.

Dicky didn't look up. 'I'm sorry,' he mumbled, 'but it's my money. I can spend it how I like. If it wasn't for Father's inheritance you'd still be sleeping under the bridge where I found you. Whoring yourself for every story.'

Jacks raised her hand and slapped him hard across the face. He fell back on to the bed.

'*Your* money,' Jacks hissed. 'It might well be your money, but look around. How many jobs would you get without me? Without all my connections? I've earned us ten times what I owe you. Don't you dare speak to me like that.'

Dicky sat up and neatened his tie. His cheek was bright red where she'd hit it.

'This isn't about money,' Jacks said, 'it's about you risking everything because of this.' She held up the pillowcase and started tearing the seam along the top edge.

With a shock, Frances realised it was one of Mrs Bianchi's. Not Frances' design, but one the old woman had shown her when she began, as a guide for what she wanted her to do. Lace scallops around the edge. As Jacks ripped, tiny packets fell out and on to the floor. Dicky jumped off the bed and started scrambling around, gathering them up and pushing them into his top pocket.

'Look at the state of you,' Jacks said. 'You disgust me.'

Downstairs, a door slammed. Agnes coming up from the cellar. Frances tiptoed quickly down the stairs, pausing at the bottom to make sure the passage was clear before teasing open the front door and stepping out, breathless, into the night.

LOWER EAST SIDE

25 November 1932

23.11

'So, you won't help me?' She felt the desperation rising up. Two days. Stan had been gone for two days.

'I am helping you.'

'I don't mean this!' Frances picked up the book and threw it across the room. It slapped against the map of the world and slid to the floor with a clatter.

Ben stood up and pushed his chair in.

'You say you don't know where he is, but you must. You've been sneaking around with him for weeks. You brought him home last time.'

'I'm sorry, I don't know where he is now. I looked for him last night and tonight. No one's seen him at the club.'

'You don't understand. He's never stayed out all night before, not without letting me know, let alone two nights in a row. He wouldn't do that. You can't have asked the right people, you can't have tried hard enough.'

He looked out of the window. Rain misted the glass. His calmness enraged her. 'I've tried, Frances, I've been trying to help him for months. Long before you came.'

'It's not my fault I wasn't here.'

'I know, I didn't mean that.'

She walked to his metal bedstead and sat down on the edge. The neatness of it – the crisp patchwork quilt, all the corners tucked in tight – made her want to scream. She had to stop herself from tearing at it.

Ben dragged his chair over and sat down in front of her. 'He'll be fine. He can take care of himself. No doubt he's in a speakeasy somewhere drinkin' away his sorrows.'

She put her head in her hands. 'He would have told me. He would have said something.' She looked up at him, her stare hardened by rage and fear. 'I know him better than you. If he'd been out and got hoary-eyed he'd be back and in his bed by now. He wouldn't want me to be alone.'

Ben nodded, his calmness slipping towards sadness. They were silent for a time, listening to the rain hitting the pane, to the sound of their own restless breathing.

'Did he ever tell you how we met?' Ben asked.

'He said you met at the club.'

'Yes. But did he tell you what he did?'

'No.'

'Did Mrs Bianchi tell you where I lived before?'

'No.' She paused. 'Yes. Harlem.'

He nodded. 'That's right, Harlem. Where I belong. I lived with my brother.'

'Stan never said you had a brother.'

'I don't, any more.' He looked away from her, out of the window again, his fingers reaching behind his head and pressing at his hair. 'My brother, Louis. Most folks called him simple. Ma didn't want to look after him, so I did. He was sixteen.'

'What happened? Didn't you like it in Harlem?'

'I liked it fine. It was other people who didn't like us.'

'What do you mean?'

The silence stretched again. Only a small part of her cared.

'The thing is,' he said, 'sometimes it's not outsiders who let you down, it's your own.'

He paused, and she could tell he was struggling to decide whether to carry on. She had learnt from other men that once they started speaking it was best to keep quiet. Sometimes asking questions only made them clam up. With women it was different. Women wanted you to ask, to be interested. Women were always relieved to talk.

'I left because of Louis. There was an accident, a fight. Some jumped-up kid called him a name and caught me on a bad day. Louis didn't understand why I got so angry. I don't think the kid did either. Poor boy. A child really. Sixteen too.' He shook his head and turned away. Frances worried he might cry.

What was he making such a fuss about? Stan would have done the same for her. He had, hadn't he? Over and over again. All those names she'd been called in the street, in the drugstore, out on the stoop. All the boys he'd shut up on account of her. It was only natural. Blood protected blood. But she didn't speak. She was worried if she agreed, or even nodded, the moment would be lost and Ben would stop explaining.

'I wasn't long home from the front, you see. The fight was still in me. All that anger you have to build up to be able to attack the enemy every day, every single day. It doesn't leave you all at once. Coming back, nothing changed. Or, at least, I didn't change fast enough.' He looked at her. She could see his eyes filling with light, and knew that if he blinked tears would fall. He stared at the rain. 'One punch was all it took. One stupid, perfect hit.'

She realised then what he meant. The shock clenched around her chest.

'God forgive me. One minute this kid was mocking Louis, spitting at his feet. The next he was dead on the floor.'

Ben looked down at his hands, turning them over, as though he was looking for an answer from them, an apology.

'After that we couldn't stay. Everything changed. He was a good kid, so they said – soccer teams, scholarships. If it hadn't been for me, he might even have made it out of Harlem. It was Stan who suggested coming here, who smoothed things out with the others. If it wasn't for him and Mrs Bianchi and old Mr Bianchi, God rest him, I don't know what we would have done. We'd have ended up out there, out in the park in Hooverville' – he nodded in the direction of the window – 'with the rest of the bums, the rest of the down-and-out ex-servicemen.'

'But you didn't mean it.' Frances couldn't stay quiet. 'Surely all the people you lived with knew that. Like you said, it was a mistake.'

'Some knew. But it didn't matter. There was enough who didn't want us there. Enough who would have made Louis' life more difficult than it already was.'

'What happened to him?'

'He died last year. Lasted a lot longer than anyone thought. Doctors had said he wouldn't live past seven, let alone make it all the way to seventeen.'

She watched the sadness ebb and flow in his face, the anguish swelling and fading as he tried to control it. It made sense now. His closeness with Stan, how he cared for Mrs Bianchi.

'I'm sorry.'

He nodded at her and looked at his hands again.

She stood up. 'I'm going to find him.'

'Where will you go? You can't run around town alone at this hour. I'll have to come with you.'

She pulled on her thin overcoat, the sleeves cooling her bare arms instead of warming them up.

'Maybe there's someone at the club who'll tell me something they wouldn't tell you. I'm going there first, then I'll have a look in his favourite bars. You know any?'

'Some of them.'

'Well then, let's get moving. You can get us a cab.'

She walked fast, dodging drunks and party girls, striding alongside all-night diners, their bright lights casting her shadow across the sidewalk. At this time of night everyone was too concerned with their own conquests and affairs, their own declarations, their own precarious journeys towards love or despair to notice her crying. She wiped her sleeve across her face all the same.

No one had seen Stan: not Willie, nor the chorus girls, nor the band members, nor Missy. None of them. At least, that's what they said. Willie had looked shifty when she asked him. Said he hadn't seen him, that he'd not come into work for a few days, but the whole time they'd been talking he'd been twisting at the gold signet ring on his finger, turning it round and round while he shrugged and smiled.

After that she'd sent Ben off to ask in the bars he knew, told him she was going home; but she wasn't, she was racing as fast as she could to Agnes, to the only place she felt safe any more.

Ten minutes later she was hammering on Jacks and Dicky's door. She knocked again, not caring if she woke up the whole God-damned square. A light came on in a room at the top. A window slid open. Jacks' head poked out. A dark silky dressing gown fell from her shoulders, her hair messed up, lipstick smeared. Still, she looked wonderful.

'Frances? What the hell are you doing?'

'Who is it? Tell them to go away.' A deep voice from inside, someone Frances had heard before but couldn't quite place.

Jacks looked over her shoulder. 'Get in that bed! Did I say you could move?' She looked back to Frances, her hands on the window sill, arms dead straight. 'What is it, Frances? I'm sorry, I'm otherwise engaged, I can't come down now.'

'It's all right, I was looking for Agnes.'

Jacks beamed. 'Of course you were. How are things going with you two?'

So she knew. Frances was glad of the dark to hide her shame.

'Fine. I wanted to see her, to talk to her. Is she in?'

'I don't think she is, dear, I heard her go out a while ago. She's probably walked up to Phillie's for a coffee. Goes there when she can't sleep. Corner of Eleventh and Seventh.'

'Thanks,' Frances said, already walking away.

'No problem, dear. We're having another party next week, you must come. Half our friends want to paint you, the other half keep bothering me to get them a dinner date. You're my greatest success so far, you know.'

'I'll try,' Frances called over her shoulder. She turned to wave and saw a man kissing Jacks' neck, his fair hair bright against the streetlight. Probably Frank.

He lifted his head and looked right at her. No, not Frank. Kane.

'According to Dicky, they've been on again, off again for years.' Agnes sipped her coffee.

Frances could still feel the swell of relief in her belly from when she'd spotted Agnes in the window of the diner. She had stopped on the other side of the street and watched her reading for a while, noting the way she held her cup by the base, not the handle, the way she twisted at the sides of her short hair as she read and tucked it behind her ears. Frances had planned to run in and kiss her on the mouth, but she didn't. She had no notion of the rules. Perhaps they'd be arrested? She was still so astounded she could feel this way about a woman. It made her look at Agnes with a kind of awe, as though she were a man in disguise. A man, or a magician, or some kind of God.

'He's violent, though,' Agnes carried on.

Frances wasn't surprised. Kane had given off an air of danger when she'd first met him at the club. It was why she'd liked him. She told Agnes what had happened, how he'd bought her drinks all night.

Agnes shrugged. 'They're all at it with everybody. Jacks saw Frank last night. Squeezing him as much for her own fun as to get information about the Mayor for her story, no doubt.' She looked intently at Frances. 'Are you all right? I know it's late, but you look shattered, different somehow. Older.'

'Thanks,' Frances said, 'that's the kind of compliment a girl likes to hear.'

'I didn't mean like that.' Agnes sipped her drink again. 'I meant you look a bit worried, that's all.'

Frances sighed and told her about Stan.

'Two days? No wonder you look like you do. And he's never gone off before?'

'Not for that long. Not without saying.' She put her head against the cool glass of the window and watched the world rushing past. 'I wish I'd never come. Nothing's been right since I got here.'

'Don't take it all on yourself. Sounds like something was wrong long before you arrived.'

Frances nodded and sipped quietly at her coffee, enjoying the warmth of it on her palms and lips. She looked across at Agnes. 'You don't look all that great either, you know.'

'Thanks! What is this? Some kind of competition?'

'No, I just think you look bothered about something too.'

'I'm tired, that's all. I can't sleep, but I'm exhausted. It's the most frustrating thing.'

'No more threatening letters?'

'No, but I've still got a week to pay up.'

'What are you going to do?'

'I'm not sure, something will come to me.'

'You don't look too certain.'

'I'm not, but what can I do? And I've been thinking. In fact I was wondering about this when I saw you looking all flustered and delightful across the street beneath that lamp over there. Would the scandal really be so bad if they lied about Stella? All these women are running around town being blackmailed because they're worried about how they might look to folks they don't even know. All that judgement. All that guilt. Is it worth the agony? It's not more painful than losing her, I can tell you. It's not more painful than watching Mother slip away. I don't want to pay, that's the truth. If you want to know how I'm really feeling, I want to punish them. I want to find them and ruin them.'

'I've still got the money, you know.'

'Frances! You should have put it back.'

'I was going to, but before Stan went off there never seemed a time when he wasn't in the parlour. And since he's gone I've been too worried.'

'Where's the money now?'

'In my drawer at home, still in my purse, pushed right at the back past things Stan would never put his hand on.'

Agnes giggled, the sound lightening the mood, striking away a part of Frances' worry.

'I suppose if your brother's not there, one good thing is you won't be missed if you get back late.'

Agnes leant across the booth and laid her warm hand on Frances' upturned palm. The touch sent a jolt down Frances' arm so strong she almost tore it away. She glanced around to see if anyone was looking. There were only two other people in the diner, a man with a stiff grey hat and a woman in a pink dress with red hair sitting close to each other on stools at the counter. They didn't turn.

'And,' Agnes carried on, leaning forward until the smell of her made Frances shut her eyes, 'there are always more photographs that need developing.'

Walking home, Frances looked at the city but saw only Agnes washed in red, her small strong hands running the length of her body, her head twisting this way and that so she might taste as much of Frances as possible. How could a thing like that be so terrifying and yet so familiar?

She felt crazy and dangerous, disgusted and electrified. It wasn't like this before, not all at once, not with the boys on the farms, not in the back of trucks as her body shook against heavy hands on bumpy roads, not sunk deep in dark theatre seats where they kidded themselves no one could see what they were doing. Everything she'd ever done before seemed boring and normal and average. With Agnes she felt so filled, so distracted, so overwhelmed, it was as though every thought, every worry, every sadness had been expelled from her body. For a brief moment she had been set free. She thought of the painting in the gallery.

If Father ever found out he'd kill her. Mother would scream. The guilt of what she had done clung to the back of her throat with the lingering stench of the darkroom, but somehow Frances knew it wasn't her shame, it was theirs. She forced herself to walk on when all she wanted was to run back and knock on the door and pull Agnes' arms tight around her like a knotted belt.

If Stan was there when she got home, she wouldn't chastise

him for disappearing. She wouldn't get angry, she'd say sorry. He'd be expecting a row, so her saying that would wrong-foot him. Things couldn't go on as they were. Of course he'd had nothing to do with that dead girl. The things in his pocket probably had more to do with a girl he was seeing than any-thing else. He'd probably helped someone out and now he was ashamed. Embarrassed, perhaps. Worried, even. If she could only speak to him in the right tone, ask the right questions, he'd tell her what was going on and she could help. Then everything would go back to how it had been.

She rounded a corner, still a few streets away from the tenement. Up ahead, a group of people had gathered on the sidewalk. A man was taking photographs. She could hear the pop, pop, pop of his flashbulb going off, the sulphur igniting over the heads of the crowd, illuminating those with upturned faces in bursts of lightning. Their expressions looked excited, manic. Somewhere a woman was crying.

Frances walked past a man going in the opposite direction with his hat in his hands. 'Oh no,' he muttered, 'shame, such a shame.' His eyes didn't leave the sidewalk.

She walked closer, pressing her body against the backs of those in front, jostling for a better view. Every time a bulb exploded she could see more of the crowd. There were children in there, their eyes blackened, their grins and shouts turned nightmarish by what they'd seen.

'Stand back, folks, stand back.' A man's voice. 'Keep clear, please, I won't ask you again!'

Frances pushed closer to the front, caught up in the crush, the smell of liquor and sweat and sugared nuts in the air, the acrid sulphur reminding her of Agnes, before it drifted over her head on the cold wind.

She was glad she was slight, it made it easier to wriggle to the front. Now she could see the photographer. His shirt sleeves were rolled up. A fat cigar threatened to fall from his lips as he moved around, searching for a better angle. Beside him, in front of Frances, three policemen were holding back the crowd, occasionally watching the photographer's progress. On the ground at their feet, splayed between the sidewalk and the gutter, was a body.

Frances could tell from the size it was a man. A stained sheet covered his head and chest. It was lagged in muck and oil. A large pool of blood seeped towards its edges, extending across the whiteness as she watched. Not long dead. On the kerb, his brown felt hat lay to one side, as though he'd just taken it off. A woman in front moved, her pinny smeared with grease, and Frances finally caught a glimpse of the man's hands, his navy pants, his shoes.

The flashbulb went off again, lighting up the street.

The conker shine on the man's brogues ignited behind Frances' lids, then faded away. No, not him. She opened her eyes. Another pop and she felt herself explode. It was him, it was. She knew it. She moved closer and looked again, doubtful now, praying, panic rising, threatening to burst from her throat, oblivious to the shoving, groping throng.

'No, no, no.' First a whisper, then a shout. She knew those hands, those legs, those shoes.

She rushed forward, her horror echoing off the brick and glass and concrete, a guttural sound that hurled itself back at her like a slap cracked across her cheek, and threw herself on Stan with such force the police couldn't stop her, then she gathered him up, the bloody sheet slipping from his lolling head, his body so heavy in her arms that she fell and rolled with him and kissed his greying face and pressed her head to his stilled heart, and screamed and screamed and screamed.

NEW YORK CITY

Winter solstice, 21 December 1932

17.10

'A bit closer, sir, that's it,' Agnes shouted.

'Damned freezing up here, girl.'

'Sorry, sir, yes, but if you could move a bit closer to the edge, I need to get the light from that building over there to hit your face so we can see it.'

'I'm fine where I am, thank you, if I get any closer the wind'll have me over the side.'

Frances was so close to his feet she could see the fine creases in the leather above the bend of his toes. New shoes, she thought. Only worn a few times, not yet lost their polish. He probably had hundreds of other pairs at home.

She wanted to push right then, had to will her hand not to reach out and grasp his ankle and pull his legs from under him, flip him over the top. She forced her fingers to stay wrapped around the tripod. It was hard to move them anyway, they were so numb they'd locked at the knuckle. She must wait. They had to get the note in his pocket first. If he fell without it they'd all be doomed. She was waiting for Agnes' signal. He was supposed to be closer to the edge now, close enough so that there'd be no doubt he would fall.

'Frances,' Agnes shouted over the wind, 'can you come back here a moment?'

'Ladies,' the man said, 'it would be wonderful if we could hurry this up. I'm not usually one to complain about the cold, but I can no longer feel my feet. I'm not sure if you're aware, but I've got a lot of drinking to do after this. Your employer said it would take no more than ten minutes. He said you knew what you were doing. I don't want to start doubting the word of a friend.'

'No, sir,' Agnes said, 'I'm waiting for the right moment. The right light.'

'Can't we wait inside until then?' he asked.

'No,' Agnes said a little too quickly. 'Not long now, sir, I promise.'

Frances prised her fingers from the tripod and walked behind the camera. The wind was so strong she almost lost her footing.

The man sighed. 'Don't suppose you'll mind if I light a cigarette, at least?'

'No, sir,' Agnes said.

He reached inside his pocket and took out a heavy lighter. Gold, engraved, swirling with decoration. 'Nice, huh?' He didn't wait for a reply.

'What is it?' Frances hissed into Agnes' ear, their faces blocked from him by the bellows and body of the camera.

'I can't do it,' Agnes whispered. 'Let's forget the whole thing. We'll be caught. No one will believe he's a jumper. And what good will it do?'

Frances scowled at her. 'What good?' she hissed. 'What good? Have you forgotten what he did?'

'No, but—'

'But nothing.' Frances could feel the anger crouching inside her. The swell of it. The livid burn. 'Think of all those girls. Of Stella. I've seen you in the middle of the night. Sweating, crying, reaching out. I know how you feel because I feel it too. Now we've got to do it. There's too many people involved. God knows who'd be next.' As she spoke she could feel her confidence growing, the words, the truth of it, convincing herself as much as Agnes. 'We have to get him closer to the edge.'

Agnes took out a shammy and rubbed it across the lens. Frances watched the shake in her hand make the job easier, wiping the smears away without the need for much motion. Fear was like that, she thought. Anger, sorrow, love – it was all the same. Sometimes the strength of a feeling could make a nasty job easier to finish.

'Okay,' Agnes said, peeking at the man around the edge of the camera, watching as he exhaled at the city, the wind whipping the smoke away, 'but I don't know if I can push, I don't think I can do it.'

'Yes, you can,' Frances said, 'we'll do it together. And if you can't manage, I'll do it myself.'

LOWER EAST SIDE

27 November 1932

02.27

Frances crawled back into bed without taking her dress or shoes off and pulled up the crochet quilt. She was desperate to be as still and quiet as possible. Soon someone would come, she was certain of that, only she didn't know who. The police, to ask more questions. One of Stan's friends, to tell her what she already knew. Ben. Whoever it was, they'd have their hat in their hands and a sorry look on their face. She couldn't bear all that.

Turning on to her side, she stared at the large crack that forked beneath the crumbling window sill. Freezing air pushed its way through, stinging her cheek beneath tears she didn't recall crying. She forced herself to breathe and slid her hand between the damp pillow and the mattress.

She could barely remember walking into the tenement. Was that yesterday or today? Since she found him (no, God, no – she pushed the thought away) some things had happened that were clear while others were blurry, locked at the back of her head behind a pane of dirty glass.

She knew the police had taken her to the station. She'd sat on a cold chair. Two men had smiled at her. The sergeant had touched her knee, his hand lingering longer than it should. He told her about the bullets. She wished he hadn't. One in Stan's heart. Another in his head. 'To make sure.' She'd nodded a lot and pretended to write her name on some papers, sipped from a mug of liquor – 'for the pain', the dishevelled woman next to her had said – and then they'd driven her home.

The city had looked strange from the back of the van. Changed. She'd stared out at the nighthawks and the flickering lights, bunching her skirt in her fists as the officers in the front seat ate cold chicken and laughed about some case they were working on. Everything was the same. Everything was different.

Only now, in the quiet, did she allow herself to think of him. She'd been resisting the pull, had rushed past his coat on the stand, her head turned purposefully the other way; but now, in the dark, thoughts of Stan surfaced and she didn't have the strength to keep them at bay.

She closed her eyes and tried to picture his face, his body, the way he stood, the whole of him, but she could only see him in pieces. The curved scar on his knee that he'd gotten years ago trying to jump over barbed wire on the farm at harvest time. The smell of one-dollar shoe-shine. The sourness of his breath when he kissed her cheek after drinking coffee in the morning. That soft look in his eyes that she'd never seen before when he met her at the train station.

The memories twisted and stretched. That rare afternoon, back on the farm – she'd forgotten how long ago – when the first rain for months had gunned down and no work could be done, so they'd sat on the front porch as the dead grass steamed and he taught her to whistle. The first New York day, fresh off the train, his hand on her shoulder, weaving her through the crowds on Broadway. The time when he was fifteen, already over six feet, and he found Father standing over her in the barn and he walked up to him and shouted, 'Enough!'

She wondered if these parts of Stan would end up being the same ones she'd always remember, as though the shock of sudden grief had frozen her first recollections of him after death and they couldn't be replaced.

She looked up and out. Fog had gathered inside the corners of the window like pockets of glittering spider's eggs. From this angle, if she pulled her eyes back until they ached, she could make out a scythe-shaped moon, scarring the sky between blackened buildings.

For once, outside it was quiet. She couldn't hear the Tonionis in the hallway or Mrs Bianchi's eldest son messing around with his cart outside. No kids screaming on the fire escapes. What time was it? She thought of a clock, then a watch, then Stan's watch, his wrist, the thick blond hairs standing up on either side of the fading leather. And just like that she began to sob. Great racking sobs that meant she couldn't catch her breath, so loud that she had to push her face into the pillow, the fear of being heard far worse than the possibility of suffocation.

The force of it scared her. The agony. The loss of him. The panic. The disbelief, but worse, the certainty. How could he be gone? He couldn't be. He was. Gone now, and he'd never come back. Loneliness rushed towards her from the black corners of the room, wrapping around her like her own death shroud come too soon, only it didn't feel like a covering, but a lack, a removal, a lessening. It was too dark to see their faces, but she could just make out the edge of their photograph on the dresser, and somehow she knew that this feeling would never fall away: his loss would tear from her for ever, as though God had picked up the photograph and begun to rip it apart, right down the middle, only he wasn't doing it quickly, he was taking his time, and he'd go on ripping from now until she died.

She cried for a long time until her heart slowed and she could breathe again, then she wiped her face with the edge of the blanket and rolled over, annoyed by the damp patches of spilt tears. She felt adrift. Usually when she cried that much, whether it was about Mother, or a cut knee when she was small, or later, about what Father had done, she'd feel relief when she stopped, but this time no weight lifted. The sky didn't clear.

She remembered Mother telling Mrs Emerson at her husband's funeral that he was safe with God now, and that time was a great healer. She hoped it was true, but she doubted it. She remembered Mrs Emerson's face too – the way she'd dabbed at the corners of her reddened eyes and clutched her stern son's arm and tried to move away as fast as possible. Mrs Emerson hadn't believed Mother either. There was only false respite in those words. Stan and all her memories of him would only get further away as more time passed. The rift would widen, the agony would expand. Like a cat with a cut, she could lick and lick all she liked, but this wound would never heal. She'd be alive longer and longer without him. One day she'd be older than he had been. Perhaps that was what people meant. It wasn't that anything got easier, it was that gradually she'd begin to forget what Stan meant to her. If she kept living, she'd stop remembering how much she loved him and that would lessen the pain.

She twisted the pillow in her fist. He was hers. They belonged to each other. She'd never let him go. And then the same thought over and over: she'd kill them. Whoever had done it to Stan, whoever had hurt him, she'd find them and kill them. The thought swelled and soothed.

Two car doors slammed outside, splitting the silence. She sat up and looked out. No need to hide, in the darkness no one could see her. On the street below, a shiny Buick had pulled up and four men were getting out. More doors banged. They weren't trying to be quiet. These men didn't care if they were seen. Not policemen. Three of them she couldn't make out, they were all similar heights and builds, but the fourth was short and thin. He took off his hat and smoothed back his sparse hair. There was something in the way he moved – a sliding, lolling gait, the walk of a much taller man, holding himself as though he was challenging someone to fight.

The guy in the automat, the one who'd hurt that woman. Joseph.

Then, all at once, she knew. The realisation emptied over her like a bucket of freezing water, goosing her skin. She stared ahead, holding the crochet to her breast as though it might protect her. They wanted the money – Stan's money. The cash under the boards that wasn't there. What else could it be? They were coming for it and she'd be in their way. Perhaps it was them who'd killed Stan. Or maybe they'd found out he was gone and seen their chance to come get it. Maybe they didn't know she was here. Maybe they did.

She scrambled off the bed. For a few seconds she stood still, her heart the only part of her in motion. She looked out of the window again. All the men were gone. Only the car was there, waiting by the kerb, looking sleek and strange and out of place, like a swan on a dried-up riverbed. They must already be inside, walking up the stairs.

She couldn't be here when they arrived. She'd go to Mrs Bianchi. Not Ben – they wouldn't hesitate to hurt him; she didn't want to take her trouble there. These guys might leave an old woman alone, but a Negro? They wouldn't need an excuse.

She emptied out the washing sack on the bed, pushing away thoughts of what was once inside. A few items tumbled out. A sock in need of darning. A chemise with a lipstick stain that made her think of Agnes. A shirt of Stan's missing a button that she pressed to her face. Pain hit the back of her throat and she reached for the bed to steady herself. Stan wouldn't bear it if she was hurt. Her mind had played a cruel trick. He was gone. She was running for herself now.

She dropped the shirt on the bed and rushed across to the dresser, pulled out the money and a few items of clothing, then shoved them deep inside the sack. Next she swept in everything on display – the photograph, her brush, the gloves and almost-gone perfume, Dicky's card, curling at the edges – and pressed Stan's shirt on top. This was all she cared about, all she had.

They might be outside by now, she had to hurry. No doubt the thin guy would recognise her right away. She must be out and into Mrs Bianchi's before they reached the end of the hall, otherwise she was done for.

She ran into the parlour and glanced around. Cracked china, worm-eaten chairs, a stained eiderdown Stan had rolled up as an extra pillow. There was nothing she wanted. Without him, everything looked rotten. At the door she pulled his coat over her shoulders – it was getting colder every day and she had no idea when, or if, she'd be back. She shuddered as the weight of it fell across her back. She wished he'd taken it. For the illusion of protection, if nothing else.

She put her palms on the rough door, listening, trying to hold her breath. Nothing. Carefully, as quietly as she could, she reached down and twisted the handle, inching it open as quickly as she dared. Behind her, a mouse scuttled beneath a cupboard. Tiny nails skittering on the boards. She turned. What if there was something else down there – something precious of Stan's – and those men found it? No footsteps, not yet. *Leave it. Get out.* But she had to check. It would only take a few seconds.

She raced back to the centre of the room and pulled up the threadbare rug, spotting the loose board, scrabbling at the edge, ignoring the splinters, the tears in her nails. In a second it was up and she was reaching inside, clawing around in the darkness. She stuck her head down. Nothing there. A waste of time.

Footsteps on the creaking floor outside. Muttering, men's voices. Too late, she'd lost her chance. What a fool she was. She straightened up, preparing to face them. Her hand glanced against something beneath the board. Not in the hole, above it. Something stuck to the underside of one of the other bits of wood. She bent down again and peered in. An envelope. She could see the crinkled sides. She pulled it free. No writing on either side, not that she could have read it. She started to rip.

A knock at the door. She froze, eyes popping, fear locking her hips, only just managing not to piss on the floor.

'Hello, anyone in?' A man's voice, low and firm, neither a whisper nor a shout. Perhaps they didn't want anyone to know they were there after all. The handle rattled.

Frances tossed the envelope into the sack. She ran to the window, opened it, climbed out on to the fire escape, then closed the sash behind her. Seconds later, a guy shouldered the door.

She crouched down and peeked through the window from the other side, trying to make sure she couldn't be seen. They swaggered in, then stopped, eyes wide. Two guys in front, another by the door with a hooked scar on his face keeping watch. The thin guy, Joseph, pushed through.

His eyes travelled, taking it all in, noting the pulled rug and the upturned floorboard. He jerked his head and the men fanned out. Two disappeared into the bedroom. Moments later the sound of crashing and tearing – of her whole life being upended – reverberated through Frances' chest, clinking the cups on the shelf. The third man closed the front door and leant against it. Frances saw a glint of metal at his waist and shuddered, pulling the sack in front of her. He smiled at no one, stretching the angry scar on his cheek so taut it looked like it might pull apart.

Joseph approached the hole in the floor and sat back on his haunches. 'Huh,' he said, 'what we got here? A little hidey-hole.' He stuck his head inside. 'Empty, eh? Now, the question is, where's it gone?'

'He must have moved it,' the guy by the door said.

'You think so?' The thin guy nodded. 'Sal, you ain't right about much, but you're right about that.'

The two men who'd gone to check the bedroom wandered back into the room.

'Nothing in there,' one of them said.

'Less than nothing,' the other one added.

Joseph nodded and started kicking their things around as though he was afraid to touch them. The guy by the door came over to see what he'd found.

'Not worth the walk, Sal,' Joseph said.

'You're right there.'

Outside, Frances heard singing in the hallway – deep, drunken, Italian voices. Mrs Bianchi's sons returning home late from a night out. The men heard it too. Each of them stepped quickly to the sides of the room, their hands inside their jackets, listening. After a time the voices faded and the men paced around the room again, upending chairs, looking inside cooking pots, rifling through drawers. The two who'd gone over Frances' room sat down and put their elbows on the table by the window. Frances ducked back.

'Nothing,' one of them said.

'Waste of time,' said the guy with the scar.

Frances could feel her breath easing, the cold night air wrapping itself around her legs. They'd go soon. There was no point in them staying. She heard the springs on the daybed creak.

'Now, Sal,' Joseph said, 'how pleased do you think the boss'll be with us if we come back with nothing?'

'Not too pleased.'

'That's right. So, we've got to get inside our friend Stanley's way of thinking. If you were creaming money off our packages, where would you hide it?'

Frances winced.

'Under that floorboard.'

'That's right, but it isn't down there, is it?'

She heard the bed creak again, then footsteps moving away, towards the door perhaps.

'So, if you don't want to hide it at home, what do you do with it?'

'I dunno.'

'Don't worry, Sal, I don't expect you to.'

Frances heard a rustle. If he was touching Stan's clothes, she'd scream. She raised her head a little and saw Joseph fingering her apron.

'You give something precious to someone you love, that's what. Mark my words, Sal. If we find his girl' – he shook the apron – 'we find the money.'

Frances ducked back down and hugged the bag, shifting her weight. The iron she was standing on groaned. Footsteps towards the window. She looked up, her heart pounding on the soft bag, the money crunching as she squeezed. Above her head the fire escape soared upwards, rusting metal criss-crossing against the black sky.

From Mrs Bianchi's, Italian voices swelled again, loud enough for Frances to hear. It was an old song they must have brought with them from home. The men grew still again, quieting their breathing. Joseph's hand paused at the sill, his head leaning towards the door.

Frances thought of the woman in the park who'd been dragged behind the car by her neck. Her toes clenched inside her shoes. She had to go. She pulled the strap of the sack over her head and started to climb, trying not to make a sound, moving as fast as she could. A coarse wind lifted the hair from her shoulders and the skirt from her legs. The sounds of the city murmured, not as loud as in the daytime, but present all the same, a constant throb of motion and muffled voices, a scream, the yell of a cat. If she could get out and over the top she could climb back down the other side and hammer on Mrs Bianchi's window. She scrabbled to the roof, shocked again at the size of the water tower, rubbing her hand across the slats of wood bulging across its round belly like thick feathers, wondering at the shining bronze roof, pointing upwards, like a puffed-up chick staring at the sky. Ducking underneath, she hugged a wooden strut. Below, she heard the sash scrape open and turned her head to the side, droplets of water leaking on to her cheek. She wished she could stop the sound of her breathing. She wished that Stan was with her like before, that she wasn't alone looking out at the swelling skyline, at the moon catching on the river.

She heard Sal say, 'Anything?'

Then Joseph, faintly: 'Nothing. Worth checking though, wasn't it. Let's get to the club. We'll squeeze Willie a little. The money ain't nothing more than change in the boss's pocket, but it's the principle of it, see, it was what Stan was gonna do with it.'

Frances heard the click of a lighter.

'We goin' then?'

'We're goin'. Fall's on the turn. Change of seasons. Can you smell it?'

Mrs Bianchi let out another cry. 'Oh, the poor boy, such a good boy, such a good man!' She blew her nose into the neat handkerchief her daughter-in-law had handed her. Two of the grandchildren, a boy and a girl, eyes still swollen from the sleep they'd been pulled from, wound themselves around her ankles.

Frances sat on the edge of her chair, clasping Mrs Bianchi's coarse hand, holding her own body still and upright, trying not to let the envelope slip from beneath her clothes, afraid the woman's tears would restart her own.

'Toni, Toni,' Mrs Bianchi said, 'fetch your Anna, where's the tea?'

Toni got up and walked into the other room, calling to his wife, the stagger gone from his gait. He looked gaunt. There was nothing like a murder to clear the head, Frances thought. Nothing like someone else's death to make you think about your own. She caught herself feeling sad for them, then remembered it was Stan and felt her breath snag in her chest.

Ben was sitting in the corner, nursing a mug of coffee. He'd helped her in through the window when she arrived. Strange he was here already, meeting with Mrs Bianchi and her sons in the middle of the night. It didn't make sense. He'd not cried when she told him like Mrs Bianchi, but his face had fallen in on itself and his cheeks still seemed hollowed out. Now his skin looked mottled and his mug was shaking in his hand. He looked up at her and for a second she felt a little less alone.

Angelo pulled his ear from the door. 'I think they've gone,' he said. 'Can't have been much else to ruin.' He tucked the large kitchen knife into the back of his belt and took up pacing again.

'Put the knife back in the dresser,' Mrs Bianchi said. 'Stupid boy, what will he do with it? Get us all killed, that's what.'

'Mama, please,' Angelo said, 'all I do is try to protect you, my family, Frances. Be quiet.'

'Respect, Angelo. You be quiet,' the other Anna said, waving her hand at her husband.

Mrs Bianchi began to sob again.

'Mama, please, quieten down, you're scaring the children.'

'They're right to be scared, Angie. Hoods at our door, Stanley dead. What next? I should never have come to this

place, should never have got on that boat. If my Vito was alive
I'd beat him, I'd kill him all over again for making us come.'

'Mama, please!'

'No, Angie, I mean it. Your nonna said don't do it, don't go.
She begged me, but I went anyway. For what? For mice in the
walls and babies sleeping on the stairs and drunk sons? Every
day I regret it.' She looked towards the ceiling. 'Nonna, Mama,
I'm sorry, you were right. I want to go home. This country! Lies,
Frances, all lies, from the moment we stepped on to the dock. No
work, no kindness, nowhere to live. We build their city, us and all
the others off the boats, and they shout at us in the street, they
smack our children, they say we are all thieves. Then this! Did
you see this, Frances? Did they tell you?' She leant over to the
table and waved a piece of paper in the air. 'Have you read? A
few weeks' notice! Then we're all out. They're tearing us down.
No warning. They must make space for improvement. Bigger
apartments. They say, they'll move us back, but they won't.
Where will we go? No, I should never have come. And now they
attack their own. What kind of place is this, what kind of safety,
what freedom? Poor girl. Anna! Where is the tea?'

Mrs Bianchi's daughter-in-law brought in a steaming pot
and the room fell silent while everyone drank. Frances felt their
eyes on her, sensed the questions behind their lips. She passed
the cup between her hands, the enamel almost too hot to hold,
enjoying the burn. Above their heads the grey parrot rattled at
his cage. She wasn't surprised about the tenement – there'd been
grumbled rumours since she moved in. Somewhere she was sad
about it, and sad for Mrs Bianchi and all the years she'd been
here, but she couldn't bring herself to say so.

After a time, Mrs Bianchi put her hand on Frances' arm. 'You
think these men that came here, they did it? They hurt Stanley?'

'I don't know,' Frances said. 'Maybe.' She glanced at Ben, but
the look he returned was blank and hard to read.

'Pigs!' Mrs Bianchi muttered. 'If they come back I will kill them myself.'

At her feet, the little girl stopped twisting her knitted doll and looked up with wide astonished eyes.

'Mama, watch your mouth,' Angelo said.

'What?' Mrs Bianchi frowned. 'I am helping them, especially this one. They must learn, Angie, the girls even more than the boys. Skin like snakes they will need. Smooth and tough, ready to shed.' She sighed.

The little boy took the doll from his sister and hit her over the head with it. The girl started to cry. 'You see?' Mrs Bianchi said. 'This is what I am talking about.' She stroked the little girl's head then reached down and slapped her lightly on the cheek. The boy laughed. The girl cried even louder. Anna bent down and cuddled the girl to her chest.

'Mama!' Angelo said. 'What are you doing?'

The girl stared at her grandmother from the crook of her mother's arm, shrinking back every time the old woman patted her swinging foot.

'She must learn, Angie,' Mrs Bianchi said, 'toughen up. If she cries every time her brother hurts her, if she waits for you or her mother to save her, what good will it do? What will happen when she grows, when a man takes something? She will cry and look around and wait to be saved. No, no, no. Not my granddaughter. I will teach her even if you won't. I will teach her to endure and to stand tall and to not take any trouble from anyone.'

'Mama, she is only four.'

'Exactly. Perfect age. Now, take her and her brother and all those tears and leave me and Frances and Ben in peace.'

Angelo stood still for a moment and Frances wondered if he was going to shout or complain. Instead he rolled his eyes and cocked his head at his wife. Anna carried the little girl through to the next room, ushering her son along without a word. As he walked past, Angelo patted Frances on the shoulder with a large warm palm. She shrank away, afraid his touch would set her off crying again.

Mrs Bianchi waited for them to leave, then bent close.

'You must run.'

'What?' Frances said.

'You're not safe here, not now.'

Frances clenched her toes. 'Why?'

'Because whoever did that to Stanley will be back for you – for Ben too, no doubt. Ben,' Mrs Bianchi beckoned to him, the word sounding like so much more than a name, 'you know how I feel.'

They both stood and held each other for a second, Ben's arms drawn wide around the old woman's girth; then he released her and stepped towards Frances. She stiffened, terrified he'd hold her too, but he put his hand on her shoulder instead.

'She's right. We need to leave,' he said.

Frances leant back. Something wasn't right.

Ben noticed her flinch. 'I'm not responsible,' he said. 'I might have done more. Before, I mean. You know how he was.'

'We all might have done.'

She let the tears stream down her face, not caring where they fell. She searched for the right words but found only moving pictures: Stan on the sidewalk, the blood and the filth and the wailing crowd searing her mind in blasts of light from the photographer's flashbulb, the scene all the more horrifying since she'd trapped the sight inside, refused to look at it, and now it was bursting to get free.

'The men that came have gone,' Frances said.

'They'll be back. And even if they don't return, someone worse will.' Ben turned to Mrs Bianchi. 'You should leave too.'

'I'm not going anywhere, not until they come to kick us out. I'm too old for running. Toni and Angelo will look after us if they have to.'

'We need some place safe,' Ben said. He went to the window and lifted the lace so he could look out.

'We can go later,' Frances said, 'after we've had some sleep. That'll give me time to gather my things, to work out where to—'

'No,' Ben said. 'We go now or we might not be able to. It's got to be some place they won't think to look, some place they'd never expect us to be, some place we can blend in. Most folks aren't used to seeing someone like me with a girl like you.'

Frances stared at him. His face was sad and soft like before, but his eyes flickered when he caught her gaze. He knew something, she could sense it. Perhaps, if she tore at his skin, if she took a hammer to his skull, if she thrust her hand into his head, she might pull the knowledge free. Her rage hovered and threatened to spill. She clenched it back behind her teeth. When she spoke she finally sounded like herself.

'I know where we can go.'

GREENWICH VILLAGE

27 November 1932

04.08

P art of Frances was annoyed they looked so excited. They'd been kind, yes. They'd helped, hadn't they? They'd taken them in and fed them. But still. At least Dicky was managing to contain it. Jacks, on the other hand, looked like a hungry dog.

'So, tell me again,' Jacks said, waving her holder around, the smoke from the almost-finished cigarette drifting across her face, 'you're in fear of your lives?' She was sitting on the table, her bare toes teetering on the edge of Dicky's chair.

'Yes,' Ben said. 'That's what I'm worried about.' He frowned. 'I wanted to get Frances out as fast as possible. Now Stan's been . . . now he's . . . now he's gone, I'm responsible, you see?'

'Yes, quite,' Jacks said, 'how very noble of you. Frances, have another. It'll take the edge off.'

Frances did as she was told. The hot bourbon burnt all the way down, settling in her stomach like a dropped stone. She wiped her lips with the back of a shaking hand.

'Top her up, Agnes, darling, won't you?' Jacks called over her shoulder.

Agnes walked in from the kitchen with the bottle and refilled Frances' glass. She moved to take the bottle back but Jacks caught her arm. 'You might as well leave it.' Agnes nodded, a sad smile flickering towards Frances.

'Well,' Dicky said, leaning back in his chair, 'you must stay as long as you need. In the meantime I think we should tell someone of your suspicions. If what you're saying is true, if Stan was murdered and now whoever did it is out to get you and Frances, I'm sure someone down at the station will take notice.'

'I'll talk to Frank,' Jacks said, 'he's bound to know something.' She reached across and brushed her fingers over the back of Frances' hand. The action was so swift Frances wondered why she'd bothered. 'So sorry again,' Jacks said, 'I know how close you were.'

Frances nodded but didn't look up. In a moment Agnes would return from the kitchen and she'd be able to raise her eyes, to breathe. She pressed her stomach and shifted on her chair, feeling the paper rustle against her skin. At some point she'd make an excuse, go to the bathroom and rip the envelope apart.

'No,' Ben said, 'I'd rather keep things quiet if that's all right. At least until I can look into it. We sure are obliged to you for letting us stay here. Can't ask for more than a safe haven. Nothing else to do, not on our account.'

Frances listened to him, anger swelling again. 'You say you don't know what happened, but you must.' She didn't look up.

Jacks raised her eyebrows at Dicky.

'I told you,' Ben said, still not looking anyone in the eye, 'we were moving packages around for Willie. I never had any notion what was in them. We'd take them to a drop-off point, give them to some guy, always someone different, and that was that, an extra fold of notes in every pay-check. Easy money, Stan said.

But then, the past few weeks Stan had been going off by himself. I kept trying to follow him, ask him what was going on, but he always pushed me away. Said it wasn't the sort of thing I'd want to get involved in.'

'And that night he was stabbed,' Frances said. 'Where did you find him?'

'At the club. He was there when I went in to play. Slumped in Willie's office bleedin' all over his chair.'

Agnes came in and lowered a tray of drinks on to the table. Her hands were shaking and some of the liquid slopped out of the glasses.

'Agnes!' Jacks chastised her.

'For God's sake, shut up,' Dicky said. 'Can't you see the girl's in a tangle? Sit down, Agnes. Ignore the beast. You've done enough. She's worried about her love, of course, who wouldn't be?' He smiled pointedly at Frances and reached across to squeeze her arm.

Frances flushed and looked at Ben. He was swirling the liquid in his glass, but she could tell from the set of his jaw he'd not missed Dicky's intention.

'It's not that,' Agnes said, sinking into a chair. She smiled across the table, fighting back tears. 'I mean, it is that, of course it is. I don't know how you can stand it.'

'I can't,' Frances murmured.

'I remember,' Agnes said. 'All you've got when it's fresh and raw is distraction. You need to keep busy. Coming here and working with Dicky after Stella died was the only thing that helped me.'

Jacks cocked her head. 'Agnes is right about taking your mind off things, but I do think we should try and figure some of this out before you forget any details. The only thing that'll make you and the rest of us feel any better is getting whoever did this locked up. You say some men came looking for something? Had you met them before? Had your brother?'

Frances didn't want to answer, to remember, to turn the events into words, but her mouth moved anyway. 'Yes,' she whispered.

Ben shot her an anxious look.

Dicky put his glass down, dabbed at the corners of his mouth with a napkin and sat forward. 'You knew these men?'

'Not exactly,' Frances said, 'I met one of them once. In a diner. Stan knew him.'

'And what does he look like?' Jacks asked.

'Joseph,' Frances muttered. 'Thin. Greasy hair. Funny walk.'

'Well, that doesn't exactly narrow it down,' Jacks said. 'Anything else? Any other details? Anything strange? Last name? I don't suppose you know what it was they were looking for?'

Ben looked at Frances again. Dicky noticed.

'Do you feel like you're in any danger now?' Dicky asked. 'Because if you do, we can help.'

'No,' Frances said, 'no, I'm all right, it's just . . . '

Ben sighed loudly and put down his glass. 'It's my fault,' he said. 'She doesn't want to say anything because I told her not to. I didn't want you to be involved. I feel bad enough bringing all this trouble to your door. The less you know the better.'

'I'm afraid I don't agree,' Dicky said. 'I see your logic, but I'd feel a damn sight safer knowing as much as you do about who might be looking for you. I have responsibilities. Not least to these two.' He gestured towards Jacks and Agnes. 'I'm sure you understand. If any of us is in direct danger, we all have a right to know from whom and why.'

Ben pressed his lips together and leant back.

'I think,' Jacks said, 'that our friend Ben here knows more than he's letting on.'

Frances looked at him. The whites of his eyes were honeyed,

like tea-stained milk. Apart from his love for her brother, what else did she really know of him?

'Come on.' Jacks bent over the table, her velvet elbows grinding on the dirty plates.

'I don't know anything more than what I've said.' Ben's voice was tight – caught around his sorrow or a lie, Frances couldn't tell.

'Leave him,' Dicky said. 'Leave him alone, Jacks, for God's sake.' He twisted at the edges of his cuffs. He looked fidgety, Frances thought, like he had an itch somewhere he couldn't scratch.

The air around the table thickened and charged.

Jacks lurched forward and threw up her hands. 'I will not be quiet. He comes here for safety, asks us to help, but why should we when he refuses to tell us what's going on? I don't know him. None of us do. You can't ask us to trust the words of a, of a . . . '

'Of a what?' Ben stood, knocking his glass over. Frances felt the liquid drip from the edge of the table on to her thigh.

'A . . . ' Jacks stalled.

'A nigger?' Ben shot the word at her. 'Is that what you were going to say?'

'Certainly not.' Jacks didn't blush, she was too angry for that. 'I was going to say two-bit sax player. We don't use that kind of language here. Dicky's donated more money to struggling black artists than anyone in this city. Hell, we had tea with Aaron and Alta last week. We aren't prejudiced here. Not in the Village, not any more.'

Agnes glared at Jacks. 'Then don't speak like you are.'

'A man's dead, Aggie,' Jacks said, 'Frances here is on the run. I'm well within my rights to ask a few questions.'

Ben reached down and picked up his glass.

Frances grabbed his wrist. 'If you know anything, you've got to say,' she said. 'Please. For Stan, for me?'

He shook his head and gripped the edge of the table.

'For heaven's sake,' Jacks said. 'I don't believe a single thing you've said since you got here.'

'I don't care what you believe.' Ben's voice was quiet, but Frances could hear the anger rasping beneath.

'You're lying to protect yourself.' Jacks had raised her voice, thrusting her finger over the table.

Frances saw the words catch and ignite. Ben started hollering. Stan's killers had set a match to him, but Jacks' words fanned the flames. He lifted his hand and threw. The glass sailed through the air and burst across the floor. Dicky stood and held his palms up, begging for calm, but Jacks and Ben kept on yelling, their voices swelling with each exchange. Perhaps, Frances thought, Ben had been lit even earlier. His fuse ran all the way back to the war, to what he had seen, to what he had done.

The louder they got, the more Frances shook. Her teeth chattered. She tried to run her fingers through her hair, but they caught on the knots. She tried to stop listening, to distract herself like Agnes said, and looked past Jacks' head to a painting on the wall, her heart pounding as though she'd run for miles. Splashes of black on a white background. Lines of bright blue. Small yellow dots as fierce and steady as wild dogs' eyes. She had no idea what it was supposed to be, but she could feel it, she could sense the chaos fidgeting within the suffocating border of the frame. A red line ran down the centre, splitting the image in half, as dark and thick as congealed blood.

She was sick of it. Sick of the lies, sick of the secrets, sick of trying to do the right thing. What did anything matter now? She stood as though electrified. 'Enough!' she shouted, feeling their startled eyes on her. She reached into her clothes, rummaged around, then flicked her wrist. The envelope spun a few times in the air and landed next to Agnes where it teetered precariously on the edge of the table.

For a few seconds no one spoke. Everyone stared at her.

'Well,' Jacks said, 'that's one way to get something off your chest.' She reached out and plucked the envelope off the table. 'Que ça?'

Ben was shaking, his eyes fixed on the envelope. 'Jacks, can you pass that to me?'

Frances glanced at him. His eyes were drawn back, his hand stretched over the table, fingers reaching for it.

'I don't know what it is,' Frances said. 'I found it underneath our floorboards. I think Stan hid it.'

'Well,' Dicky said, 'I think for all our sakes you'd better start opening.'

Jacks handed back the envelope. Frances hesitated, thinking of Stan's grin, his hands, his hat on the sidewalk, of them running together across an open field towards a full river. Of cold water rising over their heads.

'Come on!' Jacks yelled.

Slowly, Frances started to tease open one of the corners of the envelope.

Two pieces of paper inside. One was a postcard, the kind businesses use to advertise. On the front was a picture of the outside of the Catagonia Club, but it was a brighter, cleaner version of the club than she remembered. Two girls she didn't recognise, one black, one white, stood on either side of the door, matching shorts, their knees cocked, hands welcoming the looker inside. She flipped it. Two words, an 'I' and an 'S'. Some other letters she knew but couldn't pull together. She cursed herself. The usual shame rose up, but then it drained away, her cheeks cooling as fast as they'd flushed. What did it matter now?

She held it up. 'Can someone help me,' she said, 'I can't read.'

Agnes wiped her eyes with her fingers. 'You should have said.' She smiled, walked around the table and bent to look over Frances' shoulder. She read the words slowly. 'It just says – "I'm

Sorry".' She smoothed the top of Frances' head and kissed her on the cheek.

Frances looked up at her, resisting the urge to grab on to her hand and pull her away. To run and never look back.

'Well,' Jacks said, 'there's another mystery.'

Frances traced her finger across the swirling lines, imagining Stan's hand moving over the card. She'd been hoping for a few kind words, a hint of affection. An answer. Not another empty apology.

'And what about that one?' Jacks asked.

Frances nodded. The edges of the other item were creased and bent. There was a large brown stain on one side but she couldn't tell what had been spilt. Too late to stop now. She flipped it over. A photograph. Everyone crowded round to look.

It had been taken in the club. Frances could tell from the checkerboard tablecloths. Eight or nine people were squashed into the frame with their arms around each other, smiling, laughing, having a good time. There was Stan at the back, big and healthy like he used to be, head and shoulders above everyone else, grinning. She touched her finger to his face. On either side of him were two girls, beautiful, one with a flush of freckles on her cheeks – Colette. The other had long curly hair. Next to them the Mayor was smiling, whispering into the ear of the girl beside him, who had her hair tied back and looked familiar too, but whom Frances couldn't place. She was staring into the camera with a lost look in her eyes, the only one in the picture not smiling. On the other side another tall man, his back to the camera. At the front two more women, both with long hair cascading down their arms, the length unusual – not in fashion at all. And behind them, walking out of shot, his face almost merging with the darkness, his expression blurred – Ben.

'When was this taken?' Frances looked at Ben. He'd walked away to the sofa as soon as he'd seen the image and was now sitting with his head in his hands.

He didn't reply.

Agnes leant over the picture and let out a little cry. 'Oh,' she said, 'it can't be!'

All at once Frances remembered where she'd seen the sad girl before. It was Stella, Agnes' sister. Her hair was different, but it was the same girl.

Agnes snatched up the picture, pushed past Frances, and grabbed at Ben's collar as if to strangle him. 'My sister!' she choked. 'What did they do to her? Tell me! What do you know?' She held the photograph in front of Ben's face, pointing at Stella. 'Did you meet her when she came to the club? What were they doing in there? Did she look happy? Frightened? I don't care what was going on, who you get in trouble. Speak!'

Ben didn't look up.

Frances went over to him. 'I said,' she repeated, 'when was this taken?'

He looked at her. 'I'm not sure. Sometime last year maybe. I don't remember.'

'Hang on a second,' Jacks said. She moved over to a sideboard, opened a drawer and put on some gold-rimmed glasses. She plucked the photograph from Agnes' hands and held it close to her face, pointing at the man on the edge. 'Kane. What a menace he is,' she said.

'Fallen out again, have you?' Dicky said.

'Him?' Jacks said, jabbing at the image. 'I'm over him.'

'What's he done now?' Dicky asked.

'More of the same,' Jacks said. 'I'm bored of it. He disgusts me.'

'Who is Kane?' Frances asked. 'I mean, what does he do?'

'He builds things, darling. One way or another he's been responsible for half the Manhattan skyline.'

Frances felt herself getting hot. She looked at Ben. 'You need to start talking,' she said. 'I don't know what's going on but something sure is. Maybe you're still trying to protect Stan, maybe you're trying to help me, maybe you're only here to help yourself. All I know is he's gone. He's gone and there's nothing any of us can do about it. But you know something, for God's sake. Tell us, can't you?'

'I don't know,' Ben said, his eyes welling. 'I'm sorry, I can't.' He raked his hands across the top of his head and looked back at the floor. 'I'm sorry,' he said after a time, 'I can't remember much.' He pointed at Agnes' sister. 'She came in with the Mayor. Him and Kane always have girls on their arms, two or three each most nights. I think I saw her once or twice but I can't say if she was happy or sad. I was playing mostly.' He looked up at Agnes, hoping that was enough. 'Can't you ask her?' he said.

'No,' Agnes grimaced, 'she's dead.'

Ben's face contorted. 'When?'

'February.'

'How?'

'Don't worry,' Agnes said, her voice taking on a bitter tone Frances hadn't heard before, 'she wasn't murdered like Stan. She killed herself. Penn Station, front of a train. Someone was blackmailing her and she couldn't take it any more, couldn't keep paying. Now that someone is asking me for more money.'

Jacks sighed and walked back to the table looking for something to use as an ashtray. 'All right,' she said, tapping her holder on a plate, 'I don't know about anyone else, but I need a refill.' She picked up the bourbon and topped up everyone's glasses.

Frances couldn't drink. She looked at Ben. 'Talk.'

'All right,' he whispered. 'All right.' He paused and slumped, giving in at last. 'Heroin.'

'What?' Dicky twisted at the hanky in his top pocket.

'Cocaine too, if it came through. That's what was in the

packages. Mrs Bianchi got paid to line linen with it. Stan sorted it out with her. We delivered the packages where people needed it. Came back with the money. Simple, like I said. Willie had most of the guys at the club runnin' for him. A little bit extra for us at the end of the week. But something else was going on too, something to do with the Mayor's girls, and I swear on my brother's grave I don't know what it was. I asked Stan over and over, but he wouldn't say. Then when that girl turned up in the papers with her neck stretched behind that car, and I saw Stan's face and Willie's too, I knew something was going on. But he wouldn't speak, whatever I said, he just wouldn't tell me.' Ben looked up at Frances. 'I'm sorry. I swore I wouldn't tell you what he was doing. Your brother was ashamed. It was the last thing I promised him. That you'd never find out where that money he was sending you and your folks came from.'

Frances stared at him. Heroin. Some sort of drug, that much she knew. A bad one from the way everyone else's faces were looking. Drops of sweat had gathered at Ben's temples. She felt hot too. Hot and numb and sick. So that was why Jacob had paid so much for Mrs Bianchi's linen, and why Dicky had looked so broken when Jacks tipped out his pillowcase all over the floor. They were all taking it. Taking it or buying it or selling it. No wonder Stan had acted so ashamed. She reached for the back of the chair to steady herself.

'So what am I supposed to do now?' she said.

'It seems to me,' Dicky replied, sitting down, sipping from his tumbler, 'you've got three options. One – keep your heads down, your mouths closed, and stay hidden. Like I said before, you're welcome to stay here as long as you like. Then there's option—'

Jacks let out a chuckle. 'Don't be ridiculous, darling, Frances isn't a fool or a coward, she's not going to—'

'You never let me finish, do you?' Dicky said. 'As I was saying, then there's option two. Go to the club and poke around.'

'I don't think that's a good idea,' Ben said, flicking his eyes around the table.

'You're not my brother,' Frances said quietly, anger rising up again, bringing with it a moment of clarity. 'I don't have a brother any more, so I'll be doing things my own way from now on.'

Ben frowned at his fingers twisting over on themselves, as though he was annoyed at their refusal to knot. 'And option three?' he asked, turning to Dicky.

'She goes to the police. She takes all this, tells them about Stan and the men. Agnes goes too, talks about her sister, and we see what comes of it.'

'Not an option,' Ben said. 'It's too—'

'Did you not hear what she said?' Agnes put her arm around Frances. 'She'll be making her own decisions from now on.'

THE CATAGONIA CLUB
133rd ST

5 December 1932

04.10

They sat in Willie's car outside the club. Frances leant forward and wiped at the glass. Her fingertips numbed the more she rubbed. It was a waste of time: a fine drizzle had begun to fall and the smears on the windscreen were outside, not in. The car smelt exactly like Willie – smoke and sawdust and good times. The split leather on the seats scratched at the back of her thighs but she was glad to be sitting all the same.

Willie was standing outside the car, leaning on the driver's window talking to Ben. He shook his head slowly, sucking deeply on his cigar as though he was at his mother's breast, then smoothed the water from his hair and wiped his hand on his jacket.

'I told you. I can't help.'

'We ain't askin' for much.' Ben rested the photograph on his knees and rubbed at his hands, trying to warm them.

'You said that yesterday.'

'I know, but maybe you've thought it through. Maybe you've changed your mind.'

'You said that too.'

'Come on, Willie. I've always been good to you, haven't I? I've stayed late and helped all the kids with their horns. I've fixed that drum kit a hundred times. Looked out for the girls, too.'

'You have. But if I'd known you were storing all those favours up, waiting for the right time to throw them back at me, I'd have told you not to bother. I've got a business here. I got people depending on me. The only thing that makes sense is keeping the club runnin'. Anything else ain't worth my breath.' He wet his lips and sucked again, leaning back to let the smoke rise up over his head. 'I'm lettin' you borrow the car, ain't I? What more do you want?'

'The car's no use unless we know where we're headed.'

'I thought you wanted to sit here in it until you saw someone come out at closin' you felt like following.'

'That's right, but we've been sittin' for days now and nuthin'. We need you. Stan needs you.'

'Don't go puttin' that on me too. You know how I feel about him.' Willie glanced across at Frances. She could hear the regret in his voice, but she didn't care. If he wasn't going to tell them what he knew, he could keep all the sorrys for himself. Ben was getting nowhere.

She heard Agnes sigh from the back of the car. The seats squeaked as she moved around.

Frances leant over Ben and mustered a smile. 'My brother often spoke about you.'

'He did, did he?' Willie nodded at her and kept smoking.

'He said you were the finest boss he ever had.'

'Well, he wasn't wrong about that.'

'He said he could trust you, and that that was a rare thing.'

Willie eyed her. She could see he knew what she was doing and wondered if she could flatter him enough to get past his suspicions. 'Another thing he got right. There ain't many around here like Willie. I'm a man of my word.'

'That's what he said. That I could count on you. That if I ever needed anything and he wasn't around that I should come to you.'

'He said that too, did he?'

'He sure did.'

She fell quiet for a moment. The drizzle kept falling. The club thudded softly against the sidewalk. A group of girls bustled down the steps, so flushed from the spent night, they dragged their coats along the street.

'My brother was a good man.' She didn't look at him this time. 'He didn't deserve what they did to him.'

'He didn't.' She heard his voice change, the catch in his throat.

'He loved working here.'

'I know. He was a good man. And there ain't many of those.'

'Not any more.'

Drifts of water gathered and ran down the glass. She waited.

Willie sighed and tapped his cigar out on the edge of the window. Frances stole a glance at him. His face looked hard like baked earth, but something had shifted in it, as though her words had forced a crack.

'All right,' he said, 'you got me. You want the truth? You want to know what I do, what Stan helped me with? Let's say I'm a facilitator. I make things happen. Good times, friendships, business. I let these men in this picture' – he pointed at the photograph on Ben's lap – 'use this club like their own office. They come, chat a little, make friends, do deals. Simple as that. Sometimes they take my girls out. Sometimes they borrow my men for extra jobs. I get paid, they get paid, the club keeps busy, we all stay happy. But the past few months some of my girls haven't turned up for work.' He pointed at the photograph again, at the two women with long hair. 'This one and this one. And now your brother winds up the way he has. I think – and you didn't hear this from me – that some people have been covering their behinds. I'd like to tell you they're fine men, upstanding citizens, but I'd be lying if I did. Truth is, and I ain't proud of it, without them this club woulda been shut down long ago.'

He took another cigar from his pocket, bit off the end, spat it on the ground and set it alight. A man and his girl spilt out of the club and Frances heard a woman inside start up a song. She couldn't make out the words, but the voice that growled out was like nothing she had ever heard. Throaty and sweet, soaring and coarse all at the same time. The couple ran down the steps, leaning into each other against the night. The door shut and the song hushed.

'What did Stan do?' The question stuck in her mouth.

'He helped the people I asked him to. A man called Kane needed packages taken to the Mayor, real quiet. Stanley did that. Sometimes folks refused to do what we asked, so sometimes they got hurt. Stanley didn't like doing it, mind you. That much I know. Ben here tried to talk him out of it. I did too, after a time. He was getting awful wound up. White as a ghost, late for work, not a smile for anyone. Bad for business. He shouted at us, didn't he, Ben?' Ben nodded and looked at the steering wheel. 'He hollered at us for sure, told us to mind our business, that he needed the money. Sending it home, so he said.'

Frances searched Willie's face, hunting for a lie. So all this was for her? For Mother and Father and the farm? She sensed Willie wasn't telling her all of it, but that what he was saying was somewhere near the truth. She hoped he was honest about liking Stan at least, even if he was lying about the rest. Guilt throbbed through her – the most God-awful toothache she'd ever had. If only she hadn't taken the money from under the floor. The tips of her fingers and toes felt hot and itchy, all her edges yelling to be scratched. For weeks now her skin had felt like it was on fire. She wanted to crawl under the leather seats with a bottle of liquor and let the echo of the woman's voice drag her into the dark, but she had to keep asking. The only thing that mattered now was finding out who hurt Stan. Perhaps that would douse the flames. Perhaps the truth would put her out.

Agnes squeezed her shoulder from the back seat.

'And this girl? Will you tell us now?' Frances asked, leaning over and pointing at Stella's sullen face.

'Oh yes, a real ten-dollar Tess that one,' Willie said. 'Looks sad here, but I ain't never seen a girl so ready to party. I'm pretty sure the Mayor was sweet on her before he fell for Freckles. She wasn't one of mine though and I ain't seen her around lately.'

Frances glanced at Agnes in the mirror. She was staring at the rain outside with a tight look on her face, twisting a strand of hair at the back of her neck until the skin went taut.

Willie bent forward and splayed his hands on the edge of the window, the guilt loosening his tongue. 'The thing is, in an ideal world these guys would be uptown in their own clubs and we'd have enough in our pockets to keep the good times rollin'. But the world don't work like that, at least not yet, and ole Willie gotta make a livin', and the best way to do that down here is to get the rich whites in. That's why it's free drinks for all those picture stars sittin' preenin' at the back in there. Makes everyone feel nice and safe to see the faces on the screen down here in the dark, if you get my meanin'. The long and short of it is, the Catagonia wouldn't exist without those men. And not just the club, come to think of it, half the city's going up cause of those two.'

'What?' Frances said, leaning forward again.

'I mean, the Mayor makes sure his blue-eyed friend there gets all the best tenders in the city. Rockefeller, that one next to the new Empire State, most of Times Square, I heard them talkin' plenty about it. Wouldn't be nuthin' scrapin' the sky if I didn't keep the drink flowin' to those two all the way down here. And with the amount they swallow and spend, with all the other white folks they welcome here with all those deep pockets, it doesn't serve ole Willie to go around askin' too many questions about where this or that girl went or what might have happened to your brother. I'm sorry to say it, but that's the truth.'

He paused, sucked on his cigar and blew smoke into the air, then locked eyes with Frances, the sadness twisting. 'If I'd known what would end up happening to him, I mighta done things differently. The only reason I'm sayin' any of this, and I mean the only reason, is cause I owe Stanley, and now he's gone I owe you, and I'm seein' these words as that debt paid. It won't end well. Goes without sayin' I don't want you runnin' around town tattle-tailin' this to anyone and it's worth bearing in mind that those two – Kane and the Mayor – got all the police in their pocket, some say judges too. I seen 'em down here drinkin' an' dancin' an' courtin', so ain't nuthin' to be won by you goin' down the station. Anyways' – he straightened up again and blew more smoke into the sky – 'what I know ain't much and I'll deny what I do know if I'm asked.'

He gripped Ben's shoulder. 'Now I've gotta get movin' – only three more songs in Billie's set then I'm back on with the boys to keep this place movin' till sun-up. I sure am sorry about Stanley, but if I was you, I'd quit askin' any more questions. The more you ask, the more you'll be in trouble, and one thing I can say for certain is ain't everyone like Willie. Ain't everyone so ready to loose their tongues on account of paying back a friend. Most are out for themselves, and if they can put you in hot water to save their own skins they'll do it. Don't give 'em an excuse. Keep your mouth shut, your head down and your eyes open. That's the best advice I can give.'

He paused, snubbed out his cigar between his fingers then tucked what was left into his top pocket. When he looked at Frances again, his expression faltered. 'On the other hand, I might not do that if it was my brother.' He sighed. 'I guess I owe Stan, like Ben said.' He coughed and lowered his voice. 'When the Mayor leaves tonight, follow him.'

Drizzle clung to the car all the way downtown. It fogged the windows and flicked off the wipers and made it hard as hell to see where the Mayor was headed. Each time his car turned down another street, Ben cursed. More than once Agnes thrust her arm between the seats and shouted, 'There, there! That way, that way!' Then Ben would jerk the wheel and Frances would press her feet down hard into the footwell as though she was the one controlling the brake. By the time they stopped at a red light the rain had gotten so heavy the city looked like nothing more than a smudge of light and shadow.

The Mayor was two cars in front. The lights on the traffic tower changed from red to green and his car swerved down a side-street.

'He can't live here,' Frances said.

Ben didn't look at her. His face was set as though skin and bone had turned to plaster. He pulled off the main street and began to inch the car between the buildings. The Mayor's car stopped about fifty yards ahead. Rain sluiced off the fender at the back and poured on to the cobbles.

'I can't get any closer,' Ben said.

They all leant forward as the engine died, squinting through the glass, listening to the rain thudding on the roof.

Up ahead, a door slammed. Agnes blew out her breath in a

rush. The Mayor got out, pulled a large umbrella from the back seat then stepped briskly to the passenger door to help Colette.

'What's wrong with her?' Agnes asked.

'I'm not sure.'

Frances bent closer, trying to clear the screen with her palm again. The girl was leaning up against the Mayor as though her legs had failed her. She swayed away from him and he grabbed her waist to stop her from falling.

'She looks tanked,' Agnes said. 'Funny, though, she seemed fine outside the club.'

'Perhaps she's ill,' Frances said, although she didn't believe it. The fire in her hands had started up again. She squeezed them together to stop the burn.

The Mayor half carried, half dragged Colette through a small doorway beneath a single light and disappeared.

'What now?' Agnes said.

'Now we follow,' Frances said, reaching down to pull the catch on the door.

'No.' Ben's hands held the steering wheel so tightly his knuckles looked like they might split through the skin. 'I don't think we should go in there,' he said.

'What are you talking about?' Frances asked. 'What have we come here for, if not to follow? What's the point? We gotta go look in a window at least.' Frances moved to open the door again but he caught hold of her arm. She shook him off. 'What's wrong with you? You help, then you don't. You say you want to protect me, but half the time I can't find you, and when I do you're silent as a grave. Unless you speak up and give me a reason not to, I'm going.'

'Frances, calm down.' Agnes reached for her shoulder.

She flipped her hand away. 'No, I won't. I've not come this far to stay safe. I've nothing to lose now. Stan wouldn't have stopped for me and I won't for him.'

She pulled the catch and the door swung out. Freezing air wound its way around her ankles, icy drops of water spotted her skirt. She sucked at the cold, trying to breathe away the sorrow blocking the back of her throat.

'No.' Ben reached across and pulled the door closed. He sighed and sat back on the leather then rubbed his hands across his face. 'Can't you see what a bind I'm in?'

'For God's sake,' Frances said, 'what is it?'

'I've heard of this place,' he said, the words sounding as though he'd had to drag them from somewhere underground.

'What?'

'I've heard some of what happens in there, and you don't want to know.'

'You knew we were coming here?'

'No. I hoped he was heading home.'

'But when we got downtown, then you knew?'

'I thought he might be coming here, yes.'

'So,' Agnes said, jutting her head between them, 'what happens in there?'

'Things girls like you don't need to hear about, let alone see.'

Frances opened the door again. 'Sorry, not good enough, you gotta do better than that.'

Ben reached over and shut it again. 'You are the most infernal, God-forsaken woman I have ever met. If it wasn't for your brother I'd leave you here to fend for yourself. Will you not listen when someone's trying to help?'

'If that place in there's so bad, shouldn't we be helping the Mayor's girl? From the way she was sagging towards the floor she looked like she needed more assistance than any of us. We all know she's not ill.'

Ben's mouth twitched as though he was about to say something but he stayed silent and stared at her. The rain thundered at the roof. After a time he bent forward and rested his head on the wheel.

'All right,' he said, looking up, 'but if we go in it's on my terms. You two do exactly what I say when I say it. If this place is what I think it is, everything depends on it.'

At first Frances wasn't sure what all the fuss was about. It was surely a speakeasy, just like the Catagonia. She could hear the music from the street. The only difference was that the entrance was hidden away and there was no one waiting in line outside.

Ben had told her and Agnes to spruce themselves up and show a little more flesh so she'd borrowed some of Agnes' lipstick. At first Agnes had refused to change anything, but then Ben had said he wouldn't take them, and Frances had squeezed her hand and eventually she'd been persuaded. Frances suggested she take off her slacks and use her scarf as a skirt. Now Agnes' calves looked strange, quivering in the streetlight.

Ben had thrown Willie's overcoat over his shoulders and set his hat at a jaunty angle. His handkerchief peeped out of the top pocket of his jacket like a gentleman – like Dicky.

He banged on the door and Frances held her breath and fixed a smile on her face, ready to play her part.

A little shutter in the door opened and a man peered out.

'Yeah?'

'We're here to see Harry.'

'Ain't no Harry here. You're in the wrong place, friend.'

The man slammed the little window shut. Ben knocked on it again. The man opened it and Agnes giggled like Ben had told her to. She bent over and grinned at Frances and clutched her arm. 'Ooh, I feel ever so queer,' she said, and threw her head back, doing an excellent impression of Jacks at her most fried.

'Friend, I don't think you heard me right,' the man said. 'You're in the wrong place. Hell, looks to me like you're in

the wrong part of town altogether.' He peered out at them
and smirked.

Ben stepped forward, nice and easy, like he said he would.
'Look, I know you don't know me and I don't know you, but
I got a meeting in here with Harry and he's gonna be mighty
angry at you if you don't let me in. Then again, if I was you I
wouldn't let me in either.' He stroked his chin and pretended to
think. 'Harry's waiting on these ladies but he won't wait for ever
and I'm not the kind of guy to break my word. How's about I
make things easy for the both of us?' Ben reached into his jacket
pocket and pulled out the notes.

Frances winced. She hoped the man didn't notice, but she
couldn't help it. Ben was handing over a quarter of her money
from Stan, just to get inside the place. She'd agreed to it, but
now she saw the dollars pass from one man's hand to the other
she had to fix her feet to the floor and clamp her arms to her
sides and shout 'no' silently over and over to keep from reaching out and grabbing what was hers and running off down the
street. It had better be worth it.

The man eyed them through the gap, yanked the money
from Ben's hand and slammed the shutter again. Frances
jumped forward, ready to pull on it, but Ben held her back.

'Wait,' he mouthed.

After a moment the door swung open. The man stood back
so they could make their way inside. He refused to take Ben's
hand when he offered it and didn't speak. Frances passed by,
not looking at him, staring ahead while he grabbed her behind,
gathering up the flesh in his fist and squeezing until it hurt,
as though he was checking to see if she was ripe. She hid her
shock and smiled at him, thinking of her money in his pocket,
imagining her fist slamming into his doughy face.

It would have looked and sounded like any other joint in the city, were it not for the girls.

Frances huddled close to Agnes and Ben at the bar, pretending to have a good time. All around men laughed and joked and punched each other on the shoulder and puffed their fat cigars towards the varnished ceiling. In one corner a guy with his jacket off and his sleeves rolled up thumped an upbeat rhythm out of an upright piano. Waitresses milled between the tables, the same as in the Catagonia, only with shorter shorts and falser smiles, their glazed eyes a blink away from crying.

Here and there a few rich-looking women – various kinds of Jacks – sucked on their cigarette holders and sipped politely, most of them older than Frances, most of them doing a good job of pretending to have fun, their dresses expensive, the pearls in their ears grabbing the light. Frances was glad of them but she hated them too. How could they be here and do nothing? She held Agnes' eyes over her drink, willing her to keep it together. They should have listened. She should have listened.

Ben leant in and smiled so wide and stiff Frances feared his face might crack. 'Another drink, ladies?' he asked.

They both nodded, although the liquor was only making everything worse.

He beckoned the barman, and a cheer went up. Frances looked in the shot mirror behind the bar and caught sight of one of the girls standing on the middle of a table. How could they do it? She tried to look away but her eyes refused. The girl was younger than her. She had dark red hair, the longest Frances had ever seen, her skin as white and mottled as a full moon. She was naked, luminous in the lamplight, apart from a small paper skirt that was being torn from her by one of the six men sitting at her feet. As he ripped he threw his head back and laughed. The girl twisted her arms towards the ceiling, oblivious to what he was doing, her hands spiralling together as though she was in a trance, swaying to music only she could hear. Beneath her, the men clapped and chanted until the torn paper was piled on the table and there was nothing left to pull. They watched her turn for a moment, sitting back on their fat rumps, sighing, folding their hands in their laps, then the man who'd unwrapped her yanked her down and cradled her, licking her face and whispering, her eyes so empty she might as well have been dead.

All over the room the same thing was happening with other girls, each of them with long hair cascading down their backs, their bodies swaying, the paper flying, the waitresses serving, trying not to look.

Frances sipped her drink again, her eyes back on Agnes, the liquid sliding down easily enough but churning once it hit her gut. The mirror reflected everything, doubling the horror, making it near impossible to turn away. The Mayor was on a table with his friends at the back of the room. A black girl in a wig spun in front of them. Frances watched as one of the men reached up and dabbed at the sweat on the base of the girl's back with his handkerchief, then wiped it across another man's face and laughed. The Mayor laughed too, his good looks twisted, ageing in the lamplight, knocking back shots as fast as his lips would allow. The girl didn't seem to notice any of it. She looked like she'd been dancing for days.

Frances stared down at her own cracked hands, wishing she'd not come, aware that she'd never be rid of the sight and smell of the place. Still no sign of Colette. She wondered what the Mayor had done with her, what Willie had wanted them to see. Sit and wait, Ben had said. Apart from this they had no plan. She supposed he'd not thought they'd get this far. No one seemed to have paid them any attention apart from a few men scowling at Ben when he got in their way at the bar – in a world like this money was the answer to every question, and for once they had some.

Two of the men at the Mayor's table got up and walked towards them. Frances looked down, her whole body tensed. They leant on the bar and ordered some drinks, talking about something Frances couldn't quite catch.

'. . . she's out. No, the private room. With the grade As.'

'. . . sold . . . hasn't he?'

'Won't . . . her again.'

One of the men yawned. They picked up their drinks, clinked glasses and staggered back to their table. In the mirror Frances saw the Mayor get up and disappear through a door at the far side of the room.

'I need to use the bathroom,' Frances said. If she explained what she was planning they'd try to stop her.

'It's out the back, no doubt,' Ben said, his smile falling away, 'but perhaps you two should go together.'

Agnes moved to get down from her stool.

'No, I'll be all right,' Frances said, 'I won't be a moment.' She tried to smile but couldn't be sure her mouth had managed it.

'Don't go,' Agnes said, clutching her arm.

Frances held her gaze. 'Sip slow and I'll be back before you're finished.'

The hall behind the bar was dark and thin and damp-smelling. Wallpaper peeled in the corners like the leaves of the plants on Ben's window sill. Frances walked slowly. Two waitresses came out of the bathroom, one cradling the other.

'Pull it together,' the one doing the holding said, her voice as harsh as her make-up. 'We all feel like this the first week, but the money's good, the best you'll get in the city.'

'I know, but I can't . . .' the other girl sighed.

Frances was worried they might stop and ask her where she

was going, but they didn't. The girl doing the comforting looked up at her without smiling. The other girl didn't look up at all. They walked past, heading in the direction of the bar.

She wasn't sure where she was going or what she might do when she got there. All she knew was that the Mayor was back here somewhere so perhaps Colette was too. If all *that* was going on out there in the open, she daren't think what was happening back here in the dark. She wanted to run back to Agnes and grab her hand and get in the car and make Ben drive them home, but she forced herself to keep walking. Where was home now at any rate? She didn't have one with Stan gone. All she had left was a doomed apartment she couldn't go back to and a bunch of questions with no answers. If she got hurt finding out, so be it. That was better than running and hiding all the time, than looking over her shoulder, than living in fear. She needed to know, wished for it more than a hot meal and a decent sleep. Nothing was more important than the truth, least of all her own little life.

She passed two doors on the right. Both were locked. She looked round and put her ear to each of them but heard nothing. Another hall ran to the left, thinner and darker and damper than the first. About halfway along a large guy with a thick jaw was staring at his shoes next to another door. She ducked back before he saw her. That was it, in there. He was guarding something. What to do? He'd never let her inside. She peeked round again. There was a second door beside the first. If she could get in there maybe she could put her ear to the wall and hear something. She'd need to distract him and she'd have to be fast. Someone might see her if she lingered and ask what she was doing, or worse, Ben and Agnes might come looking and put themselves in danger.

A sound, a creak, murmuring. She peeked again. Another man was standing next to the guard by the door. He'd not gone past her so he must have come out of the room. He was short and slight. He almost saw her. She whipped away. It was Joseph. She took two quick steps towards the bar, towards safety. She'd find Ben and Agnes and get out. If he saw her, that would be it. The truth wasn't worth it after all. Then Joseph raised his voice. She stopped and listened.

'I'm going out back to bring the car round. He wants to take the latest accident to the new place to christen it, help the foundations along,' he chuckled. The other guy said something she couldn't hear. 'Yeah,' Joseph said, 'they need ya in there. Mr Mayor ain't happy about it, but what can he say? A deal's a deal, and it's not as if he knows where she's going. Even if he suspects something, he'll tell himself he doesn't so long and so hard he'll start believing his own lies. He's a politician, ain't he?' The guy said something again. 'No, no,' Joseph said, 'don't worry about it. You're in there, ain't you? Ain't no one gonna get by if you're on the inside. Get in there before he starts yelling. I'm sorting the car.' A pause. 'Give me my badge, would you? Might need it if we run into trouble.'

The shock dropped on Frances like slate from a roof. A door banged. Heavy feet on the boards making their way towards her. She ran down the hall as quietly as she could and ducked into the bathroom, thanking God there was no one else around. She put her hand to the wet wall, leaning over, trying to calm down, waiting until his footsteps passed by and grew faint. He was a policeman? All this time? He had beaten that woman and threatened Stan and trashed the apartment. Thank God they hadn't gone to the cops. Willie was right.

When she was sure he had gone she stepped quickly past the unguarded door and twisted the handle of the one beside it, praying it would turn.

It did. On the other side all was dark and quiet. She padded in and closed the door behind her. A storeroom. She could make out the boxes and crates on the floor, a mop leaning in its bucket, well-used linen folded in high stacks, waiting to get dirty again. She moved forward, taking care not to knock anything over and found a bare patch of wall to put her ear to. Nothing to hear except her own panic in the dark – short breaths, so terribly loud. It smelt musty and rotten. Worse than she'd expected. A little way along there was an old sink with a cupboard under-neath and one of its doors hanging off. She ducked down and looked inside. The bad smell got worse. Rusty plumbing ran through the wall. Someone hadn't finished the job very well because around one of the pipes a halo of light was big enough to get her eye to.

She crawled in. It smelt of latrines – Frances hadn't expected that – of outhouses and holes in the ground, of shit and piss and muck, but also of carcasses left out in the sun, of baking flesh and fish guts. Most surprising of all it smelt of dried-up blood, of Frances' own twisted insides, of the lump of flesh she had pulled from herself on the floor of the barn after the baby. And so, as she moved closer and looked through the gap she thought not of what she might see, but of the baby's tiny body curled in her arms, of the whisper sound he had made, a half-exhaled breath that she could still hear. She thought of the smell of him, strange and putrid and somehow delicious, like a rare but rotting fruit, of how she had wanted to put him back inside herself so that he might live a little longer.

The room next door was smaller and brighter than she expected. Along one side of the wall an unmade bed had scattered its contents all over the floor. Blankets and cushions littered the room and in the middle of it all, slumped over to one side – Colette.

She was naked, but she still had her shoes and stockings on. Frances was so close she could see the wear on her soles, the way the cold skin on one side of her buttock had begun to bruise against the wooden boards. She was staring straight ahead, looking at nothing, with her chin on her chest, the freckles on her arms extending across her body like a constellation of tiny black stars. The worst part was her face. Her glassy eyes were open, but they looked dead, like a once-loved but now discarded doll.

Frances put her hand to her mouth and moved back, banging her head on the underside of the sink, the shock making her clumsy. She sucked at her palm for a few seconds, then leant over and silently retched on to a pile of old rags, the scent of curdled liquor making her strain even more, until warm liquid gushed from her mouth like oil from a geyser, saliva stringing from her lips. She gulped for air as quietly as she could and forced herself to look again.

In the middle of the room, tapping his foot on the edge of one of the pillows, a man was standing next to the Mayor. He was big and blond, and for a single terrifying second Frances thought it was Stan, but then he turned and she saw it was Kane.

'Come on, friend,' he said, 'you knew the first time I saw you with her she was the one I'd pick. There's no point busting my balls about it now. I can't help it if she can't handle the stuff, but what I can do is fix this mess.'

Stuff. There it was again. So this was what heroin did to you in the end. Frances closed her eyes for a second, trying to shut out the shame of what Stan had been involved in, then opened them and carried on looking.

The Mayor was fiddling with his cuffs. 'I know you will, I know, but if anyone finds out . . . '

'Who'll find out? Who'll miss her? They all know already. The chief's out there, isn't he? Him and his boys. There's two judges in tonight who're here for the second time this week. You gotta stop worrying – it's no good for your ticker.' He clapped the Mayor on the back. 'And I need you healthy. How else are my buildings gonna get built? I'm doing all this for you, free of charge for as long as you help me out. If anyone talks or thinks about talking, we'll get the new Stanley over here to persuade them not to.'

Frances shivered. The guy who'd been guarding the door walked past and began pulling at Colette's ankles. He dragged her towards the door. She didn't flinch. Her fine skin shimmered in rainbow shades like the woman in the gallery painting, except the colours weren't bright any more, but dull and murky, as though Frances was looking at her underwater, as though she'd been drowned. The sound of her flesh scraping over the splintered boards wrapped around Frances' nerves so tight she knew she'd never be free of it. The guy dragging her paused to wipe his nose on his sleeve and she saw the girl's chest rise and fall, flickering with life like an almost-spent bulb.

Frances yanked her head free of the sink and stood up, gulping the sickness down. She slipped out of the room, took a deep breath and started to run.

'How much do you know?' She wanted to hit him but her knuckles were numb and shivering, pressed down in her lap.

Ben twisted the steering wheel to swerve round a parked car. 'Some of it, but nothing like what you're telling me.'

'Did you know that Stan was involved? That he was helping them?'

'Not exactly, not like this.'

'So what did you know?' she shouted again, not so loud this time, her voice bitter and hollow with hurt.

'I knew he worked sometimes for the Mayor and that guy Kane, the one building those scrapers. I knew he was in trouble. I knew he hated the work. And, and . . . '

'And what?'

'I knew that day he refused to harm that girl.'

'What girl?'

'The girl in the park.'

'Who?'

'The one,' Agnes said, leaning in from the back seat, 'that ended up pulled behind a car by her neck. Is that who you mean?'

Frances glared at Ben. 'Is she right?'

Ben nodded, his face taut, eyes bulging. 'Stan told me, said he'd refused to do it, that they'd tried to get him to strangle her. She was about to testify against someone – the Mayor I'd guess – said she had evidence on all the corruption, on the blackmailing and bribes. Stan was in such a state when I found him, said he'd seen them tying her up and he'd gone over and cut the rope, tried to stop them, but they stuck a knife in him and killed her anyway. You saw how it turned out. They beat him so bad, he thought they'd do him in there and then.'

'And you've let me run around town like a fool, finding all this out for myself, letting me put Agnes in danger when you knew all this from the start?'

'I had no choice, Stan made me promise. You kept asking and pushing and I knew you'd go look anyway if I didn't help. But I didn't want you to know what he'd been doing, what he'd been making his money from. I thought it would change how you felt about him, and I couldn't stand that. He was a good friend, loyal, honourable ... He was creamin' the money to help the girls, the ones Joseph was blackmailing. He didn't spend none of it on himself. Sent some back home to you and your folks is all.'

'Joseph?' Agnes said, her voice nothing more than a hoarse whisper. 'You mentioned him before. Who is he?'

'You don't want to know,' Frances said, looking over her shoulder. Agnes was staring at the back of Ben's head, one hand smoothing at her hair, the other in her mouth getting chewed.

'He's one of the hoods who came looking for Stan, who wrecked the place. A policeman.' She looked at Ben. 'You men and your promises. Keeping your word, honouring each other. Honour's just pride by another name, and you know what that comes before. Silence is cowardice. Heads down, mouths shut and it all keeps happening. You pretend not to see it.'

'Was he the one?' Agnes said. 'The one who sent the letters, the one who made Stella . . . '

Frances turned. 'I don't know, I'm sorry. We'll find—'

A car pulled out in front of them and Ben slammed on the brakes. Frances' head just missed the windscreen.

'Watch it!' Agnes cried from the back. 'You'll lose them!'

Up ahead, Kane's car accelerated away. Frances wondered how much of the road Colette could feel from inside the trunk. For a brief moment she hoped she was dead already.

'Do you remember the last time we were here?' Agnes whispered.

'Yes,' Frances said. 'You stood over there to get a picture of the Rockefeller going up, you said something about the light.'

Agnes nodded, although in the dark Frances didn't see her head move, she only felt her hair shift on her shoulder. 'I remember exactly,' Agnes muttered. 'I said that once this building was finished it would steal all the light from the sidewalk, that before long folks walking downtown would never feel the sun on their faces again, that the only way to get warm would be if you were rich enough to climb up high and look out.'

They were hiding behind a pillar in the basement of an almost-finished skyscraper. On the other side of the street the struts and balustrades of the new Rockefeller building sailed up into the inky sky. All around, concrete stacks, piles of bricks and iron joists cast thick shadows in the gloom. Frances watched as Joseph lay Colette beside a huge glistening pool of fresh concrete.

'I love this stuff,' Kane shouted above the noise of rumbling trains, absentmindedly twisting a large stick across the wet mixture. 'This grey sludge is building America. It's taking this great country of ours straight up to the stars. Let's have a look at her then.'

Joseph stepped back and Kane peered down at Colette. Frances tensed. She could feel Agnes' breath on her neck – little bursts of hot air.

'I'm surprised she couldn't handle it. You'd have thought the French would be used to injecting. It was their idea, after all. Although, they might have got it from the Dutch, who no doubt got it from one of those Chinese sailors. So efficient, the Chinese.'

'Yes, sir.'

'Even if she wasn't almost gone, we'd have to do this anyway. I'm sure she was hanging off the Mayor the other day when we were discussing my next building.'

Joseph nodded and started dragging again. Colette's thin body slipped in his hands and he half dropped her. Skinny limbs smacked on the concrete. Frances flinched. Had Stan seen this, or something like it? How much had he helped? How much had he really tried to stop it?

'Careful, Joe! Take your time. I ain't in no rush and nei-ther's she.'

'You want me to wrap her, sir? Or leave her like this, like the last one.'

'This is fine.' Kane walked round to one side of the pool and crouched on his haunches. If only these kids could handle their dope. Now, ease her in, nice and slow.'

Frances had been wondering why Kane was down here at all, why he hadn't just sent Joseph to do his dirty work. The look on his face told her everything. He wanted to be here. He wanted to watch.

Colette was still breathing, but only just. Frances went to run forward but Agnes caught her wrist.

'No,' she hissed. 'If you jump out now we'll all end up in there. He's got a gun, look. We gotta wait.'

'But he's going to ... she'll be drowned.'

'We don't have a choice.'

On the other side of the room, Frances could see Ben's shadow against the wall, bobbing around in the light from the lantern the two men had brought. She willed him not to move.

Joseph pulled Colette to the edge of the pool and hoisted her up by her armpits, then began sliding her into the wet concrete feet-first.

'That's it,' Kane said, rocking on his heels, clenching the stick between his fists, his piercing eyes, bright even in the gloom, fixed on the girl, her spotted pink flesh standing out against all the grey. 'Slowly, like before.'

Joseph guided her in. Frances wondered if Colette could feel it. Did she know what was happening? The horror of it slid over her like scalding water. As Colette's head disappeared, Frances thought she saw her eyes flicker. Dark curls pooled, twisting on the surface of the pale sludge. Kane poked at them with his stick until every part of the girl was gone.

'Okay, Joe, let's make a move, I'm dog tired.'

Joseph nodded and picked up the lantern. The two men walked to the manhole and disappeared back into the bowels of the city. Each grinding twist of the metal cover reverberated through Frances' body, as though the guilt of doing nothing was locking her in.

Once the sound had faded, they all ran out. Ben didn't speak. He raced to the edge of the pool and plunged his arms in up to the elbows. 'Hold on,' he said, leaning forward. They each grabbed one side of his belt. He took a deep breath and pitched into the mixture up to his waist. A few seconds passed and Frances felt the muscles in his stomach tense and she looked at Agnes and they heaved backwards as hard as they could. Slowly his body emerged, chest, then neck, then spluttering head, the concrete sloughing off his dark skin, dripping and pooling and mounting at their feet. They pulled and pulled and finally Frances saw a twist of dark hair bunched tight in his fist. She and Agnes let go of him, and bent forward, reaching their arms into the freezing pool. The silky feel of the concrete reminded Frances of batter, of Mother asking about clean hands and the sharp sting of a cuff round the ear. They scrabbled for a second, and then Frances could feel Colette's arms, her skin even colder than the liquid, and they pulled and pulled again, easing her body out, until they all fell back, gasping on the cold hard ground.

Agnes yanked her shirt over her head and began wiping the girl's face, trying to clear her nose and mouth. It was no good. Frances cradled her but Colette's freezing body didn't stir. Agnes wiped and wiped and pumped her chest and then all at once they could hear gasps, and the girl jerked forward on to her hands and knees and retched, her beautiful body made ugly by the sparse light – an unholy beast on all fours.

When she had nothing left to expel, Colette fell sideways on to the dusty ground. Frances bent close to her face and stroked her cheek. Her half-open eyes were blood-shot and caked in grey slime, rolling in their sockets, lashes matted like stone claws. When Frances finally met her gaze, it was clear that some part of her had been awake for all of it. Frances turned away then and they wrapped Colette in their clothes, then their arms, and no one spoke except Ben, who murmured, 'It's okay, it'll be all right,' over and over again.

GREENWICH VILLAGE

5 December 1932

06.27

'I don't believe you.' Jacks hugged her knees tighter and pulled at the knotted fringe on her midnight bed jacket. 'You're lying.' She took the holder from her mouth and rubbed a finger across her lips, eyeing them in turn. Frances thought she looked small, taking up less space on the chaise than before, her clothes merging into the velvet cushions as though she was becoming part of the furniture.

'Why would Frances lie?' Agnes asked, her back as straight as the chair she sat in, cradling her mug between two hands. 'Why would any of us?'

'How should I know?' Jacks shrugged out a bird-like hand. 'Probably a scam of some sort. If it's money you want, he's the one to ask.' She nodded at Dicky, who was standing by the window looking out. 'All I've got is my clothes. But I thought that brother of yours left you some money?'

The sound of Colette being sick in the hallway toilet reached

Frances' ears again. She wished she could put her hands to her head and block it out. The girl had refused hospital but now she wished they'd taken her anyway. Ben stood behind Frances, tapping at her chair like a sentry. He'd not said a word since they arrived.

'We're telling the truth,' Agnes said again. 'It was Kane. And the Mayor. The police too. Judges. I've seen some of them before at your parties.'

Over by the window, Dicky shifted with his back to them, silent, like Ben.

'I know I've picked some rotten men in my time,' Jacks said, 'and I know Kane's no saint, but come on, Agnes. You're talking about attempted murder, at the very least. He wouldn't do it. Maybe to men who deserved it' – she looked pointedly at Frances – 'but not girls. Not like that.'

'He did.' Agnes' voice grew quiet. 'I wish it wasn't true, but it is.'

'It's the truth.' Colette was standing in the doorway wearing a man's shirt Agnes had given her that went down to her knees. Frances wondered how she was staying upright.

She stood up, feeling her own legs quiver, and helped the girl across to the other end of the chaise. Colette's blotchy wrists were hot and sweating, impossibly thin. Frances tucked the blanket across her shaking knees, then walked slowly back to her chair.

'Even if it is true,' Jacks said, 'if we believed you, I can't think what we could do about it. If the police are involved and the Mayor too, like you say, there's nothing to be done. This isn't blackmail or racketeering or selling bootleg hooch from the back of a van. If he finds out that you know, that now we all know . . . ' Her voice trailed off. 'He'll get away with it. They all will.'

'He's booked me.' Dicky turned and looked at them, his arms stiff and tight behind his back, hands clutching at themselves.

'Who's booked you, for what?' Jacks asked, her eyebrows reaching for her hairline.

'I didn't want to mention it after you got so upset with him. Kane's booked me to take his photograph. Jacob arranged it.'

Jacks thrust forward, pushing at the edges of the seat, her body rising up in anger. 'What in God's name for?'

'To celebrate some new building. Wants a portrait done before and after. Jacob's been making a bust of the man's head to go on the top of the building.'

'Like a gargoyle?' Jacks asked.

'Something like that,' Dicky replied, his tone flat.

'When are you doing it?'

'I said I'd go round and take preparatory photographs on Monday. Jacob wants me to go to his place so he doesn't have to move the bust twice. I thought it would make a nice change. You know, a different background, clay all over the floor, sheets thrown on the furniture, and big old Kane in the centre flashing those mega-watt eyes. He's paying me handsomely for the privilege, of course.'

For a moment the room fell silent. Frances tried to make out what each of them was thinking. Colette hadn't looked up since she sat down. Her knees were tucked beneath her chin, moth-like hands flickering across closed eyes. Agnes glanced back and forth from Jacks to Dicky, fiddling at a flailing shred of skin on her thumb, her back still straight, her brow still furrowed. Dicky looked away and stared through the window again, the light from the lamp outside setting his stiff hair a-glow. Behind Frances, Ben remained silent. Jacks kept on smoking. The tall clock in the hallway chimed the half hour. Outside, a baby started screeching. The sound ground at Frances' nerves.

'Can't the mother shut the damn thing up?' Jacks asked. 'I didn't think anyone on the square had one.'

Dicky bent close to the window. The hollering grew louder,

and now it seemed to Frances as though the first baby had been joined by a second and they were trying to better each other, calling out for milk, for comfort, desperate and panicked and screaming for love.

'It's not a baby,' Dicky said.

'Don't be silly,' Jacks said, getting up and joining him at the window. 'What is it then?'

'Foxes,' Dicky said. 'Cubs, I think. Down by the back gate. Look there.'

'You're right,' Jacks said. 'How queer.'

Frances recognised the wild sound now. She'd heard it a hundred times on the farm – pups screaming at each other, scratching and snuffling and rolling in the dirt. The sound summoned a memory. She was eleven, not yet grown, stuck in the gap between nothing and something. She'd been unable to sleep and nothing had helped – not pacing her room, nor the warm cup of water on her stand, nor her sewing. When the cries had started up, she'd used it as an excuse to walk downstairs and on to the deck. She remembered seeing an almost-full moon clinging to the edge of the wide sky, so bright it cast her shadow across the rotting boards. She'd pulled her shawl around her arms against the wind, not worried about Father, not tonight, because she knew he'd not come home for hours. A few steps on to the withered grass she'd seen the tiny fluff balls chasing each other's tails, yelling down by the barn. She'd sat on the soft earth in the quiet and let the moths land on her arms and in her hair, watching the pups twist and turn and kick up the dust until they vanished back into the land like spilt grain.

Only after she got up and brushed off her nightshirt had she lifted her eyes and seen him. At first she'd frozen, thinking it was Father, that he'd come home after all, but then he'd raised his hand and she realised it was Stan in the rocker at the side of the house, smoking one of Father's best pipes. She had gone across and sat on the splintering chair beside him and they'd spoken for an hour or more about a lot of things, things she thought she'd forgotten, about where Stan was wanting to travel and what he hoped to do when he got there, about the town dying around them, about which of the stars shining above their heads he knew the names of. After a time she had yawned and he'd sent her back inside and she'd climbed up to her room away from the silted night and fallen straight asleep.

She opened her eyes. Piles of rugs and paintings and lamps and chairs crowded in. She glared at the closeness of the walls, at the black buildings leaning towards her beyond the window, at the lost horizon she worried she might never see again. Outside, the animals kept wailing for the dawn, calling away her doubt, until finally she knew what had to be done. She smoothed her dry palms across her lap, pushing at the creases, picking at the stains, filling her nails with dirt. She would kill him. The Mayor too. She'd kill them for what they'd done to those girls, but most of all she'd do it for what they'd turned Stan into. And she'd persuade everyone here to help her.

GREENWICH VILLAGE

12 December 1932

06.31

She walked around him, then leant in and straightened his tie. He smelt so good. Like polished wood and car fumes and burning ground.

'Richard, your assistants are wonderful,' Kane grinned, his breath on the top of Frances' head. 'Sorry we had to do this so early. I can't risk anyone seeing what we're up to. It's all about the surprise, you see.'

Twice he'd asked her how she was, twice he'd touched her arm and remembered her, twice she'd had to stop herself from grabbing one of Jacob's tools and stabbing him with it. She walked back to Agnes, avoiding her eyes.

'Thank you.' Dicky looked up from his camera. 'I try to hire the best and these girls are just that.'

Kane stood in the middle of Jacob's studio, his arm atop a giant stone version of his own head. Jacob was in the corner, fussing over something Frances couldn't see on a long low table. Apart from their lamp-thrown shadows, the walls were empty. At first the room had reminded Frances of the gallery, of its cool, clean whiteness. But beneath her aching feet the wooden floor was covered in splatters of paint and clay. How strange that the ruined places where most art got made looked the opposite of the bare rooms in which it all ended up.

'I'm finished.' Jacob held a thin slice of bronze above his head. 'Don't take any more until I've fixed the plaque on the front. Please, wait!' Dicky raised his head as Jacob rushed across the room, his smock flapping at his russet feet. Frances wondered again where he got his clothes. The dye on his stockings alone was bright enough to make her squint.

Kane relaxed a little and stretched his arms above his head while Jacob worked. 'Will it be much longer? I have a number of appointments this morning.'

'Not long now, apologies,' Dicky said. 'Once Jacob's fixed it on, if you could go back to where you were.'

Kane nodded and replaced his hand. Frances could see his annoyance, the narrowing of his eyes, the tension in his thick neck.

She bent down, pretending to help Agnes with the boxes at their feet, wondering if Kane was going back to that hellish club tonight. Agnes met her eye but didn't speak.

'Shame about the Mayor,' Dicky said. 'Now hold, hold, hold, and rest.' He pressed the trigger in his hand and the bulb popped, splintering on to his shoes.

'Is it?' Kane replied. 'I suppose so. Although, in a way, political life was never really for him.'

'How so?' Dicky asked.

'He loves women too much. He'd have courted scandal however high he went. That they've got him on corruption as Mayor is probably no bad thing. Better now than in a few years when he's higher up the food chain. He'll get off in the end, of course, but he'll not be able to work in politics again.'

'You're friends, aren't you?'

'We are, of a kind. We've helped each other. All above board, of course.'

'Of course.'

The bulb popped again. Frances squinted at the flash and tried not to scream, not to think of Stan.

'Then what do you mean?' Dicky asked.

'I mean, if they get him now while he's still young, later on he'll be able to get a position somewhere else, privately, out of the public eye. All he'll have to do is go away to Europe for a while after the trial. If he stays gone for long enough the nation will have forgiven him by the time he comes back. At least, that's what I've advised.'

'And what if he doesn't get off?'

'He will. And if he can't manage it, the result will be much the same.'

'How so?'

'A man of that standing doing that sort of crime? Involving some of the very judges who'll be implicated? You work it out.'

'I see what you mean.' Dicky brought out his head from the black cloth and turned a dial on the front of the lens. 'Please, relax again for a moment.' He paused. 'But they've refused his bail. I'm sure he can't be enjoying prison too much.'

'From what I've heard he's not suffering in the kind of cell you or I would be thrown in.'

Frances scoffed, then coughed to cover the sound. She couldn't help it. The anger was burning her throat. She'd cried when she heard about the Mayor. Cried and screamed and pounded her fist on her pillow until Agnes had run in and held her. The Mayor was out of the picture. She'd never be able to hurt him now he'd been arrested. Corruption, so they said, but what was bribery and blackmail compared to what she'd seen him do? She had hoped he'd be sent away for a long time, that he was cooped up somewhere dark and diseased. But now every word Kane spoke chipped away at her meagre relief. She stared hard at the back of his yellow head.

Dicky asked Kane to try a few more positions. He took some shots, then said, 'Well, that's enough from my point of view. I'm sure we've got plenty now. Before you go, would you mind signing the order for the prints to be made?'

'Is that necessary?' Kane asked, stretching again, straightening his cuffs.

'I'm afraid it is,' Dicky said. 'If I go ahead and make them without your consent you could sue me later on.'

'Is that so? I'm not sure I'd be too worried about a few photographs.'

'No,' Dicky said, 'but I'd appreciate it all the same. You'd be surprised at the number of people I photograph who are full of bravado in front of the lens then panic when they get home that I might have revealed something they wouldn't like the world to see.'

Frances flinched at the lie. Dicky nodded at Agnes and she pulled the paper from her pocket.

'Agnes will sort you out while we clear up,' Dicky added. 'One signature is all we need.'

Kane followed Agnes to Jacob's table. Frances could see the shake in her friend's hand from across the room. If he noticed there was a second piece of paper layered beneath the first it would all be over. This was the only thing none of them had been able to think up an excuse for. She started tidying up, rolling lengths of material, stacking boxes, shining lenses, all the while trying to breathe, to not be sick. Kane reached for a pen from his pocket. Was Agnes holding the paper right? She couldn't see. She bent over, rubbing a shammy across a circle of glass, watching her reflection slowly being revealed as the smears cleared away, unable to look even herself in the eye.

Then she heard it. The scratched scribble of a pen that meant Kane had signed his life away. His signature was all they needed. Now they could write what they wanted on the note and the world would believe them. No one would suspect his suicide was anything other than a case of misery and desperation. Which in a way it was, Frances thought, only it wasn't Kane who was hurting, it was her.

Outside at the bottom of Jacks and Dicky's stoop, Agnes put her arm around her and they walked up the steps. Frances still wasn't used to the feel of her, to the slender curve of Agnes' elbow against her waist – so much lighter than any man's, as though its lack of weight suggested how much less she might take, how much less Frances might have to give in order to be loved.

'I can't believe you did it,' Frances said, knocking on the door.

'Neither can I.' Agnes' eyes looked wild, but there was some joy in them now, some pride too. 'I was so terrified I thought I might faint.'

'But you didn't.'

'Thanks to Dicky. Who knew he was such a good liar? Kane didn't even pause to think, just scrawled his dirty name right across the page.'

The bolt on the other side of the door slid across and Jacks opened it.

'You two took your time.'

'We were helping Jacob clear up,' Agnes said. 'It would have looked strange if we'd all run off.'

'I suppose so. In you come, we're all waiting.'

They walked inside and hung their jackets on the coat stand. Frances noticed again how much the house smelt of them, of Jacks and Dicky, of tinned pomade and jasmine blooming in the dark. Of money. They followed Jacks down the hallway and Frances caught an acid whiff of the darkroom, tainting the rich sweetness. She stared at the nape of Agnes' neck, at the clipped curl of almost-black hair pointing down, like an arrow, towards her soft back. A flash of her naked torso flickered across Frances' mind, and in a moment she was hot and bothered. She wondered at the way her body still drove her on towards desire when all around the world was crumbling.

In the front room, Dicky and Ben were standing on opposite sides.

'How's Colette?' Frances asked.

'At home,' Jacks said, walking to the table, picking up a coffee. 'She's still exhausted. Her mother's there. She told her she was attacked, but not who by. The old dear believed her but she's started asking more questions, so she's off to her grandmother's in California – we lent her the money for the train. If I was her I'd go back to France but she says she hates her father.'

Frances sat down on the sagging velvet sofa next to Agnes. She looked around at them all. It was still hard to believe they'd agreed to help her. She'd known Agnes would do it. For her, if not for Stella. Ben had agreed for Stan's sake and for their own safety, as much as for the honour of the dancing girls. Jacks and Dicky had been harder to convince, but she'd managed it in the end. Perhaps Jacks had said yes because Kane had wronged her, and Dicky was doing it out of a sense of what was right and fair. Maybe they were both in it for the thrill and nothing more. She couldn't be sure. Whatever their reasons, it barely mattered now.

'Have you got it?' Ben looked fidgety, like he'd been pacing the whole time they'd been taking pictures.

'Yes.' Agnes leant back and dipped her hand into the pocket of her slacks. She brought out a piece of paper and smoothed it on to the coffee table. 'Here you go.'

Dicky and Jacks walked over.

'So,' Dicky said, 'what do we say?'

'I thought you'd know, dearest,' Jacks said. 'You've been there, haven't you? On the edge of oblivion?'

Dicky coloured but didn't speak. Frances loved him then.

'It needs to sound like him,' Ben said, 'like something he would say.'

'Well,' Jacks said, 'that's where this whole plan falls down. He's a crazed egotist, the absolute opposite of the type to take their own life.' She waved her cup around, splashing hot droplets across Frances' knees.

'So we've got to think of a reason a crazed egotist like him might want to do it,' Agnes said.

'How about an affair?' Dicky suggested. 'With someone inappropriate, someone he shouldn't be with.'

'That won't work,' Jacks scoffed. 'He's built for affairs, they're his raison d'être. He wouldn't furrow a brow over a girl, or a guy for that matter. His wife wouldn't either, you silly thing.'

Dicky pursed his lips. 'You're right, I don't know what I was thinking.'

'How about he lost all his money?' Agnes said.

'That's no good,' Frances said. 'Once they found all that money sitting in his bank they'd know it wasn't true.'

'What then?' Jacks sighed and crossed the room to refill her cup. 'We've got his name, for God's sake, that's halfway there.'

'I've been giving it some thought ever since Agnes had the idea,' Frances said. 'I've known men like him all my life. Not rich, but proud I mean. The one thing they can't stand is being wrong. What if it turned out the ground wasn't safe under one of his buildings? What if he thought he had to tear it down? What if everything he'd worked for all these years was going to get ruined?'

There was a long pause, then Jacks said, 'It might work.' She smiled over the top of her cup, and for once Frances felt the warmth of it.

'But how could we prove it?' Ben asked.

'We wouldn't have to,' Frances said, 'all it would take was a whisper. Some tall tale he might have believed.'

'But he'd have got the ground tested first, wouldn't he?' Agnes asked. 'Surely a man like him wouldn't commit suicide on the strength of hearsay.'

'You'd be surprised,' Jacks said. 'Arrogant men are mostly stupid. Even vaguely intelligent ones like Kane allow pride to override common sense. I think Frances is right. As long as the papers think he had proof, that he believed it enough to panic, it'll all add up. If he thought someone was about to pull down his precious skyscrapers, that he was about to fail in front of the whole world, that might do it.'

'So,' Ben said, 'what do we write?'

'Oh, God, I don't know,' Jacks said, moving back to the coffee table.

'I think it's less about what we write and more about how the writing looks,' Agnes said. 'It's got to seem like Kane's written it.'

'Quite,' Dicky said. 'And I think it best we say as little as possible. Kane's not the quiet type, but in my experience most anguished men don't speak much. And there will be fewer words to catch us on. If we're to pretend he's written anything at all, it must be brief and to the point.'

'Agreed,' Ben said.

'So,' Agnes said, 'who wants to write? Perhaps you, Jacks? You know him best.'

Jacks was mid-sip. She took the cup from her lips and widened her eyes in horror.

'She's right, of course, darling, you've known him longest,' Dicky said. 'He must have written you love notes at some point. Can't you dig them out?'

'Absolutely not.' Jacks looked affronted. 'Kane never wrote

me a line, not a single word. Most of the time he barely spoke to me, except in ecstasy or anger.'

'I suppose you were busy doing other things,' Dicky said, raising an eyebrow.

'Bearing in mind what these three claim to have seen him doing, I'd thank you not to remind me of that.' Jacks slammed her cup on the table. Some of the liquid sloshed out on to the paper. Agnes snatched it up and dabbed at the stain with her sleeve. 'It's not like you to be so crass,' Jacks continued, 'not at all.'

'Well, none of us are ourselves, are we, darling. It's the stress. I'll be drinking as much as you before long.'

Ben sighed, sat down on the edge of an armchair and put his head in his hands. 'None of this is helping,' he said. 'We need to make a decision. If Jacks won't do it, then who?'

'I think you or Dicky,' Agnes said. 'It makes sense it should be a man.'

Dicky pursed his mouth distastefully. 'I couldn't possibly,' he said. 'I don't mind giving advice and helping where I can but I really couldn't manage it. I can't bear to think about the man, let alone write his suicide note.'

They all looked at Ben. He still had his head in his hands.

'Ben,' Frances said, 'you could do it. You've got a good hand.'

'That's the problem,' he muttered. 'I'd be glad to, but a man intent on taking his own life ain't gonna write too tidily, is he?'

'You should do it,' Jacks said, looking Frances right in the eye. 'Ben's taught you to write now, hasn't he? Agnes was telling us.'

Frances felt startled – as much because Agnes had told Jacks about Ben teaching her as at the idea she should write. 'Yes, but I've barely tried whole words, let alone a full passage.'

'That's why it's a fine idea,' Jacks said. 'The worst writer is the best choice.'

'I don't know if I can.'

'Hush, now. Ben can talk you through it and we'll help. It'll be just like a lesson.' Jacks went across to a drawer and brought out a fine silver pen. 'This will do.' She took it to a lamp and peered at it under the light. 'In fact, I think Kane gave it to me. Ha!' She raised her eyes at Dicky and passed it across to Frances. 'Fate, isn't it, darling.'

Frances felt the weight of it. Jacks' initials were engraved down the side.

'What should I write?'

'Something pithy,' Jacks said.

Frances had no idea what she meant.

'Something the feds will believe,' Dicky said.

'Shhh,' Agnes said, frowning at them all. 'Can't you see she's thinking.'

Frances was staring out of the window, trying, for a moment, to imagine who Kane was, how he might feel stepping up to the ledge, what last words he might have to say to the world. She shut her eyes, searching for a sense of him. When she opened them she picked up the pen and slowly started to write.

They walked outside. Frances pulled Stan's coat over her shoulders.

'The diner?' Agnes asked. 'I'm desperate for something strong after all that and more booze will only muddle my brain. Coffee will do.'

'All right,' Frances said, her hands shaking, the inside of her middle finger still pulsing from where she'd gripped the pen. 'I need one too.'

She saw Agnes shiver, her shirt too thin to block the chill.

'You need a coat,' Frances said.

'I'm okay.'

The edges of Agnes' hair flickered, catching in the light from the hallway.

'You're not, you're freezing. I'll get it.'

Frances walked quickly back up the steps, happy to be of use, her body too nervous to rest. She'd told them she would do it, but that was before the first part of the plan had worked out. She'd never really believed they'd get his name on the paper. She'd promised them all, promised Agnes, but now she had no idea if she was up to it.

She padded lightly down the hall looking up at Dicky's photographs, at the fields and lakes and cities, wondering at all he and Jacks had seen. If she was caught, New York would be the last place she'd ever look out on. She'd be thrown in jail, probably, might even end up in the chair. Father had told her all about that, said he'd tell the police and lie about her if she didn't do what he wanted. He said he'd make her sound so bad they'd have no choice but to fry her. So she had let him. She'd let him touch her and beat her, and after a while she had tried not to scream or cry because she noticed this made him hit even harder. She could see his red face now, eyes bulging, sweat flicking on her, tongue lolling on his cheek like a sick cow. She'd let him do it all, right up until Stan had stopped him, because sometimes, according to Father, if the police didn't like who they had strapped into the chair, they'd turn it up real high until the person's skin and fat and innards and any other soft parts melted down to nothing and stuck to the wood. Frances wasn't certain he'd been telling the truth, but still, she didn't want to find out.

Was it worth it? Could she risk everything to splatter Kane's proud face across the sidewalk? She'd never had herself figured as a coward but now she wasn't so sure.

Behind the door she could hear Dicky murmuring to Jacks in the parlour. She stopped outside to listen.

'You seem strangely happy,' Dicky said.

'I am. I told you I liked her from the start. You liked her face, but I was the one who saw what she might become. All that intelligence cooped up behind a farm-girl facade. That fire in her belly. Remember how she leant towards us that first day on the train? I can't recall what you said now, but she was livid, lit up like a Catherine wheel. So much anger behind her eyes.'

'Yes, I remember,' Dicky said. 'You saw her potential. But I still don't understand why you're helping them do this. Don't you feel the slightest inkling of guilt? I feel sick.'

'Why would I? If they're telling the truth, Kane deserves it, doesn't he? If he got rid of her brother and sent Agnes' sister round the twist and hurt and buried all those girls, it's not like we're helping them do in a good man.'

Frances imagined Jacks shrugging, saw her flicking ash from the stump in her holder.

'Still. It's not like you to be so supportive. And you should work on dimming the tone of excitement in your voice a little.'

Frances heard Jacks suck on her cigarette. 'Well, I'm doing it for them but also a little for me, I suppose.'

'I knew it. All this stuff you got me hooked on hasn't addled my brain just yet. You don't give a fig about Agnes or Frances or those girls that might be interred underneath all those buildings. Kane could bury fifty of them down there and you'd probably have married him anyway. I know you hate him, but why? Perhaps you're still sore about that incident on the stairs.'

'I don't know what you're referring to.'

'Oh, come now, yes you do.' Dicky paused.

Frances' gut turned.

'I might not have been in when it happened but I was certainly present for the aftermath,' Dicky continued. 'One push, wasn't it?'

'He punched me. Kicked me all the way to the bottom.' Jacks' voice sounded different suddenly, as though all the mirth had been stripped away.

'I can see you getting worked up about it even now.'

'Shut up.'

'I came in, and there you were, blood all over the rug, all over your fine velvet slacks.'

'I said, shut up.'

'Called the doctor, didn't I.'

'I thanked you for that small mercy at the time.'

'You did.' He paused again. 'He told me, you know.'

'Who? Kane?'

'No. Old Doc Richardson. Worried about you, he was. Thought someone should know that you'd been with child. I figured out the rest. It was Kane's, wasn't it? That brute of a man murdered his own babe while it was still inside you.'

The shock seared, branding Frances like hot iron on horse flesh, anger swelling in its wake. She shuddered.

'No.' Jacks was whispering now. Frances had to tip the side of her shaking head until her brow rested on the door so she could hear.

'Does he even know? It's all right, you don't have to speak, I can see the truth of it,' Dicky carried on. 'You don't think I'd have agreed to all this otherwise? I'm a beast too, but I'm not that bad.'

'So you're doing it for me?'

'Yes. And for Agnes and Frances.'

'Really?'

'Oh, all right. Mainly for you. And you're doing it for yourself.'

'You don't have to sound so self-righteous.'

'I'm not. That's sadness you can hear in my voice, dearest. I didn't have you down as a coward.'

'Excuse me?'

'Getting two young girls to do your dirty work. And what will you do if they're caught?'

MID-TOWN

12 December 1932

07.10

When they got to Phillie's Diner, Phyllis, the owner, was there. Frances had thought the place belonged to a man until she saw the woman's square chin jutting over the counter like a bulldog and watched how slowly she picked up the salt shakers with her swollen fingers, setting them down neat and square in the centre of the tables, tucking the menus behind, not in a rush like a waitress, but with care, as though if she placed them just right the next customer might order a second helping of pancakes.

She and Agnes squeezed themselves into a corner and drank one cup of coffee after another, turning over the plan. Frances pushed what she'd overheard Jacks and Dicky saying to the back of her mind, next to all the things that happened with Stan and Father and the baby.

They talked and talked, trying to decide how it might happen, if it would all work out. They almost fought when Frances felt plucky and said perhaps they'd feel more normal once it was done. Agnes had looked up from the black swill in the bottom of her cup and said that that wasn't the point. That above all, what mattered was doing the right thing. Frances had hated her for a second. She'd looked out through the greasy diner windows and watched the filling streets and waited for her face to cool, for Agnes to eventually say sorry.

After a while, Agnes said she wanted to go home and sleep and Frances tried to persuade her not to. She couldn't face Jacks and Dicky. Phyllis must have noticed their back and forth, because she threw a couple of blankets at them, making it clear that since Agnes was one of her most regular customers, they could sleep in the tiny store cupboard behind the counter. Phyllis said only the depressed, the drunk or the dangerous stayed up all night, and her customers wouldn't care about two women asleep on the floor if they were in need of shelter or concealment themselves. Frances had wondered why Phyllis didn't notice how plain it was that she and Agnes were those very people – depressed at least, if not drunk and dangerous as well. On another occasion she might have made a joke.

She slept sounder than she had feared, the hard floor warmed by the pipes beneath, but she woke after a few hours with a stiff neck and a foul head all the same. She unfurled herself from Agnes' body like a snail from its shell, then they shared a plate of eggs, looking at each other but not talking much, and set back out on the sidewalk. The rain had passed over, and although it was still cold there was a crispness to the daylight that made the streets look fresh and new. Agnes kept saying she wanted to photograph everything, if only she'd remembered to bring her camera, that it all looked so striking. Frances could see what she meant – the edges of all the buildings stood out more than usual, the shadows looked blacker, the suits and dresses and hats were a touch too bright – but she couldn't admire any of it like before.

As the day wore on, Agnes talked more than usual, easing her own nerves, Frances figured. They passed window after window, most of them stuffed full of fine things, but Frances forgot to look inside. Instead she caught glimpses of her own reflection, of Agnes beside her looking panicked, of her borrowed clothes and ill-fitting shoes. Every time she saw herself – neat hair, clean face, reddened eyes, hat jammed on her head like a helmet – she had to turn away.

Agnes didn't once question why Frances wanted to keep walking, why she couldn't face going back to Jacks and Dicky. Frances guessed Agnes thought she was nervous, that she was so terrified she had to keep moving to calm her panic. She was right, in a way, of course. Frances ached to tell what she had heard, but she couldn't, not until she had decided what to do. She didn't want to be talked out of anything.

On the one hand, no doubt Kane had done all she'd seen him do. To Stan, to Stella, to Colette, to all those girls. He deserved it. But on the other, if she went through with it, she was helping Jacks do something she was too cowardly to do herself, like some desperate little lapdog. All this time she'd played her for a fool, dressed her up in fancy clothes, neatened her hair and taken her picture. Turned her into the farm girl done good. Filthy liar. And Dicky was no better, not really.

Frances coughed, brought up a spitball and shot it from her mouth into the gutter. Agnes huffed at her, making a show of her disgust. A man and woman walking towards them holding hands dodged around the mess, him pretending not to have seen Frances do it, her scowling as though Frances had ruined an otherwise perfect day. Frances bared her teeth at the woman, hoping she looked as mad and angry as she felt. The woman shrank away, grasping the man's arm as they swerved, glancing over her shoulder all the way to the corner, afraid, perhaps, that Frances would run after her and bite at her ankles. Frances had hoped her rage might lessen as she walked but it had worsened. And she still had no idea if she could go through with what she had promised.

Darkness fell thick and sudden and they kept on walking silently together, shoulder to shoulder, through the electrified streets. After a time Frances lifted her eyes from her shoes and watched Agnes run her hand along a railing like a little girl with a stick. What was the use in telling her what Jacks and Dicky had said? She didn't want to crush her the way she had been crushed. She didn't want her to feel the same weight on her chest, as though Kane's building really had fallen over and buried them both. Agnes made out she was tough, but she wasn't. Repeating what they'd said might push her some place from which Frances couldn't drag her back.

Agnes stopped. Frances walked on alone for a few steps.

'Look at that,' Agnes said, her chin tipped towards the sky, 'a new picture house.'

Frances followed her gaze, her mind elsewhere, thoughts churning like washing in a barrel.

'The Midtown Movie Theater,' Agnes read. 'About time we had one in this part of town.'

Two men were balancing precariously on top of a couple of wobbling ladders either side of a grand curved entrance. They each held a separate corner of a large sheet and were trying to pull it away from the building without falling.

'More your way, Jerry,' one of them said.

The other man jerked his arm higher, sensed them watching and almost fell off.

'Not open for a couple of weeks, girls,' he said, regaining his balance. 'Nothing to see yet. Step back, would ya?'

They did as he asked. A few more tugs and the sheet fell to the ground. Behind it, attached to the wall above the foyer, was a large stone plaque.

'Look, Frances, come and look!' Agnes said. 'It's us, don't you think?'

Frances walked closer, peering upwards. It wasn't really a

plaque but a large flat circular sculpture, black around the edge with red tiles in the centre and two women facing away from each other laid on top. The woman on the left looked sad. She had light brown skin and short jet black hair, like Agnes. Her head was tipped towards the ground, resting on one hand. The other hand was holding on to some sort of angry-looking mask. The woman beside her looked like she was dancing. Her knee was up, her head thrust out, face laughing. She was holding a grinning mask, her skin light, blonde hair a little longer.

'Yes,' Frances said, 'except the skin's the wrong colour. Mine's much darker than yours.'

'I know that,' Agnes said, 'but everything else. The rest might have been modelled on us.' Agnes walked close to her, looked over her shoulder to see if anyone was watching, and took up her hand. 'Whenever I walk past, whatever happens, I'll think of you. Of how you saved me.'

'What? Jacks and Dicky saved you already.'

'Not really. They gave me a place to stay, but I was still lost.' She tapped the side of her head. 'Up here.' She looked back at the movie theatre. 'I think this should be our place. We can come after it's all over and watch a flick. Something romantic, not violent like last time. Then, any time you want to see a movie I'll bring you here.'

Frances managed a smile. *After.* She couldn't think about after. She couldn't see past tomorrow, let alone to the other side of what she had promised to do.

'It's a fine idea,' she said, smiling, willing herself to feel the sort of joy on the dancing woman's face, to experience, just for a second, a feeling other than panic or fear or sorrow or anger.

A man walked past and whistled at them, his head cocked, eyes flashing. Agnes let go of her hand.

EMPIRE STATE BUILDING

Winter solstice, 21 December 1932

16.03

Frances sat on her hands, pressing her palms into the cracked leather – for warmth, but also so the others couldn't see them shaking. She stared through the car window listening to Agnes and Ben going over it all. The sun seemed to have set earlier and earlier this week. She leant forward and peered upwards. High above, a starless slice of navy sky split a broken path between the buildings. Mist rolled in off the unseen river towards them, muffling the lights, wetting the cobbles, as though it knew how much they needed cover.

Agnes and Ben were getting on well enough. A shared fear of the task ahead had pressed them together. It was also, Frances supposed, because they all knew what Agnes was to her now. The three of them had been easier since everyone understood their place.

She tugged Stan's coat over her knees. It felt like all she'd done for hours was listen and nod while they rushed around. She tried to remember the last time she felt so cold. Every memory took her back to the farm, to Stan hitting ice off the sills with a hammer, to Mother so wrapped up in blankets Frances couldn't see the tears burning at the cracks on her wind-torn cheeks, to Father screaming up from the cellar that they'd run out of coal. She didn't want to think about that place any more. If only it was as easy to forget somewhere as it was to leave.

'Frances, Frances? You agreed?' Ben touched her on the arm and she flinched.

'Yes, that's fine, like we said.'

'You've got it?'

Frances patted her pocket where the note was. 'You asked already.'

'I know. So, I'll be here, all right? Once we see the guard arrive Agnes is going up to convince him, she'll offer a few dimes for him to clear off and stay quiet. She'll say she wants to go up to take a picture. When he comes down he'll go into that diner, then you go up with the last bag. He's done the same every night on his break for the past few I've been watching, so he's bound to go in there. We've got an hour until Dicky told him to arrive.'

'If he comes,' Frances said.

'He will,' Agnes said. 'Dicky said he'd never seen a man more excited once he'd explained it all. You remember. He said he barely thought on it once he'd told him. All he wanted to know was which papers it would be in. That and how clear you'd be able to see his features with his new scraper behind.'

Frances nodded. The last thing she wanted reminding of was that man's face.

'I'll keep an eye on the guard,' Ben said. 'If he looks like he's moving to come back up, I'll distract him, bribe him some more, talk to him. The only thing we're really risking is him telling someone he let you up after they find the body, but I'm willing to bet he'll keep quiet and say he never saw anyone – otherwise he'll lose his job for sure. He'll never believe a little thing like Agnes would be able to push him off by herself.'

'He might be right,' Frances said.

Agnes reached for her shoulder and squeezed. 'Like Jacks said, we shouldn't need to worry about that. If we get him close enough to the edge, take him by surprise and push in the right place, it'll be all right. And there's two of us, not one.'

'I know that,' Frances said, 'but it doesn't stop me worrying on it.'

'If the wind picks up, that'll help.' Ben's words were clear but his eyes looked glazed.

The three of them sat for a moment, staring out at the twilight. Ben smoothed his hair and rubbed at a tuft that was sticking up until it lay flat.

'All right then,' he said eventually. 'That's it. I'll be waiting. We'll be gone before they have time to send out a car to clear the body.'

'And then it'll be done,' Agnes said.

Frances knew they were waiting for her to say something but she couldn't. Her voice was trapped in her throat, fluttering in the dark like a canary in a cage.

Up she went. Higher and higher. The elevator jerked and swayed and stuttered. Frances clutched the bag between her knees and tried not to fall. All she could think about were her innards being dragged through her feet. It was smaller than she had thought. Smaller and shinier and far more terrifying. She'd figured it must be as big as a room to take all those people into the sky every day, but it was only the size of a larder. How in hell did anyone stand it?

She pulled her hat down some more, checked the pins were

firm and stared up at the arrow above the door, praying the thing wouldn't stop until she got where she was going. 43, 44, 45. She hoped Agnes was right about everyone leaving. What would she do if someone stepped in beside her?

50, 51, 52.

She felt sick. Her mouth filled with the sour threat of it. She leant over, staring down at the shoes she'd borrowed from Agnes. They were scuffed on the heels and they pinched her toes, but they were still the smartest she'd ever worn. Flat men's brogues in a woman's size so she wouldn't wobble. Stan would have had something to say about them. She closed her eyes and felt the judder in her palm. If she held on to the thought of him she might manage to stay upright.

The elevator jerked then began to slow. She opened her eyes.

69, 70, 71.

The car stopped so quick, Frances landed hard on the floor. She struggled up, rubbing her knees, cursing at the pain. The door opened with a loud ping. Seventy-second floor. You couldn't get much higher, Agnes said. Best to use a room just down from the top. There was no way to be sure someone else wasn't up there waiting to jump – fixing to do themselves in from the observation deck like that laid-off carpenter. No sense in risking it.

Frances poked her head into the hall and looked around. Nothing to see. She stepped out. Nothing much to hear either, except the sound of the elevator doors closing and the bulbs buzzing inside their marbled cases overhead. Everything smelt new, as though the carpet had never been walked on, as though the walls had never been touched.

Left, Agnes had said. Go left, then third room on the right. I'll jimmy the door.

Frances picked up the bag, holding it out a little so the machinery inside wouldn't bang against her leg, and walked

down the hall, checking the doors until she saw one wedged
open with a worn leather bag. She stopped. A freezing wind
whispered through the gap, worming its way round the collar
of Stan's coat, inching up her sleeves when she lifted her hand
to knock. No answer. She knocked again. Nothing. She pushed
the door and stepped inside.

The room beyond was cold and full of wind. Frances stood
still for a moment, waiting for her eyes to get used to the gloom,
watching her breath turn to steam and disappear. There were
boxes everywhere, chairs and tables stacked at the side, rolls
of carpet standing against the walls, shadowed and stiff like
soldiers waiting to be shot.

'No one's moved into this floor yet.'

Frances swivelled, her hand at her throat. For a single terrifying second she feared she'd been caught. Agnes' voice sounded
strange up here, not like her at all. 'You could at least have said
hello first.'

'Sorry.'

Agnes walked towards her, wiping her hands on the backs of
her slacks. She was wearing a thick green sweater with a man's
navy peacoat over the top. She looked a lot like a young sailor
waiting for the off. Frances had only seen her half an hour ago
in the car, yet she looked changed. More determined, less afraid.
Flecks of light from a flickering paraffin lamp picked out the
steel in her eyes. They embraced. Frances felt shy, as though
nothing had happened between them, as though she was feeling
Agnes' arms around her for the first time. They both shivered
and squeezed a little tighter.

'I'm so glad you're here,' Agnes said into her neck. 'I could
never have managed this without you.'

Frances flinched and pulled away, thinking of Jacks and
Dicky, her own silence jabbing at her – as sharp as the guilt of
an outright lie.

'What's wrong?' Agnes said.

'Nothing.' Frances blew out her breath. 'You know.'

'It'll be all right. Not much longer and he'll be gone. We can carry on like before.'

'Maybe.'

Agnes nodded at her and forced a smile. 'I'm setting up inside. We can take the camera outside just before he arrives. Any sooner and we'll freeze to death.'

Frances followed her across the room. Agnes had already put up the wooden tripod and taken some of the camera parts out of a box. She leant over and took the bag from Frances' hand.

'That's what I need. The first rule of photography – you can't take a decent picture without a good lens.'

'Does the window have to stay open?' Frances clapped her hands against her arms, trying to stay warm. 'How much longer?'

'Not long. Another fifteen to set up, maybe. Fifteen for the right shot once he's here. Then, when I give the signal, we push.'

Frances managed to nod. She walked around while Agnes pulled lenses and shammies and strange bits of wood out of the boxes.

'It crossed my mind you might not turn up.' Agnes spoke without raising her head.

'Do you think so little of me?'

'It's not that.' Agnes paused. 'I wouldn't have blamed you if you had.'

'I'm not one for running.'

'You ran here, to the city, didn't you?'

Frances felt the scold as though Agnes had smacked her. 'I did, but that was different. I'd never run from you. Not if I thought you were in trouble, if I thought you might need me. And I wouldn't run from a promise.'

'I might have if I'd come up second.'

'No you wouldn't, you're too good. At any rate, you want him gone as much as I do.'

Agnes nodded silently. Her smile failed to reach her eyes. She fiddled with the lens.

Frances hoped the look on her own face bore some of the certainty she lacked inside. She'd made sure not to turn away when Agnes spoke, to open her eyes wide, to twist her mouth into a determined line, but it all felt wrong. She stood still and stared out of the window. All she could see were the tops of some of the tallest buildings reaching up into the darkening sky, grey and solid and proud, as though they'd always been there, like mountains. A few of the lights had already begun to turn on, giving shape to the lumpen blocks, pricking the dusk like fireflies rising from the plains. Nightfall. The magic hour. Her favourite time of day. Beneath them the city shucked and sighed, swelling with horns and running wheels, with cries and laughter. She'd never been so high.

She thought of church. Of the time Mother made her go up and help the organist polish the pipes. It was the week before her birthday. Thirteen. Just about knowing what it was to grow up, what you lost and what you gained, the pleasures and pains of mounting flesh. Mr Nickelson, the organist, was ancient. Some said he was older than the church itself. But he'd still seen fit to run his hand up her skirt a little – not so much she jumped back, but enough to put her on edge and mind herself for what might come next. She'd helped him all the same, had rubbed the smears away from the metal until her wrists ached. As a reward he'd let her sit up in the eaves for the whole of the service.

The congregation had sung so fine that day, back when the crops grew and the cattle were fat, when the dirt was wet and the rivers were full. This was before the men started hanging themselves from low-branched trees so often that kind mothers stopped letting their children run home ahead for fear of what might be waiting. And before some of those same mothers suffocated their own babies since the agony of that was less than watching them starve.

The whole service, Frances had sat leaning forward on the balcony with her wrists on the soft wooden banister looking down on the tops of all their heads, at Father's thinning hair, his scalp soft and reddened like a peach from the sun, at Mother's fresh curls, her hands running over themselves in her lap, at Stan's straight back, his chest pushed out towards the pulpit.

Mr Nickelson had thumped the keys and they'd all stood up – heels grinding on wood, bibles tucked in their grooves – and taken a long deep breath. Then they'd sung. None of the voices would have been sweet by itself, but when they rose up as one, brimming and swelling and soaring, in the glory of God, as Mother would have said, it sure had been something to hear. Frances' ears had rung with the joy of it and grown sore from the listening. She'd looked down and felt special that day, as though she was better than every single one of them, as though all was right with the world and nothing could ever be wrong.

She couldn't be sure why standing in the freezing cold looking out at the bursting city, waiting for a man she was supposed to kill, made her think of that day, but she guessed it had something to do with how high she was. Both times she'd had a job to do. Both times she'd looked down on everyone. She was lording it over every man, woman and child across the whole of this wonderful, hellish city, like she'd lorded it over those folks in church. It was some kind of power at least. She stood still and closed her eyes, not feeling the world turn, not seeing the sky grow a little darker, letting the wind nudge away some of her fear. Then she walked to the window, cocked her leg over the sill and stepped out on to the balcony.

EMPIRE STATE BUILDING to
NEW YORK CITY HARBOR

Winter solstice, 21 December 1932

17.12

'Ready now?' He failed to hide the sneer. He'd already asked Frances twice if she remembered that night in the club, if she might accompany him again. She couldn't look at him. She wished he knew she was Stan's sister, that she could watch his eyes widening and the shock settling, that he would know who she was before she killed him.

'Yes, sorry,' Agnes said, 'it's my fingers, they're too frozen to press the shutter. I needed Frances to help.'

'I'm surprised a little thing like you can use a great machine like that on a sunny day, let alone in this wind. It's to be applauded. I must admit I was surprised Dicky wasn't here to take the shot himself, but as I said, he's assured me you know what you're doing. It really is a fine new age, isn't it? Women running around with cameras recording the city as it expands.'

He paused and blew smoke towards them, but it billowed in his face. He coughed.

'I was eager to get up here and sneak around on Al's tower without his knowledge. I wish I could see his face when he picks up the paper and sees me using his glorious Empire State Building as a mere platform for a photograph of my own tower going up. Dicky says the pictures really will be something. Please, ladies, can we get on with it?'

Frances watched Agnes looking through the lens, knowing that everything she could see was upside down. She remembered Agnes showing her the day they'd roamed the city. If she thought hard she could almost hear the sound of Agnes laughing, of the cars moving, of the pigeons cooing, of the shutter clicking. Behind Agnes' head a few more windows in the nearest tower lit up. The extra light only added to the horror of it all. Frances had gotten used to the semi-darkness, to the safety, to the disguise. Now Kane's face was a little brighter she couldn't turn away – from him, or from herself.

'I never spend enough time at the top of my buildings once they're built,' he said. 'Such a shame that most of life goes on downstairs when it all looks so fine from up here.'

'That's better,' Agnes said. 'If you could move a little to the right, one half of your face will be clear and I'll be able to get my shot.'

He shuffled his feet closer to the abyss, sighing with the inconvenience of it all. The balustrade only came up to his waist. Jacks was right. His height would be his undoing. Frances slid the tripod, moving with him. His smell clung to a gust of wind – expensive tobacco, old books and metal – taking her back to his shoot at Jacob's place. She thought of all the plotting and planning. Would Stan have done this for her?

'And now turn your face out to the city a little more.'

This was Frances' signal to stand up. She waited until he

was facing away from her and eased herself on to her haunches, bracing herself against the wind. Still she almost fell and grasped the top of the camera. He didn't turn. He seemed as overcome by the sight as she was.

Frances pulled the note from her pocket and held it tight in her fist. For a second she was worried about how much she had crumpled it, then she figured it would only help make the whole thing look more believable. She took a step towards him, squinting against the gusts.

Agnes looked up slowly at her over the camera and nodded. She was crying – from the wind or the strain of it all, Frances wasn't sure. She thought of Stan, of the last time she'd seen him, of how he must have felt when this man ordered him to kill, of the strength it must have taken to refuse, knowing he would surely die because of it.

She looked at Agnes and saw Stella shivering beside the tracks, saw Colette boarding the same train to escape the city. She'd retrace part of Frances' journey, see the buildings turning back into trees, the concrete disappearing into dirt, her eyes lit by a sky she'd never have known had they not pulled her free of the ground. She thought of the ones they had saved and those they hadn't, of all the folks who would keep or lose their lives because of a choice she was about to make.

Kane put his hand to his hat before the wind could tear it away and kept shouting. 'They said it couldn't be done. You wouldn't believe the convincing we had to do, the men they had poring over the schematics, the money I spent making it happen, the bribes, the lies, the parties, the smiles. It's all I've wanted since I was a boy. To build. Nothing more and nothing less. To build as high as man can go. My own wife said it couldn't be done. Even she doubted me.'

Frances took a step towards him. Now, she should do it now. She tried to move but her body refused. He didn't seem to notice she was standing, didn't look at the note clutched in her hand. She thought of Stan's chessboard, of her own hands pushing needles against cotton, of who she had been and what she had become. She was a queen, not a pawn. She was a builder like Kane. A maker, a doer, a someone.

'Can you believe it?' he carried on. 'My own wife had no faith in me. The love of my life. Mother of my children. Six of them we've got. Did you know that? Did Dicky say? Another one on the way. The woman's an engine, a machine. She takes what I give her and turns it into flesh and bone. I take what the men of the city give me and turn it into buildings. What takes more skill? What'll last longer? I know what I'd rather be able to do.'

Frances rushed at him then, thoughts blistering like a film flowing so fast through a projector it set on fire. She ran forward, not for Jacks and Dicky, or Agnes, not even for Stan, but for herself. For the babies. For everyone.

He turned to her, laughing at first. 'What? Am I so irresistible?'

She fumbled, forcing the note into his trouser pocket before he knew what was happening, then pushed him once on his chest where Jacks had said, her eyes on his so she could see the dawning realisation, the anger shot through with fear.

He rocked back, clutching at the air.

She looked at Agnes, her eyes bulging, desperate for help, but her friend's face was blank and she didn't move. Terror scissored down Frances' spine. Kane knew what she was doing now. He grabbed her and forced her towards the edge, his face red and wild and yelling.

Frances felt her feet leave the floor, the wind catching at her body, flinging Stan's coat around her like a cape. Fear ripped through her. Her legs twisted, arms flailing until her fingers found the wooden sides of the camera and she pulled at it, trying to save herself, but then it swung up in her hand and pulled away from the tripod and the box sailed over the top of the balustrade.

Kane shook her again, forcing her into the shuddering air, and there was nothing left to do but close her eyes and wait to drop.

Someone screamed. Kane turned and let go and Frances fell beside the wall. A gunshot cracked against the rushing wind.

Ben was yelling from the other side of the room. At least Frances thought he was. She could see his mouth open, but the sound had stopped. Kane had his back to her and a gun in his hand. In front of them, Ben crumpled to the floor.

Another scream, full of rage, not fear.

Agnes crashed the wooden tripod over Kane's head. She must have taken him by surprise. She hit him again and he turned his head to her, falling to his knees. From the lee of the wall Frances felt his head smack against the stone as though the sound itself was solid. Agnes hit him over and over, her arms shunting up and down against the twilit sky like pumps bringing oil from a well. She was screaming still – a single wail dragged across the burgeoning night. Frances felt a splatter on her cheek and closed her eyes, wishing she could block out the sound of Kane's head caving in as well as the sight, her hands as useless as a veil against her ears.

Agnes stopped yelling. Frances opened one eye in time to watch the life leaving Kane's face, his eyes wild and open and shocked, finally frightened. Dark blood billowed across the grey slabs like satin. In a few seconds he was gone.

The wind wrapped around her head. Everything was muffled.

'Help me.' A voice in her head? Agnes shouting in her ear: 'I'm sorry, I'm sorry.' She was panting, her nose streaming, her eyes bright behind the tears. 'I froze, I didn't think he'd turn so fast, I couldn't move. I'm sorry, Frances, I'm sorry, I almost let him kill you.' She hid her head in her hands.

Frances looked away.

The wind harried around them.

'We've got to get him over.' Agnes pulled at his leg. 'He's too heavy, we'll have to lift together or he won't go. Quick.'

Frances wrenched herself up and grabbed one of Kane's meaty arms. Agnes took up his legs and they shoved and pulled and heaved until his body teetered on the edge.

For the briefest of moments Frances feared he wouldn't drop, that his body would hang, magically suspended above the city, or be thrown back in her face.

But then, at last, he fell.

'Stop breathing.'

'I thought you were trying to keep me alive.' Ben's voice rasped but Frances could feel some mirth in it. He'd not die if he was strong enough to make a joke. Not yet anyway.

'I mean, don't suck in so much air each time. I can't think with you sighing so loud.' Her voice juddered.

She licked the dryness from her lips and rested her head on the wheel. It felt strange to sit behind it. The last time she'd driven was back on the farm. If she could only rest a moment she might manage to stop her body shaking long enough to figure out what to do. Sweat trickled down her back. The hairs on her arms stood on end. Her feet itched. Everything hurt. She could no longer tell if she was boiling or freezing, starving or sick.

They'd done it. They'd killed him. Her head rang with the truth of it.

Agnes opened the trunk, threw in the last of the boxes and squeezed herself into the back seat.

'It's as clean up there as I can make it,' she said. 'The rain'll help if it comes. I had to sacrifice my best shammy though ... Jesus Christ, you might have warned me.'

'Sorry,' Ben said, 'I didn't know where else to put him.'

'What are we going to do with another body?' Agnes' voice was tight, the opposite of Ben's, as though no air was passing through her.

'Quiet,' Frances said. 'If everyone stops talking I might think of something.'

'How are you?' Agnes had ignored Frances' request and leant towards Ben. He was slumped to one side in the passenger seat, his forehead resting on the window.

'Not too bad.'

He was lying. Frances could see the blood oozing between his fingers. No matter how hard he pressed his jacket to the wound he'd not staunch the flow for much longer. She wondered if the bullet was still in his side, or if it had gone right through and lodged itself in a wall. If it had, they were all done for. If it was still in him she'd seen enough on the farm to know he might not last long.

Out on the main street beyond the alley another woman screamed. They stared through the fogged windows, searching for movement. It would be busy out front with folks starting to leave work, but they'd not seen a soul come their way yet. An ambulance wailed into the mounting night.

'We need to get out of here,' Agnes said.

'I know, but what are we going to do with him?' Frances nodded towards the back seat. 'We can't take him back to Jacks and Dicky. He wasn't part of the plan. At any rate, Ben says he doesn't want to go.'

'Why?' Agnes said.

'Because I don't trust them,' Ben said.

'Why not?' Agnes' voice was raised. 'Why didn't you say anything before?' Frances could tell she was barely managing to keep the panic at bay. 'Actually, don't worry, I don't care.' She turned to Frances. 'We need to leave. Any second the cops'll turn up and if we're still sat here, that'll be it. We've got to stick to what we agreed.'

'And Joseph?' Frances looked over her shoulder.

'We'll take him with us, figure it out along the way. No one'll miss a man like that now Kane's gone.'

'He's police,' Frances said. 'Course he'll be missed.'

'Not until tomorrow. He doesn't look like the type to make it home each night in time for dinner.'

'I didn't mean to do it like that,' Ben muttered. 'He wanted to come back up. Insisted. We were standing there, having a smoke, I was doing a good job of distracting him. Then he said some things about Stan.'

'What things?' Frances felt her face grow hot.

'Nothing for you to mind yourself about.' He coughed into his hand. The knuckles were swollen. Frances saw specks of blood at the corners of his mouth. 'I lost my temper.'

Frances nodded and looked back. The bottom half of Joseph's body was crumpled in the footwell behind Ben's seat. The rest of him sagged to one side. His neck rested at an odd angle against the leather. His nose was smashed across his face. Beneath the browning blood and that black scratch of a moustache, his lips had begun to purple already – the only note of vibrant colour on his otherwise ghastly face.

'You had no choice,' she said.

Ben's eyes swivelled sideways at her. 'There's always a choice.' He lifted his arm, almost a shrug, but the motion made him wince and he drew it back.

'We need to get you help.'

'Him first,' Ben said. 'You can drop me at Mrs Bianchi's after. She'll see to me.'

Frances shook her head. She stared out at the alley, at the cans of rubbish spilling across the street, at the spread of muck and filth. And then it came to her. She could see Father in her mind's eye twisting the top of the sack, could hear the mewing and herself crying. She could even feel her small damp palm tugging at his thick wrist, trying to make him stop. She squeezed the wheel. This small piece of knowledge, at least, she could thank him for.

'We'll take you on the way.' She started the engine.

'Where are we going?' Agnes asked.

Frances pressed her foot on the gas. 'Not far.'

The cold hadn't helped like she'd hoped. Joseph's body had begun to stink anyway. Not of decay, not that yet, but of congealed blood and stale shit, of sweat on starch and, worst of all, of those blackened teeth that had finally stopped rotting. They'd driven around for hours waiting for the right time, unable to open the windows for fear someone would see or smell something. Not long now. A few more minutes and the last of the crates would be unloaded from the small boat, then the sailors would all come ashore and they could take their chance.

'Is he well wrapped?' Frances asked.

'As well as I can manage. I've pulled his arms from the sleeves of his jacket and tied those round the back. Rocks in his pockets and inside his shirt like you said. Should I tie my sweater round his legs? I've got to get rid of it anyway.'

'Where did you get it?'

'The sweater?'

'Yeah.'

'It's one of Dicky's old ones. Why?'

Frances paused. 'Use it. There'll be fewer limbs to wrangle with.'

'If you're sure.'

Frances nodded but didn't turn. She watched the last man check the ropes and jump off the boat. They'd chosen a spot at the end of a pier. As far away as you could get from the city without going on to the water itself. As yet they'd been lucky. No one had stopped to ask what they were doing. She wondered how Ben was, if Mrs Bianchi had managed to sew him and save him, or if he was still lying on the floor of her parlour, already dead and gone, his blood fleshing out the pattern on her worn rug. On both sides of the dark street the crusted slats across the warehouse arches groaned in the wind. She wished they could have floated far out towards that giant statue of the woman Stan had told her about, but she didn't know where it was and they couldn't risk stealing a boat on top of everything else. Shame. It would have felt right to bury him beneath her stone feet.

Frances waited a few minutes more, listening to their breaths fall in time with the soft sighs of the water on the dock. Finally, she checked the mirror, looked around and gathered herself.

'You all right?' she asked.

'No,' Agnes said.

'I mean, are you ready?'

'No.'

'This is the last thing we have to do. Then we can rest.'

'Will we?'

'I hope so.'

'I don't think I'll ever rest again.' Agnes' voice quivered.

Frances turned to her. 'You've got to get a hold of yourself.'

'How?'

'Push your thoughts down. Don't think about anything. Shove it all into a space at the back of your head.'

'It's full.'

'What?'

'That space you're on about. It's so full I think it might burst.'

She started to cry. Frances let her. The sound of someone else's pain was a tonic.

After a time she said, 'Come on. We've not got long till the morning shift starts. I reckon dockers get up early, even in this weather.'

She'd have to take the lead, tell Agnes what to do. She opened the door. Freezing air filled her chest. She gasped at the cut of it. Her breath flared around her head. She walked towards the water, catching at the wall as she went, trying to stay upright, her feet sliding on the soaked cobbles. She stopped at the end and looked out. Apart from the dipping sway of the boats, nothing moved. Water lapped. Ropes creaked against iron.

She walked back to the car and opened the back door. They'd have to drag him together, just like Kane. Agnes was bent over with her head on her knees and her arms wrapped around her ears.

'Come on,' Frances said, 'a few more minutes and it'll be done.'

Agnes roused herself and slowly got out, but didn't look up. They rolled Joseph out, wincing at the thud of his body on the stones, then pulled him, looking all around, to the edge of the dock.

'Thank God he's slight,' Frances whispered as they bent down to roll him in, 'we'd never have managed this with Kane.'

She watched Agnes' face as they pushed him over. In the sparse light her eyes looked black. There was no way of knowing if she was still crying, if her face was wet from spray or tears. They tried to hold on to his head for as long as they could, wary of the splash. When they finally let go, his body slid into the depths as though it was desperate to return. Frances thought of the kittens in her father's sack all those years ago, of the way they'd struggled and fought to get out like they knew what was coming. She thought of Colette's hair swirling on the wet concrete, of the sound of Kane's body hitting the sidewalk that she'd been too high to hear. She thought of the fine length of muslin wrapped over her baby's face deep in the earth. Then she turned away from the water, took hold of Agnes' hand and led her back to the car, using her shoes to scratch and scrape at the tracks Joseph's body had made in the dirt.

NEW YORK CITY HARBOR

6 January 1933

07.12

'Can you see them?'
      'Not yet.' Frances craned her head above the crowds.
'But we've got time.'
      'Not much.' Agnes' face looked pinched. She started picking
up the bags at their feet, and bumped into a woman in the queue
beside them, who frowned. 'Sorry,' Agnes said.
      'It's all right.' The woman drew her hand across her brow.
'There's never enough room in these lines.'
      'Tell us how long it'll take again, Mommy, please!' A little girl
was looking up at the woman, all teeth and sincerity. She was
clutching a rag doll with a missing eye. It reminded Frances of
Annie. Had Father burnt her with the rest of the toys? Perhaps
she was still wherever he'd thrown her, lying somewhere, covered with brush and dead leaves, waiting for another little girl

to rescue her from the rot.

'It'll take as long as it takes,' the woman replied. 'I told you before, it depends on the current. We should be in France in less than a week, God willing.'

'I can't wait to see Uncle!'

'I know you can't.' The woman smiled, but Frances could see tears threatening, some unspoken pain trapped inside. Behind her, four other children were carrying suitcases and stuffed toys, taking it in turns to yawn, the older boys with slick hair and neat caps, their eyes wary, more nervous than the little ones. No man in sight.

'Are you ladies going all the way?' the woman asked.

'Yes,' Frances said, glancing at Agnes, unsurprised by the frown of warning she shot back. 'She's a photographer and I'm her assistant.'

'Ahh,' the woman said, 'I did wonder why two women travelling together had so many manly-looking bags.'

'Mommy, Mommy, Danny said he needs to use the bathroom again!'

The woman sighed, forced a smile and turned away.

'You know what Jacks said,' Agnes whispered when she was sure the woman was out of earshot, 'the less you tell people the better.'

'I know,' Frances replied, 'but it would have looked strange if I'd said nothing. Any sign of them?'

'I don't know. They're fifteen minutes late now. If they don't get here soon, we won't get on.'

Agnes put one of the cases down and stood on top of it, shading her eyes with her hand, although she didn't need to – the sun was yet to rise.

Above their heads a flock of seagulls yelled into the ashen sky, their white wings only visible when they banked. All around, families jostled and chattered. Someone said, 'Look at the size of it!' and Frances turned again to face the ocean liner docked beside them. From this angle it dwarfed the skyscrapers beyond. Some folks, probably the rich, had been allowed on already and she could see them waving hankies from the top decks.

'There, there!' Agnes called. 'I see them!' She tugged the patterned scarf from around her neck and started waving it back and forth, standing on her tiptoes.

Frances climbed on to the case beside her to look.

A Buick the colour of oatmeal, its roof and fenders as dark and shiny as a cesspit, drew up beside a pile of wooden barrels. Some of the men lifting them stopped to stare. Dicky got out of the driver's side and went over to the passenger door. Jacks stepped out, all fox fur and red velvet. One of the sailors whistled. She waved her hand at him like a movie star, like a deb, then looked up and smiled at Agnes, as though she already knew exactly where they'd be standing. Dicky put his arm around her and they pushed their way through the crowds.

'Have you got them?' Agnes called as they approached, jumping down from the case then turning to offer Frances her hand.

'Of course we've got them, darling. I promised, didn't I?'

Jacks reached into her handbag and pulled out two tickets.

'I can't believe it!' Agnes cried. She pulled Frances into a tight embrace.

Frances looked at Dicky over Agnes' shoulder. He was watching the crowd. His face seemed fatter than before, smooth but slightly puckered, like a plucked chicken waiting to be roasted.

'Thank you,' Agnes said, 'thank you so much.'

'Don't thank me,' he drawled, 'thank this one here. She's the one who pulled strings with Frank. That's the last two tickets for this liner in the whole city. God only knows what she had to do to get them.'

Jacks hit him with her gloves. 'Nothing I wouldn't have done anyway.' She laughed.

The sound turned Frances' stomach.

'So, you're off, then,' Dicky said, smiling.

Frances nodded and looked at her shoes, wishing she had kept Kane's gun.

Agnes lunged across and gave him a sisterly hug.

'And Ben's gone with his band?' Dicky said.

'Next month. To San Francisco, I think,' Agnes said, 'then touring around California.' She lowered her voice and they all drew close so no one else would hear. 'Mrs Bianchi did a fine job sewing him. Lucky the bullet landed where it did. They were packing up when we left. He'll go with the Bianchis to the new boarding house until he's well. They're levelling the whole of Frances' street next week.'

'So sad,' Dicky said.

'No it's not,' Jacks said. 'Onwards and upwards, dearest. It was a rat-infested hell-hole, wasn't that what you said, Frances?'

'Something like that,' Frances murmured, although she didn't remember saying anything of the kind.

'The sooner they tear down all those ugly tenements the better.'

Jacks lit her cigarette. Frances imagined her hair catching on it. She prayed for a sudden gust of wind, for a spark, for her whole beautiful head to set alight.

'Good, the faster you're all out of the city the better,' Dicky said. 'We don't want to take any chances. There's nothing in the papers yet, apart from the obvious. So far they've assumed the camera was Kane's, but all we'd need for you to get in trouble is one of those guards to drink too much and talk. Lucky for us, Kane was so full of himself he didn't tell anyone about the photographs. He wanted a dramatic reveal.'

'Which there was,' Jacks said.

The picture of Kane on the front page loomed up in Frances' mind, his suit still neat but his body twisted, his eyes half closed, blackness seeping from his head towards the smashed camera, dripping into a crack in the sidewalk. She saw his suicide note, her own handwriting, framed like a special announcement. The first whole sentences she'd ever managed to write:

I lived to see my buildings go up. I'll die before I see them torn down.

She imagined the photo Agnes took that the police would never find: her black and white test-shot of the city simmering in the dark, the one clue that might have led to them, the one no one would see because the camera had smashed into a thousand pieces. She concentrated on the top of the little boy's sailor hat in front so her legs wouldn't give way.

The line started moving forward. A steward with a serious face and a tall hat came by checking their tickets. Before long Agnes and Frances were on one side of a rope and Jacks and Dicky were on the other. They small-talked over the top for a time about the journey, each couple inching closer to the rusting, sour-smelling hull as the line moved along. Agnes' face glowed when they mentioned Paris. She talked of her friend who lived there, of the avenues and the parties, of the great photographers she was going to try and get work with, but none of it rang true. Her eyes were still as black as they'd been on the pier.

And then Jacks said, 'So, what will you be doing while Agnes is setting up shop, Frances?'

'She'll be her muse,' Dicky said, smiling, his brow arching.

'She'll be more than that,' Agnes said, squeezing Frances' hand.

'I'm not sure,' Frances said, flinching at the feel of Agnes' sweating palm. 'I think I'll take some time to find my feet. I want to explore.'

They started up the gangplank. Jacks and Dicky walked

beside them for as long as they could.

'You always were so sensible, Agnes,' Jacks said. 'Try and let your hair down a little for me over there, won't you? I'm going to have fun immortalising you back here, Frances. My readers are going to adore you. I'll mail you the edition when it comes out.'

'Thanks,' Frances said, without feeling. 'Thanks for everything.'

'This way, ladies, move along now, don't mind the sway, I won't let you fall.' The steward caught hold of Frances and helped her across.

She looked back at Jacks and Dicky. Agnes waved. Jacks blew some kisses, her gloved fingers fluttering like dying leaves. Dicky smoothed the side of his hair and nodded at them. A young boy in a smart suit checked their tickets and told them their bags would be delivered to their cabin.

'Au revoir!' Jacks called.

Agnes grasped Frances' hand. 'Come on,' she said, 'right to the top!'

Frances let herself be taken.

They ran up the nearest stairwell, leaping the steps two at a time. Frances felt queasy. The boat swayed, and for a moment she thought it might have pulled out of port already. They ignored the first deck and carried on past the second until they got up to the third, wheezing and coughing. Agnes pushed the thick wooden door and the breeze almost knocked them off their feet. They walked to the edge, past happy couples and racing children and young men with sad, thoughtful faces, and stood clutching the brass rail, their toes poking into the abyss.

The foghorn sounded – a deep, booming rumble that echoed back at them from the warehouses on the shore. Frances wondered if they were close to where they'd put Joseph. So much of the dock looked the same. She imagined him under them now, being nudged back and forth by the pump of the rudder.

Perhaps, once they moved, his body would be torn into a hundred pieces.

Agnes started to wave, although they couldn't see Jacks or Dicky any more, only the Buick sliding past the rows of waving people, inching its way back along the cobbles, dividing queues of people until it melted back into the city like spent wax.

Frances didn't feel like she'd expected. She thought she'd be eaten with guilt, but nothing ached. She thought she'd be terrified of getting caught, but she didn't care. She hoped she'd feel relief, but there was none. She felt flat and dull and cold, like the dark water they'd slid Joseph into, as though she was the one who was slowly, silently drowning.

Agnes was still moving her hand, grinning from Frances to the city and back again, somehow managing to keep the pain of their loss, the horror of what they had done, away from her face. She must have pushed the madness down into the deep pockets of her billowing slacks beside the rest of the money and the photograph – the one of Stan and Stella and Kane, the one neither of them could bear to burn.

Every night when Agnes cried Frances had held her, but her arms might as well have been empty. Once Agnes slept she would lie in the dark and think of Stan, of his hands and hair and voice, but she never cried any more. Only Jacks and Dicky stirred anything, but the disgust was sluggish, as useless as a blunt knife.

And yet.

The breeze caught Frances' hair. The ship moved. For the first time she felt the drifting pull of an ocean beneath her feet. She flipped Stan's collar up and looked towards New York at the crisp rows of buildings, the silvering streets and bustling docks. It was all so neat. The filth and the chaos, the stench lifting off the sidewalks and steaming in the alleys – none of it could be seen or smelt up here.

The boat rocked. She gripped the cool rail.

And yet.

A single note began to play quietly inside her chest. One finger on a lonely key, pressed down and released, over and over like a heartbeat. Like the sea. Like waves. Like the soft tug of a needle through cotton, or the scratch of a pen on paper. Like freedom. Like hope. In, out, over and back. In, out, over and back. She breathed in time with it, sucking in cold sea air, and stared ahead.

A little boy with red hair, barely older than her son would have been, ran up beside her and stepped on to the rail, waving madly, his face so full of joy Frances thought she might cry. She watched him, willing tears that refused to fall, longing for them, until his hair turned to gold; then she looked back at the city, at the sun finally rising, burning its way towards the heavens between an avenue of tall buildings, glinting off glass and bricks and concrete, striking cars and people, shining into her eyes so violently she had to close them.

ACKNOWLEDGEMENTS

I would not have had the opportunity to write this book had I not been lucky enough to win the Virago/The Pool New Crime Writer award, so many thanks to Sam Baker, Erin Kelly, Jo Unwin, Coco Khan and Emily Iredale for selecting my entry. Your decision, quite simply, changed my life. Enormous thanks to Sarah Savitt and Rose Tomaszewska at Virago – two very different but equally exacting and compassionate editors: your patience, generosity and dedication has helped both me, and this book, to thrive. Special thanks also to Jill Dawson for her sage advice, and to Nithya Rae and Daniel Balado for catching my clumsy repetitions and misplaced apostrophes before anyone else saw them – if there are any left it's my fault.

This book was born in a small writing class at the City Lit in London during a period of overwhelming grief. They did not know it at the time, but the course leader Christina Dunhill and my fellow students, especially Rebecca Craven, Belinda Murray, Helen Gunn and George McAllister – along with those first few scratches I made on a blank page – saved me. Thank you.

The courage, creativity and style of a number of great female photographers infuse the book – I am so grateful to Berenice Abbott, Margaret Bourke-White, Lee Miller, Dorothea Lange and Eve Arnold for breaking the rules, for refusing to take no for an answer and for putting art and truth above everything else.

Numerous books, films, newspaper reports, maps, museums,

galleries, paintings, photographs and testimonials of and about the twentieth century helped shape the events, locations and characters in the book. Of particular note are Abbott and Hank O'Neil's book *Berenice Abbott: American Photographer* (McGraw-Hill, 1982); David Freeland's *Automats, Taxi Dances and Vaudeville* (New York University Press, 2009); Cecil Beaton's *Portrait of New York* (BT Batsford, 1948); the original film of *Scarface* (Howard Hawks, 1932); the Tenement Museum in NYC; the British Library; MoMA; *Nighthawks* (Edward Hopper, 1942); *Christina's World* (Andrew Wyeth, 1948); Weegee; and everything Bonnard has ever painted. Thank you all for colouring my world.

Thanks to my colleagues and students on the film programme at Middlesex University for constantly reminding me of the emotional impact of time and motion and sound, of the importance of looking with intent, and of the capacity of light and shadow to shudder the senses.

Finally, thanks to my friends and family. To Chris Jude for helping me through. To Luiza Sauma for showing me this was possible. To Tom Callagher and Carlos Blanco for the art books, history chats and enthusiasm. To Rebecca Hall, Amie Jones, Poppy Stammers, Alice Edwards, Sophie Law, Grace Lilley, Hannah Tutton, Susie Foreman, Suzanne Martyr, Sophie Donaldson, Issy Jones, Polly Gregory, Annabel Blair, Liz Clements and Kate Percival for the distraction, drinks and filthy laughter. Thanks to Jojo Davies for all the childcare and support – the truth is none of these words would exist without your help. Thanks to the North London lot and the Plymouth lot, especially Nan. Thanks to Larry Thompson for showing me that the struggle to create is always worth it and to Jeanette Thompson for the unstinting inspiration and care. Lastly, thank you to my sons Luca and Gray, and to my husband Charlie Russell, for stealing time and giving it – for all the reading, for all the love.